Emilia Abraham

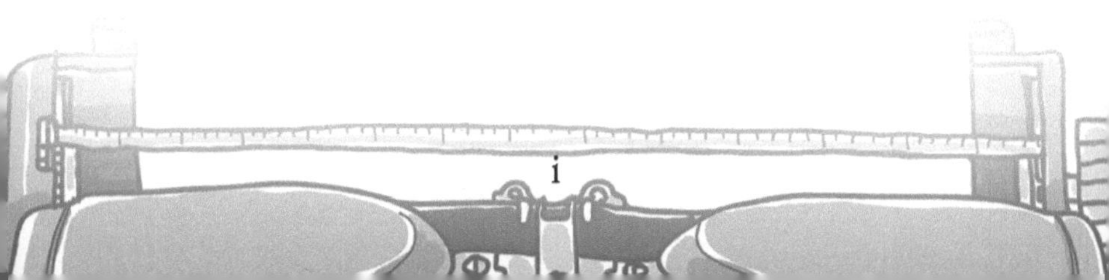

ISBN-13: 978-1-961802-07-0

Dedication

Here's to you—who has wanted something so badly, you'll do anything to get it. Even if it means exiling yourself to a cabin in the middle of nowhere. May you find your home.

And to my fellow authors, who intimately know the struggles Maddie goes through. I promise you're not alone.

Oh, and to imposter syndrome and its fickle mistress writer's block: Fuck you.

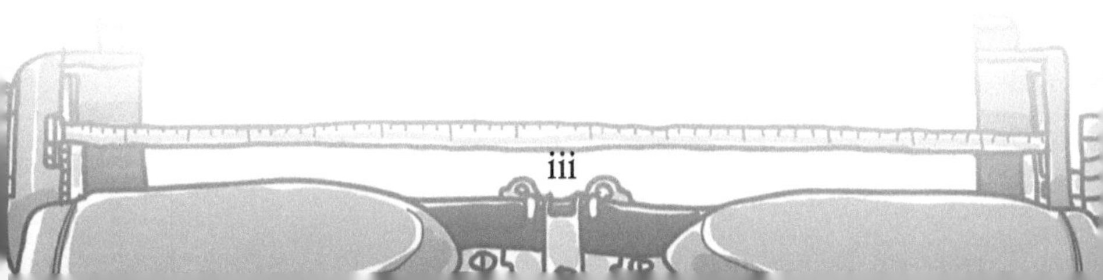

Author's Note

Content Warnings:

Adult Language

Sexually Explicit Scenes

Light BDSM (imperfect etiquette/lack of safeword)

Author's Note to Other Writers:

This is a warning and it shouldn't be taken lightly. Our main character, Maddie, is an author. Yes, she's in the middle of writer's block, but there's so much more. Imposter syndrome plays a heavy part throughout this book. Some of the emotions and realizations Maddie experiences hit close to home. Therefore, proceed with caution. I hope you can find peace within her journey. And perhaps feel a little less lonely.

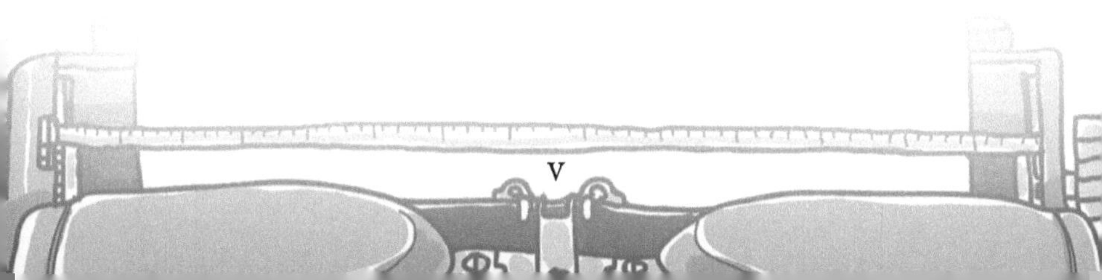

Chapter One
Maddie

A vivid world builds behind my lids, creating a realm I've never experienced before. It's not unusual for me, especially being aware that I'm dreaming. The problem arises when the colors warp, swirling through the scene and distorting the picture my psyche has created. The illusion shatters, a kaleidoscope of shards pinging to the corners of my mind. My soul weeps at the loss, despair filling every pore in my body as a buzzing hurtles me from sleep.

Rubbing my eyes, I try to focus on the text messages my best friend sent me in the middle of the night. She's one of those people who texts one line at a time. I usually wait until there's at least thirty seconds of silence before even reading her first one.

MaddieMaddie! Shit, ur sleeping. I forgot about the time thing. Quick recap. Tommys a douchebag. Screw this love thing. Best part though...I'M COMING HOME! Chicago won't know what hit them. Ur the bestest bestie if youre home when I get there. I promise I won't smother you once I get there or talk shit about your brother. Kisses, luv u.

These were sent hours ago, though, which doesn't explain the vibrations that ripped me out of my dreamscape. The sun peeks through the curtains, blinding me. I groan, throwing the covers over my head. My phone vibrates and I glance at the screen, then groan again. It's the second time she's called in five minutes. The last thing I want to do is have a conversation with my mother at eight in the morning. It's a Saturday, for fuck's sake. Doesn't anyone sleep in anymore?

I toss the duvet aside and slide off the bed, answering the phone. "Hey, Mom. What's up?"

"Are you just getting out of bed? Honey, it's late. You can't expect to get anything done if you sleep until all hours of the day."

It doesn't matter what time it is, I'm never up early enough for her. "It's only eight."

Of course she doesn't listen. That's the story of my life. "What are your plans today? Your brother is coming by to help your dad with the deck."

"Chloe is coming into town. France didn't work out. Not sure when she's getting here, though," I mumble as I stumble into the kitchen to make some coffee.

She sighs as I pop the pod into the machine. "Chloe certainly has her own way of doing things, doesn't she?"

"Don't start. She's my best friend and has been for what? Twenty years? I'm not going to drop her now just because she travels." I'm sick of having this conversation. Every time Chloe does something my mother doesn't approve of, she brings it up.

"I wasn't starting anything, and I don't know why you think I would. I'm just saying, maybe if you put yourself out there more, you'd find new friends. And then—"

"Finding a man isn't everything," I mutter, knowing exactly where this will go.

My mother has perfected the Midwestern passive-aggressiveness. A touch of righteousness, a dash of shame, and just a pinch of irritation—all mixed up into the perfect ball called guilt trip. I still haven't figured out how to combat it. Maybe it's an impossible feat. None of my high school friends knew how to deal with it, either. They all just agreed, hoping the conversation would end quickly enough for their mothers to forget about it before the next time.

"For someone who writes about relationships, you'd think you'd be better at this whole thing."

I grind my teeth, silently begging my coffee to brew faster. "Those are fictional men, Mom. They're not like actual men who don't give two shits about...treating a woman right."

It's a good thing my mother doesn't read my books. She would have a conniption and most likely disown me. Not that my parents have a lot to bequeath. It's more of the principle of the thing for my parents. They wouldn't cut me off. If they did, they wouldn't be able to bitch at me for writing about sex. And my extended family would get annoyed, which my mother wouldn't then be able to tell me off about either. I have enough talks with her about writing as a profession and her lackluster support as it is. No use adding fuel to the fire.

She sighs again and I brace myself. "Maybe it's time to get a real job, honey. You've done this for three years now and I'm not saying it was a poor decision, but it doesn't seem to be paying the bills."

I swallow the snort and the comeback I have. I've been writing forever and publishing since I graduated college. She only counts the years I've been doing it full time, though, as if the struggle to work several jobs and publish books at the same time doesn't count.

She also has no idea how well I've done. I don't tell her because it would never be enough. She'll always see it as a hobby instead of an actual profession. She doesn't know how hard I work or how much I've sold. Which is by design. The less she knows, the better. Usually, I can fend her off by changing the subject, but today I don't have the energy. Not with everything that's happened recently.

"I'm doing just fine. And I don't know why you're worried about it. I haven't asked you for money. I don't owe you anything—"

"It's not just about debt, Madelyn, which I'm sure you've got plenty of. I don't want to fight. And when you need it, we'll be there to help you pick up the pieces," she says matter-of-factly, as if there's no other outcome she can possibly imagine. "Oh, shoot. Your brother is calling. He calls me at least four times a week, but I have to take this. Come to dinner tomorrow. We don't see you enough."

She hangs up before I can respond. Not that I'd know what to say. Between the dig that I'm a failure no matter what I do and the comparison to my older brother, I'll never be able to convince her I'm enough. She means well, but the way she goes about it doesn't exactly build up my confidence.

I toss my phone on the counter and doctor my coffee with enough sugar to take down a small toddler. I make a mental note to pick up more energy drinks instead of suffering through drinking the monstrosity I've created another day.

Saturday is supposed to be my day off, but I'm so behind on everything I don't have that luxury. Especially with Chloe coming home, I doubt I'll have free time to do anything other than try to keep up with her. She's a force to be reckoned with and constantly on the move. With the time difference, we haven't been able to connect. I doubt I'll get much sleep while we make up for lost time.

After waking up my computer, I close my eyes and pull in the scent of my coffee, letting it fill my pores. I take a sip, then grimace before making my way back to the kitchen to pour the liquid into a cup with a lid. I've spilled on my keyboard more times than I can count, and I'd rather not deal with that shit again.

When I make my way back, the cursor blinks at me from where I left it last night. I wrote all of seven words yesterday and it wasn't even original.

It was a dark and stormy night.

Blink. blink. blink.

I erase the words, knowing I can't use them. At the time, I thought it would help kick-start something like it did in high school, but nothing came. I'm loath to admit I'm in the throes of writer's block. As soon as I declare I have it, the more it will consume my life. And I can't afford to have a block right now. I need to make up for...everything.

I plop my coffee next to me and tap lightly on the keys, not actually writing anything. I bite my cheek as I squint at the dark screen. Maybe if I change it to white, I'll have a better chance. A few clicks and I'm immediately switching it back. It's too bright, too much, too blindingly blank.

I pull up another manuscript I started last week. I thought I had a breakthrough since I wrote twenty thousand words. And then nothing. As soon as Sam thought he might be falling for Grace, he ghosted both of us. Asshole.

I pull up another document. And another. And another. Some are barely a page. Others include the meet cute, even if they're not entirely cute. Some are like Ryder and Sophie's story—just barely there. I avoid the one that haunts me. It's almost done, with only the reunion left.

Sitting back with a groan, I stare at that damn cursor, willing it to move. After another five minutes searching my brain for something other than emptiness, I slam the laptop closed. No use spending another hour waiting for inspiration to hit. The further I travel down this road of nothingness, the less I'm able to enjoy anything.

Reading doesn't do it. Writing obviously isn't working. Watching a show just frustrated me that those writers were able to come up with something. *They* could complete a storyline. *They* weren't experiencing the debilitating and paralyzing sensations currently flowing through me.

The front door slams open, jolting me from my doldrums.

"Honey, I'm home!" Chloe's voice rattles in my brain.

I'm already exhausted, but I shove to my feet and plaster on a smile. It's not her fault I'm a failure. It's not her fault she's able to travel all over the world. It's not her fault her sleep schedule is fucked with the time difference and my mother woke me up way too early in the effing morning.

The minute I step into the hallway and see her, everything else falls away and I squeal. We go through the usual rendition of talking over each other, jumping up and down, and the time-honored tradition of linking fingers and swaying as if we're drunk in the middle of a club. We've been doing it since we were young, though neither of us remembers why.

"Are we in crash mode or hyper mode?" I ask, pulling her toward the living room.

She plops onto the couch, tipping her head back against the cushions. Dark circles stain under her eyes and her cheeks are sunken. What the fuck did Tommy do to her?

"You look like shit," I say, cocking my head as I take in her haggard appearance.

"Love you too," she mutters before peering at me through slitted eyes. "It was a long flight."

Shaking my head, I plant my fists on my hips. "This isn't jet lag. This is something else."

"I don't want to talk about it." She sighs and I nod, even though she's closed her eyes again. "I want you to talk to me about anything other than whatever the hell is happening in my life."

I sink onto the couch next to her and tuck my legs underneath me. "My mom called this morning. Great news! My brother is still the favorite, even though it still annoys the piss out of him."

Concern flows through me when she doesn't even twitch at the mention of my brother. "You'd think she'd learn her lesson after the last time he told her off."

"Well, I may have stopped informing him whenever she compares us," I mutter, glancing away.

She grumbles under her breath, straightening to level me with a glare. "I thought we talked about that, Maddie. Ryland *wants* to help. He wants to support you. He can't very well do that if you don't give him all the information to work with."

I wave away her concern. "I'm a thirty-year-old woman. If I can't stand up to my mother, then I deserve the verbal tongue-lashing I get. Besides, it's not his job to protect me. He's got his own shit to worry about."

She raises an eyebrow but doesn't ask. Chloe understands if she needs to know, I'll tell her. And if she merely wants to know, she has to ask him herself. Which she won't. Because she's chicken shit when it comes to Ryland. I don't know what the hell happened between them, but it's been a weird dynamic for the better part of five years now. I don't pry and she doesn't ask. It's an unspoken agreement between us.

"Are we allowed to talk about how the latest release went?" Chloe asks pointedly.

Part of me screams to brush her off, to not say a fucking word because I chose this. The other part knows I need to talk about it. Everything has built up until I'm drowning. And I can't move forward until I get it off my chest.

"It fell apart. I pushed too hard and all I could think was *I need to get this out or I'll...*" I shake my head, not ready to completely unload.

"Die? Because that's an extreme reaction to not putting out a book on time." She contorts her lips as if she can convey all her disdain in my flawed thinking.

"No, but I got too far in my own head, I suppose. And it didn't work." My body slithers onto the floor and I flop to the side, groaning.

Leaning forward, she props her elbows on her knees and stares at me. "How exactly did it not work?"

I grit my teeth, averting my gaze, and mumble, "It flopped."

"Is this like that one time you thought your book was tanking when really it was just imposter syndrome attacking you?"

I let out a short laugh, though none of this is funny. "No. No, it's not."

Nothing I say can change what happened. And yet I can't move past it. No matter what I do, I just can't keep going like I am.

Chapter Two
Maddie

"Maddie, wake up! I've hit the high of the jet lag and I have a plan!" Chloe pounds on my bedroom door and I jolt awake.

Batting my hair from my face, I shiver as a stray piece tickles my nose. I rub it away as she bursts inside, tired of waiting. She throws herself on my bed and I flop onto my back with a groan.

"It's fucking early," I mumble, my voice thick with sleep. "And I don't need a plan. I have one."

"Oh? Does it include more than just randomly staring at your computer and hoping readers will forgive you?" She levels me with a look I'm not ready to address at seven in the morning.

"Yes. I'm going to write my next book and pretend the last one didn't happen. I fucked up and now I have to fix it. And I can't fix the last one, so I'll fix the next one." I throw the covers over my head.

She immediately rips them off. "That's a lot of fixing something I'm not entirely convinced is broken. Tell me about your next book that'll magically make all your problems go away."

I don't have one. Or I have too many. Either way, I don't have the capacity to tell her about any of it since I'm stuck. I'm still living in the world of the last story, wishing I would have written it differently. No, not even differently—just better. The premise was there. I wrapped up all the plot lines and gave the characters what they needed in order to be at peace. The execution...that's a different story. This isn't the first time I've finished a series. It should have been easy. Maybe not easy, but definitely not the soul-crushing disappointment it was.

"Maddie?" Chloe calls in a singsong voice, waving her hand in front of my face. "Are you still with me?"

"Stop that," I snap and swat at her while she giggles. "Listen, I have to go to my parents' house tonight for dinner. Apparently, there's some big news to talk about or something. Are you coming with?"

She raises a perfectly waxed eyebrow. "Am I invited?"

"Of course." I shove the comforter away and swing my legs over the side. "You know you're Dad's favorite."

"Much to your mother's dismay. Did you tell them I ran off to France with some douche canoe?"

"No. I told them you were doing a stint in Paris for work. Which technically you did, so I didn't lie." I pull on a pair of sweatpants and shuffle out of the room as she trails behind. I need coffee if we're going to discuss my family.

"Is your—"

"Yes, Ryland will be there. Which shouldn't matter either way. You two will just ignore each other like you have for the last five years." It's a subtle inquiry she'll ignore, but I can't help wondering what the hell happened between them.

"Where will it be?" she mutters, admitting defeat without so much as a whisper of a fight.

"Probably outside. Unless it rains. Which means you can put the fire between you two. He'll probably bail early, and my mother will make some dig about him having an actual job and needs his beauty sleep." Bitterness laces its way through my tone.

Her mouth drops open as she leans against the counter to watch me make coffee. "They did not really say that."

"Not in so many words, but they were implied, as they always are." I sigh, eyes fixed on the dark liquid sputtering into my mug. "Maybe she's right."

I mumble the last part, forgetting that Chloe has superhuman hearing. She seizes me by the shoulders, spinning me to face her. Determination and something else swims in her eyes—maybe guilt. What she feels guilt for, I don't know. It wasn't her decision to write a shitty book. She had no part in the plotting or writing or editing of it. In fact, she was the one who kept me sane through the sleepless nights. She's the one who scolded me when I wasn't eating because I was deep in edits. She was the first person who believed in me. I'll never be able to repay her for that.

"You're not fucking quitting. You don't get to quit."

I snort, averting my gaze even as my eyes fill with tears. "I might not have a choice. I *do* need to pay my bills."

"No. I refuse to allow it. You have to keep going."

"Why?" I cry, wrenching myself from her hold.

"Because if you give up, who will write their stories? You can't leave your characters to wallow in your head. That's fucking boring. Plus, if you give up..." She sucks in a sharp breath, and I turn back to her. "If you give up, then none of us have a chance. We're all out here waiting for our lives to begin and searching for the one thing that will make us feel alive. And you found it. Besides, your characters deserve their happily-ever-afters. Are you really going to be a bitch and deprive them?"

I smirk, grabbing my mug and starting another coffee for her. "I thought you liked when I was a bitch."

"Course I do, but your characters suffer enough without adding your bitchiness to the mix."

We wile away the hours pretending I didn't have a breakdown and that she's avoiding telling me what happened with douche canoe. I never liked him anyway, so I doubt it matters. We ignore the issues we're wallowing in and she never brings up her miraculous plan for me.

She regales me with her jaunts around Europe and I tell her about the schemes my father has been up to. He has a way of having some new hobby every time I talk to him, even though he's not retired yet.

"I still don't understand how he got into wood burning. Was that before or after he thought he could raise chicks?" Chloe shakes her head as she tucks her long legs underneath her.

"Before the chicks, after the actual woodworking. Had to build the coop before he could get the chickens. And he got pissy at them every time they wouldn't listen. He was convinced he could train them like dogs since they followed him around. Turns out he just had feed in his pockets."

She howls with laughter, looking lighter than she was when she arrived. As much as I'd like to press her about what happened in France, I won't. She'll tell me in her own time. And play it off like it was no big deal, even if her heart is broken. She deserves more than she's been dealt in the relationship department. I used to be silently jealous of her family's wealth, assuming she had the perfect life. How could she not with everything handed to her?

"Remember when you used to come over to my house almost every night for dinner? And every time Dad would open the door and grumble about feeding 'the brat'?" I ask.

She smiles softly. "And I'd just beam at him until he cracked? Yeah, I remember. Your family was the only one who ever hugged me."

"Speaking of the non-huggers..." I wrinkle my nose as she groans. "They ever call you?"

"Not really. I get emails from my mother every now and then. Usually it's an invite to some fancy-ass party I wouldn't attend anyways. I'm not surprised. I get more attention from them than they ever got from their parents even if it isn't anything to write home about."

"You hear from your father at all?" I grimace and tense, waiting for her to brush me off. Asking Chloe about her parents always goes one of two ways, and neither of them are particularly good.

She sighs, tipping her head back on the couch. "You know, I always thought if I got a little older, a little wiser, a little more established. If I aced that test or got into an Ivy League or brought home the right guy, he'd suddenly take notice. He'd realize I was right there in front of him. And yet I'm still waiting. There's some part of me that craves his approval."

"Could that be why you took off to France with one suitcase and a credit card with a guy you'd met all of six weeks before?"

She scowls, pursing her lips. "You're not supposed to say the quiet parts out loud, Maddie. Enough about me. We need to deal with your problems."

"I don't have problems," I mutter, pushing from my seat to wander into the kitchen.

We might be going to my parent's house in an hour, but that doesn't mean I can't snack before then. I swing open the fridge, staring at the barren shelves before closing it again. Chloe jumps onto the counter and fills her coffee mug while I slam around the room. Sipping her drink, she gives me a look over the rim and I huff.

"I don't have a problem."

"Sure you don't." She sets her coffee next to her, then hops down. "Now, this writer's block. How bad is it? Are we talking you can't write the spice? Or is it more serious? Like the time you tried to force those characters to be enemies and you had to rewrite the whole damn book."

I collapse onto one of the stools butted up against the small island. My forehead hits the granite, because of course there's fucking granite, and I groan.

"I can't write. At all. I sit at my computer and nothing comes. I pull up one of the other twenty-some manuscripts I've started and nada. They're all just languishing, waiting for me to write their stories, and yet I can't."

"Ahh," she murmurs as she sits next to me. "Have you tried...something else?"

I let out a short laugh. Chloe may be aggressively supportive of my writing, but she has no clue what it entails. She's the first to buy all of my books, and she tells anyone she can about them, yet she's never read anything I've written.

I don't blame her. She's not a huge romance girlie, which I respect. Mostly because she's never asked me to write a horror novel for her. I shudder at the thought of even trying.

"I've tried all my other techniques. I've taken a break. Went back to something new. Went back to something old. Ate a ridiculous amount of cake. Read a shit ton of books. I even tried to write fanfiction and literally nothing happened. I even tried 'It was a dark and stormy night.' Maybe I should just go back and rewrite the last book. It was shit—"

She smacks the back of my head. Hard. Probably harder than she intended. I lean away, shooting her a disgusted look, and she wrinkles her nose in apology.

"It was not shit."

"You didn't read it."

"So? I don't need to read your shit to know it's good. You hit a little bump and now you need to pull yourself out of this funk. Move on to the next story. And for the love of all that is fucking holy, do not listen to your mother. I love her to bits, but she's not exactly supportive."

We sit in silence for a minute before I sigh. "It's not just her. It's me. I feel like there's something...broken in me. Like the part that knew exactly what I wanted to do in life just winked out of existence. And I don't know how to find it again."

She wraps her arm around my shoulders in an awkward sideways hug. "You'll get your mojo back. You'll be grooving before you know it."

"Did you just combine two movie quotes for motivation?"

"Oh!" She jumps up and dashes from the room.

I rest my forehead back on the counter and wait for her return. I wonder if Chloe will be so supportive when I can't contribute to the bills for the apartment anymore. Then again, she's never asked for money. I insisted I pay for my share. Mooching off my best friend wasn't the way I wanted to go.

Did that mean a lot of shitty jobs while I wrote at night? Yeah, it did. Until this last series, I struggled for years. Every time Chloe would flounce back into town, she would scold me for burning myself out. But I had a dream, and I wasn't about to ride her coattails, or rather, her parent's money, in order to get there. I needed to do it on my own.

And I did. I made it. And now it might all come crashing down around me. No matter what I told Chloe, I know I can't go back and rewrite the last book. Readers would flay me alive. Even with a lackluster ending, it was an ending, nonetheless.

"I got you something while I was globetrotting." Chloe sets a wrapped package next to my elbow.

Picking at the ribbon, I contemplate whether I should refuse. She's always picking out the most random things. I love them, but without being able to repay her for them, I feel like our relationship is a little one-sided. Without her, I wouldn't be where I am today. Tears fill my eyes as I remember all she's done for me.

"It's just a little gift. No need to get all sentimental about it," she grumbles.

I swipe at the tears. "Sorry. Yeah, I'm fine."

I rip off the paper, my fingers trembling from the aftermath of emotions rolling through me. I need a fucking break. The constant stress isn't doing me any good. I already got sick a week after my last release. Dealing with being ill by myself isn't fun, but having Chloe there while I'm wallowing in bed would be worse.

Flipping open the small lid, I grin. Mini macaroons, only slightly crumbled from their trip across the ocean. I grab one and pop it in my mouth, much to Chloe's dismay. She shrieks and snatches the box away.

"French macaroons are not to be shamelessly shoved into one's piehole, Madelyn. Have some goddamn respect."

I grin at her with a mouthful of crumbs, and she sniffs. "If I didn't know any better, I'd swear you were raised by wolves."

"Speaking of wolves, we gotta leave. Mom will flay me alive if we're late."

Chloe rolls her eyes, then flounces off to change. The temporary reprieve I felt by her presence goes with her and I'm left bereft. Eventually, I'll have to face the fact that my mother might actually be right. Maybe I've ridden this wave as far as I can and it's time to find something else.

16

Chapter Three
Maddie

"Get the fuck in here. Dad's already cracked the scotch and Mom's been passive-aggressively commenting on the length of my hair," Ryland mumbles. "You'd think she'd—"

He clamps his mouth shut when he spots Chloe. His entire body snaps to attention and his face turns into a stony mask before he pivots and marches away. I half expected him to salute us. I glance at Chloe, but she's too busy scowling at my brother's back. She stomps inside as he turns the corner to the living room. I'm sure he'll hide until dinner, then sit as far away from her as possible. Not that there are a lot of people to hide among.

Slowly, I shut the door behind me and lean against it. Chloe veers into the kitchen, probably to avoid Ryland in the living room. Mom's greeting echoes through the house. For as much as she disapproves of Chloe's life choices, she never fails to pamper her.

"Kind of feels like she's the daughter Mom never had, huh?" Ryland calls just softly enough for Mom not to overhear.

I stumble into the living room and collapse next to him on the couch. "Not like it's anything new. I'm used to it. Plus, it's not her fault."

He grunts, fixing his eyes back on his phone. I lean over, peeking at the screen. He glares at me from the corner of his eye and tilts it away from me.

"Why are you looking for a new place to live? They kick you out of your apartment for excessive mopiness?"

"Mopiness isn't a word, first of all. Second of all, they're raising the rent by a thousand. I'm not paying that much for a shitty apartment. And don't tell Mom. She'll want me to move back in." He glances over his shoulder to make sure she's not lurking in the doorway.

"Your apartment is like six blocks from the pier. You lucked out getting that place. I'm surprised it took this long for them to up the rent. Doubt you'll find another one for even close to what you're paying now."

He shakes his head. "Which is exactly why I'm looking now. I've got two months. I'll find something by then." He wrinkles his nose. "Even if it is in the suburbs."

"Oh no. Not the suburbs." I shudder in mock horror, then cackle. "Maybe it'll get Mom off my back. She'll be focused on you settling down and starting a family. You'll have the home for it."

His horror isn't faked at all. Slipping his phone back in his pocket, he mutters a curse. He gives me a look before wandering off to the backyard. I watch as Dad turns from the grill and grins. Soon they're laughing and slapping each other's backs. I sigh, wondering if anyone would notice if I left.

"Snap out of it, Maddie," I breathe and shove to my feet.

I know I haven't been feeling like myself, but I am not this mopey bitch. So I'm lost with what I'm supposed to write. Who cares? Doesn't mean I need to fade away into obscurity, playing a tiny violin as I go. I shove aside the doubts I have about work and throw my shoulders back before going to the kitchen.

"Oh, Madelyn," Mom says as I plop down at the table. "I didn't realize you came in."

"How else would Chloe get here?" I ask, dropping my elbows onto the wood and resting my chin in my hand. Seconds later, I'm sitting back and folding my hands in my lap.

"Don't be snippy, Madelyn. Chloe always knows she's welcome—with or without you. Now, come set the table."

I hop up and grab the plates while Chloe brings bowls filled with salad and potatoes to the table. Mom never got out of the habit of making enough food to feed an army. Chloe was a constant fixture at the table. And once Ryland was a teenager, he was always bringing his friends by. I only ever had Chloe. There were other friends we hung around, but none I wanted to bring home.

"Are you seeing anyone, Chloe? We both know Maddie isn't. She's too busy falling in love with fictional characters." The censure in her voice is clear. Chloe laughs as if she's joking. She's not.

Chloe flicks her blonde hair over her shoulder and plants a hand on her hip. "There may have been someone who turned out to be a not-so-great of a someone. So, I ditched him in a foreign country and never looked back."

"Poor bastard," Ryland mutters as he slinks through the door, earning a glare from her.

"Well, that's too bad, dear. He clearly wasn't worth your time." Mom gives me a pointed look, though I have no idea what she wants.

It's not like I've brought home a man for her to be disappointed in recently. Or ever. Every time I've snagged a date, they run for the hills as soon as they find out what I do for a living. It's just another reason Mom has to point to why I should pursue something else. They all cite one of three reasons, but it always comes back to my job.

One, I clearly must be looking for someone to support me. Two, I have unrealistic expectations and they'll never match up. And three, writing romance is disgusting. I could counter each and every one of them with plausible responses, but it's not worth it. They don't care that I probably make more than them. If they're insecure about comparing themselves to fictional men written by women, that's more of a them thing than a me thing. And the last point isn't even worth addressing. Telling them it's the largest genre with the biggest readership and the highest grossing market wouldn't sway them. And I don't want to.

"Madelyn." My mother's sharp tone cuts through my musings and I whip my head up. "The drinks?"

Chloe spins and grabs glasses from the cabinet. I push to my feet once more, rolling my eyes as I open the fridge.

"I saw that," Mom mutters as she passes with another bowl filled with corn. She's cut it from the cob just for Chloe since my friend doesn't like getting the strings in her teeth.

"Maddie," Dad calls from the grill, and I peek over the door.

He waves me outside with his tongs, and I practically toss the pitcher of lemonade on the table before hustling to him. My dad may not always approve of the choices I've made, but he always has a twinkle in his eye when he sees me. I launch myself into his arms and he envelops me in a hug. Ryland's voice rumbles through the air, followed by Chloe's snarky reply. Mom closes the glass door, cutting them off from us.

"Your mother isn't happy with you. Apparently, you were short with her yesterday," Dad says as he flips the burgers sizzling on the grill.

"Well, I'm not exactly happy with her, either. She's harping on me about being like her golden child."

"Your mother and I don't play favorites." He sighs, shaking his head. "You know she's just worried about you. Her methods aren't always the greatest, but she wants what's best for you."

I roll my eyes, knowing I'll never get him to see things from my point of view. Dad may be firm in his convictions, but his love for Mom outweighs even the deepest of his beliefs. He won't tolerate an ill word against her. As frustrating as it is sometimes, I can't help but admire how much he loves her. I'd be lucky to find what they have. Not that I'm in any danger of that.

"Are Ryland and Chloe biting each other's heads off yet?" he asks, gaze fixed on the cooking meat like it'll jump from the flames if he doesn't keep a close eye on it.

"Pecking, more like. I wish I knew what changed," I murmur as I stare through the sliding glass door at them studiously ignoring each other while Mom flits about the kitchen.

Dad chuckles. "Puberty."

I roll my eyes. "I doubt they hit puberty and thought, *hey, that person seems like a good one to hate*. Doesn't work like that, Dad."

He gives me a peculiar look I can't decipher before he turns back to the grill. It hits me that Dad thinks they're sweet on each other. They're not. At least, according to them, they're not. Ryland refuses to say a word about her other than a snarky comment here or there. Chloe, on the other hand, might not have told me anything, but she did show up at three in the morning sobbing. She didn't say much other than raging against Ryland. The next time she woke, she was emotionless and wouldn't say anything else. She refers to it as "the incident."

"They're not in love with each other."

Dad sends me a smirk over his shoulder. "Not yet."

He slips inside and sets the food down, scowling when no one cheers. Mom tries to scowl, yet her lip twitches as Ryland pounds the table and Chloe claps. It's ridiculous and completely normal for us. A pang rolls through me.

Even in my own family, I feel like an outsider. I've spent so long being the odd one out. I didn't lie to Ryland. I don't blame Chloe in the slightest. The only love she's found is with my family. And my family loves me. I just never quite seemed to fit in their puzzle.

"You coming?" Ryland calls, concern flashing across his face.

I force a smile and make my way inside. I settle between Ryland and Chloe, not pissed in the slightest that I have a table leg splitting my knees apart. It's my usual spot, so I should be used to it. Chloe hands me the bowl of mashed potatoes as she widens her eyes. Her warning falls flat since I wasn't paying attention to their conversation while I was out back.

"Madelyn, I was telling Chloe about how I ran into Casey's mother. She's finishing her residency at Mayo. Have you talked to her recently?"

I peek at Chloe, who shrugs. "I have no idea who you're talking about, Mom."

"Oh, you remember Casey. You went to camp with her when you were younger. Her birthday parties were always at that fancy hotel downtown." She waves the serving spoon around until my father grabs it from her.

"I still don't know who you're talking about. But good for her. Mayo is a good hospital." I shovel a forkful of corn into my mouth, praying she doesn't keep harping on this random person I can't remember.

She huffs, shaking her head. "Well, Barbara, Casey's mother, was with Janice. You remember Janice. *Her* daughter started a restaurant. Or she's managing it or something. She said her daughter could probably get you a job there if you were interested."

And there it is. I knew she'd find some way to use this dinner to goad me into finding a "real" job. Chloe's knee hits mine and pushes my leg into the table. The whole thing rattles and I snort as she blushes.

"Madelyn, knock it off. You're not getting out of this conversation. If you won't accept a job from your own brother, then you might as well look for other avenues."

"I don't need a job, Mom. I have one, if you'll recall," I say calmly.

She waves away my words. I catch my dad's eye, but he just gives me a sympathetic grimace before turning his attention back to his plate. Ryland won't help, mostly because I told him not to interfere. It only lands me in more trouble when he does. My brother can do no wrong, and I get blamed for his attempts.

"Except you're not even able to afford your own place. You're mooching off poor Chloe, who clearly won't say anything about it since you've been friends for so long."

"So, engaging in nepotism by taking a job from Ryland is totally okay, but living off Chloe's generational wealth is a no-no. Got it." I pop the spoon in my mouth, then choke on it when Ryland's knee slams into mine.

Mom glares at me from the other side of the table. I'm poking the bear, but I can't seem to stop myself. She's constantly pushing my boundaries in the name of my wellbeing. How do I fight something like that? How do I look at my mother, who truly loves and wants the best for me, and say she's fucking this up? I don't. I take whatever she slings at me and brush away the negative feelings—burying them under the guise of her love for me.

"What the fuck," I mutter under my breath.

"Madelyn Rose Benson. You will not speak that way in my house," Dad snaps, his usual grin nowhere to be found.

My cheeks heat as I duck my head and mumble an apology. At thirty I should be able to drop the occasional f-bomb, but clearly not in my parent's home. Ryland gets away with it. That argument won't fly. Better to say I'm sorry and move the fuck on.

Chloe's hand finds mine, hidden away from my parent's prying eyes. She squeezes, lending me whatever strength she can. I squeeze back and glance at her from the corner of my eye. Her bottom lip slips between her teeth before she squares her shoulders.

"I'm going to get a job," she states to the group.

Ryland's fork freezes halfway to his mouth. The kernels of corn slip off one by one, plopping back on his plate. Dad clears his throat as his gaze darts from Chloe to Mom and back again.

"Well, that's just fabulous, dear. What were you thinking of doing?"

"Burlesque...dancing."

I turn wide eyes to her and panic flashes across her face as she peeks at me. Our only hope is that my parents don't know what burlesque dancing is. I don't even know where she got the idea from.

Ryland bursts out laughing, his deep chuckles filling the silence. Dad joins in, shaking his head. When Mom smiles, her giggles are stilted. Either she doesn't know what it is, or she doesn't want to embarrass Chloe. Either way, my best friend has once again rescued me, just as she always does. If only she could save me from the disaster I've found myself in with my books. If she could pull that off, I'd be peachy keen.

Chapter Four
Maddie

My parents' front door shuts behind us, leaving us staring at the dark street, and we both heave out a sigh of relief. After Chloe's announcement, the rest of the dinner went off without a hitch. At least, Mom went back to passive-aggressive comments instead of an outright attack. The number of times she asked if I'd be willing to let her set me up sent my head spinning. I only had so many excuses before she beat me down.

"Well, that was…interesting," Chloe mutters.

"If by interesting you mean like running a gauntlet, then yeah."

The door opens again, and I scramble down the stairs. I skid to a stop at the bottom and swing around. There's no way I can pretend like we weren't camping right outside.

"Pretty sure that's the fastest I've seen you move in years, Maddie. Good to know all I need to get your ass in gear is to sic Mom on you," Ryland chuckles.

Chloe snorts, then smothers the noise behind her hand. Ryland's head snaps toward her. She tips her chin up, whipping her hair around and smacking him in the face with the strands, before she flounces down to me.

"I'll order a car, Mad." She points down the block. "Over there."

I track her as she walks away, blonde hair blowing in the soft summer breeze. When I turn back, I find my brother's eyes fixed on her as well. I cross my arms, tilting my head, content to see how long it'll take him to pull his gaze away from her. He finally does, scowling when he catches me watching him.

"Don't even start, Maddie."

I hold my hands up. "I wasn't going to say a damn word. You know she could probably help you find a place to live. Oh, and the next time I need to get out of Mom's path of destruction, I'm totally throwing you under the bus."

"Why the hell do you think I didn't tell you before? I've known for three months I have to move." He sends me a lopsided grin, then tromps down the stairs. "Listen, in all seriousness, you know if you need anything, I can help, right?"

"I don't need—"

He holds up his hand and I snap my mouth shut. "I know you don't *need* help. Doesn't mean you can't ask for it. Sometimes shit gets hard and I want you to know you can always count on me."

He wraps his arm around my shoulder and leads me toward Chloe. "Are we going to sing a duet together now? Maybe do a blood pact or something? Because I don't know where your hands have been, and I'm not sure I'm comfortable asking."

"Hardee har. If you need a job, especially one where Mom and Dad won't find out, just text me. I can find something at the company for you. Might not be glamorous, but it'll help supplement what you're bringing in from writing."

I sigh, the ache in my chest burrowing deeper. Chloe might be the only person in my life who truly believes in me. Even if I didn't write another book for a year, I'd be fine. None of them think I'm telling the truth other than my best friend. Which I suppose is why she holds that title in the first place. She's unwaveringly supportive.

"I don't need a supplement. But I may need help getting out of the date Mom is going to set me up on."

His arm drops from my shoulders, and he shakes his head violently. "No can do. If she's not setting you up, she'll turn on me. No way in hell am I going out with some sycophant she's conjured from the depths of her friends' daughters."

He shudders before spinning around. He waves without turning around and disappears into the dark. Chloe tracks him as he vanishes, an odd look in her eye. She wipes it away, then smiles at me.

"That wasn't so bad," she says as the car pulls up along the curb.

I climb in the other side and put on my seatbelt as she greets the driver. "If you count me getting roped into a date and told fourteen different ways I'm failing as a human being and daughter, then yeah, it wasn't so bad."

She waves away my words. "I've got an idea for how to get you out of that date. I know the guy she's talking about, and he hasn't showered since we graduated over ten years ago."

"Is this idea better than the one where you proclaimed to my family you were taking up burlesque dancing?"

She grimaces, then glances out the window as the city lights up around us. "It was the first thing that came to mind. Actually, it was the second. The first was being a professional volleyball player, but I didn't think they'd buy that."

"Hate to break it to you, but burlesque dancing isn't any more plausible. However, it does bring me to my next question, which is..." I pull in a deep breath and brace myself. "What are you going to do now that douche canoe is no longer in the picture?"

She shrugs, a melancholy look crossing her face. "I honestly thought he was different. The minute they find out I come from money, their entire personality changes. I realize how extremely privileged I am. I'm not that out of touch. Doesn't mean I don't deserve someone who cares about me, right?"

"Of course not. You deserve love just like everyone else. And it's not like you're not trying to do something with your money. Douche canoe wasn't the reason you went off to France. You just took him with you. You met with those investors and got them to give tons of money to that organization...the one with the food."

She smirks, waiting for me to butcher the French pronunciation. I stopped attempting it after the first time she gave me shit for it. I raise my eyebrow and she giggles.

"Yes, I did. But it's not enough. I thought I could just donate all my money to worthwhile causes and I'd get other richies to do the same and I'd fall in love with someone and I'd live happily ever after. Like in your books," she says wistfully.

"Except I write about magical creatures and billionaire bikers and lots of fucking. Which I suppose could happen in real life, but it's...different."

The driver chokes and I grimace. Sometimes I forget polite society has a proverbial stick up their ass when it comes to romance novels. Then again, maybe it was my proud proclamation that I write about people fucking. The driver whips around the corner and screeches to a halt outside our apartment building. He doesn't even bother telling us to have a good night before speeding off.

"I think you scared him," Chloe laughs as the doorman swings open the glass for us.

"Good thing I didn't start talking about monster peens, huh?"

The concierge nods his head to us as we pass the front desk. This place is more than I could ever afford on my own, but I'm not going to complain. Even Mom usually doesn't say anything about where I'm living because of the security. I wonder if there are any apartments available here for Ryland. Chloe, as much as she seems to hate him now, wouldn't let him be homeless. She might put him off long enough to move back into our parent's house for a couple months though, if only for the laughs.

I collapse on the couch, tipping my head against the back. "You didn't answer my question about what you plan on doing now."

She plops next to me, mirroring my position. "I don't know. Maybe I should get a job. Might be easier than gallivanting around the world begging people to care about those who don't have vaults of money to swim in."

"Or you could do what you want to do," I murmur, and her arm twitches against mine. "All the supplies are still in the closet. Wouldn't have to buy much."

"Actually, I've got an idea for *you*." She sits up, twisting toward me as she tucks her leg under her knee.

"If it's just sitting down and writing, I've tried that. And let it be noted that I know you're avoiding the discussion, but I will require us to revisit your future at a later date."

"Duly noted. And it's not just sitting down and writing. Tell me, when was the last time you left the house?" She levels me with her serious look, and I close my eyes.

"About three minutes ago." I can practically feel her eye roll.

"I mean, for reals got out of the house and tried writing somewhere else."

I sigh, sitting up as well. "I tried the coffee shop on Fourth. The pier. The courtyard." Ticking them off one by one on my fingers, I try to remember all the places I've gone.

"Okay, I get it. But all those places are in the city. Maybe a change in scenery—like a huge change—is in order."

I'm shaking my head before she's finished. She'll suggest a vacation. I'll remind her I can't afford it. She'll say it's on her. I'll argue that I don't want to mooch off her. She'll ignore me and we'll be in Bora Bora by tomorrow. And it still won't cure my affliction. I'll lay on the beach, drink way too many mai tais, and pretend my problems don't exist. And I'll come home without any new words written. Without any progress. With nothing to show but a sunburn and an affinity for coconut.

"I can't—"

"Stop it. I know what you're thinking, but I'm not saying we run off to Monaco. My uncle has a cabin up north."

I narrow my eyes. "Which uncle?"

"The good one, not the creepy one. Or the one who embezzled all that money. I'm pretty sure that one's in prison. Or he disappeared overseas. I can never remember." She bites her tongue, then shakes her head. "Anyways, this is the one who cares about something other than how high he is on the societal ladder. But he has a cabin."

She says it with such conviction, I'm pretty sure I'm supposed to react in some way. "Cool. Good for him."

She huffs, gripping my arms and shaking me. "He. Has. A. Cabin. In. The. Woods. Pull your head out of your ass, Maddie. You can go there and touch some goddamn grass. Get in touch with nature. And break whatever the fuck is going on with you. It's perfect. Plus, bonus points because your mother will have no idea where you are and there's barely any cell service up there."

"So, you want me"—I point to my chest—"a self-proclaimed city girl, to go off into the woods and find my spark again. In nature. With bugs."

"Maybe you'll find a lumbersnack, and he'll whisk you away from your gritty life in the city, and you'll stay lost in the woods." She giggles, then sobers. "You can't keep avoiding this, Maddie. You need something to shake you up."

"No way in hell our friendship would survive if we were stuck in the woods together," I snort, trying anything to get out of her wild plan.

"Fuck that. No way in hell am I going with you. You'd use me as procrastination and wouldn't get shit done."

Her hands drop from my arms, and she settles back again. She fixes her gaze on me, daring me to dispute her. She's not wrong. But that doesn't mean she's right. I'm not built for the woods for more than a few days. Glamping is as close as I usually get.

"I've got about three nights in me before I start to worry the trees will eat me..." I wiggle my eyebrows at her, and she smiles, but it's not the normal one I'm used to.

"Maddie, stop hiding."

I drop the dopey look from my face and heave out a breath. "This release took it out of me, Chlo. I'm pretty sure this isn't just burnout. Or writer's block. Or imposter syndrome. Or one of the many other things that plague people like me. I think I might just be done."

Saying it out loud doesn't make it any easier to deal with. Nothing could have prepared me for the deluge of emotions swamping me. Terror, shame, anxiety, guilt—all of it blends together, leaving me to choke on the remnants of my reality.

"You're not done," Chloe snarls, snapping me from my dark thoughts. "You are going to go to this cabin for...four months. And you're going to get in touch with nature. You're going to find your inner writer and kick fucking ass. This is what you're meant to do, Madelyn Rose. You're meant to share your stories. Are you really going to let your characters down? No. You're going to get your ass up and do the thing."

My body vibrates, anticipation overriding the other sensations flowing through me. Despair creeps back in, fighting against the tide threatening to pull me under.

"And if I fail?"

"You won't. I won't allow it."

My stomach coils and I close my eyes once more. "Guess I'd better pack for a road trip, then."

Chapter Five
Maddie

Chloe bounces on the balls of her feet, waving wildly at me as I pull away from the curb. I stick my hand out the window and return the gesture. My eyes keep darting to her shrinking form in the rearview.

I don't know how she pulled everything together so quickly. It hasn't even been a week since she pitched this scheme, yet here I am. She even dealt with my family. Well, everyone but Ryland. I had to call him on my own. Chloe refused to tell me what my mom said, which means it wasn't good.

As I turn onto the freeway, I crank up the music and leave them behind. Even if this doesn't work, at least I'll have some time to myself. Not that I get out much as it is. Writing is a lonely existence no matter how many people I surround myself with. No matter how many readers I have or author friends to confide in, I'm still alone in my stories. Characters make for great companions unless they get pissed off. Or when I kill them off. But they're still fictional.

As the miles tick by, I lose myself in the music blaring from the speakers. The car Chloe leased is fancier than I'm used to, and I might be in love. I won't be using it for much more than going into town, which is apparently the size of a postcard, for groceries. As I pull onto another highway, the sight of chrome temporarily blinds me.

Motorcycles stream by me as I merge. I swear there's at least a hundred of them. A few nod as they pass. The rumble of the engines drowns out whatever song comes on, but I don't care. I'm mesmerized by the way they glide along. I was always too terrified to get on a bike, so I wrote about them instead.

Snorting, I remember how out of place Chloe was when I dragged her to a shop and badgered the bikers with questions when I was doing research. Most of it didn't end up in the book anyway, yet it was the highlight of my year.

I wave to two bikers riding side by side. The smaller of the two waves back, then revs their engine. Grinning, I wonder where they found a pink bike. They're gone before I can study it more, and the tail of the group whizzes by me.

As the front of the pack crests the hill, the sun hits the horizon and I squint. Fumbling with the visor, I finally get it in place. It won't block the light for long, especially since I'll be on this road for a good hour before I have to veer north. I don't think there's even a town for at least thirty miles. Which is why I peed at the last gas station. I studied the route more than I usually would, afraid I'd miss a turn and end up in Nebraska.

I'm still half a mile away from the hill when the reflection from the last bike flashes through the air. I feel like I should mourn their leaving me behind. I haven't seen another vehicle for a while and I'm afraid with the straight roads I'll get tired. It doesn't feel so lonely when there are other people traveling too.

My phone rings and I glance at the high-tech screen in the dashboard I'm scared to touch. It looks too sophisticated for me to figure out. Chloe's name flashes across the display, and I find my smile again. Hitting the handy button on the steering wheel, I wait for her giddy greeting.

"Hey, girl! How's the drive? I figured I should call now since you'll lose service soon. That is, if you haven't chickened out and turned around," she says haughtily.

"I have not turned around. I've lost service once, but it came back. And the drive is boring now. My ass is numb. Oh, and I just saw a bunch of bikers on the highway, so that was..."

I narrow my eyes as I reach the top of the hill. The sun still cuts across my vision, but I can clearly see the road for a good two miles ahead. Yet there are no motorcycles. No one else either, but they shouldn't have been able to get so far ahead of me I wouldn't see them now. Unless they turned off. I glance at the map on the screen as Chloe calls my name.

"Hold on," I mumble, eyes darting from the road to the GPS. "That's weird."

"What's weird? Are you okay?"

"I'm fine. Sorry. I just saw a bunch of bikers. Like at least a hundred of them, but now they're gone."

She snorts. "Are you sure the drive isn't getting to you? Did they get abducted by aliens?"

"Funny. No. They went over a hill, but I can't find them now. And there's no turnoffs." I scan the road, then ease off the gas. I didn't notice how fast I was going, subconsciously hoping I could catch up to them.

"Maybe you're tired." The line clicks as she types something out. "You've got a town about forty-five minutes away. It doesn't have a hotel, but you could at least stretch if you need."

I shake my head. "Nah, I'd rather just get there. My mind was wandering, so I'm sure it was just me being distracted. Did Ryland stop by?"

She huffs, the beeping of the coffee machine echoing down the line. "Yes. And he was just as pleasant as normal. He got the box and flounced back out."

Chuckling, I shift in my seat. Even with the ergonomic design, my ass is still numb. Maybe Chloe is right and I should pull over to stretch my legs. I'm already going to be getting into town too late to go to the cabin right away. I'd rather not sleep in a hotel an hour from my destination, but Chloe wasn't sure what condition the cabin would be in. And I'm not convinced I'd win in a fight for squatter's rights against a raccoon.

"Listen, I know you two have this whole song and dance going on—"

"We do not have any such thing," she sniffs. Whenever she gets flustered, a wild accent shows itself.

"Whatever you want to call it doesn't matter. He's got a small issue that could turn into a big issue, and I just want someone else to be in the know." I bite my lip as I blink against the dying sun's final gasps of light. It slips below the horizon, creating a tapestry of colors threading their way through the sky. It's the type of scene I'd try to describe and fail miserably.

"Fine, tell me what it is. Wait, he isn't sick, is he?"

The concern in her voice is clear, but I decide not to point it out. "Nothing like that. They're raising his rent. By a lot. And he's going to have to move by the time I come back to town. Can you just make sure Mom doesn't jump his shit if he has to move to the 'burbs?"

It's not entirely what I want to ask of her, but she probably wouldn't volunteer to help him find a place. He wouldn't accept her help, either. They're both too stubborn and hung up on the past for something like that.

"You really shouldn't have told me that. Now all I want to do is watch him move there. You think your mom would let me sit there quietly while she tried to find a partner to match the aesthetic?" Her peals of laughter fill the line and I wait for her to get it out of her system. After three minutes, I'm not sure it'll come any time soon.

"Pull your shit together, Chloe. My actual fear is he'll live in his beater of a car because he's too stubborn to ask for help."

Chloe's giggles die out. "Oh, you honestly think he would do that?"

"What do you think?" I sigh, my eyelids becoming heavier with the darkness swirling behind me.

"I promise I won't let him do that. And if need be, I'll run interference with your parents. I'm going to be around for a while, so it shouldn't be a problem."

"Thanks, Chlo. I appreciate it."

She clears her throat. "Listen, I didn't tell you before because I knew you'd argue. You know how I said you won't have a signal up there? Well, I don't want you driving into town to call me. I fully expect not to hear from you until the fall. In fact, if you try, I'll only ask if you're done."

"And if I'm not?" I ask as nerves bubble in my gut.

"I'll hang up on you. Unless it's an emergency, but I'm like hours away. Focus on your writing." She's trying to sound stern, yet failing.

"Fine. I won't call you."

She snorts and I can practically feel her eyes rolling. "No texting either."

Dammit. That was exactly what I was going to do. Her cutting me off is what I need. I'd allow her to distract me and procrastinate, returning four months later with nothing accomplished.

"Gah. I hate that you know me so well."

"You love me. Now, tell me what else I missed when I was in France."

She stays on the phone until my signal drops the call. My stomach knots, wondering when I'll get to talk to her again. I have no problem being alone. Doesn't mean I won't miss her, though. I tried to get her to push back this idea until we could spend some time together, but she wasn't having it. She has more faith in me than I have in myself. I wrap her confidence in me around my heart as I drive onward. Her faith is the only thing I have left to cling to.

My phone pings and I glance at the screen on the dash, then chuckle. I pull to the side of the road, checking my mirrors, though I'm sure no one else is around. Chloe's last gift before I drop off the face of the planet is apparently to force me to rest. I set the GPS to my new destination before heading out again.

An hour later, I pull into a dusty parking lot, eyeing the bed-and-breakfast Chloe booked for me. She didn't need to do all the planning, but she insisted. She probably thought I'd back out if she didn't. And she'd be right.

An old woman steps onto the porch, the light illuminating her white hair. As I climb from my car, she raises her hand. I grab my overnight bag before climbing the stairs. She smiles warmly, gesturing me inside.

"You must be Madelyn." She doesn't wait for me to answer before she's ushering me past a makeshift front desk and through a swinging door. "You must be starving after your drive. Come eat. The boy will bring your bag to your room. Don't worry, he knows better than to go through them."

The boy she's referring to doesn't look much younger than me. He clearly has an edge to him, but the affection in his eyes for the older woman combats the darkness swirling around him. He dips his chin to me and holds out his hand for my bag. I hesitate, then pass it over.

"Be careful. My laptop is in there," I blurt out. Instantly I regret the words. If he wanted to rob me, I just gave him a reason to do so.

"Won't be tossing it out the window, ma'am." He turns to the older woman. "I'm heading out after this, Marie. I've got to get there by tomorrow night."

She pats his cheek, smiling. "Don't forget to take the cake I baked you two."

He scowls, but not until she turns away from him. When he catches me staring, I duck my chin to my chest and settle onto a stool by the island. He shuffles away, disappearing through a door I didn't notice before.

Marie sets a bowl in front of me, and I stare at the soup. A spoon appears by my elbow. The smell of homemade chicken soup wraps around my senses and my eyes flutter shut. It's been more than a few years since I've had it. The last time was when I was still living at home.

"Eat up, dear."

"Do you know Chloe?" I ask as I dip the spoon in and take a bite.

I almost audibly groan, it's so delicious. If I didn't know any better, I'd think my mother broke in and cooked this. She made it every time Ryland or I, and sometimes even Chloe, was sick. Chicken soup, saltine crackers, and a Sprite were her cure for most ailments. And somehow it always worked. A piece of apple pie appears next, and I smile in thanks at Marie.

"No idea who Chloe is, but I'm sure she's one of the good ones if we're crossing paths. This journey you're on will take more than some good food, but I have no doubt you'll figure everything out." She bustles around the room, gathering ingredients I can't imagine will be used together.

Chloe must have put something in the notes when she booked this place. "We'll see, I suppose. This is delicious, by the way."

"I'm glad you like it, dear. I've made plenty a goodies for people over the years. Some are a little trickier than others. More than a few have given me a run for my money. Can't complain, though. I've got a mighty fine legacy from them, if I do say so myself."

I'm not entirely sure whether she's talking about desserts or people, but I nod along anyway. Arguing with the one who feeds me is not something I'm willing to risk. I dip my spoon in the bowl once more. The metal scrapes against the porcelain and I frown. I don't remember eating the whole thing.

"Don't worry yourself, Madelyn." She snatches the bowl away and nudges the pie closer. "Hurting people rarely realize how hungry they truly are. All they need is a good meal to fill them up and they're on the path to recovery most of the time."

"How long have you run this place?" I ask before stuffing a forkful in my mouth. It's divine, just like I knew it would be.

The explosion of sweet and tart dances on my tongue. Flakes rain down on my plate, and I lick my lips before diving in again. Marie might be spouting a lot of stuff I don't understand, but she's right. Her meal is certainly healing something within me. At least for now.

"Not as long as you'd think. Yet the passage of time is often one I can't pin down. Which is fine. I'd much rather live within the pages of a book." She turns her kind eyes to me, pining me in place with a look. "Don't you agree?"

I set the fork down, the plate cleaned of pie. I can't pull my gaze away from hers. It's as if she's staring into my soul, judging whether I'm worthy of her advice.

"Yes," I whisper finally. "I agree."

Chapter Six
Maddie

My mind is so muddled by the time I fall into the bed, I don't even notice my surroundings. When sunlight streams through the sheer curtains, I groggily open my eyes. I may not have been with it while I went to sleep, but I was pretty sure there was more lace. Now the room looks like it's been abandoned. Sitting up, my eyes dart around and I pull the covers to my chin. My bag sits innocently on a solitary chair, untouched. I didn't even change when I got up here.

"No way that old woman drugged me," I mutter, flinging the comforter back.

Slipping from the bed, I sway, pressing my fingers to my temples. A throb of pain hits me behind my eyes, then disappears. I shouldn't have gotten up so fast. I stumble to the en suite and do my business. Shaking out my hair, I wonder if I should shower or find someone for breakfast first. I opt to get clean first, then figure out what the hell is going on.

As the water splashes across my skin, I close my eyes. Usually, my thoughts are absorbed with my latest story. Or the latest idea that's popped in my head. Instead, I'm left puzzling over the words Marie spoke last night. She seemed to know exactly what I needed to hear. And her food was amazing, even if it was poisoned.

When I'm done, I dress quickly and check my phone. I almost forgot about it, which is not normal. Every other day, it's the first thing I grab. Mornings are spent scrolling and pretending I don't have to get up. This place is starting to give me the eebie jeebies. I resign myself to getting out of here as quickly as possible and making it to the cabin before noon.

I try to call Chloe, but it won't connect. Sending her a quick text, I watch the spinning wheel for what feels like forever before it fails. I guess I really won't be contacting her for a while.

I sigh, then grab my bag before stepping into the hall. The stairs creak as I make my way down to the main level. Everything is the same as last night. The makeshift front desk with six keys hanging behind it is right there. Potted plants frame the front door, which should give it a homey feel, but it just falls flat. I realize they're fake and goosebumps erupt along my arms. I almost feel like I fell into a mystery novel. Or maybe a horror...

Shaking my head, I push open the kitchen door and it swings shut behind me. The deserted room sends another chill up my spine. Nothing looks out of place, but the vibe is definitely off here. It's nothing like the cozy feeling I had last night. A plate with a towel over it sits on the island with a note stuck on top.

"Hello?" I call, glancing around.

My name graces the front of the paper in flowy script. This had to be from Marie. Peeking under the towel, I expect something to jump out at me, and my stomach flips. I breathe a sigh of relief when I find scones. I probably shouldn't eat them, but my stomach grumbles and I snatch one up. I may be the first to die in a horror movie, yet I won't be hungry when I meet my demise.

It crumbles in my mouth and an involuntary moan leaves me. I stuff more in my mouth before unfolding the letter. More of the same elegant handwriting splashes across the page. Apparently, Marie had a food emergency that couldn't wait. I grab another scone and shove it in my mouth. Of course, she tells me I'm welcome to stay as long as I'd like and take all the scones with me if I need to leave.

Don't forget to be prepared for whatever life hands you. The best things in life are often handed to us while wrapped in a surprise we weren't expecting.

I wish I could talk to my best friend. How the hell did she find this place? Marie didn't even seem to recognize her name, even though Chloe booked the room. I glance over my shoulder, half expecting the man from last night to appear. He doesn't, of course. The bed-and-breakfast is quiet as a tomb other than my own heartbeat.

I shove the rest of the scones in the plastic bag and seal it, then grab my bag and head to my car. Marie said nothing about locking the door, so I leave it the same as I found it. Dashing back inside, I almost trip on the last stair. I scribble a quick note to Marie, thanking her. I wish I had cash for a tip, but I'm pretty sure Chloe left one when she booked. She usually does, anyway.

"Alright," I mutter as I climb behind the wheel again. "Let's get this shit on the road."

I glance around, waiting for someone to catch me talking to myself. Just like everywhere else, the area is deserted, thankfully. The number of times people have caught me mumbling under my breath should be embarrassing. I don't apologize for it anymore. It's the way I deal with being by myself most of the time.

My tires hit a pothole as I bump down the driveway, and I grimace. Easing to a stop at the entrance, I check both ways. A beat-up truck rumbles down the road, kicking up dust as it goes. A man in a cowboy hat scowls as he passes, but still lifts his fingers in a half-hearted wave. I lift my hand a second too late, then burst into laughter. At least four goats sway back and forth in the bed of the truck. I'm sure they're bleating out their distress, but I can't hear it over the song that starts up on the radio just then.

I glance at my phone, not recognizing the song. The cover shows a man who would be labeled a silver fox by my author friends.

"Hayes Griffon, you can definitely sing me to sleep every night."

The ballad continues, and I hum along as I pull the opposite way the truck was going. The dust has settled, leaving the road desolate. As Hayes sings out the last note, I smile. My phone beeps and my music cuts off. I switch to the radio and the speakers crackle as I search for a station.

I turn onto the highway finally, still scanning for anything to come in. I hate driving without music, but at least I only have another hour to go. I'll end up talking to myself again. Maybe I'll figure out some of the plot points in the many manuscripts wallowing on my computer.

Finally, a station picks up, and once again, it's Hayes Griffon. He's singing the same ballad as before. This time around, I sing the chorus. He's pining after someone, proclaiming how shitty he's been and how he'll make it up to her.

The speakers crackle again as the song ends, then cuts out completely. Grumbling, I fiddle with the radio as my tires eat up the road. Of course there's nothing. My phone isn't connecting. I resign myself to an annoyingly silent final leg of my journey.

By the time I pull into the small town, I'm a ball of anxious nerves. I have no idea what to expect and I just want to put it off a little longer. A small grocery store sits next to the post office, but there's nothing else other than a few houses scattered here and there. I'm surprised they can get mail way out here.

I park in front of the store, hoping they're open since it looks deserted. The bell over the door rings out and I glance around. Three aisles stuffed full of products are laid out in front of me. I grab the only basket, nodding to the woman behind the counter.

Meandering through the small space, I grab whatever looks good. Marie's scones will only last me so long and I'll have to stock the cabin. I'm not about to plan out my meals since I mostly snack when I'm writing. It's not healthy, but it's gotten me this far in life.

The bell jingles again, and I glance toward the door. A woman dressed in all black skips inside, followed by three men. They have the same air as the man back at the bed-and-breakfast. I avert my eyes, not wanting to have small-town chitchat. Now that I've stopped here, I just want to get to the cabin. If I would have gone there first, though, I wouldn't emerge again until the scones were polished off.

"She's right there. Can't I just—" the woman whispers.

"Leave it," one of the men snaps.

I can feel their eyes on me, but I ignore it. I'm sure a stranger in this tiny place is a sight. How many people even live here? Chloe said it was in the middle of nowhere. I didn't expect to have to deal with a lot of residents. Or their ogling of a newcomer. Making friendly with them might not be that bad, especially if I need help with something. When I look up to greet them, though, they've vanished. Peering around, I don't see them anywhere.

I shake my head and plan on a nap once I get to the cabin. The last two days—hell, the last week, has been a whirlwind. I probably pushed myself too hard getting ready to be gone for four months. Add in the anxiety of whether this venture will work to jump-start my writing and I'm not surprised I'm discombobulated.

Grinning at the woman, I set the basket on the counter. Her lips twitch as if she's attempting to smile back at me and failing. She scans the items one by one, scowling at the ancient machine as it beeps at her. A scar runs from her cheek to her jaw, pale and barely visible. I narrow my eyes before I realize I'm staring. Poor woman probably gets that enough, especially when it was fresh.

I smile again when our gazes meet, and she huffs. I'm not one to force small talk. Especially when the other person seems annoyed as hell. I can't blame her. Working in this place probably isn't the most exciting job.

A man appears out the front window and raps his knuckles on the glass. The woman's head whips around, and he raises an eyebrow. She shakes her head and shoos him away.

"Sorry about that. He's protective," she mutters. Her voice seems familiar.

"That's fine. You look like you could snap me in half if I had nefarious motives." I laugh awkwardly, grimacing. Why the fuck did I say that? I really hate small talk.

"Not really my thing. The others…" She snaps her mouth shut and slams her hand onto the machine.

She shoves the items into two bags and thrusts them at me. Gingerly, I take them. I have no idea what just happened. Maybe she's just having a bad day.

"Uh, how much do I owe you?"

"Nothing. Just…" She glances out the window and whispers, "Do right by them."

"What was that?" I ask, flabbergasted. There's no one around and Chloe said no one has been to the cabin in years.

She clears her throat, shaking her head. "Go right on Second. The bridge is out."

She hurries away, leaving me standing there, holding bags of groceries I haven't paid for, in a place that shouldn't exist anymore. It should be one of those ghost towns they do documentaries on. Yet all the people I've seen are not only wildly out of place, but they're all around my age.

I push it from my mind as I settle in the driver's seat. Another ten minutes and trees close in around me. The turnoff to the cabin is almost obscured and I wrench the wheel. The canopy overhead casts shadows across the road, and I slow to a crawl as I bump along. The trees open up, revealing a quaint little cabin. Quaint and little aren't the right words to describe it since it's a lot bigger than I imagined, but it gives off that vibe.

A swing hangs by the front door with a pair of rocking chairs on the other side. Craning my neck around, I spot more seating along the side. It looks like the porch wraps most of the way around. The sun breaks through the clouds, bathing the whole scene in a golden sheen. It's like a fairy tale come to life.

Craning my neck, I scan the area. Large swaths of emerald green lawn expand on each side of the home before abruptly hitting a line of dense trees. I eye the shadows cast by the trunks and a shiver rolls down my spine. Hopefully, I'll be able to calm my nerves enough to venture in there while I'm here. I should have asked Chloe what animals to watch out for.

I push my door open and lean out, the sounds of nature filling the air. I can't see very far from here, but it seems as if there's a steep drop behind the cabin. Chloe didn't tell me much about this place other than the plumbing and electricity worked. I'm kicking myself now for the oversight.

I leave my things in the car and make my way to the front door. I didn't realize how loud the woods would be between the breeze blowing through the trees and the birds calling to one another. As worried as I was, a peace steals over me, relaxing my muscles. Maybe this won't be so bad after all.

I pull in a deep breath, then twist the knob and push on the front door. It doesn't move. Chloe said it wasn't locked and sometimes would stick. Her exact words were "put your back into it." I giggle as I knock my shoulder into the wood. Of course it doesn't move still. Because why would anything to be simple?

Taking a few steps back, I cross my arms. I glance over my shoulder, making sure I'm alone before a grin spreads over my face. I've always wanted to smash through a door. It probably won't work and I'll hurt myself, but when else am I going to have the opportunity to try? Never.

I brace myself, then skip toward the barrier and kick my heel into the wood. Yelping, I stagger back, hopping on one foot. That was not my smartest move. It's a good thing I'm not strong enough to break my foot.

"Ow, ow, ow. That was not smart, Maddie. What the fuck," I mumble, trying to clutch at my injured heel.

My other foot hits the lip of the stairs and I whimper. My arms pinwheel as I fall in slow motion through the air. No one will find me out here. Chloe won't be expecting me to bother her for at least a month. I'll be rotting away in the dirt. And that's if the animals don't find me first. Just the image of a coyote dragging my dead body into the underbrush sends a shiver through me.

I squeeze my eyes shut, hoping I don't hear my bones crunching when I hit the ground. Instead, strong arms wrap around me, cushioning my fall. My breath hitches, pulling in the scent of old parchment paper. It's so distinct my eyes fly open and my mouth drops. A gruff man, swathed in a black shirt, stares down at me. His blue eyes, lined with concern, bore into me.

And then he opens his mouth and the huskiest voice I've ever heard asks, "Are you okay?"

Chapter Seven
Emmett

Golden. It's the only way to describe the woman in my arms. She was a fiery phoenix, flying through the air. I couldn't leave her to crack her skull on the ground. Losing her feels like it would be a loss to the world at large.

Her golden hair slides over my arms, tickling my skin. Her golden eyes stare up at me as if she's as mesmerized by me as I am by her. Her golden skin shimmers in the sunlight and my breath hitches. I wonder if every inch of her is golden.

My fingers tingle as I right her. My hands fall away from her when she steadies, and I mourn the loss. Shaking my head, I try to come to grips with this turn of events. I'm only here to fix up the cabin—nothing more, nothing less. Falling for this golden girl is not in the plans. Not that I'm in danger of that. I'm perfectly content with where I am in life.

"Are you okay?" I ask again as she gapes at me.

"Where did you come from?"

Even her voice gives off a golden quality, lilting and musical. It weaves around me and I bite my cheek.

Running a hand through my hair, I pull my eyes away from hers. "I was out back. Now, answer the question."

"I'm fine," she whispers, then shakes her head. "I'm sorry, who are you?"

My mind glitches, fog seeping into the corners of my mind. I flex my fingers, swallowing hard. It's rare I meet anyone else. I'm content being a loner, but sometimes it's hard to remember how to do small talk.

"Emmett. I, uh, I've been fixing up the cabin. Hasn't been tended to in a while." I gesture at the structure behind her.

She glances over her shoulder, then back at me, and the corner of my lips twitch. She has no idea what I'm working on. I doubt she's spent a lot of time in the woods like this. The fancy car sitting in the driveway said as much, but the look on her face confirms it. I could go through all the things I'm fixing. Not many people care about that stuff, though. They just want the job done.

Alarm flashes in her eyes. "Does Chloe know you're here?"

"I don't know a Chloe, gorgeous." The pet name slips out without warning and my muscles tense, waiting for her reaction.

She sighs, gazing up at the clear blue sky peeking through the trees. "Of course you don't. Because Chloe doesn't own this place. Sorry, I'm Madelyn. Maddie. I'm supposed to be...I probably shouldn't be telling you any of this."

"Why is that?" I ask, raising an eyebrow and crossing my arms over my chest.

She narrows her gaze and leans away from me. "Are you an axe murderer? Or...a thief? Wait, that's not what they...is this a B and E?"

"If I was an axe murderer, I'd have an axe. And I probably wouldn't have caught you as you were falling off the porch. Also, I'm not the one who was trying to karate chop down the door. If anyone should be worried, it's me."

Her mouth drops open, an indistinguishable noise coming from the back of her throat. I can practically see the gears turning in her mind, attempting to refute what I've said. She spins around and stomps a few steps away before pivoting to face me again. When she juts out a finger in my direction, I almost crack. As it is, I'm having a hard time holding back a smile. When she was falling into my arms, she was awash in a fiery blaze, but this? This is something wholly different. The passion flaming in her eyes while she's searching for a way out is something I've never seen before.

"You're like well over six feet. You could easily snap me in half. Or rip my heart from my chest while it was still beating. Or...drag me into the woods and bury me in a fallen log with a bunch of bloody meat, creating the world's most vicious wolf treat."

"Where the hell did that come from?" The descriptions she came up with are ridiculously specific. And slightly terrifying.

Her cheeks redden and she tucks her chin to her chest and mumbles, "Comes with the territory."

"What territory? Being a serial killer?"

Her head whips up and she rolls her eyes. "I'm an author. I've written about things like this. Why the hell are we even talking about this? Listen, thank you for making sure I didn't break my neck. How long will it take you to finish whatever you were fixing?"

I rub my hand along my jaw, scanning the cabin. Part of me wants to tell her it all could wait. What if I end up running her off? I don't know why she's staying here, and I doubt she'll tell me. There's something there, though, whispering in the back of my mind, telling me she has to stay. Something in her calls to me, insisting I need to convince her everything will be fine. I shake my head, forcing the thoughts from my mind.

"Honestly, a while. The roof needs patched. The deck is rotting in places. Some of the electrical is out and the second bathroom needs some work. Not to mention the parts of the porch railing need replacing. Couple of the doors need work and—"

"Okay, I get it. The place is falling apart at the seams. Have you been crashing here?"

I nod, though that's not technically the truth. I planned on staying here, but the last few weeks have been fuzzy. I think I fell asleep on the beach after gazing at the stars last night. It's time to find a new purpose and being in the middle of nature might help. Changing the trajectory of my life is top priority. This project was the first step toward that.

She sighs, running her fingers through her golden locks. It's distracting, with the sunlight glimmering off the strands. She pulls her hair up into a ponytail and it swings behind her as she glances around.

"Well, I suppose I can always go back home." Her defeated tone puts an ache in my chest, dangerously close to my heart.

"The cabin's big enough. You can do whatever you need to while I fix things up around you. I can start with the deck so you'll have some place to go while I work inside. There's two bedrooms, one upstairs and the other in the lower level, so that won't be a problem. Two bathrooms, though there's only one working shower."

Her lip twitches and I raise an eyebrow. "Is there only one bed?"

"I just said there were two bedrooms. Plus, about seven couches. Why they need that many is beyond me," I mutter.

Her face falls the slightest bit, and she turns away. "Well, can you open the door? Chloe said it wasn't locked and the latch sticks, which is why I was trying to kick it down. I didn't think anyone would see me, though."

"It's fine. Always wanted to try it myself." I grimace as she glances over her shoulder. "I did lock it. Didn't want anyone wandering in."

I produce the key from my pocket, though I don't remember slipping it in there. In fact, I can't recall locking the door. I didn't come to until I heard Maddie's car. Sleeping on the ground took it out of me. I should have gone into the cabin once I got tired, especially being next to the woods. Surprised an animal didn't attack me while I was passed out.

She marches up the stairs, grabbing the railing as she goes. The spindles wobble and I rush to catch her if she falls again. My hands hover as she hustles the last few steps. She slides to the side and gestures for me to pass her. I swallow hard, trying to block her view as I put the key in. I jiggle the lock and say a prayer as I turn the knob. It pops open and I breathe a sigh of relief.

I slip out of the way and present the way to her. "After you, Maddie."

Her gaze darts to me, then skips away as she steps inside. Her feet stutter as she crosses the threshold, and my hand shoots out before I think better of it. She leans into my touch and my vision flashes. I blink against the brightness, dropping my arm. I blink again, and the next thing I see is Maddie's concerned face.

"Are you okay?"

"That's my line," I say, then grin.

She huffs, but I catch a small smile before she turns around. I track her movements as she peeks into the small half bath next to the door. I need to fix the sink in there and check the toilet. My palms itch to catch her as she stumbles over a loose rug in the short hallway. I make a note to remove it before she cracks her skull open.

I glance toward the kitchen to the left. The oven doesn't work, and half the pendant lights are out over the tiny island. I wonder if I should expand the area by taking out the closet across from the half bath. Shaking my head, I push the idea from my mind. This place isn't mine. I can't just go tearing down walls to suit my plans.

If I could, though, I'd gut the entire place and rework the entire floor plan. The stairs to the lower level would have to stay, but I'd move the bedroom on this level and expand it into the living space. It's sectioned weird with two separate sitting areas that probably rarely get used

I hurry after Maddie as she wanders toward the back of the cabin. The space opens up, revealing a sunken living room with massive floor-to-ceiling windows overlooking the back deck.

Clearly, all the money from the last renovation went into this area. I wrinkle my nose at the massive dining table taking up a third of the area. It doesn't look intentional—as if they stuck it there without thought to how the room would flow.

"Chloe didn't say anything about a deck. It's huge," she whispers, pressing her nose against the glass.

"Who is Chloe exactly?" I cross my arms, watching her from the landing.

"My best friend. Her uncle owns this place." She whips around, wide eyes finding mine. "And she knows exactly where I am and when I'm supposed to be back. And I'll be checking in with her regularly."

"I'm not an axe murderer, Maddie. And I'm not going to drag you into the woods to turn you into a wolf chew toy. Or drown you in the lake."

"There's a lake?" she exclaims, whipping back around. She raises on her tiptoes and cranes her neck.

Loping down the three stairs into the living room, I make my way to the sliding glass door. I open it with a flourish, presenting her the way yet again. She rolls her eyes, hiding another smile. In the fifteen minutes I've known her, I've gotten the impression she doesn't hand them out easily. Each one feels like a balm to my injured soul. Which is ridiculous. I don't even know this woman.

I grab her arm as she skips over the threshold, almost putting her foot through a soft spot. "Why don't I go first so you don't end up with your feet dangling through a hole you've created?"

She nods as her body shivers. I intended to keep my hand on her upper arm, but she links them together, clutching at my bicep instead. I could tell her it's not that serious and she'd be fine, but I'm enjoying her clinging to me too much to say anything.

If I had the time, I could extend the deck to attach to the side porches. Having stairs leading down from here would be nice, too. I doubt I'll have a moment to spare with the other repairs. Attaching stairs to a two-story deck isn't a small task. I edge her around the rotten parts of the wood until we're at the railing.

"Don't lean on this. Some of the posts are missing and, as previously established, you can't fly." I smirk as she continues to clutch me to her.

"It's like something out of a fairy tale. How the hell did Chloe never take me here? Why would they let it fall apart?"

"Technically, it's not falling apart. And people get busy with their lives. They buy these places and mean to spend time at them, but life gets in the way." My hand covers hers, which is wrapped around my arm. The extra connection sends tingles through my skin.

"I suppose. But if I had a place like this…"

"You'd live here?" I ask, chuckling.

She snorts, brushing the hair from her face when the breeze picks up. "No. I'm not exactly a woodsy kind of girl. Spent my life in the city, so I don't really know why I said that."

"Kind of magical, though, isn't it?"

"The kind of place you fall into without even meaning to," she whispers.

She gazes out at the area, the crystal blue lake, the water lapping gently on the shore, and the whole array of trees circling the scene. But I'm not looking at anything but her. For some reason, I'm drawn to her. I've never felt this way before. It's as if a fog has lifted from my mind, allowing me to see clearly for the first time in my life.

I bite my cheek and look away as pain radiates from the wound. It centers me just enough to pull away from her. Whatever spell she's put on me, I need to break free of it. Nothing good can come from this. I'm not in the right place to get involved with a woman like her. No matter how much it hurts to turn away from what fate is placing in my hands.

Chapter Eight
Maddie

Every thought going through my head is contradictory. Emmett led me back inside, muttering about getting back to work, then disappeared. I have no idea where he went. I didn't ask, but I wanted to. Then my inner monologue took over. Instead of my brain crafting a story, filling in plot holes, and revealing character arcs, it warred with itself over whether I should jump the man's bones.

In jeans and a black T-shirt, it's not like he was flaunting his body. Yet when he caught me, I could feel the definition of his muscles—both in his biceps and his stomach. Actually, everywhere. Every inch of him was sculpted by some god long since moved on from this world. I could get over that. Usually, that just meant they were obsessed with working out and that is not something I'm even remotely interested in.

But then his brown hair flopped over his forehead, and I was captured. The strands glittered in the sunlight, almost a caramel color. His eyes waver between green and blue, I swear matching the photo of Lake Michigan I took years ago. I loved the shades so much I had it made into a canvas and hung it over my desk when I finally had a space of my own.

When his eyes bored into mine, demanding an answer to whether or not I was okay, I was pretty much a goner. It's like my perfect book boyfriend was plucked from the pages and set down right in front of me.

My lip curls as I lug my bags inside. I *was* completely smitten with him until my better sense caught up to me. He might not be an axe murderer, but he certainly has snark lacing every word that drops from that perfectly formed mouth. I could disregard that if it wasn't for the look on his face. Describing it would take every thesaurus I have sitting at home. Not that I use any of them. They're more for nostalgia. Thesauruses are a dime a dozen online, and usually have all the slang in them as well.

I drop the last of my bags on the bed in the bedroom situated off the living area. Emmett said there were two bedrooms, but I didn't bother searching for the other. His things aren't in here, so I assume this was the one I was supposed to post up in.

I dump the contents on the bed and paw through my clothes. None of them are cute, but that shouldn't matter. No, it *doesn't* matter what I'm wearing. Because I'm not trying to impress anyone, least of all Emmett. He's probably pissed at me anyway for interrupting his work.

Shoving my clothes in the drawers, I mumble under my breath about all the ways this could go wrong while my pussy tries to convince me this is a perfect situation. Apparently, she has a mind of her own now. And she's certain he's the one thing we need to break through this writer's block. Even if it doesn't help my issue, then at least we'd get a good dicking down out of it.

She's ridiculous in her tenacity, and it's pissing me off.

"Jumping his bones would be incredibly uncouth," I mutter. "Just keep your head down and deal with it for a week."

"So, you'll only be here for a week?" Emmett asks from behind me.

I squeak, tossing the remaining clothes in the air as I perform a pirouette I'd be proud of at any other time. Of course I was holding my bras and underwear. And of course, they're now plopping around me like live grenades, just waiting to go off at the slightest touch. Maybe if I don't move, he won't notice the pair of panties on my head.

He saunters forward, lips twitching. "You have a little something...right there."

He plucks the underwear off my head and drops it into the waiting drawer. A gentleman would have shut the door and pretended he hadn't noticed a goddamn thing. In fact...

"The door was closed. Do you often barge into people's rooms indiscriminately?" My haughty tone doesn't hide the redness of my cheeks. Still makes me feel better, though.

"If you would have checked the other room, you would have noticed there wasn't a bed in there. And the walls were torn up. It's uninhabitable." He makes his way to the attached bathroom, leaving the door wide open.

I breathe a sigh of relief when he starts washing his hands instead of peeing. In most circumstances, I wouldn't have assumed he was going to take a piss with me right here, but I can't put my finger on this guy. Shocked would not be one of my reactions if he whipped his dick out right now.

I shake my head, wondering where the hell that thought came from. Sure, he might barge into rooms and lean on the sarcasm, but there's nothing to suggest he'd do something like that.

"Perhaps you can take one of the seven couches then," I say sweetly over the water while I shove my unmentionables into the drawer.

"Except all of them are in the living room and face a massive wall of windows that have no curtains. And as it's summertime, the sun makes an appearance ridiculously early. I'm doing hard labor and need my beauty sleep," He flashes me a smile, showing way too many straight, white teeth. It kind of looks like he's going to eat me. My pussy purrs at the thought, and I mentally beat her back with a broom.

My fists land on my hips so hard I wince. "So what am I supposed to do? I can't sleep on the couch. And that car may seem super fancy, but it isn't exactly comfortable to sleep in."

He leans against the door frame, crossing his arms. "I'm not going to make you sleep in your car."

"Well, that's just peachy. Where exactly do you suggest I sleep then? And why do you get *this* room? None of your stuff is in here. I figured this was a first come, first serve kind of situation." I purse my lips, glancing around again to make sure I didn't miss his bag stuffed in a corner.

His eyebrow pops up. "You sure about that?"

His eyes dart to the dresser drawers next to the open one with my underthings spilling out of them. I checked all the drawers. I remember searching each of them to make sure I wasn't the interloper. My hand trembles as I reach out slowly, then glance at him.

"Are you fucking with me?" I ask, narrowing my gaze.

He rolls his eyes, gesturing me to continue. I frown, snatching the handle and ripping the drawer open. Neatly folded clothes greet me, and I silently curse.

"Those were not there before. When the hell did you sneak in? While I was getting my bags from the car?"

The irrational urge to toss his perfectly pleated pants out the window overtakes me. My palms itch and I curl my hands into fists. I'm usually an even-keeled kind of gal. Being around this man has thrown me off. I'm either wanting to climb him like a tree or run screaming into the woods to get away from him.

A flash of confusion crosses his face. "They were always there. Perhaps you didn't check."

My blood boils and I pull in a deep breath, holding it until my rage is at a simmer. Assuming he's trying to gaslight me isn't healthy. Maybe I really didn't check well enough.

"How did you even get here?" I ask, using the innocuous question to center myself.

"Truck's parked on the forest road about a half mile away. It's old and didn't quite make it here. I'll have to fix it later."

Of course he doesn't have a working vehicle. Which means I'll feel bad if I actually leave. Annoyance bubbles through me again. Not at him, in particular, but the fact I can't abandon him without helping him. It's the way I was raised.

When I have my shit under control, I pivot and grab an armful of my clothes from the drawer. I'll deal with the couch or find another room I can drag some cushions into. He's probably exaggerating about the other bedroom. It can't be *that* bad.

I swivel and drop my underwear into my open suitcase. Spinning around again, I attempt to school my face into one of neutrality. I pull open another drawer and grab the next bundle of clothes. When I turn to drop them in my bag, I catch Emmet clutching a bunch of my thongs. I freeze and my gaze meets his wide-eyed one.

"So help me, if you sniff them..."

He scowls, then tosses them in the drawer before pivoting and stomping back to the bathroom. I roll my eyes and drop the clothes. By the time I gather my underwear again, he's back, unpacking my bag. Tipping my head back, my nostrils flare as I attempt to calm the hell down. I won't be able to have a civil conversation if I can't get my emotions under control.

"What are you doing?" I snap, snatching them away from him.

"Pretty clear. I'm stopping you from running away, gorgeous."

I roll my eyes again at the nickname, but let it go. No use picking another fight when we're already in one. Unless we're not arguing at all and I misread the situation. Fuck, I hate dealing with people. Interacting with characters is so much easier. When they talk back, I can just tell them to shut up. I can blame them for a messed-up situation and they can't argue. Mostly because it's their fault they decided to go off the rails with the plan. Sure, they fuck shit up sometimes, but when they piss me off, I just walk away from my computer for a while. They still scream at me in my head. Eventually they get tired, though.

Handling actual people is a whole other ball game. And I'm not very good at sports. They have all sorts of emotions and feelings, yet most of the time they keep them hidden. Makes for very frustrating interactions. I always end up tripping over my words and saying something that probably should have been an inside thought.

"We can't both stay in this room," I mutter even as my thighs clench. I'm studiously ignoring the signals racing through my body.

"Why not? We're both adults. Unless you're still worried I'm secretly an axe murderer." He sends me another smirk, as if that's supposed to ease my worries.

I clear my throat, glancing away. "We don't know each other. We met, what, an hour ago?"

He nods, staring over my head, and he adopts a pensive look. "We'll alternate until you're comfortable, then. You can stay here tonight, and I'll take the couch. Tomorrow night we'll switch."

I narrow my eyes and my chest aches for some reason I'm not willing to explore. "Until I'm *comfortable?*"

"I'm sure before long you'll be begging to sleep in my bed."

My mouth drops open. Before I can collect my thoughts, he pivots and strolls out the door. The audacity of that man. It took me a ridiculously long time to come up with an excuse why we shouldn't share a bed in the first place. Finding a comeback worthy of his asinine statement will take me years.

Still, I plant my hands on my hips and shout, "It's not your bed, asshole!"

His chuckle echoes through the house, and I stomp over and slam the door shut behind him. Clenching my jaw, I stare at the swirls of wood, wondering how I got myself into this situation. This trip is supposed to be calming. Chloe insisted if I just touched some grass, I wouldn't feel like I fucked my whole career. With this new addition, I imagine most of my days will be spent either bickering with Emmett or avoiding him so I don't soak through all my panties.

I don't have time for this.

The thought pulls me up short and despair crashes over me. I spin around and sink to the floor, pulling my knees to my chest, then wrap my arms around my legs. I have nothing *but* time. Four months seems entirely too long, yet too short to accomplish all my goals. I'm afraid I'll put off writing until the time to leave looms over me. I'll go home with a pitiful attempt at getting my shit back on track.

I can't keep going like this. Either I buckle down, no matter if Emmett hangs around or not. Or I take this time to reevaluate my life. Maybe being in the woods won't be so bad. Having Emmett here might help stave off the boredom when I'm staring at a blank screen. I sigh, knocking my head against the door. Writing was all I ever wanted to do, but maybe I should find something else. Something more guaranteed and less stressful.

Today I'll wallow. Tomorrow I'll figure out whether I give up on my dreams.

Chapter Nine
Emmett

A wolf howls, jolting me from sleep, and I jerk upright on the couch. Light pierces into my brain via my eyes and I groan, flopping back again. It can't be more than five in the morning. I silently curse Maddie, blaming her for my early rise. It's not her fault, but if she wasn't here, I'd be in that bed, slumbering away.

I shouldn't have suggested we share. When the idea popped in my head, the words tumbled out. I'm not usually so forward, especially with someone I just met, but there's something different about Maddie.

It's as if she's everything I've been searching for without even knowing it. Between her sass and awkwardness, I don't know which is more endearing. I scrub my hands over my face, trying to push her image from my mind. I should not be this fixated on her after less than twenty-four hours. Except someone whispers in the back of my mind, telling me she was written just for me—the perfect woman for me, drafted from my fantasies and splashed across the page.

I groan again, attempting to kick the blanket I found off my legs. Instead, the fabric twists around my ankles and before I know it, I'm rolling toward the floor. Crashing onto my hands and knees, I bite back a yelp as pain radiates through my bones. I drop my forehead to the ground and squeeze my eyes shut. This is the other reason I didn't want to sleep on the couch. None of them are wide enough for me, and I always end up in this position.

"Why are you on the floor?" Maddie croaks, and I lift my head.

She presses the heel of her hand to her face, rubbing the sleep from her eyes. With her golden hair jutting every which way, she looks like she's been rolling around in a ball pit. When she blinks sleepily at me, a bolt of desire runs through me, making my morning wood all the more painful.

"Don't worry about it. Go back to sleep," I mumble.

There's no way I'm standing up right now. I'll stay right here with the blanket still wrapped around my feet and my hard-on concealed from Maddie's prying eyes. Not that she looks awake enough to notice anything. I could brandish an axe at her and she'd merely yawn. My lips twitch and I drop my head again.

"Did you fall off the couch?"

"I'm fine. Go back to bed, Maddie. It's too early to be awake."

Exhaustion from staying up way too late, fruitlessly hoping Maddie would change her mind about sharing a bed, makes my arms tremble. Even sitting back would expose me since I'm only in boxer briefs. They don't leave much to the imagination.

She yawns loudly and I glance at her through my lashes. I zero in on the small strip of skin peeking from the hem of her tank top as she lifts her arms over her head and stretches. I should look away. Ogling her will only make my situation worse. My eyes have a mind of their own, though, as they sweep over her body.

The sunrise cresting over the horizon sends beams through the trees, creating a halo around her. The glow highlights the white shirt, accenting the curve of her breasts. My gaze darts farther down before I start drooling. She doesn't deserve me lusting after her.

"You can check me out if you want," she says sweetly, then slaps her hand over her mouth.

I shake my head, snorting softly. "Are you always this forward in the morning, Madelyn?"

Her pert nose scrunches up in the most adorable way. "Don't call me Madelyn. My mother calls me that, and it's just...don't."

"Well, Maddie, why don't you go back to bed?"

She crosses her arms, pushing up her breasts until they're almost spilling from her loose neckline. I avert my eyes, then slowly pan back and take in her tiny sleep shorts. I swear I'd witness half her ass cheeks hanging out the bottom if she turned around. My cock throbs, begging for attention.

"Why aren't you getting up?" Her arms drop and she hops down the two stairs. "Did you hurt yourself?"

I hold up a hand to stop her, and my other wrist threatens to give out. "I'm not hurt. But you should go."

A sly smile overtakes her face as she skids to a stop. I drop my hand, scowling. Now that she knows my problem, I doubt she'll let it go. She sinks to her knees in front of me, tilting her head and my gaze falls to her lips. When she pulls the flesh between her teeth, I swallow another groan.

"Do you need some help?" she whispers, as if this is some big joke. If her pussy was throbbing, begging for me to fill her up, she wouldn't be laughing.

"Unless you're offering to bend over the couch while I..." I snap my mouth shut and drop to my forearms. "Sorry."

"Apparently, I'm not the only one who's forward in the morning. Although you seem to have a dirty mouth at any time of the day." She pushes to her feet and shuffles away. "Maybe once I've determined that you're not going to roast me over a spit, we'll come back to your little fantasy involving the couch."

She saunters away, adding an extra sway to her hips, and my chest heaves with my silent suffering. As soon as she disappears into the bedroom, I shove to my feet. I need a cold shower and a little alone time with my hand. That woman has already infiltrated my mind, taking over every corner with her intoxicating presence. I doubt it will get much better the longer we stay here together.

Stumbling into the bedroom after her, I ignore Maddie's gasp. Once in the bathroom, I kick the door shut behind me and start the shower. A grunt leaves me when I ease off my underwear before gripping my cock. It throbs in my grasp, and I stroke up my length once. The move does nothing to ease the tension riding me.

Freezing water splashes me as I step inside, and goosebumps pebble my skin. I barely notice as I brace my forehead against the wall, still gripping myself. My hand won't be nearly as satisfying, but I won't push Maddie. This isn't a one-night stand where we'd both get our rocks off and go our separate ways. This situation calls for coffee in the morning while rocking on the front porch. A perfect little future laid out in front of me. The thought sends a shiver down my spine, and I stroke my cock.

Closing my eyes, Maddie's image floats behind my lids. I imagine it's her hand gripping me instead of my own inadequate one. My cock hardens even more, if that's possible. I thought it had been pushed to the limits. Putting Maddie in the mix of my mental fantasies has added fuel to the fire. I groan, tipping my head back as I stroke faster. In my mind, Maddie's sly smirk graces her face, and my muscles tense. I swipe my thumb over the tip, imagining it's her tongue.

Two more passes and I'm moaning her name as my release hits the shower wall. I pant as I watch the evidence drip toward my feet. It wasn't enough. I have a feeling no matter how many times I fuck my hand, it'll never be enough. Only Maddie will slake this thirst raging through me.

Rinsing my hands in the lukewarm water, my eyes glaze over. Not from coming, but the idea that Maddie is so important. I've never felt this way about a woman, much less one I barely know. It's as if there's an invisible force pulling me toward her. I don't know how comfortable I am with that, as I like making my own decisions. It's why I came here in the first place. Allowing others to direct my life wasn't working. I needed to forge out on my own.

I crank the handle and the water warms, sending a shudder through me. I grasp at the memories of my past floating just out of reach. My brain is still fuzzy, probably from lack of good sleep. There's no way in hell I'm making Maddie stay on the couch. She'll probably be stubborn and refuse my offer to be a gentleman. We'll bicker about it, and I'll have to convince her I'd rather stay where I am. It's going to be fucking miserable, but there's not much else I can do.

A soft knock reverberates through the small room, and I run my hands through my hair, pushing the water out of my face.

"Ye—" I clear my throat, praying I don't sound like I just busted a nut all over the shower. "Yeah?"

"Did you call for me?" Maddie's voice is still thick with sleep.

I wonder if I'm going to have to tuck her back into bed to get her to stay put. My cock twitches and I grit my teeth.

"No." I'm done telling her to go back to sleep. I'm pretty sure I've said it a dozen times and it's not even six in the morning.

"Do you want coffee?"

"Do you want to join me?" I mutter.

"Maybe tomorrow." Her footsteps fade away before I can respond, leaving me reeling.

Until Maddie is out of the house, I think my days of escaping into the shower for alone time are over. I quickly finish washing, then drying, and tug on my boxers. The irony of hoping Maddie didn't go to the kitchen doesn't escape me. If she's lounging among the sheets, my cock will harden once more, and I'll end up right back in the shower.

I need to plan better for crashing on the couch. Maybe I can keep my shit in the living room for now. I don't particularly like the idea of living out of a suitcase, but it's better than waking her up every time I need to change in the morning.

Soft hums float from the kitchen when I crack the bathroom door, and I breathe a sigh of relief. Slipping into the bedroom, I scan the crumpled bed sheets. The room smells like her, a mix of old books and citrus. It infiltrates my senses, tickling my nose. I quickly change, my head swimming the longer I'm surrounded by her essence. My jeans are tighter than normal, but that can't be helped. Not without another trip to the shower.

When I make my way into the kitchen, coffee percolates, overwhelming her scent with that of roasting beans. I stumble into the counter when I spot Maddie bent over and rummaging through the fridge. There isn't any food inside, at least not that I know of. Last night I waited until she'd shut herself in the bedroom before venturing back inside and going to sleep. My stomach gurgles and I wonder when the last time I ate was.

She wiggles to the song in her head, breathy notes escaping her every once in a while. I swallow hard as she bounces her ass to a mysterious beat. Her tiny shorts struggle to keep it all in check. When she straightens, my mouth waters. Fuck, I could live in that crease. I turn away, shaking my head.

I lower myself onto the stool pulled up to the island. The kitchen is almost not big enough for two. There are only a couple places to sit. The dining room juts off to the side of the living room. I make a note to not drink too much while sitting there. I'll end up falling down the stairs and sailing over one of the many couches, then crashing into the end table.

The clink of a mug on the counter catches my attention, and I glance back. Steam wafts from the coffee, warming me before I've even taken a drink. Maddie's already spun away and fills her own cup, doctoring it with a bunch of additions. I don't even recognize half of the shit she's dumping in her drink.

"How much more you going to put in there? Surprised there's any coffee left to taste." I pick up my mug, hiding my smirk behind the rim.

"I usually don't drink coffee, so I need to mask the flavor," she mutters. She takes a sip, shuddering.

"Why would you make coffee if you don't like it?"

She sighs, gazing mournfully at her cup. "Because I like the smell and I forgot to grab my energy drinks at the grocery store. Plus, I figured you'd drink some. I'll probably have a headache later, but what can ya do?"

She leans against the counter, sipping and grimacing, before starting the process all over again. I duck my head, not wanting to stare at her.

"Do you want breakfast?" she asks, interrupting my staring contest with my mug.

"You going to make it?" The coffee she made is bitter. I'm slightly worried about her cooking skills.

"Uh, actually, I was going to throw a granola bar at you." She grins at me, then glances away. "I got some eggs, though. I can make a mean omelet."

I can think of a lot of things I want for breakfast, but it doesn't include eggs. I'd rather spread her out on the dining room table and feast on her. I stand abruptly, my hand shooting out to stop the stool from clattering across the floor. It might be time for another shower.

Chapter Ten
Maddie

Emmett stomps from the kitchen without a word. I have no idea what I said to set him off, but it seems like this is a thing for him.

"If you didn't like eggs, you could have just said that," I mumble, then take another drink.

The bitterly sweet concoction rolls down my throat like a spoonful of molasses and I gag. Dumping the rest down the sink probably isn't great for the pipes, but Emmett can fix it if this sludge clogs them. Sugar coats the bottom and I crank the hot water to full blast to rinse it out. No reason to give Emmet more to complain about.

I glance at my backpack lying innocently by the door. Inside holds all the things I could possibly need to write remotely. I probably overpacked since I brought every resource book I had minus a dictionary. Sticky notes, legal pads, and not one, not two, but three planners, all of which I use whenever I remember they exist. My computer is in there, but I'm ignoring that fact. If I don't think about it, the problem will work itself out.

At least that's what I've been telling myself. For the last four months, I've been teetering between wallowing and trying to force it. Chloe was right. I need to get away from the screen, reconnect to whatever muse used to visit me, and center myself again. Pushing myself won't accomplish anything. I'll keep staring at the blank screen, wishing the words into existence.

I scrub my hands down my shorts, then glance down. "What the fuck am I wearing?"

Groaning, I tip my head back. Five a.m. was much too early. I tried to go back to sleep after I caught Emmett hiding his erection in the living room. Then he burst through the room to shower. After a good five minutes, though, I knew I wouldn't accomplish anything other than fantasizing about him under the spray. I plan on taking a nap later. The problem is, I forgot to change, rolling out of bed without a care in the world.

My pajamas have holes randomly scattered about the fabric, including one by my bellybutton. I gasp when I realize how fucking thin my tank top is. I cover my nipples as I squeeze my eyes shut and try not to sob. Now I understand why Emmett kept staring at his coffee. Oh, and why he ran out of here like a bear was chasing him. My shorts aren't any better since they barely cover my ass. And my backside isn't small.

"How long was I mooning him when I was digging in the fridge?" Embarrassment flashed through me and my skin flushes.

I'm not used to living with someone. Chloe disappears from one week to the next, leaving me alone for months at a time. Even when she's at the apartment, she doesn't care what I wear. Hell, I could parade around naked, and she wouldn't bat an eye. I feel like I'm fifteen again, living with my family, and I had to bring my clothes to the bathroom so no one would see me in a towel.

"It's not that big of a deal. We're both adults. It's not like he's never seen a woman's body before."

I slide around the island and make my way to the bedroom. I've got the door halfway open before I jump back, slamming it shut. Staring at the wood, hand still wrapped around the knob, I swallow hard.

"Emmett?" I call, squeezing my eyes shut while I wait for a response that never comes.

A heavy breath leaves me before I open the door again. Still, I peek inside and scan the room for signs of life. The bathroom door stands open, empty. Unless he's hiding in the closet, I won't be busting in on him. There's no lock, because of course there isn't. That would be too easy.

I dress quickly, eyes darting toward the exit every few seconds. Which results in me falling on the bed with both legs stuffed in one hole of my leggings. I struggle to extricate myself, grunting all the while. Once I finally kick them off, I huff, flinging my limbs out. I didn't even remember to put on underwear I was so distracted. The beams crisscross over my head, and I gaze at them while my mind wanders. And wander it does—straight back to Emmett.

When I found him on the floor this morning in only his boxers, I couldn't pull my eyes away. I may have been half asleep, but that didn't stop me from tracking his back as his muscles flexed. His arms that held me so effortlessly were taut, and I swear I drooled a little. Then he had to open his mouth and start talking about bending me over the couch, and I couldn't handle it.

The things he's slipped into our conversations, and we haven't even known each other for a whole day. I could easily slide into his bed, letting him take care of my needs. But then what?

This isn't a one-night stand where I can sneak out in the early morning light. We're both here to stay, for at least a while. Having him here, like we're playing house and living happily ever after...it'd be strange. Throw in the fact we don't know each other, and the idea is dead in the water.

Unless...

Unless we're adults about it. We work during the day, pretending we're just two people occupying the same space. At night, we fall into this bed and fuck our worries away. My eyes flutter shut as I imagine what it would be like to have his hands on me. Would he be gentle like he was when he caught me? Or does he lean more on the rough side, like his dirty mouth? Would he call me a good girl or demand I get on my knees? If he was the perfect book boyfriend, it'd be both.

My fingers curl into the rumpled sheets as I fight the urge to touch myself. An exasperated sigh leaves me before I give up and cup my breast. Biting back a moan, I roll my nipple until it's a hard nub. My other hand joins in and I bite my lip. It's not the same as Emmett touching me, but it's enough to have heat gathering between my legs.

His image floats behind my lids, with the sun creating a halo around his head. A smirk graces his face and all the dirty words I've written in my books whisper through my mind. My fingers slip under my waistband, dancing along the sensitive skin. Heat radiates from me and I shudder. When I swipe my finger along my pussy, I whimper. I've been wet since I woke up, but this is excessive. Just fantasizing about Emmett is enough to have me soaking my panties.

My fingers circle my clit, and my back arches from the pleasure sweeping through me. This would be enough, but my mind wanders to the toys I stuffed in the side pocket of my bag. I probably couldn't get away with using any of the functions. They're not exactly quiet, and the last thing I need is Emmett busting through the door. The worry has my eyes flying open and my hand stalling between my legs.

I listen intently for any footfalls outside the room. When there's nothing, I shuffle my body around until I can see the entrance clearly. My eyes become slits as I attempt to find my rhythm again. A thrill skitters down my spine as I envision him on the other side of the wood, intently listening to me pleasure myself. It's enough to have a fresh wave of wetness coat my hand.

Slowly, I thrust my fingers into my pussy, just how I assume Emmett would. He doesn't seem very timid. The more I think about it, I'm convinced he's domineering in the bedroom. He wouldn't hesitate when he touched me. He wouldn't take it easy, worrying whether or not I was ready. He'd know from instinct and the desire dripping from me how much I wanted him.

I drag my fingers from my pussy and rub my clit hard and fast. I could really use one of those toys right about now to clamp down on. My arms aren't long enough to do both. But I'm afraid I might tumble back down pleasure mountain if I stop now. I'd end up cranky and empty with no relief.

I squeeze my eyes shut as my breath saws out of my lungs. Bending my knees, I attempt to keep quiet as euphoria builds within me. The elastic from my leggings cut into the back of my hand and my fingers ache from how hard I'm working my clit. I'm so fucking close, ecstasy dangling just out of reach.

Groaning softly, I stop, gently pressing on my clit. My muscles protest as I straighten one leg. I'd rather not hobble around the rest of my day from a cramp I got while masturbating.

Reaching toward the headboard, I stretch to grab a pillow. I yank it to me, almost smacking myself in the face, and tuck it under my head. My temples pulse while the blood seeps back into my body. I should get another one for my hips, but I feel like that's pushing it.

Emmett won't stay away for long. He tends to pop up randomly. It's both slightly terrifying and exceedingly exhilarating how quietly he moves. He's the poster boy for a chase scene in the woods.

My legs jerk and my hips kick up when I imagine him stalking through the trees after me. I haven't done half the things I've written about, but I've concocted so many scenarios it's hard not to wonder if I'd truly like them or not. The last guy I slept with wasn't exactly adventurous in bed. He was the type to think doggy style was super kinky. I didn't have the heart to tell him I've read things hotter than what he did to me.

I sigh as I stroke my fingers on either side of my clit, shivering when my pussy spasms. Soft footfalls from deeper in the house reach my ears and I lick my lips. I might not ask Emmett to chase me, or even fuck me right now, but I can certainly role-play in my head. Maybe he's closer than I thought. Perhaps he's just waiting for me to be teetering on the edge of oblivion before he'll open the door. He could be waiting for the right moment before he tells me to scream his name like a good girl.

My fingers dip into my core, then return to my clit to start once more. With the added bonus of the scene I've created, my orgasm builds much faster. I shouldn't be using him for mental fodder, especially with him lurking somewhere in this house. Doesn't stop me from pinching my nipple as my other hand works between my legs.

As the edge looms nearer, I slam my eyes shut. Stars burst behind my lids, creating a kaleidoscope of color—a firework show just for me. I press my lips together, my moan coming out more like a whine as I sail into oblivion. Panting, my movements become erratic as I pull out my orgasm as long as possible.

Knuckles rap against the door, and I freeze, lifting my head. "You need any help in there, gorgeous?"

Is it my imagination or is laughter dancing in his voice? Was he really standing outside the door, listening to me touch myself? Thankfully, I didn't say his name when I came. There's no way he'd know I was thinking of him while I was touching myself. Was there?

I clear my throat. "No. I'm just getting dressed."

"You sure? Sounds like you could definitely use my help."

I was right. There is laughter in his tone. Bastard.

"I'm perfectly capable of putting on my pants by myself, thank you. Go away."

His chuckle fades along with his footsteps, and my head drops back to the pillow. If I have to go the next couple weeks without an orgasm, I'm going to lose my mind. And I won't be able to help myself if he keeps walking around without a shirt on. Or sleeping in his underwear. Or spouting nonsense. I'll end up climbing him like a tree before long. I'm not entirely sure that's a bad thing.

A bolt of pleasure rolls through me and I realize I've been touching myself the entire time he was standing mere feet away with only a few inches of wood separating us. Disgusted with myself, I tug my hand from my pants and lurch off the bed. I sway and my hand slams on the wall to keep myself upright.

I can't keep this up. He'll end up catching me. And the next time, I won't be able to resist his offer of help.

Chapter Eleven
Emmett

My eyes keep darting toward the forest. I've been working on the side porch railing for a good two hours now, but I'm barely making any progress. Maddie disappeared between the trees, claiming she was going to commune with nature to get her mojo back, whatever that means. I waved her off, pretending I wasn't tracking her every move.

I'm convinced she was touching herself when I knocked on the bedroom door yesterday. I walked away with a hard-on and a chuckle. Hours later, I was no longer laughing. The rest of the night was torture and my sleep was shit. Even today, she's occupying most of my thoughts.

Every time I think I've pushed her from my mind and calmed my cock down, she pops back in. Then I have to start the whole process all over again. If she wasn't so lovely to look at, even in my mind, I'd be annoyed.

"Where are you, Maddie?" I whisper, dropping my tools and gripping the back of my neck.

I'm half tempted to go in after her. What if she tripped and hurt herself? What if an animal attacked her? What if she wiggled her way into a log trying to get away from a wolf and really did make herself into a chew toy? Fear slices through me and I'm trotting to the front before I register what I'm doing. I'd vault over the railing if I could, but it'd probably break on me and then I'd be fucked.

I'm halfway across the yard when a high-pitched scream echoes through the air. I sprint toward the sound, heart pounding in my ears. As I reach the tree line, Maddie crashes into me, head turned to look behind her.

As I wrap my arms around her, a growl erupts from my chest. I pick her trembling body up and spin us before racing back for the cabin. Her fingers dig into my shirt and her cries are muffled by the material.

Once inside, I grab her arms and attempt to pry her fingers from the fabric. There's no give and I cup her face instead. Bending, I stare into her wide eyes. Fear mixes with something else within the deep golden depths.

"Are you hurt?" I demand, my voice harsher than I intended, and she flinches. "Maddie, are you hurt?"

She shakes her head, peeking over my shoulder at the open door. She swallows hard and her lip slips between her teeth. My thumb catches the plump flesh and pulls it from her mouth. She sucks in a soft gasp and her hands flatten on my chest. This isn't the time, but my cock doesn't care. It strains against my jeans while my mind screams to kiss her.

I clear my throat. "What happened?"

She blinks, pulling away from my touch and rubbing her hands down her leggings. I've studiously ignored the fact they're skintight the whole fucking day. At least I pretended I wasn't staring at her ass as she vanished into the forest.

"So, I went down by the lake first. I wanted to see if there was a dock down there. And there totally is, so if I fished, I could catch dinner. But I don't fish, so that doesn't matter, I suppose." She paces away, then back as she waves her hands around. "So, then I walked around the lake, and I wasn't going to go into the woods since I'm not exactly outdoorsy. But I didn't get very far, and my feet were getting tired. I thought about coming back..."

"But you were avoiding me. I got it. Can we cut to the part where you run out of the forest screaming your pretty little head off?" I raise an eyebrow, palms itching to grab her even as a flash of annoyance crosses her face.

"You asked what happened." She plants her fists on her hips and cocks her head. "Don't be pissy when I start from the beginning. And I wasn't avoiding you."

I smirk, tucking my hands in my pockets. "Sure you weren't, gorgeous."

"Anyways." She pulls out the word, glancing over my shoulder again, and I follow her gaze. There's nothing there. "I'd been in there a while and got hungry, so I started in the direction I was pretty sure the cabin was."

I hold up a hand, then pinch the bridge of my nose. "Are you telling me you went wandering in a forest you've never been in for hours and you also don't have any sense of cardinal directions?"

"Listen, I was blessed with a lot of things, but knowing which way is north wasn't one of them," she snaps. "Are you done interrupting me?"

"We have a lot of work to do," I mutter under my breath.

"Seriously, I haven't even gotten to the good part yet!"

I tip my head back, silently pleading to whatever god will listen to save me from this woman. "So help me, if you tell me you were chased by a wild animal and that's the *good* part..."

"Well, it didn't chase me, but Emmett—" She jolts me from my thoughts as she latches onto my arms. "I think I saw bigfoot."

My first instinct is to scoff, then laugh, but she's so sincere I can't do anything except stare at her. Excitement replaces her fear, and she bounces on the balls of her feet. I run my tongue along my bottom lip and her eyes dart down. She flushes, her cheeks turning such a pretty pink. I don't want to kill the joy radiating from her.

"What's he look like?"

My question must catch her off guard. She blinks rapidly, brows pulling low. When she sucks her cheeks in, making a fish face, I can't stop the burst of laughter from erupting from me. If a scowl could kill, I'd be dead.

"He was obviously hairy. And tall. And stomping through the trees." Her mouth drops open, and she smacks my chest. "You. It was you, wasn't it? You were fucking with me...wait. That doesn't make any sense."

I kick the door shut with my heel, then wrap my arm around her shoulder, tugging her to my chest. "Did you hurt yourself when you were fleeing from bigfoot?"

"No," she snaps, her voice muffled again by my shirt. "Why are you hugging me?"

"Because you scared me half to death and my lungs haven't remembered how to breathe properly yet." I tighten my hold, closing my eyes as I bury my nose in her soft hair.

"Your heart is beating really fast," she murmurs, and her arms slip around my waist.

I sigh, brushing my hand down her back. It's the most I've been able to touch her since...yesterday. It's been a mere forty-eight hours since we've met. It feels longer—like a lifetime has passed. I shove the thoughts aside. They do me no good while she's in my arms. I'll end up obsessing over why I'm so drawn to her.

"Do you want me to go scour the woods?" I bite my cheek to keep my laughter inside. "Bigfoot couldn't have gone far."

A disgusted noise leaves her, and she shoves away from me. I should have kept my mouth shut, but I couldn't help myself. She glares up at me, then smacks my chest again.

"I'm going out to find whatever it was, or I won't be able to sleep tonight."

She pushes past me, and I snatch her elbow, swinging her around to face me. "You're not going back out there by yourself. And if you need help sleeping..."

I smirk as I drop my hold on her and open the door. I'm halfway across the yard before she catches up. The canopy overhead casts shadows on the forest floor as we step into the muted area.

"You know, I never realized how loud it is in the woods," Maddie whispers.

"Why are you whispering? Are you afraid we'll scare him off?"

"I've had enough of your comments, sir," she snaps.

A shiver rolls down my spine, and I open my mouth to tell her she can call me sir anytime. I think better of it since I'm not entirely sure how I'd be able to control myself if she continues. She'd probably pull it out in the middle of a spat just to throw me off my game. I'll end up bending her over the nearest piece of furniture. Glancing at her, I don't know whether that'd be a bad thing or not.

"How far in?" I ask, catching her elbow when she trips over a divot hidden by the leaves covering the ground.

"I don't..." She stops, then slowly spins around. "I jumped over a...there."

She points at a fallen tree, joy splashing across her face. The leaves shiver overhead and sunbeams dance across her hair, producing a golden shimmer around her. Her hands land on her hips, and my heart skips a beat. Her wide eyes meet mine in a look I can't decipher.

"Uh, what?" I ask, mimicking her stance.

"You're staring at me instead of looking at the log. Plus, shouldn't you be, I don't know, leading the way or something?"

I roll my eyes and turn, making my way in the direction she pointed. Twigs snap behind me as she follows, and soon we're walking through the brush side by side. My palm itches, and I wish I had the courage to grab her hand. Any another time, this might be a romantic date.

Her nervous energy infects the space between us. I doubt I could seduce her out here. At least not right now. I'll have to wait for another time when I've convinced her we should explore this attraction between us. I'll bring her out here and hopefully the date will end with her back against a tree while I fuck her senseless.

I shake the fuzziness from my head, rubbing the back of my neck. Even in my own head, I'm not usually so possessive...or dirty. At least I don't think I am. Every time I try to recall my past, the memories slip from my grasp. I assumed it was from the time in the woods or the lack of sleep. Now I'm not so sure. Did I hit my head while I was camping? Nothing aches other than the muscles in my back from crashing on the couch two nights in a row.

"Shit, shit, shit," Maddie whisper-squeals.

Her hand latches onto mine and tugs me behind a tree. It's not nearly wide enough to hide us both. Apparently, she comes to the same conclusion, and she shoves my back into the trunk, then presses her body to mine. Instinctively, my arms circle her waist, my grip holding her upright as she leans to peek through the forest.

"He's right there," she mouths, pointing to some far-off place I can't see.

I shuffle us around until her back rubs against the bark and she's scowling. I smirk, then duck to spy whatever she thinks is a mythical creature that most-assuredly does not exist. Squinting, my gaze skips from one brown thing to another. They're all trees and logs and branches. Nothing else is there. When I start to pull back, she makes a noise in the back of her throat. My hand covers her mouth as I spot something swaying between two trunks.

When I lean forward, her body molds to mine. One half of my brain zeroes in on her curves fitting into mine like two puzzle pieces finding their home with each other. The other half focuses on the slight movement that disappears, then reappears ten seconds later.

Retreating, my lips brush the shell of her ear, and she shivers. "Stay here. I'm going to check it out."

"What?" she screeches, all while still trying to be quiet. It doesn't work. "You're not leaving me here. What if a moose comes out of nowhere and gouges me?"

"You'll be able to see a moose come. Plus, I doubt they're roaming about around here. But come if you want. Just stop yelling."

Do I really think it's bigfoot hiding in the trees? No. It's more likely a bear, though I don't think it's one of those either. Most likely, it's just a shadow playing off a canopy of dried leaves from a fallen branch.

The closer we creep, though, the less likely that theory holds up. Whatever it is, it rises and falls in a rhythmic pattern as if it's alive. I hold my breath, almost wishing I brought a weapon.

"If it's a bear, we're going to move slowly. For fuck's sake, do not run. We'll shuffle sideways unless it starts following us, then we stop."

She latches onto my arm, nails digging into my skin through the fabric of my shirt. I glance at her, finding her pale and trembling. I wish I would have made her stay at the cabin now. I thought whatever I found would be silly, but now I'm second-guessing myself. Finding a wild animal in the north woods isn't unheard of. I should have been better prepared.

"What if it's something else?" she mumbles, and I swear there are tears in her voice.

"Just don't run. Or scream," I murmur. If she screams, she'll end up in my arms with my hand over her mouth. I wouldn't mind so much if she wasn't terrified we were about to be mauled.

Twigs snap under our feet no matter how hard I try to avoid them. Birds still sing out their songs and insects still fill the air, thank fuck. Maddie stumbles when the breeze picks up, shaking the leaves overhead. I slip my arm around her waist to keep her steady. I'd rather have both my hands free, though. Not that I'd be able to fight off a bear with my hands, but the alpha male in me screams that I totally could. I really couldn't. I'd end up mincemeat and Maddie would be next.

As we slide around a small group of trees, I burst out laughing. Maddie gasps, attempting to slip from my arms to turn and hightail it back to through the trees. I tighten my grip on her, holding her closer as she fights to get away.

"Let go," she cries, hands pushing at my arm. "It's going to eat us."

"Stop it. It's just...look." I force her around, gripping her chin in my hand to see her mysterious mythical creature.

Her body stiffens and she sniffs. "What the fuck is that?"

Chapter Twelve
Maddie

"It's an old hunting blind. Looks like it was blown in from a field or the lake," Emmett murmurs in my ear.

A shiver rolls through me and my muscles tighten. The canvas hangs in tatters, fluttering in the light breeze. I don't understand why it was so rhythmic, like it was breathing. The camouflage blends with the trees, and I roll my eyes. Of course it blends in. It's a fucking hunting blind. I've never been in one, but I've seen plenty in the stores back home.

"The thing I saw was furry," I grumble, crossing my arms.

Emmett shuffles us around the last trunk blocking our way, and I wonder if he's keeping me close for his benefit or for mine. I'm no longer worried something will jump out at me. Explaining to him I thought it was a bear, which is much more plausible than bigfoot, would have taken too much energy. And I needed a lot of energy for running.

"There." He points at the side of the blind and a sound of protest leaves me.

"Who the hell puts a realistic mural on the side of their hunting blind?"

He chuckles and his hand slides from my waist to my hip. "Someone who wanted to be funny. Did a good job, though. The fur certainly looks real."

It does, but I'm not going to admit that he's right. I glare at the life-size replica of a Sasquatch, brown fur blowing gently in the breeze. It ripples with the wind, making it seem as if *he's* moving as well. I'm not surprised I was mistaken. If I give in to Emmett, though, it's just more fodder for him to use. There are more than a couple people in my life that would never let me live this down.

"Well, okay then. We can go back now." I shimmy away from him, and he hesitates a second before dropping his arm.

As he examines the shelter, I fan my cheeks, desperately trying to ease the heat gathered there. When I turn, he's staring right at me, his one cocky eyebrow raised so high, I'm surprised it hasn't merged with his hair.

"What?" I snap, and his other eyebrow joins the first under the curl of caramel locks resting across his forehead. "It's hot out here."

He nods, then gestures to the blind. "Anything else you want to explore?"

"No. I'm hot and hungry and I want to go home."

Do I sound like a petulant child? Yes, but I hate the feelings flowing through me right now. I'm old enough it shouldn't bother me that I was wrong. The fact he's here to witness it shouldn't matter, either. But I'm out of my depth. Too many changes when I'm already feeling unmoored. I'm stuck in the woods with a man I've never met. I have no idea what I'm doing with my life anymore. I'm drowning. And there's no one there to save me. No one to throw me a life ring. Sure, I could ask Emmett to scratch the itch in the bedroom, but then what?

Fucking Emmett won't fix my writer's block. Sleeping with him won't magically make the last book better. And it really won't help me decide what to do with the rest of my life.

I sigh, spinning away from Emmett's prying eyes, and stomp back to the cabin. I make it all of ten feet before Emmett grabs my arm. He swings me around before I have a chance to snap at him for yanking me around like a rag doll. His hand drops and he points the other way. My cheeks heat again. Or maybe the blush never left.

"You can wait for me while I check out the inside. Might be able to find who it belongs to." Emmett wanders back to the hunting blind.

I huff, crossing my arms. "I don't do well with people bossing me around."

He glances over his shoulder, confusion swirling on his face. "Besides the fact I have no idea what the hell you're talking about, I figured you wouldn't want to go running off into the forest by yourself. Especially since you were going the wrong way not two minutes ago."

"I also don't like people insulting my intelligence," I mutter.

He turns slowly to face me and tucks his hands in his pockets. "Are you intentionally picking a fight?"

"Why the hell would I do that?" I snap, then press my lips together.

He's entirely too perceptive. I am picking a fight. If he asks me why, I'll have to make something up because I don't have a reason. Not like I'm going to tell him I'm embarrassed. Or floundering. Or horny. I'm definitely not going to tell him I'm horny.

"Alright, gorgeous. Why don't we just go back, and I'll feed you. I suspect you're undercaffeinated as well. I can come back and check this out while you work."

His hand wraps around my elbow and tugs me in the right direction. After a few feet, I yank my arm away. I consider snapping at him again, but the energy to fight drains from me. Whatever is going on with me feels like a lot more than not being able to write. It feels like an ending of an era—of a dream.

I trail behind Emmett, trusting him not to lead us astray. As the trees thin, the sunlight dances across his tanned skin. I swear he's stepped straight from the clouds, a golden god descended to earth. His form wavers, shimmering in the beams. I shake my head and glance away.

A branch jumps from nowhere, catching my toe, and I almost fall on my face. I've righted myself before Emmett can react, thank fuck. The last thing I need is him having to save me from myself yet again.

Thankfully, the cabin comes into view, and I rush forward. Maybe I can take a shower. Or a nap. My head is starting to hurt, and I'd rather it didn't turn into a migraine. I'm sure Emmett wouldn't fancy having to take care of me. Plus, he mentioned me not sleeping on the couch tonight. I was planning on insisting, but if my head is pounding, the last thing I want is to be woken up at the ass crack of dawn.

"Why don't you go take a shower," Emmett says as he hauls himself up the stairs. It's not a question, more of a demand.

"Yeah, fine."

I push past him, my heartbeat pounding in my ears. The pressure in my head has only gotten worse. My vision dims at the edges, throwing off my depth perception. I snatch my backpack up and rummage inside until I find my meds. I barely notice Emmett slipping by me and into the kitchen. Just as I pop the top of the bottle off, a glass of water appears by my face.

I shoot him a grateful smile before taking the meds, praying they work quickly. Maybe I got bit by something in the woods. More likely, I just overdid it. I'm not a stranger to exercise, but it mostly consists of walking to the corner store less than a mile away. And strolling through the city is a lot less taxing than stumbling through the forest. I should have come back earlier, but I let my fear get in the way.

Mostly I was afraid I'd jump Emmett's bones. No matter what he says, I doubt he'd appreciate that. Squeezing my eyes shut, I try to focus on something other than the throbbing in my temples. It's radiating down to my ears and making my neck tight. One wrong move and my head will snap clean off my body. At least that's what it feels like.

"Do you need help getting to the shower?" he murmurs, and I open my eyes to slits.

Concern flits across his face as he crouches next to me. I could kiss him just for not talking at a normal volume. I clear my throat, the sound reverberating around my head. He grabs the glass before it can hit the floor.

"I'll be fine. A shower should help."

My eyes flutter shut again and his hand wraps around my wrist. He guides me upright, and I swallow the nausea threatening to overwhelm me. If I puke now, all the meds I took will come up with it. I'm sure it would be embarrassing as well, but I won't notice until my head stops pounding.

"I'm going to pick you up." His deep voice washes over me, easing the ache in my chest.

A whimper escapes me as he slowly swings me into his arms. Tucking my face into his shirt as he cradles me, I revel in the woodsy scent woven into his clothes. The headache came on so suddenly. I shouldn't have stayed out in the heat for so long. Not that there's anything I can do about it now. I'll have to deal with the consequences.

If I was alone out here, I would have been fine. Having Emmett here to help me is infinitely easier, though. Actually, I can't remember the last time someone took care of me. Chloe hasn't been around enough to help. It's honestly like living alone most of the time. It's one of the few times I wish I had someone who cared enough to check up on me. My mother would come and take care of me if I was sick, but I never felt comfortable calling her unless it was an emergency. I got pretty good at dealing with sickness alone.

"You're mumbling, gorgeous." Emmett's voice cuts through my mind's rambling. "What do you need?"

He lowers my feet to the ground gently, and I realize we're in the bathroom. With no windows and the lights dimmed, I'm able to open my eyes a little more without it feeling like someone is stabbing my sockets. I don't know how he knows what I need. Maybe he gets migraines too. I lean against the counter as he turns on the shower. I can't even admire his ass as he bends over. My stomach flips again, and I close my eyes once more.

Emmett clears his throat and I peek at him. "Do you need me to help you undress?"

Usually, I'd have a snarky comment or a witty reply. I just don't have it in me, though. Plus, he's clearly trying to help me, not proposition me. I'd rather not have him see me naked for the first time while I'm in this state.

"I can manage. I'm used to it. Can you just grab my sweats? The black ones. They're—"

"I'll find them and leave them on the counter. As soon as you get out, just get dressed and get in the bed. I'll check in on you in a bit." He's out the door before I can respond, and tears fill my eyes.

"Thanks," I whisper in his wake anyway.

The hot water splashes down my body. I don't even remember undressing. I end up on the floor, arms wrapped around my legs as the spray hits my neck. It helps, but not enough. My mind wanders, following the threads of the various stories still dancing through my mind. My characters are revolting, winking in and out of existence in protest while I attempt to figure out how to write their happily ever afters. Should I be thinking of something else? Probably. Except the only thing I ever think about in the shower are my books.

I groan when the water turns lukewarm. Emmett's hand snakes through the curtain and turns the knob. A towel appears, and he shakes it around.

"Off the floor, Maddie. Do you need me to dry you off?"

"Are you propositioning me while I'm naked?" My voice slurs and I sway, almost tipping over.

He snorts, shoving the towel closer. I can practically hear his eye roll, though he's still tucked behind the curtain.

"It would definitely remove a step. Now if you don't stand up, I'm going to be seeing you naked, regardless."

I swallow another groan as I push to my feet, and my head lolls on my neck. It clearly has a mind of its own. My shoulders shake as I wrap the towel around me, desperately trying to keep my giggles inside. They turn into silent sobs as the pain in my head doubles. The curtain flies back and Emmett catches me around the waist before I hit the tile.

He swings me up in his arms once again and my stomach rebels. I barely notice it through the throbbing pain in my head. The meds clearly aren't working. The shower only kept it at bay while I was in there, and I can't spend the rest of the day under the water. I really want some caffeine, but there's no way I'm going into town. I don't even remember there being any there, anyway.

"Why's it so dark?" I whisper. With two windows in the room, even with the curtains drawn, there should be light filtering through.

"I hung some blankets over the windows."

I'm practically enveloped in the bed, and he tosses the comforter over me, then tucks the sheets around me. I curl onto my side, burrowing in until only my eyes remain, and barely make out Emmett's form shuffling around. My mind drifts, never fully settling on one topic. When the mattress dips, I whimper. I'd finally found the one position where I could handle the pain rushing through me.

"Sorry. I'm going to help you drink this. It'll help."

His arm slides around my back, helping me to sit up. I sway, not fully in control of my limbs. It takes me three times to grab the glass. It's water, but I desperately want an energy drink. I don't have enough caffeine flowing through my veins right now. I could use some sugar too. Ice cream, to be exact. I doubt Emmett has either of those things lying around, though.

I take a couple sips before it starts to taste funny, and I quit. Emmett sighs as he takes the glass from me, then guides me back into the fluffy cloud of blankets.

"Get some sleep. I'll check on you in an hour."

I'm out before he's even closed the door.

Chapter Thirteen

Emmett

I've paced by the bedroom door at least a dozen times in the last hour. I haven't heard a peep from Maddie and it's starting to mess with my head. When I threatened to tuck her in, this wasn't what I had in mind. She was so pale, yet flush at the same time. She was basically waterlogged when I fished her out of the shower, and she probably wouldn't have been able to get out on her own.

"Fuck it," I mutter, pushing the door open.

She's bundled in the blankets exactly how I left her. It takes a minute to figure out if she's even breathing. The panic slowly recedes, flowing out of me. Brushing her hair from her forehead, I scan her face. She's still pale, but she doesn't look as bad. When I pull my hand away, she chases after my touch. I'm tempted to crawl in next to her just to make sure she keeps breathing.

I sigh, rubbing my hands down my face. Waking her would be cruel, and if I jostle the bed, she's sure to notice. Instead, I drag a chair into the room and resign myself to keeping an eye on her. If I have to be here all day, so be it. Sleeping upright won't be any worse than that damn couch. I settle in as the soft light slowly fades.

It doesn't feel like it was just two days ago that she was falling off the porch and into my arms. Actually, it's almost as if we've been here before—her tucked into bed with her head hurting and me keeping vigil as she slept. I press my thumbs into my temples, trying to pinpoint why I'm so fucking out of it.

Before I came here, I was lost. I didn't have a purpose, much less a plan. I bounced around from place to place, wishing I'd find somewhere I could settle down. When I got the call about the cabin needing to be fixed up, there wasn't anything tying me down. Moving around with the few things I own is how I've been living for years. I never stay in one place for long. I figured the cabin was just another pit stop on the way to something else. Hopefully something better.

I didn't anticipate Maddie. Living out here for the next few months alone would have been fine. I don't particularly care for people, so it didn't matter to me the cabin is in the middle of nowhere. I could live out my days here, getting snowed in during the winter, enjoying the lake in the summer.

Maddie coming along was an unforeseeable complication to my solitary time here. And I don't know how to handle the change. We've spent most of the time tiptoeing around one another or bickering. I barely know what she has planned for the next week she's here. She clearly can't wander around in the woods by herself. I'll end up babysitting her, making sure she doesn't get eaten by a bear or attacked by a mountain lion.

Even if I could convince her to fall into bed with me, I doubt it would change the end result. Eventually, we'll go our separate ways, and I'm afraid she'll leave me with another gaping hole I'm unable to fill. I'm dealing with enough of those, I'd rather not add more.

Maddie groans, throwing her arm over her head. I lean forward, hand hovering over her body. She's not awake and I'm afraid if I touch her, she'll jolt upright, making her headache worse. I should go make her food, even if it's something small. Then I'll have something to offer her if she's hungry. I can't force my feet to move, though. Instead, I end up tracking every twitch and sigh she makes, wondering if I should be doing more.

Eventually, I settle back again, watching her through slitted eyes. The sun sets, casting shadows through the cracked door. The minutes tick past slowly and my eyes grow heavy. The next thing I know I'm jerking awake, disoriented, with my neck cramping.

"Oh fuck," Maddie moans, and my gaze shoots to her.

I can barely make out her form as she sits up and drops her head in her hands as she trembles in the near-dark. I flip on the bedside lamp, and she shies away from the light.

"Sorry," I murmur. "What do you need?"

My hand lands on her back, rubbing it gently, and she leans into my touch. I scoot closer, practically wrapping my arm around her body as she cuddles into me.

"Shower," she whispers, but doesn't move away from me.

I swallow hard, then sigh. I've been pussyfooting around, waiting for her to tell me what she wants. It's not working, since she's not getting better. It's got to be after midnight, so she should be on the mend if it's a migraine. Instead, she looks just as miserable as when she got into bed.

I pull away and slip my fingers under hers to cup her cheeks. Tilting her head up gently, I hope she doesn't bite my head off. Dull eyes meet mine and concern flashes through me.

"Your way isn't working, Mad. I'm taking over. Got it?"

Her lip twitches like she wants to smile but doesn't have the strength. She nods and I steel myself for her to potentially throw up on me. I scoop her up, cradling her against my body. The smallest movement has her whimpering, and my heart clenches. Somehow, I'm able to turn on the shower while still holding her.

Her body trembles as I step over the lip, keeping the spray off her face. My back hits the far wall and I slide down, settling her on my lap. Thank fuck whoever redid this bathroom had the foresight to put in an oversized tub.

Steam wafts through the air, wrapping around us. I pull in a deep breath and find myself swaying back and forth. She blinks up at me as her cheeks warm to a healthier pink. At least I hope it's healthier and she's not burning up. I can't tell with her tucked into my body and the hot water seeping into my clothes.

"You're getting wet," she murmurs.

She struggles to sit, then tucks her head under my chin. I thought she'd pull away, run from whatever swirls between us. Maybe she's too tired to fight it. More likely, she's not even concerned with me. I'm just a warm body here to help her through a migraine. I can't imagine dealing with them alone, though I get the feeling she's used to it.

"I'm fine. Unless you're trying to get me naked. In that case, all you had to do was ask."

She snorts softly, burrowing into me further. I wrap my arms around her and lay my cheek on her wet hair. The spray from the water is annoying, but it seems to be helping her. I can handle the discomfort.

"I need…" She sighs, her words dripping from her face along with the water. Or maybe they're tears. I can't tell.

I slide my hand up her back to her neck. Gently, I flex my fingers, massaging the tense muscles. She groans as her chin drops to her chest. It's not easy with her hair, but I manage. I move my thumb behind her ear, rubbing on what I'm pretty sure is a pressure point. The noises she's making send a bolt of desire straight to my cock. No matter how much I try to brush it aside, I can't. I grit my teeth, continuing to ease her pain while ignoring my own.

"What else do you need? I've got an energy drink for you, but it's probably warm now. I'd have to grab another one from the fridge."

She lifts her head, wide eyes finding mine. "You got me some? When?"

"I already had some. Kept them in the mini fridge in the basement. I don't usually drink them, though, so you can have them."

Honestly, I don't even remember buying them. I stopped on my way into town and stocked up on things, but I can't recall half the things I saw when I was searching for something with caffeine for her. Hopefully, she enjoys the snacks I picked up since I won't be eating them.

"Basement. Is it really a basement if it's just a lower level?"

"I should probably know the answer to that, but I don't. Also, I wouldn't go down there if I were you. It's mostly unfinished with some shoddy work on the things they did do."

"I'm hungry," she hums as the water slowly cools.

"Well, let's get you fed, then."

She slides off my lap and wraps her arms around her bent legs. The water hits me in the face, I'm so distracted making sure she's okay. I sputter, whipping my head back and forth to keep from waterboarding myself.

Twisting the knob, I cough and swipe my hand across my face. She giggles and relief slips through my veins, easing the tension in my muscles. I've been riding the edge for so long I'm going to need a massage now.

"Are you okay to stand, or should I carry you?" I ask, wondering how the hell I'm going to carry her while not tracking water throughout the house.

"As much as I'd love to say I can't walk, I can. My head still feels like there's little men who've taken up camp with tiny hammers, but I won't puke on myself anymore, I don't think." She pushes to her feet, then swipes her hands down her face.

Her mouth parts while I attempt to keep my gaze on her face instead of rolling down her exposed body. If I thought I was hard before, it's nothing compared to what's happening now. If her own eyes dip down, she'll find my cock outlined by my extremely wet clothes. A chill runs down my spine, though I can't tell if it's from being cold or from the flame of desire flaring to life in her eyes.

I clear my throat, running my hand through my sopping hair. The excess drips down my temples and tickles the back of my neck. The shower isn't big enough for me to put any distance between us. I fling the curtain back, saving us both from further embarrassment, and grab two towels. She snatches one from me, and I raise my eyebrow.

"Sorry, I'm just freezing now," she mumbles as she wraps it around her.

I dry my hair, using the time to figure out how the hell I'm going to get myself dressed along with her. I spend a good thirty seconds longer than I normally would and when I emerge, I finally have a plan.

"Okay, I'm going to step out, close the curtain, get out of these wet clothes, and then I'll get us both some dry stuff. Then I'll feed you." I peek at her before glancing away when I find her adjusting her towel.

"Yeah, okay." Her voice is laced with exhaustion and another pang hits my chest.

While I've been coming up with ways to make sure she doesn't notice I'm hard as a rock, she's been in pain. Sneaking a peek is probably the furthest thing from her mind. I step out, shutting the curtain behind me, and shuck off my clothes in record time. I wrap the towel around my waist, then stutter between the curtain and the door. Shaking my head, I stomp from the room.

I don't know why she sends my brain into meltdown mode. It's like as soon as she comes into view...hell, when she crosses my mind at all, I glitch. As I pull on a pair of sweatpants and a shirt, I realize I'm going to need to have a talk with her. After a few days with her, she's already got me in knots, bending over backwards to take care of her.

I grab her some clothes as well and shuffle back to the bathroom. Knocking softly, I wait for her response, but none comes. The longer I wait, the higher my heart rate soars.

"Maddie? I've got your clothes." Still, she doesn't answer. "Answer or I'm coming in."

The door cracks open and her hand appears, fingers wiggling until I give them to her. She doesn't bother to close it behind her, and I pace away. I could go get some food ready, but I'm afraid I won't be able to hear her if she calls for me. If she tips over and hits her head, I won't know. Plus, I have no idea where the nearest hospital is.

"Can we eat now?" she asks, exhaustion lining her tone.

"Yeah. You need me to carry you? Help you around? I really don't want you passing out again," I mutter.

"I didn't pass out. I was just a little woozy. Walking shouldn't be a problem. I'm just hungry, now."

She shuffles past me and my hand hovers around her lower back as I follow her. The house isn't that big, but she keeps turning the wrong way. When she almost wanders down the steps to the living room, I wrap my arm around her waist and guide her in the right direction. I settle her on one of the stools, hoping I'm not making any mistakes.

I feel like I've been making them all my life. This is the first time in a long while I've felt like I'm exactly where I'm supposed to be. If Maddie tells me to leave her alone, though, I don't know what the hell I'm going to do.

Chapter Fourteen
Maddie

"What do you want to eat? Anything sound good?" Emmett asks, opening the fridge.

"Whatever," I mumble, and he glances over his shoulder. "I'm not picky."

Now that I'm mostly in the post-migraine haze, I'm regretting a lot of things. I'm pretty sure at one point I was clutching at Emmett, begging him to stay with me. That might have been a dream, but my wet hair means I took a shower with him. He was fully clothed and I was completely naked and I didn't give two shits at the time. Sitting here with him while he insists on feeding me? Yeah, I'm definitely giving a shit now.

"Tell me what you want, and I'll make it. I don't care if you're picky. I'm going to feed you whatever you're craving so you actually eat it."

"Bold of you to assume I know what I want to eat."

"You strike me as the kind of person who knows what they want." He turns back to the fridge and rummages inside.

"You'd be surprised," I mutter, glancing away.

I used to think once I moved out of my parent's house I'd broken out of my ways. I made decisions and took risks. Being an author was everything I wanted, and I went after that dream. It was hard learning all the things that went into it, but I knew what I wanted. And I went after it with everything in my soul.

I spent months—years really, trudging along. There are a dozen books in my backlist that no one reads. Or at least, they didn't use to. I worked two jobs and wrote at night, barely getting any sleep.

"What's that supposed to mean?" he asks as he drops a bunch of things onto the counter. His body blocks my view of the ingredients, but at this point my stomach might eat itself, so I don't care what he makes.

"Well, when I was growing up, I didn't know how to stand up for myself. I thought being the good kid meant doing what everyone else around me wanted. Made me kind of a doormat. Then I went to college, and I had a hard time breaking out of that cycle. I figured out I couldn't let people walk all over me and do nothing for myself. I was bleeding myself dry."

"How?" he grunts as he bangs around on the stove. The fact he's paying attention even a little sets me on edge. Most people don't care *how* I got to where I am unless they're other writers.

"A lot of it was fate. Or luck, I suppose. My best friend had an apartment and wanted me to move in. It freed up a lot of money for me, so I was able to focus on what I wanted to do instead of working a dead-end job. I publish a lot of books that are only now making me some money. I sunk every extra penny I had into publishing. And just when I thought that was going to be the rest of my career—"

"Wait." He spins around and leans against the counter. "What do you mean?"

"Uh, well...publishing is hard. Writing the story is easy in comparison. I had a handful of readers who got me through, but I thought I had hit a ceiling. All of my author friends seemed to be killing it and I was just...there. I was making money, but not enough to *make* any money, you know?" I rest my chin in my hands while he nods, a pensive look overtaking his face. "And then it happened. I wrote a series that took off. Not a lot, but enough. And then I wrote another one. A year later, running off the high of what I thought was my big break, I started a trilogy."

I close my eyes, remembering the hope and excitement I felt when I first started writing the story. The characters were clear and motivated. There was so much potential. No matter what happened, I knew I was telling a tale that was worth it. And I was doing it justice right up until the end, when I crashed and burned. The small smile I had falls from my face.

I clear my throat and open my eyes, looking everywhere but at him. "Unfortunately, I got in my own head and rushed the end. The last book flopped, and I lost...everything."

I've never told anyone the whole story. Even my author friends don't know what the hell happened. I don't know why I'm telling Emmett all of this. Maybe it's because he took care of me for hours while I had a migraine. Or because he saved me from breaking my neck. Or maybe it's just fate stepping in again, placing the exact person I need in my path. Whatever the reason, it's as if a weight is lifted from my shoulders. I hate to admit it, but Chloe might have been right. This time away was precisely what I needed.

"Did you really lose everything? Did all your readers run away or something?"

I chuckle despite the heaviness in my heart. "No, but it was pretty clear they didn't like it. People started talking about how sad it is when promising authors end up flaring out. It was—"

"Not great, I'm guessing. Why did you listen to them?" He genuinely looks perplexed.

A second later he jolts, then spins around to stir our lunch—or rather dinner since it's so late. Either way, I'm grateful since it gets him to stop staring at me. His deep blue green eyes are unnerving when they're fixed solely on me. Unnerving in the way it shoots bolts of desire through me and makes my head throb again. If we do come to some sort of agreement on our sleeping arrangements, it won't involve any sexy times tonight.

"It was hard to get away from it. I promote my books online and the videos seemed like they were everywhere. I couldn't avoid them unless I went offline. If

I go offline, I don't make money. Eventually, I put out a statement I was taking a break, set my ads, and went dark. A little too late, though."

"So that's what you're doing here?" He glances over his shoulder. "Going dark?"

"Not exactly. Chloe said I need to touch some grass. I haven't been able to get anywhere with my WIPs." I roll my eyes, slumping in my seat.

Confusion washes across his face before he smirks. "You packed whips for a trip to the woods?"

Rolling my eyes, I can't stop a shiver from shooting through me and settling straight between my legs. "Works in progress. I've got...a few."

"How many is 'a few'?"

"The air quotes are a little much," I mumble.

"Maddie." He pulls out my name. It rolls around his mouth and off his tongue with ease and sensuality, sending another bolt of desire through me.

"It's only like ten. Maybe fifteen," I mumble. His eyebrows disappear under the flop of hair that's fallen over his forehead. "Your food is smoking."

He jerks around and starts stirring furiously. Whatever he's cooking smells divine. Honestly, I'd gobble down whatever he put in front of me at this point. It hits me I'd probably still be wallowing in bed and starving if it wasn't for Emmett. And I just lied to him.

I clear my throat. "It's twenty."

"What's twenty?" he asks distractedly.

I pull in a deep breath, bracing myself. "I have twenty stories in the works. A few of them are close to the third act, but most of them are barely halfway. One of them only has bits and pieces floating around my head. Actually, there's quite a few that aren't even on paper other than one or two lines."

I press my lips together, waiting for his reaction. When Chloe stumbled upon my notebook with all of them listed, her eyes went cartoon-wide. My author friends and I joke about how many we have. But to have started that many and not get anywhere is embarrassing. They're all happily writing their books, publishing without a care in the world. Rationally, I know they're struggling as well, but none of them have writer's block like me. They're all writing and I'm here watching a gorgeous man make me food. I probably shouldn't be complaining about that.

"Why don't you finish the ones that are almost done, then?" He's too busy grabbing bowls out of the cupboard to see the look of pure disgust on my face.

"Because writing a book is like weaving a tapestry. You have to thread things together in such a way you don't accidentally pull the wrong one too hard. Unfortunately, I'm all thumbs right now and I fucked up the colors and now things have unraveled into a hot mess. All the tapestries are mixed up. And I'm pretty sure I'm going to have to stuff them into a closet I don't even fucking have." My chest tightens and nausea bubbles in my stomach. Spots dance in my vision and I squeeze my eyes shut.

One of the bowls clatters against the island, followed by silverware that hits my elbow. Emmett's hand skims across the back of my neck, startling me out of the spiral I was trapped in. He leaves a tingling sensation in his wake as he drops onto the stool next to me. Steam wafts up, filling the air with an intoxicating smell. My mouth waters as I stare at the noodles doused in white sauce.

"Not going to get in your belly by gawking at it." He nudges my fork, then concentrates on his own bowl.

"Are there any peas in this?" I ask, poking at the green pieces in it.

"Nope. Broccoli. Don't like peas?" he asks between bites.

"They're disgusting."

I gather too much onto my fork, but I'm committed now. Shoving it into my mouth, I instantly regret it. Not because it doesn't taste good. It's delicious, the flavors exploding across my tongue. The moist chicken is seasoned to perfection, and the pasta has just the right amount of bite to it. So many people overcook their noodles, leaving a gummy residue behind.

"There's more in the pan. You don't have to eat it all in one bite."

I don't bother to respond. He shakes his head as he slides from the stool and makes his way around the island. When he sets a perfectly buttered roll next to my bowl, I become a little more suspicious.

"Where'd all these ingredients come from? It wasn't in the fridge earlier. And I didn't buy them."

"There's another fridge downstairs. I just moved everything up here instead." He says it likes it's totally normal. Unless one is for beer and in the garage, I've never heard of someone having two fridges in a cabin.

"So, what do you do?"

I take another bite, hoping we can have a normal conversation. All our interactions have either been laced with sexual tension or I've been semi-conscious. If I get him talking, I might be able to decide whether I should sleep with him or not. I snort, then stuff another bite in my mouth to cover the sound. As if the only thing keeping me from fucking him is because I don't know what he does for a living.

"Um, right now, I'm a chef." He shoots me a smirk before returning his attention to his food.

"And before that?"

"A nurse."

"Hardee har."

"Before that I was a bigfoot hunter. Though I suppose I wasn't technically hunting him. Are all bigfoots male? I assume there's some female ones out there, too. Right?"

My nostrils flare and I wonder if I'm going to have to go through the whole list of things he's done for me. He seems like he's waiting for an answer, too.

"I don't know anything about bigfoot. Except for what he...she looks like. Are you always this obtuse about your occupation?"

My mind races, and I glance at him from the corner of my eye. He's hiding something, though I can't imagine why it matters whether I know what he does for a living. Unless he's embarrassed. Does he not have a job? Did he lose the one he had? Or is there something more nefarious he's hiding?

Chapter Fifteen
Emmett

Stuffing the entire bun in my mouth to avoid answering Maddie isn't my smartest move. Her question isn't out of line. I should be able to tell her what I do for work. The problem is, I don't know. Right now, I'm a contractor who's fixing up this cabin. I don't think it's what I've been doing in the past, though. My head aches the more I search for the information. It's like I'm wading through a thick fog, desperately waiting for the sun to rise so it can burn it all away.

"I'm not being obtuse. Things have been complicated." My head throbs once more, a stabbing pain behind my eyes, and suddenly my mind clears. "I've been doing construction most of my life. My father had a company when I was a kid, and I started working for him when I was in high school. I took some business classes with the thought I could take over for him when he retired."

Her body sags the slightest bit, and I realize she was worried about my answer. From her point of view, it probably seemed like I was a hitman or something. With the way she reacted when we met and the fact she's an author, her mind runs to the wildest options available.

"But you didn't?" she whispers, and I jolt, realizing I've been staring at her while I'm lost in my thoughts.

"My life hasn't exactly worked out how I thought it would." I grab our empty bowls and take them to the sink to rinse them out. "How long are you staying here?"

I hold my breath while I wait for her reply. I'm both terrified and anxious of her answer. If she's only here for a week or two, it won't be enough time. I already know that. If she's here longer, it just gives me more opportunities to fuck this all up. Releasing the pent-up air slowly, I fill the dishwasher as I resist the urge to glance at her.

"Four months. Chloe said if I come back before then, she'll throw me out of the apartment. And I'd never survive at my parent's house. Not with my mother trying to change my career every other day."

I give in and peer at her, relief flooding me. "Guess we'll be learning a lot about each other then, hmm?"

Her cheeks heat and she turns her head. "What exactly are you hoping you'll discover?"

"I'm sure we'll figure it out." I catch her smile before she ducks her head. "Why don't you get your computer and try writing? See if touching some grass earlier helped."

She groans, dropping her forehead onto the counter, and mumbles, "My head still hurts."

"Does it really? Or are you merely avoiding your responsibilities?" After I close the dishwasher, I cross my arms and lean against the counter.

"I'm in my post-migraine haze. I'll do it tomorrow. Today. Whatever. Or maybe next week. I've got time."

"Is four months enough to write twenty books?" I have no idea how long it takes or what it entails. If she's really staying for that long, maybe I'll learn.

She mutters, but I can't hear her. I clear my throat, and she picks her head up slightly.

"Twenty-seven."

"You just said it was twenty. Don't tell me you came up with ten new ones while we were talking," I chuckle, but she doesn't join in.

"Well, I was rounding up from seventeen. One is actually a five-book series. So that would be twenty-two. There's a novella in there I didn't count, so there's twenty-three. Another is one I'm putting on my website one chapter at a time. I should probably do something with that." Her eyes glaze over for a good thirty seconds, then she shakes her head. "Oh, and one is a trilogy. Like the series, though, I only count it as one idea, but it'd be three books all together."

I raise my eyebrow and her eyes widen. "Still doesn't add up to twenty-seven."

Rolling her eyes, she sighs. "I came up with another one on the way up here when I heard a song on the radio. Which usually doesn't matter because they float away into the ether to be picked up by someone else, but this one stuck. Which is really effing annoying."

"Doesn't sound like you have time to mope around here waiting for inspiration to strike. And while I would love to take another nap with you—" Her eyes snap to mine while my cock hardens once more. My fucking mouth is going to get me into trouble with this woman.

I clear my throat again. "I have work to do. Just like your stories won't write themselves, this cabin isn't going to fix itself. Stay off the porch. And the deck. I've got the railing tore up right now. Wouldn't want you taking another tumble without me being there to catch you."

Her nose wrinkles in the most adorable way. "Thanks for feeding me. I'm going to go take another shower. Promise I won't pass out."

I want to argue, demand I go with her. For her safety, of course. I hold my tongue, though, tracking her as she wanders from the room. I sit for another minute, thinking about how I'm totally fucked when it comes to Maddie. She's going to worm her way under my skin and I doubt I'll care.

Six full days of having Maddie pop up randomly has me riding the edge of distraction. The entire week we've been pussyfooting around each other, ignoring the building feelings between us. I've thrown myself into the various projects the house needs. Every time I finish one, I uncover three more that need to be done. I knew this reno was going to take me a while, but now I might be here longer than Maddie.

I brush my hands on my pants as I survey the deck. Replacing the rotten boards took longer than I anticipated. At least it's done now. Maybe I can get Maddie out here. Motivate her to start writing again. Her book bag containing her computer and whatever else she's hauling around hasn't moved from the front hall. It's collecting dust at this point. If we were friends or something else, I'd unpack it for her—tell her to get her shit together and just do it. Unfortunately, we're not there yet.

"Looks good," Maddie calls out from the safety of the screen door, and I spin around. "Is it safe to walk on now?"

I plant my hands on my hips, glancing around at my work. "Yeah. I'll need to stain it, but that can wait."

"I don't know how to do any of this kind of stuff. Dad taught me how to fix a toilet and change my oil. Oh, and fix a flat. He didn't want me to have to rely on someone else if I was in the middle of nowhere if my tire blew out."

"Good advice. I could—" I suck in a deep breath, my words dying as the sun slips from the shadows of the house to bathe her in a golden ring of light.

Fuck, she's gorgeous. It's not like I forget that fact when she's not in front of me. She's been living rent-free in my head for days. Having her pop up, though, sends bolts of desire through my body. I get lightheaded and flustered. Even as she is now, she lights a fire in my gut that never truly goes out. She picks at a loose thread on her shorts as her teeth worry at her lip. Her thin T-shirt has some design on it I've never seen before.

"You could what?" Her hair slips over her shoulder as she tilts her head, the strands glistening in the sunlight.

I clear my throat, glancing away. "I could teach you some things. Not the shit where you could get hurt, but there are some projects you could help with."

"Just don't make me paint. It's tedious and annoying. And I'm capable of doing other shit." She crosses her arms, drawing my eyes to her chest.

I mirror her stance. "Didn't say you weren't, gorgeous. And I won't make you paint, mostly because there's not really a lot of painting to do, anyway. But I'm also not going to let you work on the electrical. You'll shock the shit out of yourself, then probably blame me."

"I wouldn't…" She purses her lips, then rolls her eyes. "Yeah, you might be right. Oh, and no plumbing. You're not going to flood the house, right?"

"No, I'm not. I'm trained, Maddie. I'm not going to let the cabin fall down around you. But maybe you should be focusing on writing instead of learning how to hang a door."

Her cheeks redden and she won't meet my eye. "I'll get to it."

"Can't get to it if you let your computer wallow in your bag," I mutter.

I don't bother to wait for her response as I pivot and make my way to the corner I found a safe spot to stack the chairs and table. I spend the next ten minutes arranging them back on the deck. Maddie watches me, probably because I glared at her when she tried to help. When I've got everything where I want it, she grabs the cushions I tossed in the living room. We work in a comfortable silence.

I collapse onto one of the deck chairs. The lake glitters far below us and a soft breeze rustles the trees around us. It's peaceful and my mind starts conjuring all sorts of scenarios. Scenes from a time far into the future dance around my head—us sitting on a swing as the sun sets over the lake, me cooking while she types away at the kitchen island, us walking hand in hand along the shore. A future I never imagined unfolds before me, then slowly fades away.

"This is really peaceful," she murmurs as she sinks into the other chair. "Perfect place to relax."

"Nice spot to work," I murmur, glancing at her from the corner of my eye.

She huffs, resting her head against the back of the chair. "Why don't you just stick to fixing shit, and I'll worry about my own things."

I don't know why I keep bringing it up. She's a grown-ass woman, capable of taking care of herself. If she doesn't want to write, so be it. If she can't bring herself to even try right now, then who am I to tell her different? For some reason, though, there's an itch inside my brain. I need to get her to finish her stories. I don't know what will happen if she doesn't, but the situation feels dire.

"The whole reason you're here is to get back into the groove of things. Seems like you need someone to hold you accountable."

Her head lolls as she whines under her breath. Her foot stomps on the newly laid boards, sending her rocking back and forth. When she tucks her legs underneath her, I glance away so she won't see my smile.

"Fine. I'll write, but not until after I take a nap." She shoves from her seat and grumbles the entire way into the cabin.

Glancing over my shoulder, I watch as she nears her bag. It's as if she's approaching a wild animal. When she finally gets her computer out, her shoulders slump. Maybe I shouldn't have pushed her so hard, not that I thought I was shoving her into something she didn't want.

The other option is to fill her days worshipping her with my head buried between her legs. I'm not entirely sure either of us is ready for that step. She's intoxicating in a way that will completely overwhelm me. I won't be able to stop myself from falling under her spell.

"You don't need the bathroom, right?" she calls through the screen door, and I raise my hand instead of answering. I doubt I'd be able to now that I've got the image of her writhing underneath me bouncing around in my head.

As her footfalls fade, I adjust myself subtly in case she's still watching. At some point, I need to make a decision when it comes to her. Waking up hours before her to hide by the lake while I jack off to the images I've collected in my head isn't sustainable. She'll either be my salvation or my downfall. Even if I'm able to claim her, though, the time we have together is fleeting. And I'm not sure if once I have her, I'll be able to let her go.

Chapter Sixteen
Maddie

It takes another three days for me to take Emmett's advice. Every day was another step forward, but most of it was spent procrastinating. At least I plugged my computer in. There used to be a time I was terrified to turn it off, thinking I'd lose all my progress. Thankfully, it was all there when I booted it up the next day. As much as I'm forcing myself to do this, I don't want to lose any of the actual progress I've made.

Day two was spent organizing my files. They were scattered in various places, as if I thought a different program would spark my creativity. It didn't, obviously. Emmett gave me the side-eye when I told him this was necessary. He didn't question me. I don't know if I would have been able to explain it, anyway.

When the sun rose this morning, I showered right away, thinking it would motivate me. I have nothing else to do other than write unless Emmett has a project. He's been using them as a carrot to encourage me to get shit done. If I write something today, he'll let me help him on the roof. I'm not entirely sure I'll stay up there, even if it isn't particularly steep. Then again, I tripped over the threshold when I was coming out to the deck ten minutes ago.

The cursor blinks at me, daring me to start a sentence. The last one I wrote in this story was the end of a chapter. I think it's a particularly good one. "Not yet, my queen. Not yet" sent shivers down my spine at the time. Hell, it still does. But I have no idea what's next.

Plus, the blank screen apparently hates me. It's throwing me off. Years have passed since I was intimidated by an empty document. Usually it fills me with excitement, adrenaline at starting another story, another chapter, another journey. Lately, all the old feelings of insecurity have rendered me useless.

I sigh, clicking out of the document. Those two will have to wait. They're pissed at me since I left them on a bit of a cliffhanger, but they'll deal. All my characters are dealing. Not well, but they're handling it. Most of them are screaming or grumbling. One is prowling around in the back of my mind and randomly kicking things. It's annoying as hell.

"What are you working on?"

I've pulled up another WIP, another cursor mocking me. "Just Eve and Axel's story."

"How far are you?" He leans over my shoulder but keeps his eye on me.

"In this one? None. Thought I might start a new one."

He settles into the chair next to me, gazing at the view. "What's it about then? Or do you not know?"

"Uh, Axel is a hockey player. Eve isn't. I think they're in college and were on a project together. Wait..." I close my eyes, searching through the files in my mind. "Her brother is a hockey player. He told her to stay away from his teammates. Axel used to be her friend, I think. At some point she's at a party and someone spikes her drink. Axel finds her and the team rallies and takes care of it while he takes care of her. That's all I've got though. I don't know if I want to write a college romance, though."

"When you say 'I think', what do you mean?"

"I write the story, but it's the characters who call the shots essentially." I peek at him from the corner of my eye, assessing his reaction. Half the time people nod like that totally makes sense. The other half can't seem to grasp the concept of people living in my head.

"If they're calling the shots, wouldn't it be their fault you can't get their stories out?"

He's got a point, but unfortunately, I have no one to blame but myself. "Since I'm the one who actually writes the book, I don't think so. I like your thinking, though."

"Well, get to it, then." He waves at my computer that still has the blinking cursor of death.

I spend the next half hour staring at it before I give up. I pull up another document, then another, and another. None of them spark even the slightest bit of creativity. After an hour, I'm ready to give up. In a last-ditch effort to get something—anything—on the page, I start reading one of my old WIPs. It's disjointed and not how I construct things now. I start tinkering with the sentences, then give up after a page. If I keep messing with it, I'll get sucked in and seeing as how this book is halfway done, I'll end up spending the entire four months I'm here editing instead of writing.

A growl builds in my chest until I finally let it loose, slamming my computer closed. Emmett's hand brushes my arm and I jolt, almost upending the table.

"Holy shit, you scared me," I gasp, pressing my fist to my pounding heart.

"Forget I was here?" He grins, a twinkle entering his eye. "Why don't you take a break? We can go swimming."

"Thought you needed to get the roof done," I say while I push from my chair. "And I really should try to do *something* productive."

He chuckles and his hand rests on my lower back, sending tingles along my skin. "You did do something productive. It may not be what you need in the end, but maybe it's enough for right now."

It's a good thing I packed my swimsuit. Chloe insisted I'd need one, then threw in two more for good measure. It takes me a good five minutes to decide whether I wear the bikini or the one piece. In the end, I opt for enticing Emmett. I want to see the blush staining his cheeks when he first spots me. Nothing could prepare me for the instant desire in his eyes. I swear they darken, though I thought that was something that only happened in romance books.

He clears his throat, running his hands through his hair. "Ready? The water should be plenty warm by now."

I grin, bouncing on the balls of my feet. "Lead the way."

The steep stairs leading to the lake prove to be my downfall. I'm trying so hard to not trip, I end up catching my heel on the previous step and tumbling into Emmett's back. His arms swing around and catch me as he grunts.

"Sorry," I cry, attempting to right myself. Now my cheeks are the ones burning.

Somehow, he maneuvers me in front of his body. His arms wrap around me and lift me effortlessly until I'm over his shoulder, my barely covered ass resting right by his face. All he'd need to do is turn his head and he'd be able to take a bite. The thought sends a bolt of desire through me, and I wiggle.

"Stop moving or I'll end up dropping you. No point taking the hard way down to the lake, gorgeous."

His hand rests on my thigh and goosebumps scatter across my skin. By the time we reach the shoreline, I need a cooldown. As soon as my feet hit the rough sand, I'm skipping away from him into the water. Cool water laps at my ankles and a squeal leaves me. Emmett's laugh rings out over the lake. I scowl, refusing to retreat. I'm going to need to force myself deeper just to save face.

"Need me to toss you in?" he asks, wading in next to me.

His fingers skim along my hip before coming to rest on my lower back. If he keeps touching me like this, I'm going to reenact the fantasies I've been having while falling asleep. Twice this week I've woken up cupping my own tit. Once my hand was down my pants. My dreams have been wild, always starring the man currently throwing a cheeky grin at me.

His hand drops and he charges into the water while ripping off his shirt, then dives smoothly under the surface. I didn't realize the lake was deep enough this close to shore. Instead of excitement over the revelation, I'm suddenly not okay. I retreat to the edge, waiting for him to pop up.

After what feels like forever, bubbles disrupt the surface. His head slowly appears, and I swear the move is straight out of a movie. It's the slow-motion hands through the hair. Not to mention the droplets of water rolling down his body. I didn't realize contractors were so fit. He has at least six abs rippling down his stomach. When he spins around, I about swoon over the view. I never focused on someone's back, but Emmett's just might be a work of art.

I shake my head, glancing away. If I keep staring, I'm liable to become one with the lake. I shuffle along the shoreline, attempting to put more space between us. At some point, he's going to look for me and I'd rather he not notice I'm about to combust. As cold as the water is, at least it'll cool the desire swamping me right now. Getting close to him while in the water won't help, so I need to put some distance between us.

I'm a good twenty feet away when he finally glances around to find me. I've wandered in up to my waist, but I can't force myself any farther. My elbow dips into the water and I yelp, holding my hands higher as goosebumps spread along my arms. Floundering along, I'm half expecting to step into a sinkhole.

Emmett's strong arm wraps around my waist, and he pulls my back against his chest. Instantly, my body relaxes and molds to his. When my feet leave the sand, I bite my tongue and kick them back and forth.

"Relax. I'm not going to dunk you," he whispers in my ear.

I let out a shaky breath, and his other hand runs down my side. "That didn't even cross my mind. I was afraid we'd hit a hole or something."

"I won't let that happen," he says, chuckling as he wades deeper. "And if it did, I'd be going down with—"

And then I'm underwater, my body cushioned by his. Arms tightening around me, he squeezes what little breath I have left in my lungs. I'm only under a few seconds before I'm upright. I'd love to say I handle the entire situation with poise and grace, choosing to laugh it off. Instead, I cough violently, clinging to his arm as I dig my nails into his skin.

"Whoops." His body shakes as he floats us away from the sinkhole of death.

"Why do I feel like you did that on purpose?" I gasp, resting my head on his chest.

"I most certainly did not. Don't punch me."

I open my mouth to ask what the hell he's talking about when he tips back and we float. It's a strange sensation, being held while drifting. I should swim away, put space between us, something. But I can't force myself to move. My eyes flutter closed, and I wonder if this is what it feels like to be safe. To be protected from the outside world. A peace I've never known steals over me, like the waves lapping at my sides.

"Do you hear it?" he murmurs after a few minutes.

"Hear what?"

"The trees are singing. A song you'll never hear again. They only sing it once and then it'll be gone, lost to the wind. And we're the only two who will witness the symphony. They're playing it just for us."

I concentrate on the breeze wafting through the forest, rustling the leaves, then disappearing. Another gust ripples above us and the world around us shivers. I wonder if this was what Chloe had in mind when she forced me up here. I've never felt a particular affinity for nature. There was no pull toward the forest like some people talked about. The closest I ever got to camping was setting up a tent in the backyard of my childhood home. I now understand the desire to disappear into the wilderness. At least a little bit.

As we float along, though, I wonder if it's Emmett and not the forest calling to me. He's drawing me in a little more every day. I just keep waiting for the other shoe to drop. Until I know his flaws, I'll never be able to fully trust him. Right now, though, I'm going to enjoy this moment while it lasts.

Chapter Seventeen

Emmett

I didn't know how Maddie would react when I pulled her into me. This wasn't my plan, but now that I'm holding her, I refuse to complain. I swear she's barely even breathing as we float around the lake. She needs this break, regardless of how little she's accomplished since she got here. And I need her in my arms.

When she stepped out of the room in her gold bikini, I saw the glint in her eye. She wore it on purpose to either entice me or see me blush. Joke's on her—she could have worn a Snuggie and I'd react the same. I want her no matter what she's wearing.

"Maddie," I whisper, my fingers flexing on her hip.

"Hmm?" She sounds like she's about to fall asleep. As happy as I am that she trusts me to keep her safe, I'd really rather not have to wake her up in the middle of the lake.

"Look to our right."

Her head turns, then she shivers when the water hits her ear. I chuckle, slowly tipping us upright. I keep hold of her as my feet hit the bottom. She wiggles, forcing me to grit my teeth as her ass rubs along my cock. There isn't nearly enough fabric between us to hide my reaction to her. When she gasps, I wince, convinced she'll swim away.

"Are those ducks? They don't even look like they're fully grown."

About seven ducklings waddle through the underbrush, disappearing from view.

"They probably aren't. Soon, though."

I wade us closer to the shoreline, assuming she's done swimming. She wiggles again and I loosen my grip. I suck in a sharp breath when she spins and loops her arms around my neck. My hands settle on her hips, awkwardly holding her while the water attempts to push us together, then apart. She smirks as she glances down, as if she'll be able to see my hands on her body.

Her legs loop around my waist and her body melds to mine. Her breath ghosts across my lips and I groan, tipping my head back.

"You've been feeding me for the past week, but I'm still *really* hungry," she says, and a laugh bursts out of me.

"I hope you're better at having your characters flirt than you are."

Her bottom lip pops out, drawing my gaze down. "Because I'm not the one saying those things. My characters are. And I'm in their head when they're saying them. Unfortunately, that doesn't translate to my own language, apparently."

"Good thing I'm not judging you on your dirty talk," I murmur, resting my forehead on hers.

She huffs, then clears her throat as she closes her eyes. "It shouldn't feel like this yet, should it?"

Part of me wants to question her, feign ignorance. I can't, though. I know exactly what she's talking about. Something is driving us together, throwing us into each other's paths. I've never particularly believed in fate, but there's an outside force driving our connection.

"I don't know. I've never been through this before," I murmur. Her gaze snaps to mine and I chuckle. "Not like that. Never felt like this before."

A small smile blooms across her face milliseconds before I pull her mouth to mine. An explosion of colors burst behind my lids, lighting my world up in a way I've never experienced before. Sliding my tongue along her bottom lip, I breathe her in.

When she opens for me, I'm lost, wholly and completely giving myself over to the sensations running riot through my body. She tastes like sunshine and moonlight. Like coming home after a long day. Like dreams come to life.

She pulls away, gasping. "That was—"

"Transcendent."

I swoop in, kissing her again. Our movements become frantic as I run my hands along her sides. Water laps at our bodies, snapping me out of the spell I'm under. I won't be able to carry her all the way to the house. Not with the steep stairs between the lake and the cabin. Throwing her down on the shoreline and fucking her sounds great in theory until we're covered in sand.

My foot hits a rock and I yelp, ripping my mouth from hers. She squeals as I slip and fall backward. My head goes under, and I shove her away from me. Instead of her saving herself, her legs clench around me, squeezing tightly as the sky disappears. I scramble to set my feet, wondering if we're both going to drown because I couldn't wait to fuck her.

Her garbled cry reaches me as I finally find the bottom. Maddie's legs tug me upward, probably thinking she's helping when really she's making it harder. Finally, my head crests the surface and I sputter as I wipe my face. My other hand slides around her back and I haul her into me.

"Holy shit. Are you okay?" Her hands cup my cheeks, then run down my neck to my shoulders. Her touch burns away the last of my anxiety over thinking I was going to drown in the lake before I truly tasted her.

"I'm fine," I gasp, still catching my breath as I hold her closer.

"I don't think you should carry me while in the lake." Giggles erupt from her, and she ducks her head.

"Maybe we should just enjoy the lake from the deck from now on." I smirk and more giggles flow out of her.

It's the most relaxed I've ever seen her. She's had a cloud of anxiety coating her movements since she got here. The pressure she's putting herself under had to break at some point. I'm just glad she fell into my arms rather than sobbing alone in the shower.

Her legs unwind from me and I set her down, then grab her arm to steady her as we make our way out of the water. I imagined this scenario a lot differently when I suggested we go swimming. As we climb the stairs, random bursts of laughter erupt from her, and a grin graces her swollen lips.

When we reach the cabin, I tug her inside, straight to the bedroom. As much as I'd love to throw her on the bed and strip her bikini from her damp body, we need to shower. I should be a gentleman and let her clean up in peace, but I won't. She's too tempting for her own good. I'll be consumed with images of her naked just feet from me.

"Are you coming?" Maddie asks, and I realize I'm hovering in the doorway.

Stepping inside, I grin and my palms itch to touch her. When she leans over to start the water, I step behind her and grip her hips. She glances at me over her shoulder, biting her lip. I swear she's fiddling with the knob unnecessarily just to feel my hands on her a little longer.

I lean, covering her body with my own. "Are you trying to tease me, gorgeous?"

"Is it working?" She gasps as I run my hands along her skin, then toy with the tie between her breasts.

"You don't have to work very hard. Every time I see you, my cock stands at attention. Every time you cross my mind, I'm overwhelmed with the need to be near you. And I suspect I'm not the only one. Do I need to prove that? I bet your pretty little pussy is soaked right now, isn't it?" I pause, closing my eyes while I wait for her response.

She may have kissed me, pressed her body against mine, blushed every time I dropped a hint of how much I wanted her. Doesn't mean she wants to sleep with me. I've met women who like to flirt, thriving off the thrill of a man wanting them. Hell, I've done it as well. I don't mind, but I certainly don't want to push her if she wants to leave it there. Her body might want me and yet her mind might not.

She pushes upright, forcing me to straighten as well. With one hand gripping her hip and the other splayed under her breasts, I duck my head.

"Why don't you see for yourself?" she breathes as she tips her head to the side, giving me access to her neck.

I brush my lips along her shoulder all the way to behind her ear. She shivers and her fingers dig into my thighs, keeping me close to her. I toy with the tie between her breasts again. It takes everything in me to leave the knot as it is. Goosebumps erupt along her damp skin as I run my hand down her body.

"I'm clean," I murmur. "And I got snipped."

She hums as she drops her head to my shoulder. "Me too."

I chuckle and she shivers. "Good to know we're doubly protected."

"You know what I meant," she hisses.

Slipping my hand under the waistband of her bottoms, I nip at her jaw. I've dreamt of this moment since she fell into my arms. Now that it's happening, I want to savor every second, yet my cock isn't on board with that plan. As soon as my fingers reach her pussy, I groan.

"So fucking wet for me, gorgeous." I stroke her as she shudders in my arms. "Do you need me to take care of this?"

"Please," she breathes, her hips moving with me. "I've waited long enough."

Her words send a shiver of satisfaction through me. She wants me just as much as I want her. I flick her clit, then slide my fingers down to her core. Slowly, I thrust them into her, swallowing hard at how easily her pussy gives in to me. She rides my hand, breathy noises ghosting past her lips. A whine leaves her when I pull from her, and she sags against me.

"Why don't we get you in the shower?" I tug at the tie between her breasts and the fabric falls away from her body.

I cup both of them, flicking my thumbs over her nipples. She gasps and her nails dig into my thighs again. She's leaving marks along my skin. A possessiveness overtakes me, the urge to mark her as well almost choking the air from my lungs.

Leaning down, I sink my teeth into the soft flesh of her neck. Her moan echoes through the small room, goading me onward. I lap at the indents, then press a kiss to the brand. It'll fade before I'm done worshipping her body, but that's okay. I'll just leave another when it does.

"I swear, Emmett, you're going to regret it if you make me wait," she growls, and I chuckle.

"Shower. Now."

She rolls her eyes and steps into the tub. When she hooks her thumbs in the waistband of her bottoms, I cover her hands with mine. She raises an eyebrow, and I slowly shake my head. I'm going to unwrap her like a present just for me. My gaze dips to her chest, following the water splashing across her nipples. My mouth waters and I duck my head, licking at one of the hard nubs. The spray hits the back of my neck, soaking me. With a grunt, I straighten, though I don't want to. I want to bury my face between her thighs.

I step in after her, then drop to my knees. Tugging the rest of her swimsuit down her legs, I lick my lips. Her hand lands on my shoulder and she steps out of the holes. The bottoms land on the tiles outside the tub with a splat. Her top follows and my cock twitches in my trunks. I wrap my hands around the back of her thighs and bring her closer.

Burying my face between her legs, I groan as her scent fills my senses. She smells like home, which doesn't make a lick of sense, but I refuse to question it. Not with her ready and waiting for me to pleasure her. She shuffles her feet apart, giving me more access. Using my tongue, I circle her clit and she holds onto me to stay upright.

When I slide down to her core, her body curls over mine. As much as I want to make her come, I need to see her as she explodes, and I can't do that from this angle. I flick her clit once more, then stand. Her glazed eyes find mine. Her tongue darts out, licking at the drop of water on her lips. Steam floats around us, lending a magical quality to this whole scene.

I take off my trunks and they join her swimsuit on the floor. We'll need to clean it up later, but that's a future problem. I'm too focused on Maddie to care. I stroke my length and tip my chin toward her.

"What?" she asks breathlessly.

"Wash your hair. Don't touch your body, though. I'll take care of that," I murmur.

It takes her a minute to process what I've asked her to do. She tips her head back, rewets her hair, and does as I've commanded. Having her obey me without question has my cock hardening even more, though I didn't think that was possible. My hand is the only thing keeping me from grabbing her and sinking into her heat.

When she's done, I twirl my finger, waiting until she presents her back to me. Gathering the washcloth and soap, I lather up the suds before running it over her body. She moans when I massage one breast and then the other. Her nipples pebble, and her breath comes out in short gasps. I've barely even touched her and she's already worked up. I could probably make her come from this alone. The idea has me nudging my cock between her legs, and she pushes her ass into me.

Dipping between her legs, I slip my finger around the washcloth and circle her clit. Thirty seconds later and she's panting. My other hand wraps around her and I hold her upright while I continue playing with her body.

"Emmett, please let me come," she whines, and I pull away to finish cleaning her skin.

The ragged cry that leaves her almost has me giving in. Almost. I should clean up as well, wash the lake off me. Her body is too tempting, though. Stepping away from her carefully, I run the washcloth quickly over my arms, then chest. She leans against the tiles, trying to catch her breath. Before long, she's going to get pissed. Even now she's playing with her nipples. It only makes me want her more.

I rinse quickly, then shut off the water. I'll deal with my hair after I've made her come. When I'm out of the shower, I hold my hand out to her and help her out as well. As soon as she's on the rug, I haul her body into me and cover her mouth with mine. She moans and I swallow the sound. I fit my fingers into the crease of her ass and lift her. Setting her on the counter, I continue to devour her.

She forces a grunt from me when she grips my cock and rubs the tip along her soaked pussy. Her legs end up around my waist, trying to force me closer. I rip my mouth away from hers and glance down. She lines me up and the tip slips in. I groan as her pussy clamps down.

"You're going to have to control yourself if you want me in any farther, gorgeous."

Her pussy quivers around me, and she throws her head back. "If you'd take control, I wouldn't have to."

I wrap my hand around the back of her neck and yank her toward me. "Be a good girl and let me in."

Her mouth parts and her tongue darts out to wet her lips, her gaze fixed on my cock rocking against her. Inch by inch, I slip into her more. She shudders, finally relaxing, and I tip her chin up. Our eyes meet and I slam into her.

I groan as her heat envelops me and she sails over the edge into oblivion. I didn't expect her to come so soon, and I rest my forehead against hers, mesmerized by the ecstasy blossoming on her face. Her pussy spasms around me, her eyes falling closed. I roll my hips, covering her mouth with mine. I want to drink her in, devour every sound, and bask in every moment. Her body shudders once more and I slowly pull out of her, then slam back in.

"Harder," she breathes, clinging to my shoulders.

"Hang on, gorgeous. I'll be sweet and gentle next time, but right now, I need to fuck you."

Her legs tighten and she digs her nails into my skin. I thrust into her hard and fast, forcing a whimper from her every time I hit the deepest parts of her. Her ass slides along the counter and she drops her hands next to her hips, holding the lip to stay in place. Slipping my hand into her hair, I grip the strands and tug until her head tips back.

"Oh fuck. Yes, right there," she cries as her pussy quivers around my cock.

I pound into her, chasing my release. Gritting my teeth, I stare at her as she falls into oblivion once more, my name on her lips. I follow close behind with a shuddering moan. I swear the lights blink out and I'm thrust into an alternate universe. One where stars hang above my head, exploding through the air around me. It's transcendent in a way I've never experienced before. And I fear I never will with anyone else. Something within me clicks into place—a piece I never knew was missing. It's in that moment I realize I'm completely fucked.

Chapter Eighteen
Maddie

A deep peace resonates in me as Emmett plays with my hair. It might be the rumbling coming from him, though. We've been cuddling the entire morning, enjoying the aftermath of finally giving in to our attraction. I'm not going to complain.

We spent the rest of yesterday exploring each other's bodies, only leaving the bed to pee. He did bring me food in bed, which, again, I'm not going to complain about. I wouldn't mind a repeat of yesterday. Another day of blissfulness seems like the perfect way to spend my time here.

This whole situation could turn out incredibly amazing or ridiculously chaotic. I've been studiously ignoring any thoughts of the future. When our time is up, we'll go our separate ways. An ache settles in my chest, and I wonder if this is how my characters feel when I've put them in an impossible scenario.

I close my eyes, snuggling closer to his side. He presses a kiss to my forehead, then goes back to his book. It's a thriller and not something I would usually read. Every once in a while, he'll snort, but when I asked him what was funny, he said nothing. When he does it again, I dig my fingernails into his bare chest.

"Something you needed, gorgeous?" he murmurs as he turns the page.

"You keep making noises and I'd like to know why."

He chuckles, making my head bounce on his shoulder. "Every time they make a discovery that I've already figured out, I can't help reacting. I already know who the murderer is, I'm just waiting for them to figure it out."

"Ahh." I chew on my lip. "So, who's the killer?"

"No one, actually. It's all in the guy's head. He's probably in prison, telling the story to his cellmate. At least that's my guess. Aren't you going to ask me?"

"Ask you what?" I push up, resting my head in my hand.

"Why I read books when I already know the ending?"

I snort, then giggle. "Dude, I write Romance—with a capital R. They all end the same way, essentially. They end up together and in love, even if it's just for now. Like yours, it's more about the journey."

His nose wrinkles, and he sets his book down. "Did you just call me dude?"

"Uh, yes." It comes out more like a question than an admission.

He grins, then rolls on top of me, forcing me onto my back. I squeal as he grabs my wrists and forces my hands over my head. He grinds his hips into mine and my breath catches in my throat. When he nuzzles my neck, a sound I've never heard before escapes me. It's a cross between a moan and a whine and is utterly primal. He responds by growling, then sinking his teeth into the soft skin of my neck.

"Are you going to melt under my touch again, gorgeous?"

"Mmmm," I hum, tilting my head so he'll mark me again.

I've never been one to indulge in the fantasies running through my mind. I reserve that for my characters, convincing myself they deserved those experiences. But never me. I'd never met someone I felt comfortable with enough to even bring up the subject. Emmett seems to know instinctually what my body is yearning for, though. If he were one of those perfect book boyfriends, he'd demand I tell him exactly what I want. He'd make me beg.

"Give me your words like you'll give me your body, Maddie. Tell me what you want me to do to you."

I jolt, eyes flying open. Did he just read my mind? Did I accidentally say it out loud? I may talk to myself when I'm alone, but I've been hyperaware of his presence since I got here. I didn't want to scare him off by muttering about random plotlines or having imaginary conversations with my characters.

He nips at my jaw as his hand runs down my arm and settles on my breast, kneading the flesh. My eyes flutter closed again, and I arch into him. I lick my lips, gathering up the courage to tell him to fuck me—mostly because I don't know what else I would ask him to do. Sure, I could tell him to fuck me doggy style, but saying it out loud seems crude.

His breath ghosts across the shell of my ear, leaving me a puddle underneath him. "Do you want me to slip my cock into your pretty little pussy and fuck you hard and fast like before? Or do you think you can stay still while I feast on you instead?"

I swallow hard, then bite his shoulder when his hand slides between our bodies. He doesn't hesitate to push two fingers into me, pumping them leisurely, as if we have all the time in the world. I suppose we do for now. My hips kick up, meeting his shallow thrusts, and my clit hits his stomach each time, sending a mini shockwave through my body.

He pulls them out and a soft cry leaves me unbidden. "Emmett, please."

"Please what?" His thumb circles my clit gently—never enough to get me anywhere near the edge. "You didn't answer my questions. I think I'll make you beg for it now. Beg for my cock. Beg for my tongue. Beg me to fuck you."

Holy shit. This man can't be for real. He said he didn't read anything other than thrillers and mysteries, but I wonder if he's hiding the fact he reads spicy romances. Otherwise, he must be a figment of my imagination. Maybe I hit my head and I'm currently in a coma, dreaming of a whole other life. When he sinks his teeth into the top of my breasts, I dismiss that theory.

And then I'm swept away. His lips travel down my stomach, hands roving over my skin. He seizes my ankles and bends my knees. My legs fall open and he groans as he stares.

He tsks, shaking his head. "Such a mess you've made."

"Your fault. Better clean it up." The words tumble from me, and my cheeks burn.

He grins and my muscles relax as I breathe a sigh of relief. "I like it when you're bossy."

He doesn't give me time to respond before he buries his nose in my pussy. I squirm, grabbing onto the slats of the headboard to keep myself still. He swirls his tongue around my core, then licks up to my clit. Tipping my head back and closing my eyes, I moan. It's been too fucking long, and this isn't something I can recreate with toys. He sucks the sensitive bud into his mouth, and I clamp my legs around his head.

He chuckles against me, easing my knees down again. When he presses a kiss to my clit, I glance down.

"You are *not* going to just stop." It was supposed to be a question. He grins again, and I have the sudden urge to smack him.

"Don't move," he says, then tosses back the covers and slips out.

My mouth falls open and I'm about to lambast him, but a pillow flies through the air and lands on my face. His hand wrap around my wrists, keeping my own hands on the headboard. When I start to close my legs, his knee and other hand stop me.

"Stay just like this. I want to have you ready and waiting for me. Be a good girl and don't move."

I snort, my voice muffled. "You want me to be all splayed out like fucking dessert for you while I have no idea what's happening?"

"Wouldn't want to ruin the surprise."

I freeze, my interest piqued. Damn my horny body. If my pussy wasn't such a greedy bitch for his cock, I wouldn't have a problem demanding to know what this supposed surprise was.

When he's satisfied I'll stay put, he releases me. I can't hear where he goes. He could walk straight out of the bedroom and I'd have no idea. Still, I strain for any crumb to give me a clue of what he's up to. Hopefully, he's not taking pictures of my naked body and putting them on the internet to make fun of me.

I'm just about to move when his fingers trail up my side, sending shivers through me. I close my eyes, focusing on his touch. He lifts the pillow from my face, and I struggle not to peek.

"Look at you being such a good girl," he murmurs in my ear.

I shouldn't be into this—not with someone I barely know. His praise shouldn't affect me so much. I shouldn't crave it. Yet something unfurls within me, filling in the cracks in my soul. Naming whatever it is wouldn't be smart. Not while I should be focused on what he's doing to my body—his fingers skating across my stomach, his breath on my nipple, his hair brushing my skin.

"Such a beautiful canvas, waiting for me to paint with pleasure," he whispers, then wraps his lips around my nipple.

I arch my back, gripping the slats tighter as I resist the urge to grip his hair and shove his face into my chest. He'd probably suffocate since I'm more than a little well-endowed up top. Emmett hasn't complained about my curves or my boobs. With the way he's squeezing and biting every extra bit of skin, I'd say he's a little obsessed.

"Tell me where you want me," he breathes, then nips at my bottom lip. His hands continue their quest to map my entire body.

"I need more," I whine, shaking with need.

"More what?"

"Of you," I gasp, not sure how to be more clear. Every time I open my mouth, I'm barely coherent. Mostly it's moans and whimpers.

"More where? You're not going to get away with letting only your body do the talking." His lips brush along my jaw and I lean toward him.

I mull over his words, my mind at war with my body. Convincing myself to get over my embarrassment isn't as easy as I thought it would be. I can't believe he wants me to tell him, that he cares so much about my pleasure. I always thought I'd lucked out with my past partners. They might not have put my pleasure above their own, but I usually got off. I know a lot of women who don't get that. Now I wonder if I was merely expecting the bare minimum.

His hand slips between my legs, cupping my pussy, and I moan. "Seems as if you need me here. Say it. Demand I fill this pretty little cunt."

"What the fuck," I gasp, arching against him. I grit my teeth until he starts to pull away. "Please. Fuck me, please. Don't make me beg."

"Oh, my sweetness." He pinches my nipple and slides his finger along my folds. "You already have, like the good girl you are. Nothing wrong with begging."

My eyes fly open, a surge of confidence rolling through me. "Then fill me the fuck up or I'll do it myself."

He smirks, then slides his palm down my face and I close my eyes again. "Keep your eyes closed."

"Or what?"

"You're not ready for what will happen if you disobey."

I'm about to question him when a buzzing fills the room. My body spasms when he runs my vibrator along my inner thigh. My legs quiver and I fight the urge to snap them closed. I don't want him to stop, yet the need to have it inside me scrambles my brain.

"More," I moan, jerking my hips toward him as I seek more.

Lightly, the vibrator runs over my clit, and I whimper. He plays with me as I writhe underneath his touch.

"Harder," I gasp, arching my back off the bed.

He chuckles as he presses down on my clit, then eases off. Again and again, he repeats the move until I'm begging for relief. He pulls the vibrator away, and a whine leaves me. My hips jolt toward him, chasing the high of the orgasm dangling just out of reach. His fingers dance along my ribs, and goosebumps erupt on my skin.

"How far will you let me go?" he murmurs as he brushes my inner thigh, making my legs quiver.

"As far as you want." I bite my lip as soon as the words leave me.

"You shouldn't give me a free pass, gorgeous."

"I...I don't know why I said that."

"Because your body wants everything, but your mind says it's too early. You tell me what you want, and I'll do it."

It's easier to have this conversation with my eyes closed. I wanted to peek before—see what he was doing, read the emotions on his face. These moments aren't always easy. Then again, I don't usually get this far. My hook-ups are few and far between. My last boyfriend preferred vanilla sex in the dark. I didn't have to worry about discussing boundaries because he only had two moves and they never got me anywhere. Not that he noticed. I don't think I'll have those same issues with Emmett.

He finally dips his thumb between my legs, teasing the core. As soon as the vibrator hits my clit, he plunges his fingers into me. I gasp, my ass leaving the bed. Whatever he's whispering is lost in the buzzing of the toy. I'll ask him about it later when I'm not teetering on the edge of oblivion.

My palms ache as I grip the slats of the headboard while a shockwave of pleasure rolls through me. I yelp when rips his hand away, the vibrator still pressed to my clit. A shuddering sob leaves me. He's left me empty, my pussy spasming around nothing. The toy disappears and my eyes fly open.

"What the—ahh." A strangled cry leaves me as his hands grab the back of my knees and yank me to the edge of the bed.

He plunges into me, my orgasm blooming once more. The vibrator returns, settling on my clit, and a low moan leaves me. With every thrust, another wave of ecstasy crashes over me. It's as if he can read my body and knows exactly what I need. I give myself over to the euphoria, curling my fingers into the sheets as I writhe underneath him.

He tosses the toy aside and pinpricks erupt from the sensitive bud. The line between pleasure and pain blurs. He doesn't slow, his fingers digging into my flesh. Another orgasm hits me without warning, though it might be the same one as before. His head tips back, the tendons in his neck standing out as he groans.

He collapses on top of me, and I wrap my arms around him as he kisses his way across my chest. I hold him close, not ready to let him go. Whatever is between us, I'm ready for this. I'm ready for the beginning of my own story.

Chapter Nineteen

Emmett

A whole two weeks of christening the cabin has been the best time of my life. We're in our own bubble, losing ourselves in each other's bodies. I never expected this to happen. I'm not going to question it, though. It's more than being inside of her, watching her fall apart in my arms. It's the quiet parts in between, her soft smile when she's gazing out at the lake, or the explosion of laughter when I chase her around the cabin.

We never talk about the future, never question what we're doing here. We're just enjoying something new, I suppose. It's too soon to speculate where we go from here. If she pushed me, I'd admit I don't want to give her up. Ever. That thought alone terrifies me in a way I've never experienced before.

I nip at her inner thigh, and she shudders in my hold, the patio chair creaking under our combined weight. I slide my knees onto the deck and tug her ass closer to my mouth. Grinning, I glance up at her, waiting until her gaze meets mine. Desire drips from her golden eyes and they darken as I lap at her pussy.

"Emmett," she gasps, jerking her hips up. "I can't."

I hum as I swirl my tongue around her clit. "You can and you will."

She's already come three times, but she's been so good, obeying my every command, she deserves one more. I slip two fingers into her core, pumping gently while I wrap my lips around the already sensitive bud. The most delicious sounds fall from her, echoing through the ever-darkening sky. I'll make her see stars as the real ones emerge above us while night falls around us.

Her legs shake as I crook my fingers, stroking her faster. She moans, hips moving in time with my thrusts. My cock hardens once more, and I reach down to grasp my shaft. The pressure doesn't ease. My only relief lies in me burying myself into her soaked cunt. I let go of myself and dig my fingers into her thigh. I could ignore my own need if she'd stop panting my name, urging me on.

When she's right on the edge and I can't take it anymore, I pull my fingers from her and straighten. A cry of desperation leaves her, but it quickly morphs into a groan as I bury my cock in her. She flutters around my length, and I rub her clit. I thrust into her over and over, the chair skidding across the wood. Latching onto her hips, I keep up my pace. She wraps her fingers around my wrists and her nails dig into my skin.

"Come for me, gorgeous," I growl, another orgasm looming on the horizon for me.

Her pussy spasms around my cock, sending me into oblivion with her. Those stars I wanted her to experience explode behind my own lids, exposing a whole new world I never knew existed.

I cover her body with my own as our gasps fill the air. Her arms snake around me, holding me close. I kiss her damp skin, burying my face in her neck.

"Fucking magical," I murmur.

"Mmm." I can hear the smile in her voice.

I groan as I slip from her heat, then gather her in my arms. She giggles as I struggle to stand, her body slipping from my grasp.

I huff, dropping her onto the lounger, and finally stand. "It's not funny. Do you know how fucking low this thing is?"

She grins, not bothering to cover her luscious body. She's come a long way since our first swim. Most of the time, she walks around in one of my T-shirts with nothing underneath. It drives me wild, but at least I have easy access to her pussy. She always seems to be wet for me. All I need to do is look at her and she's climbing me like a tree.

"Come here or I'll end up fucking you again," I growl.

She rolls her eyes. "As if I'd complain about that." She pushes upright, and I help her stand before leading her into the house.

The last of the sunlight disappears beneath the horizon, leaving smudges marching across the sky. A single lamp illuminates our path to the kitchen. I need to install new fixtures, but I've been putting everything off in lieu of spending as much time as possible with Maddie. Eventually I need to get back to it or I'll run into snow, making my job a whole helluva lot harder. Plus, Maddie needs to get going on her stories. I hope she's relaxed enough to get out of her head. She hasn't brought it up once, though. And it's starting to worry me.

"Go get dressed. I'll make some food," I say as I pull on a pair of sweatpants I left on the couch.

She saunters by me, swaying her hips suggestively. I smack her ass, smirking as she yelps and her skin reddens.

"Better be careful or we'll never eat," she calls as she disappears into the bedroom. Seconds later, her head pops out and she wags her finger. "And don't tell me you've got plenty of sausage to fill me up."

I chuckle as I make my way to the kitchen. I need to go into town soon to pick up more groceries. Leaving Maddie hasn't been easy. The only thing left is eggs or cereal. I grab the box of sugary goodness and pour it into bowls. We have a few peaches, so I cut up two and call it good. It's not fancy, but I doubt she'll care.

"I was thinking we could walk down by the lake tomorrow. Maybe see if we can find those ducks again," Maddie says as she plops onto the stool.

Placing the bowl in front of her, it hits me how much we've been putting off. It's not just about the food situation. She hasn't been doing any writing and I'm woefully behind on my projects. I sigh, handing her the milk. There isn't much left, and I might be eating dry cereal.

"What's wrong?" She takes a spoonful and shoves it in her mouth, raising her eyebrow.

"Nothing," I mutter.

"Doesn't look like nothing. Looks like you're making potato chips in your head."

I open my mouth, then snap it shut as I shake my head. "What?"

"I watched a documentary about how they make chips from start to finish. They start with a potato that's less than twenty-four hours old, and it goes through all these different machines to make them into chips. It was fascinating. Probably makes me a nerd or something, and I shouldn't have told you all that." She bites her lip. "Anyways, they go through the whole process in like fifteen minutes. You looked like your brain was making potatoes into chips in the time I was gone."

"I don't know if that's...you know what? Never mind." I pull in a deep breath, suddenly nervous. "I have to go get some groceries. Maybe we should do something else."

She tips her head back, a hearty laugh leaving her. I don't know if I'm supposed to join in, but after her comment about potatoes and her current reaction, I'm at a loss. She continues giggling, then snorts as she covers her mouth.

"Sorry, it's just...is this really happening? Shit. I did not see that coming. Well, fuck."

"What the hell are you talking about?"

She shakes her head, a rueful expression overtaking her face. "So, you're going to go into town and leave me here. And we should find something else to do. Am I getting that right?"

"Yes?" I still don't see what the problem is. "You could—"

She holds up her hand and I snap my mouth shut. She brings her bowl to the sink, then turns and leans against the counter. With the island between us, I feel like we're on opposite sides of an argument. One I didn't sign up for, nor am I totally prepared for.

"So, which one of us is taking the couch?" She glares at me, but there's a quiver to her chin.

"Why exactly would one of us be relegated to the couch? Honestly, Maddie, I think you're—"

She crosses her arms, and I lean back. "I swear to fuck if you tell me I'm overreacting..."

"I don't have a death wish, gorgeous. Pretty sure you're on a different page than me." I slip off the stool and round the island. I cage her in with my hands on the counter, pressing my body close to hers, and her breath hitches. "No one is going to sleep on the couch. No one is leaving you anywhere. And while I would love to spend all fucking day buried in your sweet little pussy, we do have other things we need to get on with."

She tips her chin up, clearly not willing to admit she misunderstood. "Sorry I kept you from your work."

"Nope. We're not going to do that. Get out of your head and stop thinking I'm going to throw you away when I'm done with you. Because I am nowhere close to done with you."

Dropping her arms to her sides, she ducks her chin and whispers, "What exactly did you have in mind?"

I slide my arm around her waist and meld her body to mine. "I think I'll go into town. And you're going to get your computer out and write. When I get back, I'll reward you."

Her body twitches, and she slides her hands up my bare chest. She presses her lips together, eyes avoiding mine.

"What kind of reward?"

Slipping my hands to her ass, my cock hardens. I knead her flesh and her forehead rests on my chest. I skim my fingers underneath her shirt, leaving goosebumps in my wake. No matter how many times I touch her, I swear I'll never get enough. We might still be in the honeymoon phase, or maybe it's the post-sex haze we've been floating in for the past two weeks.

"Depends. How much do you think you can write by the time I get back?" I have no idea how any of this works. She could write one sentence and I'd be impressed.

"Hmm. We usually measure in words. When I was writing consistently and it was a good day, I could get like five thousand words without batting an eye. Now. Well, you've seen what it's like now." The misery in her tone rings through clear as a bell.

I tip her chin up until our eyes meet, then kiss her softly. "For every hundred words you get, I'll let you come. If you don't get any, though..."

She snorts. "What? You won't give me any? That's not very nice."

"I'll eventually give you one, but you'll have to make up for the words you don't write by begging."

A flush splashes across her face and her lips part. "We could always skip the store and writing. I could bank words. That's how it works, right?"

"Like banking hours?" I chuckle. "I suppose so. But that's not an option here. Get your computer and write some words."

"What if the store isn't open? This is a small town."

Reluctantly, I let her go and grab my dishes. "Then I'll go to the next town over. Should give you plenty of time to grumble and procrastinate. We need more than that small gas station can provide, anyway."

She follows me into the bedroom, leaning against the door frame. "So you'll be gone for two hours? What happens if a bear attacks me?"

"Or bigfoot appears again?" I ask, then pull a shirt over my head and she makes a face.

"Okay, but really, what do I do if a bear shows up?"

"Maddie, a bear isn't going to knock on the door and hand you a cup of sugar. If one shows up, you keep the doors and windows shut, and don't try to pet it."

She purses her lips, not fully convinced. What was she planning on doing if I wasn't at the cabin when she showed up? I'm not sure she would have survived four months here alone.

"I wouldn't try to pet a bear, no matter how fluffy he was. Bigfoot would depend on a couple different factors, I suppose."

I snag her around the waist and kiss her soundly. "No orgasms without me, gorgeous."

"Take my rental. It's got built-in GPS."

"Don't really have another option right now," I remind her.

I kiss her again, then make my way out the door. As soon as my feet hit the ground, my head throbs. I press my thumbs to my temples and close my eyes. It slowly recedes and I chalk it up to the temperature change from the air conditioning to the hot summer night. Climbing behind the wheel of Maddie's car, I hope I'm making the right decision leaving her by herself. Despite the nerves building in my gut, I pull around and head to town.

Chapter Twenty
Maddie

I check the clock again and realize thirty minutes have passed since Emmett left. I did pull out my computer. Even turned it on and set out all my notebooks. I spent a good five minutes just clicking my favorite pen. Sitting at the dining table isn't as great as I thought it would be. I thought it would help me concentrate, but the chair feels weird, and the table isn't the right height.

Now I'm lying on the floor in front of the couch, staring up at the stars through the skylights. Any minute, something will come to me. I'll have an epiphany and be rewarded for the thousand words I'm about to write. That's what I'm telling myself, yet the motivation just isn't there. It's as if my characters are caught in a tornado and I'm only able to catch the occasional cow flying by. Snippets of words that don't make sense flit around my brain and I start muttering, hoping they'll make sense if I say them out loud.

It doesn't work. Because of course it doesn't work. Nothing has worked so far. I don't know why Chloe thought this would be a good idea. No amount of touching grass will rid me of this feeling of inadequacy. I'd give up right now if it wasn't for Emmett. If orgasms aren't enough to kick-start my brain into being a functioning author, then I doubt anything else will. The excitement I felt when he drove off died off not long after—right about the time I opened my computer.

I sigh, throwing my arm over my eyes. Bemoaning my vanishing career won't help. Then again, nothing else has either. I just want to wallow for a while longer.

I must fall asleep, because the next thing I know, I'm jolting upright to a knock at the door. My heart pounds in my chest, and I cover my mouth. Peeking over the couch, I have a clear view of the front of the cabin. The light over the oven barely illuminates the space and the hallway is bathed in shadows.

"Bears can't knock," I whisper. A hysterical giggle works its way up my throat, and I swallow it down.

My unexpected visitor knocks again, and I scramble to my feet. I grab one of Emmett's hammers from his tool bag next to the couch. I've tripped over the thing twice, but he still hasn't put them away. Where "away" is, I have no idea. My toes wish he'd find some other place, though. The stairs to the living room are enough to almost kill me, yet he insists on putting more obstacles in my path. Maybe he really is a serial killer. A very hot, exceptionally good at sex, serial killer.

I grip the wooden handle, weighing it in my hand as I make my way past the kitchen. My eyes catch on the knife block, but I dismiss the idea of replacing the hammer with a sharp object. Stabbing isn't my strong suit. Then again, neither is bashing someone's head in with a blunt object. I leave that to my characters. I *do* know exactly where to hit them to get them to stop moving from my research. I know where to stab people, too. No guarantee I'd be able to hit the right spot or hell, even go through with the act.

I shake my head as I slip into the hallway. A shadow plays across the glass next to the door. It's distorted, thank fuck. I'm pretty sure it's a woman, and my mind flips from someone trying to kidnap me to wondering if she's in trouble. Not that women can't be nefarious. Usually, the more badass femme characters I've written are much more capable than the men. Keeping my guard up is the smart thing to do.

I tuck the hammer behind my back and inch open the door. A pretty woman with chestnut hair and clever light brown eye stands there, wringing her hands together. She smiles nervously, then glances over her shoulder.

I follow her gaze, but I can't see whatever she's looking for. "Can I help you?"

"Oh, I'm sorry it's so late. I didn't really think about that." She tucks her hair behind her ear and smiles again. "I just saw someone was staying here and thought I'd come and introduce myself. I'm Grace."

I return her smile and use the hammer to scratch my back. I'm not entirely sure I buy her story. Maybe this is a normal occurrence in remote areas like this.

"Maddie. So, you're from around here?"

"Something like that." She bounces from one foot to another. "I didn't think this would be so awkward. We don't get a lot of people vacationing up here."

When she glances over her shoulder again, my stomach turns. "Just needed a change of scenery. My husband should be back soon, though. He knows a lot about the area. Got here a bit before I did, actually."

Husband? Where the fuck did that come from? Emmett isn't even my boyfriend, much less someone I married. All the instructions my mother hammered into my head to keep myself safe scroll through my mind. Never letting someone know you're alone was top of the list. I suppose telling her Emmett would be back soon counts.

"Oh, I'd love to meet him. Listen, I didn't mean to put you on edge. I promise I just wanted to say hello. Maybe we can chitchat another time—when it isn't so late, and I don't seem like I'm about to feed you to a bear or something." When she checks behind her once more, the hairs on the back of my neck stand up.

"Did you come with someone else?" I want to ask if she's in trouble, but if she does plan on robbing me or something, she'll probably lie.

She sighs and deflates, the tension flowing from her in a wave. "No. I thought my...friend might show up, but he's been avoiding my calls." When she sees the look on my face, her eyes widen. "Oh, not here. But the road to my place is right out there. I was hoping I'd spot his headlights."

"He ghost you?" I ask, my lip curling without warning.

She opens her mouth like she'll deny it, then she sighs again. "Seems like it. I *might* have said some things he *may* have interpreted as me having feelings for him. I think I scared him off."

"Fuck him," I snap, then chuckle at her shock. "Most men aren't worth the effort. Unless they're cinnamon rolls, then by all means, get it, girl."

She shoots me a sad smile before ducking her head. "Guess we'll have to see. He's kind of an asshole. Shit. I shouldn't be unloading on you. Can I come by in the daytime, maybe? It's a bit lonely out here. No worries if you want to say no. I'm sure you want to spend your vacation with your husband."

I bite my lip, weighing the risks of letting her come back. Emmett did say he needed to get some work done around here. We've already lost two weeks. Well, I've lost three weeks technically. He only slacked off for two, I suppose. Since writing clearly isn't on the horizon for me, it might be nice to hang out with someone while he does his own thing.

"I'd like that. He has some projects he needs to get done. He fixed the deck already, though, so we can hang out there. It's got a great view of the lake."

She nods once, delight dancing in her light brown eyes. "Perfect. We can get to know each other and who knows, maybe you can help me with my love life."

I laugh lightly, shaking my head. "I don't know about that. I'm sure you've got it all handled."

She waves her hand, dismissing my words, and turns. When she gazes back at me, a wave of familiarity hits me. I'd say it's déjà vu, but honestly, it's something else.

"Sometimes you just need someone else's perspective to help finish your story."

I freeze, my eyes blurring as the darkness swallows Grace up. When I finally snap out of the daze her words hurtled me into, she's gone. She must know the woods pretty well if she's willing to risk walking alone at night without a weapon. At least I didn't see a gun or anything she could use to protect herself from the wildlife.

Slowly, I close the door and set the hammer down. The whole interaction was wild, but her words play on repeat as I wander back into the living room. Plopping onto the couch, I sigh. The more I think about it, the more familiar her face becomes. I'm sure we've never met. Maybe we crossed paths at some point. The mind only holds so many faces, so maybe Grace's was buried under the hundreds of others I've seen.

I jump from the couch when the front door swings open. I didn't even lock the door after Grace left. Rookie mistake. Emmett appears hauling several bags, and I breathe a sigh of relief. His foot connects with the hammer, and it skitters down the hall. I wrinkle my nose as a blush creeps across my cheeks.

"There a reason you were digging in my tools, gorgeous? If you want to fix something, great, but I'd rather you didn't hurt yourself."

I plant my hands on my hips. "Bold of you to assume I wouldn't be able to hammer a nail in on my own. Kind of sexist, don't you think?"

He smirks as he sets the groceries on the island. "Normally I'd agree with you. I've also seen you almost smack yourself in the face with this very same hammer."

I roll my eyes and make my way toward him. He snags me around the waist and pulls me close before brushing his lips along my forehead. A shiver rolls down my spine and I cling to him.

He's only been gone a couple hours, but it feels like much longer. It must be the newness of everything. I'm not used to someone caring whether I was around unless I count Chloe. She's so erratic with her comings and goings, though, I don't know when she'll be home these days. This is an entirely new experience.

I ease from his hold and start putting the food away. For some reason, I can't look him in the eye when I'm confessing I opened the door for a stranger at eleven o'clock at night. I can't imagine he'll be entirely happy with me, even though nothing really happened.

"Remember how you said bears don't knock?" I ask as I shove the milk into the fridge.

"Don't tell me a bear actually showed up," he chuckles.

"Ah, no. But a person did come by. I think she's staying nearby and wanted to say hi."

"At this time at night? You didn't tell her you were alone, did you?"

My cheeks redden, and I hide my face in the fridge. "I said you'd be back any minute. She didn't realize it was so late, I guess. It was a little awkward, but she's going to come by tomorrow while you're working on whatever you're going to do."

There's no way I'm going to admit I called Emmett my husband. Grace will probably out me tomorrow, anyway. It's a problem for future me. I peek at him, hoping he'll let it all go, but his hands are on his hips and he's glaring at me.

"She's probably going to break in and steal things. She was casing the place for her and some dude who's going to sell our shit on the internet, Maddie."

I wave away his concern. "I doubt that would happen. There's nothing here to steal, anyways. Plus, it's not *our* stuff. Most of the things here are Chloe's uncle's shit. They'd probably sell it to a pawnshop before they fuck around with the internet since we're in the middle of nowhere."

"Why do I get the feeling you're being deliberately obtuse?"

"Maybe because I don't want you to lecture me about opening the door. I had a weapon if I needed to bludgeon them in the head."

He wraps his fingers around my wrist and spins me to face him. "You're a grown-ass woman, Maddie. I don't need to lecture you. You're capable of taking care of yourself. I just want you to be safe. I just found you and I'd rather not lose you so soon."

Butterflies erupt in my stomach, and I melt a little inside. There's no way this man is for real. No one I've met has ever spouted poetic lines—not to me. Men like this must exist in the world, yet my life has been sorely lacking them. It's going to take more than a couple pretty words strung together to convince me he's for real. But I really hope he is.

Chapter Twenty-One

Emmett

My wrench slips from my fingers for the third time, and I let out a curse. My mind keeps wandering off, or rather, back to this morning. Waking up next to Maddie is an experience. With her golden hair a fuzzy mess around her head and her sleepy eyes blinking up at me, I don't know if I've ever seen a more stunning sight.

I tried to slip out of bed without waking her. I kept her up pretty late exploring her body more and she needed the extra sleep. She caught me and whined about taking my heat from her. It didn't take much convincing on her part to get me to rejoin her and wake her up properly. It's biting me in the ass now, though, because I can't stop reliving the moment.

"Emmett, she's here," Maddie calls from the top of the stairs.

I throw the wrench down and rush upstairs, wiping my hands on a rag as I go. No way is she letting some random woman in the cabin without me meeting her. I'm still not convinced Grace is completely moral. Maddie strikes me as a person who is entirely too trusting for her own good. It took her all of an hour to assess my character. It's entirely plausible I was a serial killer and she would never have questioned me.

"Slow down. She's not going to be standing there with a shotgun." Maddie rolls her eyes as she skips down the hallway.

"Why don't you let me answer the door, anyway?" I yank her back and stuff her behind me and add, "Just in case it isn't her."

She sighs, but stays put, thank fuck. A snort leaves her when I try to peek out the windowpanes framing the door. It's ground glass, distorting the outside, yet allowing enough visibility to figure out what's on the other side. In this case, a woman's lone figure holding something in her hands. It doesn't look like a shotgun, at least.

I swing open the heavy wood wide enough to have a conversation without seeming rude, but with my body still covering most of the entrance. Maddie smacks my back, yet I refuse to move. The woman in front of me doesn't seem dangerous. She presses her lips together, a nervous air to her. That in itself isn't suspicious.

Maddie slides around me, shoving me back with her ass. "Hey, Grace. How's it going?"

"Oh hi, Maddie. I think there's something wrong with your door. Might need to get that husband of yours to fix it."

My brows pull low, and I stare at Maddie's profile. A blush creeps up her neck and settles on her cheeks. Her eyes dart to me, then back to Grace. I was not aware that Maddie had a husband.

I pivot and stomp down the hallway. She probably has an explanation, but I'm not about to have a conversation about whatever the hell is going on in front of her new friend. No need to air dirty laundry. And if she didn't tell me, I'm sure there was a good reason. Unless she was just too ashamed to admit she was sleeping around.

"Shit," Maddie mutters. "Come in, I just need to...fix this."

I'm halfway down the stairs by the time she catches up to me. I need to finish installing the toilet in the next few hours. I don't have the time or the energy to deal with whatever game she's playing.

"Emmett, wait. I can explain," she whispers.

"I'm sure you can, Madelyn. I have shit to do, though. And you left your friend upstairs by herself. We can talk about this later."

"Would you stop running away? It won't take that long. Just stop."

I swing around and she slams into my chest. Instinctively, I reach out and steady her, then drop my hands. My cock hardens and I scowl. He doesn't care she lied. All he knows is how amazing it feels to be buried in her pussy. Her face is awash with panic and my mind starts rebelling at my actions along with my body.

"Well?" I cross my arms to keep myself from wrapping her in my arms and comforting her.

She rubs her hands along her thighs, eyes fixed on my shoulder. "Last night when I figured out I shouldn't have told a stranger I was alone, I said you were going to be here any minute. But I didn't say your name…I said my husband. It just slipped out and I don't know why I said it. I could have said literally anything else, but I panicked."

I rear back and drop my hands to my sides. "You told her I was your husband?"

"Yes? And it's not exactly something you can backtrack on in that situation. She'd think I was lying and if she *was* a bad guy about to kidnap me, then clearly I wouldn't want her to think I was lying." She holds her palms out, imploring me to believe her.

I run my tongue over my teeth, but I can't keep the grin from my face. "Well, gorgeous, I think it's a bit soon for a proposal, but if you insist."

She scowls and wrinkles her nose. "Funny. I'll tell her we're not married, explain the whole thing. I'm sure she'll understand."

She turns back to the stairs, and I grab her hips, then pull her back to my chest. Ducking my head, I nuzzle her neck.

"You can call me your husband. No reason to derail a new friendship by telling her you lied. I can play the part of a doting spouse who brought his sexy-ass wife up to the cabin for the summer. You can create a whole backstory for us—whatever you want. Do I need to pretend to be in the mafia? Or maybe I'm a retired professional hockey player?"

"At the rate you're going, I'm going to make you an accountant," she mumbles as she tilts her head, giving me more access to her delicious skin.

"As much as I'd like to push you against the wall and fuck you senseless just to show you how amazing you'll feel having an accountant's cock buried in your wet little pussy, you should go back upstairs."

She shudders in my hold, then straightens, and I let her go. "Save that thought for later. Come, let me introduce you, *husband.*"

I follow her up the stairs and find Grace hovering around the front door. Shit, we should not have just run off like that.

"I'm so sorry. This is Emmett, my husband. He's a little protective. Being a former adventure guide, he's always got safety in mind."

I swallow a laugh and hold out my hand to Grace. Shock flits across her face as she gently shakes my hand. She glances at Maddie, then back to me. A question swims in her eyes and I wonder if she'll ask it out loud or keep her thoughts to herself. She pulls away, gaze still bouncing between us.

"It's nice to meet you. I promise I'm not scary, no matter what my father says." She smiles and her suspicion is replaced with calculation.

"Emmett was nice enough to make us a fake charcuterie board without all the nasty parts. We can sit on the deck and let him get back to work."

Grace trails behind Maddie, who's talking a million miles a minute. I slip around the island and grab the platter from the fridge before she can and hand it to her.

"Your nerves are showing, gorgeous. Slow down," I mutter. "Well, I'm off to finish the bathroom. Let me know if you two need anything."

Maddie moves toward the deck, food in hand, but Grace stops me with a hand on my arm. She quickly pulls it away, then tucks her hair behind her ear.

"Does she know?" she whispers, leaning around me to track Maddie's progress.

"Know what?"

She narrows her eyes at me, then sucks in a sharp breath. "Oh. Oh, you don' t...okay. Never mind. I thought you were someone else. Your name is Emmett?"

"Yes," I say slowly, wondering who the hell she thinks I am.

"My mistake. I'm going to go join her before she starts talking to herself."

"Wouldn't be the first time," I chuckle. "She's an author. Comes with the territory, apparently."

She nods, slipping around me and makes her way to the deck. Maddie gives me a questioning look, but I shake my head and smile. I don't understand what that was all about. No use worrying Maddie with it. If it becomes a problem, I'll say something. For now, I'll let her enjoy her new friend.

Several hours later, I finally finish my work. It was a bitch to put in the standard toilet since the hole wasn't big enough. Not to mention the pipes I had to replace. The thing doesn't leak anymore, which is a job well done in my book. I'm not a plumber, so I feel even more accomplished than I normally would. Maddie checked on me once, insisting I eat as she shoved a sandwich in my mouth. The excitement bubbling from her was contagious and I couldn't keep my eyes off her.

I need a shower and a drink. It's the only way I'll be able to keep my hands off Maddie. I head straight for the kitchen and grab a bottle of water from the fridge before turning toward the large windows. Maddie nods along as Grace relays what looks to be a very interesting story, her hands waving around. They've been out there for hours, which means they're probably hungry. I down the rest of my water and make my way to the sliding door.

Popping my head out, I clear my throat and they both turn. "Didn't mean to interrupt, but I'm going to get in the shower. You two hungry?"

"Oh, you don't have to feed me. It's okay," Grace says, then bites her lip.

"Am I capable of feeding myself? Yes. Would I rather him make food for me? Also yes. He's a great cook and you know the way to a woman's heart is through tacos."

"Tacos it is, then." I grin and Maddie mirrors me.

"Thanks, honeybun." She bursts into laughter, probably at the look on my face.

I rap my knuckles on the glass, shaking my head. "Find another one, gorgeous. I'll whip up some white person tacos when I'm done getting clean."

They both giggle as I shut the door, and I can't keep the smile from my face. After the last week, she's smiled and laughed, but not like this. She's been present—happy even. There's something missing, though. Even now, there's a gleam in her eyes, as if part of her mind is somewhere else. I imagine if she got back to writing, she'd find that missing piece. Maybe I can talk to Grace and have her encourage Maddie to try again.

All through my shower and while I'm cooking, my thoughts are consumed with making a list of projects to get done. Maddie keeps creeping in, derailing whatever I was planning. As the sun marches across the sky, the light catches her hair and creates a golden halo around her. She's literally glowing and it's fucking distracting. When I finish the food, I bring it outside with the intention of retreating back inside.

"Where's your food?" Maddie demands, even as she's stuffing food in her mouth.

"Didn't want to interrupt you two. Seemed like things were getting intense out here," I say, running my hand through my hair.

She rolls her eyes, then points with her taco at the empty chair. "Sit. Eat. You made them and you're feeding us. We're not going to make you eat by yourself."

Grace nods, and I resign myself to obeying my fake wife. My skin tingles every time I think the word. She may think it's hilarious, but the thought of us being married settles something in my soul. Tucked away in the woods with no influences from the outside world, it's easy to imagine spending the rest of my life with her.

We don't really know each other. Sure, I know the sounds she makes when she comes. And the look on her face when she's working something out in her head. And that she's wicked smart, which sometimes gets in the way of her common sense. It's not enough to build an entire future on, though. Not yet anyway.

"It's a start," I whisper. "All we need is a beginning. The rest of the story will write itself."

Chapter Twenty-Two
Maddie

As the sun slowly sets behind the tops of the trees, I sigh. Grace left a little bit ago, and I wandered back to the deck while Emmett disappeared into the lower level once more. Talking to Grace felt like catching up with a long-lost friend. I started to anticipate her responses and asking her questions I normally wouldn't ask of someone I just met. She took it all in stride, sharing about her relationship with her parents and her new job. Being a teacher sounds stressful and utterly exhausting. And then the conversation turned to her love life.

When she said her neighbor was an asshole, I laughed, but he really is wishy-washy. When I mentioned he sounded like a specific type of book boyfriend, she got a strange look on her face, then changed the subject. Not everyone reads, so I dismissed it. Now I'm wondering if she *does* read and took offense to the comparison. I'm second-guessing our entire conversation, wondering if I've fucked things up before they've even started. I'd be fine spending my entire summer with Emmett. It would be nice to have someone else to talk to, though.

Emmett collapses on the chair next to me, tips his head back, and closes his eyes. In the dying light, he's mesmerizing. I've spent enough time with him to know he hides a spectacular physique under his shirt. It's hard to keep my eyes off him. Add in the fact that he's good with his hands in more than one area and he likes to keep me fed, and he really is the full package. I keep waiting for him to screw up, which is probably fucked up, but I can't turn it off.

He passes me an energy drink, and my heart melts a little more. I crack it open and take a drink, savoring the flavor as it slides down my throat. Most people have a glass of wine or a cold beer at the end of the day, but I prefer a jolt of caffeine. It just hits different for me.

"Thank you for getting me more," I say as I set the can on the table between us.

"Of course. Can't have you lacking caffeine. Little warning, though. I will scold you if you have too many of those during the day. I'd rather you outlive me in this marriage."

I roll my eyes, even while the thought makes my insides squishy. It is entirely too soon to be thinking about anything other than the next couple days when it comes to us. The idea of acting out a book trope sends my head into a bit of a tizzy. It's a thrill I didn't realize would have this effect on me.

"Speaking of marriage...I confessed to Grace. I couldn't handle her not knowing we're living in sin."

He snorts, rolling his head toward me. "You don't strike me as religious."

"Oh, I'm not. Went to church a few times with my grandparents, but that was about it. It didn't feel right to lie to her, though. She got a kick out of it. Said she wouldn't say anything and let us keep pretending if we wanted." I take a deep breath. "I like her. She's really nice and has such an interesting story."

"Did talking to her jump-start anything for your writing?"

I make a face before I can stop myself, and he raises an eyebrow. "Not really. I just enjoyed being, you know? It's been a while since I didn't have the crushing weight of responsibility sitting on my shoulders. Though, you are certainly an excellent distraction."

I slide from my chair to straddle him. His hands find my hips and I run my palms up his chest. Maybe he'll stop talking about my inability to write if I seduce him. From the way his cock is hardening underneath my ass, I doubt it will be very difficult.

"Are you trying to get out of this conversation, Maddie? Because eventually you'll have to talk about it, you know."

I sigh, curling my body and tucking my head under his chin. "I've tried everything, but nothing works."

"I don't know a lot about writing," he confesses. "Have you tried doing an outline? That's what they made us do in school."

"If I do that, then I'll have already written the story and it won't be interesting anymore. I know that sounds like a cop-out, but my brain doesn't function that way. The words are there, I can almost reach out and grab them. Every time I get close, though, they disappear. It's like my head is a silent tomb and my characters are trapped in their coffins with no way to get out."

"Well, that's a fucking horrific thought. Have you tried reading from the Book of the Dead?"

I huff as my stomach turns. I know he's trying to make me laugh, but I don't have it in me. Nothing's going right and everything's a mess. My mind picks up the rest of the lyrics and I start humming. He rubs my back and a peace I haven't felt in a long time, if ever, steals over me. If I don't write another word in my life, I'd be devastated. Being here in this secluded place with Emmett might make up for it.

"You talk about your characters like they're alive. Did you notice that?" he murmurs as he rubs the tension from my neck.

"To me they are. They may live in my head, but that doesn't mean they're not their own people. They're three-dimensional beings with hopes and dreams and worries just like us. So to me, they're real. Once I write them, they live on the page. It's funny. If I write about them later on, after their story is told, it's hard to get them to show up sometimes."

I don't know if that makes any sense to him, but I feel him nod. He drops a kiss on my hair, and I close my eyes.

"Why can't you just tell them to get their shit together if they live in your head? You created them, so you should be able to boss them around."

I chuckle, sitting up, and his hands fall to my hips again. "Not how it works. Characters have their own ideas for how they want their stories to go. If I force them, they rebel and go silent."

He tilts his head as his fingers slip under my shirt. "You think that's your problem now? You tried to force them?"

"Nope. I've gotten pretty good at listening to them and letting them do their own thing. Sometimes the story goes off the rails, but I'm able to rein them in usually. This is straight up writer's block. I know what I want to write and where I want everything to go, but the words just aren't there."

He pulls me to his chest once more and I cuddle closer, taking advantage of his warmth. It isn't cold out, really. With the breeze coming from the lake, though, I'd usually throw on a sweatshirt. Using Emmett as a blanket is better.

"You'll find them. Maybe you just need a little more inspiration to kick-start all those creative juices."

His fingers march up my spine under my shirt. The fabric bunches, halting his progress, and he growls, the sound reverberating through me. I grind my pussy into him, and a soft groan leaves him.

"What sort of inspiration did you have in mind?" I ask as I move my hips.

He doesn't bother to respond. Instead, he grips my ass and stands. My arms latch onto his shoulders as he carries me into the cabin. We don't even make it to the bedroom before he's dropping me onto the couch and ripping off my shirt. He drops to his knees, tugging at my shorts.

"Lift your hips, gorgeous, or I'll end up tearing them from you," he growls, and I obey, hoping he'll call me a good girl again.

Before I know it, I'm completely naked and he's towering over me. His gaze burns as it travels down my body, leaving licks of flames in his wake. He's not even touching me and my thighs are soaked. I bite my lip, my palms itching to do something, anything, whether it's undressing him or touching myself. I clear my throat and his eyes dart to mine. When he tips his chin at me, I lick my lips. I have no idea what he wants.

He smirks, his brows pulling low. "Spread your legs. Let me see how wet you are."

Lust flares in his eyes when my knees fall open. He crosses his arms, but not before I catch the tremor in his hands. Between that and the bulge in his pants, it's not hard to see the effect I have on him. I didn't realize how powerful I felt from his reaction alone. I've never felt this...desirable.

"I'd love to watch you touch yourself, but I don't know if I'd be able to stop myself." His fingers flex, nails digging into his skin. "Then again...why don't you start, and I'll make sure you finish."

He pulls his shirt over his head and his hand falls to his belt, then stops. When he raises an eyebrow, it hits me he's waiting for me to start. We've done a lot over the last few weeks. Never this, though. I focus on his fingers toying with his buckle and cup my breasts. Slowly, he slides the leather through the loop. I pinch my nipples, and my eyes dart to his face as the clinking of his belt fills the quiet space.

I slide my hand between my legs and swallow a whimper as my fingers slip easily between my folds. His groan fills the air, and my eyes snap to his. His gaze is fixed on my pussy and he licks his lips. I continue to stroke myself and he groans again. Before I know it, I'm floating, tipped over his shoulder as he stomps to the bedroom.

He drops me onto the bed, desire burning in his eyes. "Hands and knees."

My mouth goes dry, and I flip around. I glance over my shoulder as the mattress dips. His palm skims across my ass and I tuck my chin to my chest, biting my lip. A resounding crack echoes through the air and my ass cheek burns. A choking sound leaves me as he rubs the mark he's surely left behind. His fingers dip between my legs and he strokes me.

"You okay?" he murmurs, reminding me of our conversation earlier. He promised he'd take care of me, demanding I tell him when I needed to stop, and even asked about certain things he wanted to do.

My breath stutters in my chest. "Do it again."

His hand connects with my skin again and I gasp, my back arching. Wetness coats my thighs and his hand, and he chuckles.

"Such a dirty girl, getting wet for me while I spank you."

A primal noise leaves me when he pushes two fingers into me, then curls them. He slowly builds me up until I'm bucking against him, pleading for release.

He pinches my nipple as he continues his exploration of my pussy. "You know I love it when you beg."

His cock nudges my opening when he pulls his fingers from me. He sinks into me, groaning as he bottoms out. I expect him to continue his slow assault on my senses. Instead, he digs his fingers into my hips and thrusts into me over and over. Before I can catch my breath, I'm sailing over the edge into oblivion.

I grip the comforter and my forehead hits the mattress, the new angle allowing him to hit the deepest parts of me. The covers muffle my screams of pleasure as he continues to bury his cock in me. His fingers find my clit and another orgasm builds swiftly.

"Come for me," he demands through gritted teeth, and I shudder as I slip into a weightless rapture once more.

He groans out his own release, hips jerking as he comes. He collapses to the side, taking me with him, and his cock twitches inside me. As he cradles me, he murmurs against my skin. Not that I can hear him over the ringing in my ears. As the fog clears from my mind, I shiver.

"Was that inspiration good enough?"

"Better than good enough," I breathe. "So much fucking better."

Chapter Twenty-Three

Emmett

As the sun beats down on my shoulders, I wipe the sweat from my brow. Maddie's footfalls rattle the loose boards I tore out from the side porch this morning. I sigh, shaking my head. She's been out here seven times since I started three hours ago.

She's bored out of her mind, even if she won't admit it. She insisted I start working on the renovations almost a week ago, which I'm sure she's regretting now. Finding the willpower to pull myself away from her isn't easy. I watch from the corner of my eye as she tiptoes her way around the holes.

"Fucking criminal," I mutter.

"What is? And why are you down there when the porch is up here?" She tilts her head, surveying my work.

"Don't lean on the railing. It's not secure on that side. In fact, get your ass down here." I step to the side and hold my arms up for her. She practically tumbles into them, giggling when I stumble back. "Not what I had in mind, but okay."

Setting her feet on the grass, I catch her intoxicating scent and bite back a groan. Every bit of her calls to me, reeling me in a little more each day. No matter how much time we spend together, I can't seem to get enough. It's as if she was made just for me, quirks and all. I drop a kiss on her forehead before letting her go. I need to finish this before the sun sets and I'm already working on borrowed time. Crouching, I survey the beams underneath the porch, trying to figure out if I need to add extra support.

"What's criminal?" she asks, peering over my shoulder.

"Looking that good, gorgeous. It's fucking criminal."

"Will you pay my bail when they haul me away?"

I peer up at her, a grin spreading across my face to match her own. "I'll think about it. You get any writing done?"

She straightens, then grabs the hammer I left on the deck. I should make her put on safety glasses so she doesn't take out her eyeball. She'll start swinging it around before long. I still can't figure out if she's trying to use it as a baton or a weapon. As if on cue, she flips the tool in the air, attempting to catch it. The claw sticks in the ground, inches from her toes.

"Those are tools, not toys, Maddie. If you want something to practice with, I'll buy you a dagger." I grab the hammer and put it back, and her face lights up. "A very *dull* dagger."

"We could go to one of those axe throwing places. There's gotta be one around here, right?" She glances around like one is going to appear out of nowhere.

"Probably be driving at least a couple hours for something like that. Besides, they use hatchets, not axes. Throwing an axe would be incredibly difficult."

She plops next to me and leans against one of the posts. I eye the wood to make sure it won't smash into her skull. She doesn't seem to understand I can't save her from herself when she's flitting about where I'm working. It would be a miracle if I could. Her trust in me is admirable, yet misplaced, and probably stems from how we met.

I clear my throat. "Don't think I didn't notice you didn't answer my question. You said you had an idea earlier. Did you get any words in?"

Ever since her visit with Grace, she's been randomly stopping to stare off into space. When I finally asked her about it, she said it was a process. Whatever that meant. She found my kryptonite, though.

Every time I ask her about her plans with her career, she distracts me with sex. I'd love to say I can resist her charms, but the temptation is too great for me. I'm not built to turn her down. If I keep pushing, she'll probably jump my bones and I'll let her.

She groans, tipping her head back and closing her eyes. "I don't want to talk about it. They're bitches and I'm ignoring them."

I still don't fully understand how she's able to separate her characters from herself, but I'm learning. She talks about them as if they're real, which makes it easier.

"Are you ignoring them because they're ignoring you? Because I don't really think that tactic will work how you want it to." I grab my tape measure and start recording the numbers I'll need to replace the boards.

"They keep throwing random ideas at me, expecting me to just know what the hell they're talking about. Newsflash—I don't. Oh, fun fact. I have a character named Grace too. I need to ask the real Grace about what her situationship's name is. Wouldn't it be so wild if it was Sam?" She laughs, but my eyes blur. I squeeze them shut and swallow hard.

"I need a break. I think the heat is getting to me," I mutter, staggering to my feet.

Her small hand grabs my bicep, attempting to steady me. "Are you okay? Shit. Let's get you inside and I'll make you something to eat."

She leads me indoors, my head pounding with each step. She deposits me on the couch and shoves another bottle of water in my hand. I slowly sip it as she retreats to the kitchen. Before she gets done making food, my vision clears, and the pain vanishes as quickly as it came on. I don't understand where it came from or where it went.

I push from the couch, and Maddie makes a noise in the back of her throat. "What are you doing? Sit down before you trip down the stairs."

She rushes toward me, hands outstretched like she's going to shove me down herself.

"Whoa there. Honestly, I'm fine. Why don't you make yourself a sandwich and we'll eat together."

She doesn't look convinced, but she lets me guide her back to the kitchen. I end up devouring my sandwich before she's even finished making her own. I should get back outside and finish. There's no rush, but I want to get it all done before sunset. Not having a timeline for this job should work in my favor. As long as I complete the outside projects before winter sets in, I could stay as long as I like.

I jolt from my thoughts when she sets another sandwich on my plate, then settles onto the stool next to me. I mumble a thanks and eat slowly this time.

"This place is weird, right?" she mumbles.

"What do you mean?"

She sighs, eyes fixed on her plate while she picks the crust off her bread. "The bigfoot thing was funny, but I keep thinking I'm seeing things in the woods."

A chill rolls down my spine. "Like animals? Or..."

"Maybe? I think I saw a cougar the other day. But I swear there were a couple people running through the trees. Almost like they were...I don't know. Never mind. It's not a big deal."

She shoves off her stool and dumps her crust in the garbage. Her movements are jerky and her hip slams into the corner of the island. She yelps and I'm up, gathering her into my arms. An ache spreads from my chest, panic quickly taking over.

"I'm fine," she gasps, trying to push me away.

I drop to my knees and yank her shorts down to see what she's done to herself. The mark is red, but not bruised. At least not yet. I press a kiss to the hurt and goosebumps scatter across her flesh. Slipping my hand around her thigh, I resist the urge to bury my face between her legs. Whatever she's talking about clearly needs to be discussed. We can't fuck all our discussions away.

"Tell me what you saw," I murmur as I pull her shorts up, then gaze at her.

"It's honestly not a big deal. I'm sure my imagination is just running wild." She tries to step away, and I tighten my grip.

"Sounds like someone squashed your creativity. What did they do in the woods?"

She sighs, rubbing her face with her hand. I stand and lead her to the couch, pulling her into my lap when I sit. She curls into me, her head on my chest, and I wrap my arms around her. Every once in a while, I wonder if we're moving too fast. These deep conversations are usually reserved for relationships. We haven't even defined what we are to each other. Yet we're acting like we're married. The thought hits me in the chest, making it hard to breathe.

She sniffs, pulling me back to reality. "It was like they were floating, but fast. Like they were drifting. Chasing each other. Shit, words are hard. What the hell is wrong with me?"

I chuckle, rubbing her back. "Nothing is wrong with you. I'm sure it happens to a lot of writers."

She huffs, plucking at my shirt. "You need a shower, by the way. You haven't seen anything, have you?"

"No, but I haven't paid attention to the forest. Our brains do strange things, though. Doesn't mean you're not spotting something we just haven't figured out yet."

"Like ghosts?" she snorts, tipping her head back.

"Ghosts, werewolves, vampires." I smirk. "Bigfoot."

"Ha, ha. I don't think they were vampires, but maybe fae. I don't care what anyone says, there's other dimensions out there we just haven't discovered." She sits up and straddles me, resting her hands on my shoulders. "Or maybe we have and they're gaslighting everyone who talks about it. So the only outlet we have to discuss it is by writing fantasy."

Her eyes light up and she's practically bouncing in my arms. Her excitement overflows the confines of her body, spilling into me and infusing me with her enthusiasm.

"Who are 'they,' exactly?"

"Probably the government. Or skeptics. How amazing would it be if there were different dimensions? And they probably wouldn't even think the way things are were wild to us. Can you imagine stepping into another world and there was magic? And if they came here, would they think the things we're doing are magical?" Her eyes stare over my head, taking on a far-off look. She's lost in her own head, fantasizing about a world beyond our plane of existence.

It's not that I don't believe her. I just can't seem to wrap my head around places with magical creatures, much less them spilling over onto earth. She gasps and her eyes dart around the room. Everything in me wants to ask her what she's figured out. Which pieces of the puzzle just slipped into place? Which thread did she pull to complete the tapestry? I keep my mouth shut. She'll tell me when she's ready.

"What if..." she breathes, then stops. "I mean, it could be like..."

I bite my tongue and dig my fingers into her hips. Her chin drops to her chest and she mutters under her breath, too quiet for me to hear even with her so close. I tip my head back and close my eyes. Exhaustion settles deep in my bones, and I drift in that space between waking and sleeping.

"Emmett," Maddie whispers, her voice rolling through my mind along the waves of colors exploding behind my lids.

Her warmth seeps into me as she settles onto my chest and I hum, contentedness washing over me. Whatever revelations or breakthroughs she's had can wait for later. For now, I'll bask in the tranquility of just existing with her in this dimension. If there are others out there, living their lives with no knowledge of our own, doesn't matter. Their existence doesn't affect what Maddie and I have. Maybe one day worlds will collide, forcing us to deal with the aftermath. But not today.

Today I just want to hold her in my arms and pretend like the rest of the world, including any others we don't know about, doesn't exist. I'll encourage her to write tomorrow.

175

Chapter Twenty-Four
Maddie

Laughter and shouts rouse me from sleep. My neck aches since I'm cuddled up on Emmett's chest while he sits on the couch. He's still out cold, soft snores emanating from him. I lean back, trying not to disturb him as I unravel my arms from around him. He mumbles, but his eyes stay closed. Water splashes followed by several voices cheering from outside.

I tiptoe to the door and ease the glass open. Glancing back once, Emmett slips down, feet still planted on the floor. It's probably not comfortable, but I'm loath to wake him up. Another splash from the lake sets my feet in gear. I lean against the railing, trying to spot whoever is swimming. The cabin is so secluded I didn't think anyone else would be close enough to hear, even with sound traveling over the water.

The other places around here are tucked away in the trees, not visible unless I was in a boat. Chloe said this was a private lake with a few other houses, most of them vacation homes. Grace may be staying around here, but that could mean she was a mile away from us. I'm surprised she knew someone was staying at the cabin in the first place.

I finally spot the group of at least ten people laughing and splashing around. It looks like they've found a rope swing and are making good use of it. I smile, their giddiness infiltrating the air even from so far away. I watch them for several minutes before a wave of sadness crashes over me.

Sighing, I turn away from the scene of happiness. Their shouts reach me, and I lean against the railing. Immediately, a shiver hits me, and I jump away from what I'm sure is about to be a fall to my death. Emmett may have fixed the thing and I trust him, but I can't convince my body of that. Not with the ground being so far away.

I settle into one of the chairs instead, content now that I'm not about to die. The grief remains, though. I miss Chloe. She might not be around a lot these days, but her erratic schedule is a constant. Most of my other friends from high school have drifted away, living their own lives. We keep in touch through social media posts and whatever information is passed through the mothers. College should have been where I made a lot of friends, and I did. They're scattered across the country, though. Life moved on and took us all in different directions. It's not uncommon, which rationally I know. Doesn't make it any easier to deal with the solitude.

When I started writing, it was a relief. I didn't have to put up a front and engage in small talk like I did at the jobs I didn't care about. They were a stepping stone and nothing more. The co-workers were an added bonus some of the time. Others not so much. The further I got into my writing, the less I interacted with people. I didn't care because I was living my dream. I didn't realize how much I missed socializing.

Meeting other authors online helps, but it's not the same. I can't just drop everything and go for coffee with them. I can't meet them for book club where we drink wine and talk about everything *except* the book. Getting together is a production that requires schedules and money and traveling.

Grace coming over was amazing, but it only reminded me of how lonely my life is sometimes. If Emmett wasn't here, I'd probably be halfway back to Chicago by now. Hell, I would have left after the first week. This trip would have felt like a bust since I haven't written a single word. I wonder how long he'll stick around. It's a conversation we'll have to have sooner rather than later. Because when he goes, I probably will too. I'll go back to my mostly solitary existence and watch my world burn around me. At least my mother will be happy I'll have to find a different job.

The door slides open behind me, but I don't bother to turn. Emmett clears his throat and I tilt my head. He drops a kiss on my forehead, and a smile blooms across my face involuntarily. I'm not ready to let him go. He's too fucking perfect to let ride off into the sunset. He bends over the railing, eyes fixed on the group still playing in the water.

He turns, not having the same qualms about the sturdiness of his work as he leans against the wood. "What are you doing out here by yourself?"

"I heard them." I wave toward the ruckus. "Didn't want to wake you."

He crosses his arms, glancing over his shoulder. "Think they'd like some company?"

"Uh, I'm not crashing their little party. They'd probably think we were going to yell at them or something."

He gives me a look, raising his eyebrow. "We're not old, Maddie. And we're not going to tell them to get off our lawn. Besides, you could use some more people to talk to."

I shake my head. "What's that supposed to mean?"

"Not to sound sullen, but you need people. Maybe not a lot of people or for long. Short bursts of interesting people might help you. After Grace was here, you were…" He looks around, searching for the right words. "Animated. Your characters started talking to you. You opened your computer. Stands to reason interacting with others will jump-start even more of those creative juices."

I grimace, wrinkling my nose. "Don't use that word."

"Juices? Why the hell not?"

I shudder as he laughs. "Reminds me of vagina juices." I fake gag, pretending to retch. "I read it in a book once and it instantly gave me the ick. Now, I won't even write about someone drinking juice."

He saunters over and plants his hands on the arms of the chair. He runs his nose along my jaw and my breath catches in my throat. I swear this man has some spell over my pussy. He could brush by me, and she'd perk right up, ready for whatever he has in mind.

His lips brush the shell of my ear, and I shiver. "I'd drink your vagina juices every morning if I could."

He pulls back, face completely serious. My jaw twitches, and I stab my nails into my palms. He smirks, then purses his lips like he's propositioning me, and I lose it. I double over, gasping for breath as giggles forces their way out of me.

He straightens and I peek at him, then lose it again. He's scowling, but there's a glint in his eyes. His face reddens as he tries to hold back his own laughter. Eventually, he can't hold it in and joins me. I swipe at the tears streaming down my face as he collapses into the chair next to me.

"Why would you do that to me? Now every time you're down there, I'm going to giggle."

"Well, it's a fun experience, so a little giggling wouldn't hurt. Plus, if you're laughing, my cock will enjoy it."

Slowly, I turn to face him. "Why would your cock be happy that I'm laughing?"

"Every time you laugh while I'm buried in that pussy, she rewards me by clamping around me. Same for coughing, but that's not quite as fun for you. Although it's nice to know I take your breath away." He gives me a sly grin. I glance away and duck my chin so he won't see my smile.

"You're ridiculous," I mutter.

He tangles his fingers with mine. "I'm just glad I was there to catch you when you fell for me."

"Oh my God. How many more lines do you have stored away in that brain of yours?"

He shrugs as his thumb rubs the back of my hand, then gazes out at the view. The party on the lake seems to have died down, though I didn't notice when. Emmett is a walking distraction. The outside world falls away when we're together.

Maybe I don't need a bunch of friends to hang out with. Maybe I just need one person. Glancing at him, I wonder if he feels the same way. I refuse to ask the question. Not yet anyway. I'm not ready for the answer. If he rejected me, I'd be mortified. Even if he merely said it was too soon, I'd be embarrassed. I'm just not ready.

"Oi," a man shouts from the lake, and I sit up. He sounds closer than the group was before. I can't see the water's edge with the chairs set so far back.

"Doubt they're talking to us," Emmett mumbles, his head tipped back and his eyes closed now.

"Ahoy, neighbor," another man yells and Emmett sighs.

"Stay here. They might be vampires from another world," he says, and I smack his arm as he pushes from his seat. "Yeah, they're talking to us. Come here, gorgeous."

I join him at the railing, finding two of the guys loitering halfway between us and the water. The rest of them hang back on the beach, matching nervous looks on their faces.

One of the two waves, a grin fixed on his lips. "Hey there. I'm Beckett and this is Austin. You wanna join us? We're going to have a bonfire on the beach, roast hot dogs, and all that."

Emmett glances at me and I waggle my eyebrows at him. "Up to you, gorgeous. I think it'd be good for you, but if you'd rather stay here and have me—"

"If you say vagina juices, I'm going to push you over the railing," I snap, then press my lips together. I turn back to Beckett. "Do you need us to bring anything?"

Beckett glances at Austin, who gives me a strange look, then subtly shakes his head. I don't think it's that strange of a question. I glance at Emmett, who shrugs. They're the ones who invited us, so it's not like they're trying to get out of having us there.

"BYOB. If you've got some ice, we always run out. Oh, and wood. Never seems to be enough of that shit." Beckett grins again. Grooves around his mouth suggest he does that a lot.

"What's BYOB?" I mutter from the corner of my mouth.

"Bring your own beer." Emmett waves, but neither of the guys wave back.

Austin runs his fingers through his dirty blond hair and peers over his shoulder before turning back to us. "Just come down when you see the flames."

They turn with a final wave and retreat to the others. I'm not about to stare at them while they walk away. I grab Emmett's arm and haul him back into the cabin. When the door closes behind us, I round on him.

"That was strange, right? I wasn't imagining their reaction when I asked what we could bring?"

"Nope. That was definitely not the reaction I was expecting." His brows pull low, and he runs his fingers through his hair. The move is so similar to the one Austin did I get a chill like someone's walked over my grave. It's unsettling enough I grab his arm and tug him closer.

Swallowing hard, I play the move off as me wanting a hug. As I grab my wrist around his back, I bury my face in his chest. I may have just been ruminating about how lonely I get, but actually being around people is terrifying. It's why I've connected with so many others online. They understand me because they're in the same boat as I am. The group we're meeting at the bonfire seems like a lively bunch, ready for an adventure.

"You're trembling," he murmurs, gliding his hands along my back, up and down, over and over. The repetitive motion centers me.

I struggle to find the words to explain how I'm feeling. It's more than their reaction. It's more than hanging out with a bunch of people I don't know. It's fear of never being what other people axpect—of never knowing if someone really likes me or if they're merely tolerating my presence. I thought surrounding myself with my characters would heal that part of me, but they've abandoned me, too. And that might be worse than anything else.

Chapter Twenty-Five

Emmett

Flames leap into the sky, much higher than I'm comfortable with. I doubt the bonfire they've built will start a forest fire, but as the crackling of the logs fills the air, the fear remains. A spark floats around the makeshift ring they've built, and I stamp it out with my boot. No use tempting fate.

Maddie's laugh overtakes the low murmur of conversations as she talks to Andie, who is apparently dating Sebastian. The man hovers nearby, glancing between the two as if they'll jump in the lake any second now. The tightknit group flits from one discussion to the next, streaming to and fro with ease. It's fascinating to watch the ebb and flow.

Devin plops into a chair next to me, his gaze fixed on his wife Harper. They're clearly still in the honeymoon phase with their stolen glances and subtle touches. From what I can tell, he's more serious than the others. He merely rolled his eyes when Beckett suggested they scare the girls later in the night.

"Did you know when you got here?" he asks, his voice low enough not to travel to the others.

"Know what, exactly?" I match his tone as my muscles tense. They've all been throwing curious glances at me since we got here.

"Who Maddie was. Did you know? Because it seems like you two are both getting to know the other, yet are completely in tune."

I hide my smile behind my hand, rubbing it away before he can see. "Newlyweds. Still in the honeymoon phase. And don't ask me what's going to happen when summer is over. Your wife already did, and I have no idea."

Shock flits across his face almost too quickly for me to catch. "When summer is over? You don't think we'll be gone by then?"

"Everything will work out the way it's supposed to. Whatever Maddie decides, I'll have to be okay with." I don't know why he's concerned about us staying or not. We just met these people, yet they act like we've known each other for years.

He sighs, then brushes some ashes off his pants. "We just want everything to go well. It's hard being in this predicament."

"What predicament is that?"

He tenses and his entire leg jiggles. He doesn't seem like the type to beat around the bush, yet it feels like he's dancing around what he really wants to say. Between this conversation and the side-eyes I've been getting all night, I feel like I'm missing something. They're acting like we're in this together, but I don't know what *this* is.

Devin clears his throat. "Just being out here, mostly secluded. Meeting new people to hang out with. I could tell how tense Maddie was when she first showed up. I know Harper just wants this to go well so we can have some friends while we're here."

He's lying. At least partially. It's in the tilt of his head and his leg still bouncing around. It's in the tension in his shoulders and his fingers gripping the arms of the chair. For some reason, I don't think he's hiding something nefarious. If I thought Maddie was in danger, she'd be over my shoulder and we'd be halfway back to the cabin.

Maybe I just want to keep her locked away for my own purposes. Sharing her company with others isn't as easy as I thought it would be. I want her to interact, even if it's at the expense of keeping her all to myself. It's a hard line to walk.

"Feels like it's a little more than that." My eyes dart to Maddie, wondering if I need to get her out of here.

"Ah, shit, man. We honestly thought you were her brother. It wasn't until Maddie said something about you being her husband..."

My chest throbs, a stabbing pain echoing through me as his voice trails off. It was the same when she told them who I was. Until she introduced me, they completely ignored me. I didn't care as much as Maddie did. She took it as a personal affront, which didn't bode well for the rest of the night. Andie and Noelle seem to have smoothed it over.

As the pain recedes, I rub at the spot above my heart. Maybe we shouldn't be lying to people. It could be my conscience flaring up, reminding me she's not even truly mine. The urge to wife her up right now overtakes me and I shrug it off. Proposing would be ludicrous. And she'd reject me. Or worse, laugh it off. The more time I spend with her, I'm convinced she's made for me. We're meant to be. Whether we've known each other for four weeks or four decades, that won't change.

"You just went through some shit, didn't you? Seen that look on a lot of these guy's faces." He chuckles, shaking his head. "Don't let it go too long or you'll chicken out."

He claps me on the shoulder before wandering off. I push from my seat and wave off Maddie when she throws me a questioning look from across the fire. I just need a minute to myself. We've spent a lot of time in each other's back pockets recently. I need to clear my mind and figure out if my feelings are real. I've dated before, but nothing like this. It's never been this intense. Finding someone to spend my life with wasn't on my to-do list.

The trees swallow me up, cutting off the others. The farther I go, the more the night comes alive. Crickets sing their songs, creating an underlying background. An owl calls to its mate, who responds in kind. A rustling to my left has me instinctively turning toward the sound. It's probably a fox or rodent, and I slow.

The noise stops and so do I, afraid I'm about to get a face full of racoon. Instead, a flash of white ducks in and out of the trees a hundred feet in front of me. I crouch down, squinting into the dark. A figure hides behind a tree, peeking around the trunk to our left. With a ski mask pulled over their face, it's hard to decipher anything about them other than a slim build encased in black with one white glove. They skip over a fallen log and stop once more.

"You can't run forever, little prey," a man's low voice calls. I can't pinpoint where they are, but the figure seems to know exactly where they'll appear.

I expect fear to flood me. Or the urge to protect them from whoever is chasing them, but I don't. It's like watching a fight scene in a movie. There's a sense of detachment—an understanding that I shouldn't interfere. I almost feel like I'm intruding on whatever game they're playing.

"Run, run, as fast as you can," she murmurs in a singsong voice, then scrambles away. Heavy footsteps follow her, his shadow stretching across the forest floor as the moon makes an appearance. They disappear into the woods, only a giggle on the wind to mark their passage.

Maddie told me she'd seen things in the woods. These two weren't floating or dashing, and they were clearly human. I wonder if they've been playing in the woods around here for the last few weeks, unintentionally messing with Maddie's head. At least I'll be able to tell her she's not seeing things.

I turn, intent on going back to the bonfire, but another rustling distracts me. Pivoting, my feet move without thought, following an overgrown trail. A trill floats through the air, light and musical. My vision blurs and I trip over a vine strewn across the path and crash to my knees. A woman's low chuckle, laced with malice, echoes around me. A chill rolls down my spine, and my body freezes.

I bite my tongue, blood filling my mouth, and whatever spell I was under is broken. Staggering upright, I shake my head to dispel the last of whatever plagues me. When an owl screeches, ice floods my veins, and I force my body around. It's like walking through quicksand, each step more labored than the last.

After what feels like an eternity, I reach the vine I tripped over. My heavy boot barely clears the plant, but as soon as I do, the weight sloughs off me and I crash to the ground once more. Another chuckle chases me as I gain my feet and race through the trees, leaving whatever the hell that was behind.

I stumble around for a while, trying to find my way back to the bonfire, but my hands tremble the entire time. I huff out a sigh of relief when Maddie's laugh rings out, guiding me back to safety. My shoulder slams into a tree, knocking me off balance. Wrapping my arms around the trunk, I concentrate on steadying my breathing. I can't walk back to the others like this. Maddie will know something is wrong and I'm not entirely sure I should tell her anymore.

I don't want her to think she's the only one, but whatever the hell is going on in these woods isn't normal. The first couple was clearly having a good time chasing each other. The spiteful air that hung in the air with the second encounter isn't something I ever want to experience again. Alternate dimensions aside, I don't have an explanation for what just happened.

When my heart stops pounding, I slowly make my way back to the group. They're oblivious to what I've been through, laughing around the dying bonfire. Sebastian, Andie's boyfriend, catches my eye and throws me a questioning look. I shake my head and search for Maddie.

My stomach flips when I don't find her in the chairs. Sebastian elbows one of his buddies and nods at me. He's started a chain reaction of everyone nudging one another until they're all glancing at me, and the conversation dies out.

Maddie's voice hovers in the silence and the tension in my body eases. My hand twitches, wanting to grab her. She'd mentioned walking through the woods tomorrow while I finished the side porch. No way in hell is that happening. Letting her out of my sight isn't an option. I won't put her in the position to run into whatever the hell I just did.

"You okay, man?" Beckett asks, the jovial voice he's had all night gone.

"Maddie and I need to leave. I'm sorry."

He stops me with a hand on my arm when I try to slide away and whispers, "Did something try to bite your dick? Because I have tips to deal with that."

"I...what? No, nothing bit my...what the fuck are you talking about?"

His hands shoot up, a smirk gracing his face. "No worries. I just wanted to help. You wanna talk about what *did* happen?"

"No. Just—" I run my hands through my hair. "Just don't go into the woods. At least not at night. Or at all."

Beckett glances over his shoulder, eyeing the shadows. "You think I could get Jordan to wander in there?"

I latch onto his arm, shaking him until he looks at me. "I'm serious. Don't fucking go in there."

His eyes widen and he nods. I drop my hand, then move toward Maddie. She mumbles something to Andie. Hopefully, she's making an excuse as to why we need to leave. Convincing her to go when she's clearly having a good time isn't what I want to do, but I need her home. I need her safe. And being this close to the forest isn't safe. Not right now. Tomorrow I'll deal with the aftermath.

"Let's go," I growl, my voice coming out much harsher than I intended.

"We were going to have s'mores." She sidles up to me, resting her hands on my chest. "Can't we just stay another ten minutes?"

I duck until my lips brush her temple. "We need to go back to the cabin. Now."

Her body shivers as if she feels the residual anxiety I'm sure is clinging to me. She nods, concern in her eyes as she tips her head up. She says her goodbyes and makes plans to meet them later. With the conversation I had earlier, I don't know if that's a good idea, but now isn't the time to deal with it.

One thought echoes through my head—*protect her.*

Chapter Twenty-Six
Maddie

"So let me get this right. You saw something in the forest, but you won't tell me what it is. Based on this mysterious interaction, you don't want me going near the woods without you. Is that what you're saying?" I ask for the third time.

Once he got me home last night, I fell asleep almost immediately. I didn't realize how tired I was after a few drinks. Not enough to be hungover, thankfully. I'm glad we didn't have this conversation then. I would have been even more confused.

"That's what I'm saying." He tightens another screw on the kitchen cabinet.

"And you won't tell me what you saw?" I grit my teeth, wondering when he'll give in.

Why he's holding out on me doesn't make sense unless he's scared. I can't think of anything he would be afraid of. Something's holding him back. It's as if he physically can't tell me what he encountered in the woods. Waking up this morning, he was groaning like he'd been hit by a truck, then sent through a meat grinder. He didn't have any bruises, though.

"You don't need to know. Just don't go into the woods without me and everything will be okay."

I open my mouth to argue more, but a knock at the door has me glaring at him before stomping down the hallway. My frustration permeates the space. It'll hang around until he caves and tells me what the hell is going on. I just wanted to have a fun night with new people.

I rip open the door, then immediately regret it. The woman on the other side raises a perfectly manicured eyebrow. Her black pencil skirt and white blouse screams how out of place she is. Add in the low heels and my lip twitches. I don't even know how she managed her way across the gravel and I'm hit with a tinge of jealousy. She's much more put together than I ever am and she makes it look effortless.

She clears her throat and I plaster on a fake smile. "Sorry, hello. Can I help you?"

The woman sighs and checks the binder in her hands. "Yes, I'm Ms. Frost. I'm the executive assistant for Mr. Aiden Sullivan."

I lean against the door frame and cross my arms. "Never heard of him. Are you trying to sell something? Or campaign for him?"

She smirks, then presses her lips together. "Uh, no. Neither one of those. He's looking to relocate to a more...secluded spot, and I've been sent to find a place. I was just wondering if you're looking to sell."

"I didn't think people actually did shit like this."

Ryland mentioned trying to get someone to move out so he could rent their place, but I didn't think he was serious.

She sighs, clearly annoyed. Whether it's with me or her boss, I'm not entirely sure. If she gets snippy with me, she caught me on the wrong day. Usually, I'll avoid the confrontation if I can. With Emmett's inability to communicate, I'm ready for a fight. She glances from side to side, then leans closer.

"He's ridiculously rich, kind of an asshole, definitely the closest thing to a recluse, and I'm supposed to tell you he'll make you a *very generous offer*." She waggles her eyebrows, then rolls her eyes. "He's an asshat who thinks money can buy anything."

"Well, he'll be barking up the wrong tree here. I don't own this place. In fact, I doubt a lot of the people around this lake own the cabins. I think most of them get rented out," I say, grinning.

"Yeah, I told him that. Of course, he didn't listen. He's got marbles in his ears every time I talk. I'm sorry to bother you." She steps back, a forlorn expression on her face.

I'm about to offer her something to drink or to come inside when her phone buzzes. She sends me a pained smile before stepping back and holding up her finger. I was going to give her some privacy. I hate standing around while someone talks on the phone. It's annoying for me and embarrassing for them. I glance behind me, trying to find where Emmett wandered off to. If he thinks our conversation is over, he's got another thing coming.

"Yes, Mr. Sullivan?" She pauses and rolls her eyes. "As I told you before you sent me to bumfuck nowhere, no one here is willing to sell. Most of these people don't even own the cabins they're staying in."

She grimaces, pinching the bridge of her nose. "By all means, if you think throwing millions of dollars at these people will magically transfer the deeds over."

I snort, smothering the sound behind my hands. "Magical indeed."

"Sure, fine. Come up here if you think you can do any better. But you do realize that will require you to *talk* to people, right?" She tips her head back, her exasperation evident. "Well, bring a tent then. And do not bring only one."

She hangs up while he's still barking orders at her. I'm impressed she's able to keep her cool. I would have quit long ago if I had to put up with his arrogance. Not that I know him. I've written plenty of characters like him. Those asshats end up groveling and professing their love for their assistant. Things like that don't happen often in the real world.

"Sorry. Fuck, I feel like I'm constantly apologizing for shit that isn't my mistake. I should stop that. And now I'm unloading on you. I really am sorry. I won't bother you anymore. I promise I'll keep him away from your place."

She turns and my stomach flips. "Do you want to come inside? It's almost lunchtime and I was going to eat anyways."

She glances over her shoulder at me. "I was just going to find something in town. Don't worry about it."

"Unless you're good with gas station snacks, you won't find anything else in town. There's like three buildings. Unless you were going to go an hour away. I can ask Emmett what's there."

Shock flits across her face, and she pivots to peek over my shoulder. "I figured you'd be here by yourself. How does that work?"

"Uh, well, he just stays here, too?" I don't entirely know what she's asking. Unless she thinks he owns the place, and I was holding out on her. "He doesn't own the cabin either. It's my best friend's uncle's place. Which is a mouthful now that I've said it out loud. I promise it's not a big deal if you want to eat here. We could commiserate about how awful your boss is."

I hold the door open wider and she tentatively steps through, heels clicking across the hardwood floors. A blush splashes across her cheeks, and I wonder if I've just put her in an impossible position.

"I'm Rylie, by the way. You don't have to call me Ms. Frost." She grimaces and I bite my lip.

"I'm Maddie. You honestly don't have to stay if you don't want to. I won't be offended or anything. But Emmett's been pissing me off today, so I could use the distraction." I probably shouldn't have told her that.

With every person who shows up lately, I seem to spill some random personal shit they don't care about. I've been stuck in my own little world for the last couple years, and I swear it's killed my peopling skills. It's exhausting making small talk and I avoid it whenever I can. Except my avoidance paves the way for all the things regular people don't admit to strangers.

"I haven't had an actual meal in a week, so I appreciate it." She flips her black hair behind her, revealing a row of piercings marching down her ear. Maybe she's not as straightlaced as her skirt implies.

I gesture at the stool and she hops up, setting her binder and phone next to her. "Do you want me to help?"

"Nope. I'm going to find Emmett and see if he had anything planned for lunch. Help yourself to whatever you want to drink."

She smiles, waving me off. I skip away, my bad mood from earlier slipping off my shoulders. Emmett isn't in the bedroom or the bathroom. I check the lower level next, though I hate going down there. It's fine for a cabin, I suppose. Emmett has most of it torn up, though, and I'm just waiting to step on a nail. I can't remember the last time I got a tetanus shot. I don't fancy trying to find the closest hospital.

The door to the patio under the deck doesn't work, and I huff. I'm halfway up the stairs before it hits me he might be in trouble. He talked about getting up on the roof. He was going to wait until I could make sure he wasn't going to fall off, though. If he climbed up there because he was annoyed with me...

I rush through the rest of the upstairs, nerves bubbling in my gut. The first floor is devoid of his electric presence. I've spent the last few weeks wrapped up in his energy. Now that it's missing, a hollowness invades me.

"Maddie? What's wrong?" Rylie sets her can down and slides from the stool.

"Nothing. I just can't find Emmett. He's probably outside. I'll just be a minute," I call as I race down the hallway to the front door.

I blast outside, my feet tripping over themselves. Rylie's hand wraps around my arm and hauls me upright. I take the stairs two at a time with Rylie on my heels. I'm not exactly light on my feet, but her keeping up with me in heels is impressive. Later, I'll be awed by her abilities—after I've found Emmett safe and sound.

"Emmett," I call as I round the porch.

"Do you think he went for a walk? Or went swimming?"

"No." My head whips back and forth as I try to remember what he was wearing today. "Emmett!"

"The lake. Check the lake." Rylie gasps, then throws out a curse. Her heels go flying the next second, hitting the lattice of the porch.

Her footsteps fall behind as I take off. I should slow down since the last time I descended these stairs, I almost broke my neck. I can't stop, though. Something picks at my brain. Something is wrong even if I can't figure out what it is. My nerves won't settle until he's in front of me, safe and sound.

My foot connects with a rock and I wince. It'll hurt like a bitch later. I stutter to a stop and scan the shore, then the water. Nothing. Not even a breeze ripples the surface. The wind died the minute my feet hit the sand. What the fuck is going on around here?

"Is he down there?" Rylie yells from the top of the hill.

I swallow hard, tears filling my eyes. I shake my head as I continue to search the area for any sign of Emmett. My voice has fled, leaving me without enough breath to even call for him anymore. It would be really great if I had anyone's numbers right about now. I could call up Andie or Bailey from last night and ask for help. Grace would come running if I asked. Why didn't I get any of their numbers?

My knees wobble and I dig my nails into my bare leg, using the pain to center myself. I can't fall apart now. He's around here somewhere. I just have to find him. And if I collapse on the sand, I won't be able to. He could be hurt and alone, not knowing if I'm coming for him. He probably thinks I'm too annoyed to look for him. Maybe he's unconscious and bleeding out. My mind races with all the possibilities, and a choked sob leaves me.

"Fuck," I breathe out, gripping my hair. "Get your shit together."

I spin and race back up the stairs. Rylie, bless her, is searching along the tree line, peering into the forest every couple steps. This poor woman just wanted a fucking meal. And now I've roped her into a crisis.

"I'm going to where we were last night," I call, and she whips around. "We were down by the lake over there."

I point toward the bonfire, not that she can spot it from where she is. I doubt Emmett would go down there. He was freaked out when he came out of the woods. I thought he'd just gone to pee, but he was pale as a ghost when he came back out. I assumed it was a bear or a cougar. We heard wolves howling when I first got here. Spotting animals like that in the day is scary enough. At night would be worse. But when he refused to tell me what it was...

I could take the stairs again, but I'm too worked up and end up crashing through the brush. My ankle rolls at one point, almost bringing me to my knees. I'm going to hurt myself before I even find him. When we reach the remnants of the bonfire, I stop to catch my breath. I'm not used to running around like this.

"You had a bonfire here? Are you sure?" Rylie asks, planting her hands on her hips as she glances around.

"They must have cleaned most of it up. But this is where we were."

I poke around, not sure what I'm supposed to be looking for. I don't write thrillers or mysteries. Finding clues isn't the way my brain works. I don't even read that genre. Not that reading or writing a mystery is going to help me here. This is the real world, not a book. Research is all well and good, but it doesn't make an author an expert.

"Uh, Maddie. What's that?" Rylie's hand rests on my arm.

The edge of the trees shimmer, green light cascading through the trunks. "Maybe it's just the sun reflecting through the leaves."

"It looks like a...portal." She grips my wrist as if I'll dash toward it.

"Trick of the light," I murmur.

Between one blink and the next it vanishes, and the breeze picks up, rustling the leaves. I step forward, Rylie's hand falling away. I may be smart enough not to run headlong into a magical portal, but I still wander toward the place it vanished. If it sucks me into another dimension, so be it. Maybe it would finally shove me out of the slump I'm in.

I shake my head, concentrating on the actual problem. Emmett is missing. The panic hits me again full force and my chin quivers. I peek into the woods, staying far away from where the supposed portal was. A flash of red catches my eye and my knees give out. Emmett appears, his eyes darting around, never fully settling on anything.

"Emmett?" I whisper.

His gaze snaps to mine and I swear I catch a flash of bright green in his dark eyes.

"The trees speak."

Chapter Twenty-Seven

Emmett

Stars explode behind my lids, and something digs into my back. I groan and roll, getting a face full of sand. Grimacing, I stretch my muscles, an ache settling in my bones.

"Emmett?" Maddie's voice floats through the air and I shudder. "I'm right here. Don't move."

My eyes snap open and I grab her arm. "Did you go into the woods?"

"No. No, I didn't go into the woods. I promise." Tears splash down her face and I cup her cheek, brushing away the wetness. "Where'd you go?"

"They—" I shake my head, not sure whether or not I should tell her. Or if I can. "I blacked out. When I came to, I was in the trees. They—"

"They spoke? You said the trees speak," she whispers.

I shudder, a voice echoing through my head, the words unrecognizable. "They listen too. But not here."

I sit up, pulling her onto my lap. The urge to hold her is too great. Eventually, I need to tell her everything. I bury my face in her hair, letting her scent fill the holes left behind by my journey into the woods.

She's yours. Make her see reason.

The words echo through my mind over and over. The advice wasn't a request, nor was it particularly comforting. Hell, it wasn't even advice, really. They, whoever *they* are, commanded me to make her see reason. I don't know what it means. Delivering what they want isn't possible without all the information. And they weren't very forthcoming. The rest was nonsensical words thrown at me.

"What do you mean by 'not here'?" She straddles me and cups my cheeks.

"I don't know. I'm—" My eye catches a woman hovering by the water's edge. "Who the hell is that?"

She glances over her shoulder, then back at me. "That's Rylie. We were going to have lunch."

"How the hell do you keep meeting these people?" I whisper.

"I don't know. They just show up. We need to get you back to the cabin." She climbs off me, then mumbles, "I should take you to the hospital."

I struggle to my feet, my head swimming. "And how do you think that'll go? Yes, he's my husband, but not actually my husband. Oh, and he's talking to trees. I'm sure they'd take my blood pressure and let me go."

She puffs out her cheeks, then exhales. "Fine, but if you start slurring your words, I'm taking you in."

"Maybe I'm just dehydrated."

Rylie comes closer, concern on her face. "Are you okay? She was really worried about you."

Maddie grimaces, then turns toward her. "I'm sure he'll be fine. I'm really sorry about this. Probably not any less stressful than dealing with your boss."

"Uh, this is the most exciting thing to happen in a while. Plus, I'm pretty sure I'm never going to run into a portal to another world. So this was a goddamn trip to remember." She grins, rubbing her hands together.

"Portal?" I ask, my voice cracking.

Maddie swings around again to face me. "There might have been a little glimmer in the trees. We weren't sure it was an actual portal. But I told you this forest was fucked. Which you totally knew but wouldn't tell me. Maybe if you would have, we wouldn't be in this predicament."

Her gaze flicks behind me, and her eyes widen. Her fingers latch onto my arm, nails digging into my skin. A chill rolls down my spine and my mouth goes dry. It's the same feeling as last night, with malice swirling through the air. The magic—I'm convinced that's what this is—chokes off my breath. An invisible force wraps around my head, squeezing until I drop to my knees, gripping my hair as a silent scream is ripped from me.

"Stop," a woman's voice murmurs, steel lacing her tone and the pressure releases.

A hiss from behind me sends another shiver through my body. Maddie's hand grabs my shoulder, shaking me as if I don't know shit is going down. I stumble to my feet and spin, shoving Maddie behind me. I may not entirely understand what the trees were whispering, but the message was clear—protect her. I can't fight magic with my fists, though.

A lead stone drops in my stomach when a woman slips between the trunks. Her features scream there's something *other* about her. Her brilliant green eyes bore into me, and she tilts her head, her golden-brown hair shimmering as the strands slide over her shoulder. Her gaze snaps to Maddie, who's leaning around me. I blink rapidly as the woman dissolves before my eyes. I swear her skin shimmered, which may have been the mist she vanished into.

"What the fuck was that?" Maddie breathes.

Another woman in her mid-twenties steps from behind a trunk, and I shove Maddie behind me again. Rylie giggles, practically clapping her hands like she just watched a magic show. The longer we stay here, the more I'm convinced everyone we've met is a part of some elaborate prank. Or we actually have stepped into an alternate universe.

"Sorry about her. She's still learning how to interact with...others. She won't bother you again." She steps back as if her explanation makes any sense at all.

"Wait. That's it?" Maddie asks, stepping next to me. My palms itch to step in front of her and I curl them into fists.

She grimaces, eyes darting to Rylie, then back to Maddie. "You're not ready, love. When you are, well, we'll be here."

"You've got to be kidding me. That doesn't explain anything," Maddie cries, and I lace my fingers with hers.

The woman's lip slips between her teeth. She glances over her shoulder and sighs. Hopefully Maddie can convince her to give us something—anything—to explain what the hell is going on around here. When she faces us again, I realize that's never going to happen.

"I'm sorry. I can't. Not yet." She tucks her chin to her chest and mutters, "Even if I really, really want to know what's going to happen."

"What's happening?" I mumble as I grip the back of my neck.

"Forget I said that," she rushes out, wide eyes finding mine. "Sometimes you just have to wait for the story to unfold."

She steps back, disappearing into the trees. There's no grand exit with someone dissolving or swirling portals. In fact, she's still tromping through the trunks, making a racket that sends birds scattering in her wake. Soon, the normal sounds of nature take over, but I can't stop searching the forest for more strange occurrences.

"Well, that was interesting. Should we go have lunch?" Rylie says, breaking the silence.

Maddie shakes her head, then turns to follow Rylie as she treks back to the cabin. I sway, torn between waiting for more shit to walk out of the woods and staying close to Maddie. Of course, she wins and I rush after her. I really should have a conversation with her about how I'm feeling. Now might not be the right time since we just crossed over into...I don't even know what to call it.

"Maddie," I call, and she spins and walks backward. "Turn around before you fall."

She rolls her eyes and spins back around, wiggling her fingers behind her. I grab her hand, a shock racing up my arm at the contact. Tugging, I try to create some distance between us and Rylie. She glances at me, and I shake my head.

"We need to talk about what just happened," I mutter.

"I know, but I really think we should get some food in you. And I did invite Rylie, so kicking her out now would be rude. We'll just wait until she leaves, then you can tell me how you wandered off into the woods."

"That will be a short conversation. I don't remember. One minute I was looking at the deck supports out back and the next I was waking up to your face hovering over me. Your new friend's reaction to everything isn't normal. Neither is yours."

She pulls me to a stop when we reach the patio under the deck. She waves Rylie on, though I'm not sure I want her in the house without one of us. If she isn't involved in all this and just assumes this is a prank on our part, we shouldn't make her prepare lunch for us. She should be a guest.

Maddie swings around to face me and crosses her arms. "I don't have any reaction because it's better than screaming and running into the lake. And Rylie probably thinks this is a trick or something. Also, while I don't entirely know what to think about all of *that*, I'm not surprised. I *told* you I saw weird things in the woods. I *told* you there were things we couldn't explain. Why is it so hard to believe that others might think that too?"

"Because it's—" The words stall in my throat. Explaining away a portal and disappearing women would be easy if I had a head injury. A gas leak or drugs could produce hallucinations, I'm pretty sure. But none of those excuses fit.

"See? You don't have any answers either. So, right now I'm going to go in there and pretend this didn't happen. At least until I've eaten. And we'll just wait to see if something else occurs." She presses her lips together, a pleading look in her eyes.

I sigh, running my hand through my hair as I glance at the peaceful lake. I thought this place was paradise when I got here. When Maddie showed up, I thought fate had handed me exactly what I needed. Sure, I couldn't remember half the shit I should know, like how I got here or who sent me. But I was so enamored with her, I didn't realize how many questions I can't answer. It's as if my past pops into my head, presenting itself as an old memory, yet isn't. As if someone else is telling me what my life was and who I am today. It's disconcerting.

"And what happens when we can't handle the next thing?"

She wraps her arms around my waist, resting her head on my chest. "We'll do it together. Just don't go wandering off again."

I run my hands up her back, shaking my head. "Didn't wander off. I literally don't know what happened."

"Maybe it's just the trees telling you to see reason and tell me shit." She leans back, grinning.

She unravels her limbs and skips toward the cabin. I'm frozen, her words repeating over and over in my mind. It mirrors the message from the trees so well. *Too* well. Different dimensions aside, I don't think we can stay here. Convincing Maddie won't be easy. She's taking the sudden display of magic in our world much better than I am. Maybe it's because she didn't experience what I did. The woman in the trees, the one who disappeared, was filled with spite and hostility. She was like a cat playing with a mouse seconds before she snapped the poor thing up.

Once Rylie leaves, I'll just have to persuade Maddie to leave with me. I refuse to leave her here by herself, no matter how freaked out I am. I trudge up the stairs and across the deck. Rylie and Maddie chat away in the kitchen as they pull ingredients from the fridge. They look like they've known each other for years. I watch them for several minutes, resisting the urge to snatch her up and toss her ass in the car.

I shake my head, glancing over my shoulder at the spot in the forest I stumbled from. Nothing moves, not even the leaves rustling in the wind. It's as if that particular section is dead. Or alive with more than the natural world. My muscles tense and I shake my head again, glancing back toward the women.

I startle when I see Grace has joined them. I wouldn't be surprised if the group from the bonfire shows up next, stumbling into the cabin as if we planned a dinner party. The front door stays shut, though, and I resign myself to waiting. By tomorrow, I plan on getting both of us out of here.

Chapter Twenty-Eight
Maddie

"Emmett, do you really think kicking the tires will get it to work?" I ask, leaning against the railing as I watch his frustration build.

"This thing is brand new. It shouldn't just not start." He grips his hair, staring at my car.

He's adamant that we're leaving. While I understand his reasoning, I think he's overreacting. Emmett doesn't agree, of course. Our bags are already in the trunk of the car Chloe rented for me.

"Where exactly are we going?" I tilt my head, then straighten.

The heat from the summer sun beats down on me and a trickle of sweat hits the collar of my shirt. Gathering up my hair, I lift the mass from my skin and pull the strands into a ponytail. The days are growing longer, and the ball of anxiety in my chest expands. If I don't get to work soon, I'll end up choking from the panic. It's as if my future slips away a little more every night as my computer sits untouched on the table.

"We'll go wherever we can. I'm taking you somewhere safe, Maddie. Don't argue with me on this," he growls.

I sigh, wondering how long I should let this go on. I don't want to leave. This whole experience is off-putting and completely wild, but it's the most amazing thing that's happened in my life in...years. I've probably thought more about the supernatural than the average person on account of being an author.

I've had countless conversations with friends about the most random things—what animals could shift, what a vampire smells like, whether an angel's wings would get in the way during sex. Most people would probably give us funny looks if they saw our messages. Even Chloe shoots me the side-eye when I throw out a particularly wild what-if.

"So, I'm not arguing with you, but I don't think the car is going to start. And walking into town would take a while. Not to mention they probably wouldn't have a new battery, if that's even what's wrong with it. Since you haven't fixed your truck, that's out. And hitchhiking to the next town over would be futile. Why don't you just wait until one of the others comes over and ask them for a ride?"

He shakes his head, still staring at the car like he can will it into starting. He laces his hands behind his neck, and I slink down the stairs. Wrapping my arms around his waist, I press my cheek to his back. Instantly, his muscles ease and a heavy sigh leaves him. His hands drop to mine, which are laced over his stomach.

"I think they're in on it," he murmurs.

"Doubt it. Let's just go inside and you can tell me how I'm too calm about this."

"You'll just distract me," he grumbles.

I slide around him, tucking under his arms. "How exactly do I distract you?"

He scowls, but there's no heat behind it. I wiggle my brows and purse my lips. He swoops down, capturing my mouth with his. I melt into him as heat gathers between my legs. It's only been a little while, but it's been too long.

"See?" he growls against my lips.

I yelp when he pulls away and throws me over his shoulder. Giggles erupt from me as he bounds up the stairs and smacks my ass. I expect him to take me to the bedroom. Instead, he heads for the dining room. My ass hits the table, and he forces my shirt over my head. I didn't even bother putting a bra on this morning, despite his insistence we were leaving.

He pushes me onto my back, covering my body with his. I rake my nails down his back as his lips run over my skin. He lifts his head and grins, a twinkle hanging in his eyes. I loop my legs around his thighs before shoving his shirt up. I struggle to pull it off while his hands skim across my breasts. He forces a yelp from me as he pinches my nipple and rolls it between his fingers.

"Take it off," I grumble, and he grins again.

Finally, his shirt joins mine somewhere on the floor. Straightening, he runs his fingers through his hair and I kick my hips up.

"Something you needed, gorgeous?" He grips himself through his pants, raising an eyebrow.

I lick my lips, my breath stalling in my throat. The bastard knows exactly what I want, yet he'll make me say it. I'm not as worried as I was before, but the anxiety of voicing those things out loud still has a slight hold on me. I swallow hard as I drop my legs from around him and brace my feet on the edge of the table. He steps back, tracking my movements.

Lifting my hips, I try to not slip off the smooth surface. That wouldn't be sexy at all, and I *really* want him to fuck me. Which he won't do if I hurt myself. I shimmy my shorts down, my skin smacking against the wood as I drop my body while I kick the fabric from my feet. He sucks in a sharp breath, eyes fixed on my pussy.

"No bra," he murmurs as he forces my knees apart and steps between them. "No underwear." He grips my hips, probably leaving bruises behind. "Seems like you had a plan to seduce me today. Is that what you want, Maddie? Do you want me to fuck you until you scream my name?"

He drags his finger across my stomach, then down to my pussy, swiping through the wetness, and my back arches off the table. A whimper escapes me as he gently circles my clit. And then he's gone, stepping back once more.

"Emmett," I whine, my hands cupping my breasts like they have a mind of their own.

He seizes my wrists and forces them above my head. "Be a good girl and answer the question. Do you want me to fuck you so hard your cries of ecstasy echo across the lake?"

"Yes," I gasp, a rush of wetness seeping from my pussy.

"Say it. I want to hear you beg for my cock."

My gaze snaps to his as he backs away and slowly unbuckles his belt. He pauses, tipping his chin at me. The intensity of his gaze threatens to send me up in flames. He's ruined me for anyone else, including myself. Every time I've tried to touch myself in the shower, it's never as good as when it's him.

I clear my throat and tip my chin up, though the move probably doesn't have the intended effect. "I want you to make me scream."

He rewards me by unbuttoning his pants. He stops once more and I pout, but he doesn't give in. Bastard.

"I want you to fuck me so hard I scream your name." I clear my throat and he smirks. "And then you'll call me a good girl."

He drops his jeans and kicks them off. His boxers follow, and I bite my tongue as my gaze slides to his cock. He grips his length and strokes himself, his thumb brushing over the tip. My mouth waters, but I doubt he has plans to get me on my knees. His focus is on counting how many times he can make me come. He told me his goal was nine, and I laughed in his face. I doubt we'll be counting today. From the blazing desire in his eyes, I have a feeling this will be hard and fast. Not that I'm complaining.

"We'll see," he murmurs.

He drops to his knees and tugs me to the edge of the table, draping my legs over his shoulders. I open my mouth to ask what he's doing, but all that comes out is a breathy moan as he licks me from core to clit. My fingers grip his hair, keeping him in right where I need him. My eyes roll back in my head as he devours me.

My muscles tense and my legs shake as my orgasm hangs just out of reach. He flicks his tongue against the sensitive bud, then he pulls away. My hands fall away, and I squeeze my legs closed, trying to keep him where I want him. He chuckles, his breath caressing my skin.

"Why?" I cry, slapping my palms against the table.

He stands and shoves my legs apart to stand between them. "When you come, it'll be around my cock, gorgeous."

He plunges into me and I moan, locking my ankles behind his back. His forearms hit the table on either side of my head and his lips brush against mine.

"So fucking perfect," he whispers.

He groans as he pushes upright and grips my hips. He smirks as he slowly pulls out and his eyes dip to where we're connected. When he eases back in, I whimper.

"Emmett," I gasp as he does it again.

"Hmm. Look at how well you take my cock," he murmurs., as if he's talking about a delicious piece of cake. The way his eyes glaze over looks like he's salivating over my pussy.

I hum and roll my hips to urge him faster. He doesn't, just continues his slow torture. His thumbs press into my hip bones, then slide along the creases of my legs. My ankles slip when he thrusts hard and my legs fall.

I used to struggle to keep my mind focused during sex. Too many thoughts swirled around my head, distracting me from what should be a desirable experience. With Emmett, I only have enough bandwidth to focus on him and the pleasure he pulls from my body.

He abandons his pursuit with his hands and latches onto the back of my knees. I whimper when he lifts them higher, his cock hitting a spot deep within me. My eyes roll to the back of my head as he places my feet on the edge of the table.

"Play with your clit," he growls, and my fingers obey immediately, diving between my legs.

A flame sparks in my gut, spreading fire across my skin. I arch my back, my ass leaving the table as he pounds into me. He groans as he destroys me from the inside out. I give myself over to the sensations flooding my body and sail over the edge into ecstasy. He doesn't slow, fucking me through my orgasm. My hand falls away and I slap the wood, unable to stop myself from writhing underneath him.

He hisses when I tumble into another climax, clenching around his length. "There's my good girl. One more, gorgeous. Give me one more."

I shake my head, whimpering, and he pulls out of me suddenly. A choked sob leaves me, but he doesn't leave me empty for long. He tugs me upright until my feet hit the ground, then spins me around and pushes me down again.

The coolness of the wood on my hard nipples has shock rippling through me, and I shiver. He slams into me once more, resuming his rough pace. When his arm snakes around my waist, his fingers finding my clit, another sob echoes around the room. He rubs frantically, pushing me further than I've ever been. I'm on my tiptoes by the time I shudder out one more release.

He groans as he follows me into ecstasy, his movements slowing. His body covers mine, fingers dancing along my damp skin. I'm practically purring as he presses kisses along my shoulder, whispering words of praise.

"You did so well, coming for me." He rolls his hips and pinpricks of pleasure erupting between my legs. "Your pretty little pussy knows exactly who she belongs to, doesn't she?"

I hum in response. A weightlessness overtakes me, making it hard to speak. I'd agree to almost anything he said right now. Whatever he wants, I'll give it to him, if only he continues to make me come and keeps feeding me. I never knew how much I'd enjoy his possessiveness—his claiming of me.

I whimper as he pulls out of me, turning into another hum as he gathers me in his arms. As he cradles me against him, heading for the bedroom, a contentedness spreads through me. He tucks me between the sheets, then crawls in behind me. My eyes flutter shut and a smile tugs at my lips. If we really are stuck here, I don't think I'd mind all that much.

211

Chapter Twenty-Nine

Emmett

I shouldn't be out here. Nothing good ever came from staring into the woods. At least I convinced Maddie to stay in the house. Ever since our encounter five days ago, she's been staring at her computer. It's different from before. I can practically hear the gears turning in her head. After a while, she'll heave out a heavy sigh and close her laptop, but it's an improvement.

I glance behind me at the cabin, making sure she's still sitting on the deck. When I'm sure she's safe, I walk between two thick trunks, running my hands down the bark. It bites into my palm, crumbling under my touch. This area isn't as... malevolent as the area by the bonfire. I'm not worried about portals popping up or creatures appearing out of nowhere. It's calm here, a soft breeze rustling the tops of the trees.

Maddie refuses to leave and I refuse to take off without her. Not that we'd be able to go anywhere. We're too far away from civilization to do anything other than wait. None of the people Maddie has met have been by. It's as if they disappeared as soon as the incident in the forest happened. Every time my mind wanders back, I lose more of the details. I grasp at them, desperately trying to make sense of what happened. It's no use, though.

"Can you even throw a football?" A man's voice echoes through the trees, and I stumble back, seeking the safety of the lawn.

A woman giggles, and I search the woods for whoever it is. "He'll have to learn if he's going to play."

Another man snorts and a group appears, tromping through the forest. "Of course I can throw a football. Stop trying to impress her. You're punching down and girls don't like that."

"Good thing I'm not a girl then, huh?"

"Uh, hate to break this to you, P, but you're definitely a girl. Unless you haven't told us something," the first one says.

"I am a *woman,* not a girl. You'd do well to remember that."

A chorus of "ooohs" ring out as they approach. I track their movements, waiting for them to either shimmer or disappear. When neither happens, I realize they might just be regular people.

Turning, I steel myself for another conversation with Maddie about getting the hell out of here. The more people who show up, the more on edge I am. And I'm not about to put her at risk any longer.

"Maddie, we need to go," I yell as I blast through the front door.

She turns, confusion stamped across her face. I rush to the bedroom and grab her empty bags. She unpacked after the car wouldn't start.

"Emmett, what happened? You didn't go into the woods again, did you?" Her footsteps echo through the cabin and my stomach flips.

"I'm packing your shit if you don't." I throw one of her bags on the bed.

Her hand latches onto my wrist, halting my progress. I pant, my vision blurring. I've spiraled, unable to see the future clearly. Maybe my jaunt into the woods earlier messed with my ability to think clearly. I'm not even listening to her as she continues to ask me questions. I need to focus on her and what she wants instead of forcing her into anything—even if it is to keep her safe.

"Are you even listening to me?" she cries, throwing up her hands.

"No, I wasn't. I...there are people outside. I just want to keep you safe," I whisper.

She sighs, stepping into me and wrapping her arms around my waist. I grip her tightly, afraid she'll disappear if I let go. I bury my face into her hair, letting her warmth, her scent, her essence fill in the missing pieces.

"Do you believe in fate?" she asks, her voice muffled by my shirt.

"I didn't until I met you."

She laughs softly, tipping her head back, and meets my eyes. "Give me a kiss."

Maddie purses her lips, then sucks her cheeks in. I can't stop my grin, the anxiety that's been gripping me instantly falling away. She's all I need to center myself. I give her a peck, then grab her hand and tug her toward the door.

"Who were the people? Did you talk to them? What did they want?"

I glance back at her. "No idea who they are or what they want. They were talking about football."

I lead her out to the deck, hoping she's a better at finding out their motive than I am. From now on, I'm deferring to her. It's the only way I'll be able to handle everything this place is throwing at us.

She tugs on my hand, forcing me to stop. "Do you really think this is something supernatural and not a gas leak?"

I bite my cheek, not sure how to answer. Checking the lines was the first thing I did when I got here. And then again after the bonfire. My father taught me a lot about houses and the potential hazards. Not enough to know everything, though. I'd never be able to learn every risk out there. It's entirely possible there's an environmental reason behind everything. My gut tells me it's more than that.

Pulling her through the door, my eyes dart to the forest, then the lake. She huffs, probably thinking of all the ways she can get me to talk.

"Try to not collect these people the way you did the others," I mutter as we approach the railing.

"Are you saying I shouldn't make friends? Because this is the first time in forever I've actually met people I like. Or think I like. Most of my friends are online." She leans over the railing, and I grab the back of her shirt.

"Of course I want you to make friends. I'd rather you not find out your friends are shitheads who would put you in harm's way."

She turns, her brows pulled low. "I don't think they'd hurt me. Any of them."

"Rylie clapped when that shit went down the other day. Grace knocked on the door at eleven at night. And Andie and Beckett and Jordan? They invited total strangers to a bonfire. Not to mention Devin's questions were off the wall. I'd love to think they're not nefarious, but I'm not willing to risk it."

"Did you really just use the word nefarious?" She snorts, running her nails under my shirt. A shiver skitters down my spine as she continues raking across my skin.

"Keep that up and you won't get to meet these new people," I murmur, ducking to press a kiss to her jaw.

"Except I think they disappeared, so we've got time to kill." Her lip slips between her teeth and she worries the flesh. I tug it from her mouth, then grip her chin.

"Is that all I am to you? Time to kill?" I smirk, skimming my hand down her neck and wrapping my fingers around her throat.

She shudders, tipping her head back as I step closer, caging her between my body and the railing. The urge to bury my cock into her while she's bent over the wood, the whole of the world to hear her cries of ecstasy, overwhelms me.

"Clearly not. If I was looking for something to kill, I'd venture into the woods with the very dull dagger you promised me."

I grin, unable to stop a chuckle from erupting from me. "I'll get you whatever you want as long as you keep me around."

She skims her fingers along my sides, then pulls me closer. I swoop down, sealing my mouth to hers. Slipping my fingers in her hair, the soft locks cascading over my arm. I grip the strands, angling her head to deepen the kiss. She's the only one I want to lose myself in. Whenever I'm with her, the world shrinks to just her.

"Oi!" A man's voice echoes through the still air, and she jerks back.

Whipping her head to the side, she snaps, "Well, that's rude."

She untangles her limbs and I reluctantly do the same, following her to the side of the deck. Her mouth drops open as she stares into the woods right where I was standing not fifteen minutes before. A shirtless man stands with his hands on his hips, a scowl plastered on his face. He's at least half a foot taller than me and covered in swirling tattoos that seem to slither across his skin in a hypnotic fashion.

"Oi," he shouts even louder than before as his eyes dart around the yard.

"Can I help you?" Maddie yells, an edge to her voice. She glances back at me, widening her eyes.

The color drains from his face and his hands drop to his sides. "Oh, uh, hello."

"Something I can do for you?"

His jaw clenches as he bounces from one foot to the other. "Yeah, can you finish, please? Because I'm getting real sick of blasting into places and getting my ass singed."

His eyes dart to me and he raises an eyebrow. I don't know what the hell he's talking about any more than Maddie does. She grips my arm, nails digging in. My reaction is very different from just moments before. My gut turns as I study the man who doesn't seem to fully belong on this plane of existence.

"Uh, I'm sorry? That's not exactly—I mean, the idea of exhibitionism is one thing, but to actually do it..." She bites her lip, squeezing my arm tighter.

Alarm flits over the man's features and he hastily steps back, holding his hands up in surrender. I burst out laughing despite Maddie's serious tone. I snort, bracing my hands on the railing and doubling over. How she came to that conclusion is beyond me. Unless he saw us kissing. Or could read my thoughts. The idea pulls me up short and I sober.

"No, no, no," the man yells anxiously. "That's not what I want. I need you to finish—"

Grace runs from out of nowhere, shoving against his chest to get him back into the woods. Shadows wrap around him, and I shake my head. Maybe his tattoos weren't swirling after all. Maddie's mouth drops open, and I slide a hand around her waist, ready to whisk her away at the first hint of danger.

"Stop it, Kol," Grace hisses, her voice floating to us on the summer breeze. "You're going to ruin everything."

"Knock it off," he growls, and Grace drops her hands. He doesn't stop moving, though.

It's as if an invisible force latches onto him and tugs him back, almost taking him off his feet. "Fuck, Rune. Let me go. You want this shit, too. We need to find Evalie, and we're not going to do that if she doesn't get her shit together."

I'm so focused on the scene in front of me, I don't notice Maddie moving until she plops onto her ass and drops her head between her knees. She mutters under her breath, and I crouch down.

"Rune. Evalie. Kol. Rune. Evalie. Kol." She repeats the names over and over, then gasps. "Where the fuck is Nix? And Dez? Shit. Oh shit. They're all...every single fucking one of them."

"Maddie," I whisper, my hand hovering over her. I don't want to startle her, but she's starting to worry me. "Maddie, are you okay?"

I finally brush my fingers along her arm, and she jerks away from my touch. Her wide eyes find me, and she scrambles into the corner of the deck. I mirror Kol's stance, holding my hands up.

"Are you? No, I never wrote about you. Not all of them were named, but why would you just randomly be here? You're not one of them, are you?" Tears fill her eyes and spill down her cheeks. All I want to do is wrap her in my arms and take away whatever pain she's going through. I'm pretty sure I'm the source, though.

"I don't know who those people are, Maddie. I'm just me. I'm Emmett who has no fucking clue what the hell is going on." I glance at the others, still arguing in the yard.

"I know who they are," she whispers, almost too low for me to catch.

Her eyes meet mine, indecision swirling in the depths. She peers between the slats, then scurries over to me. She shoves my arms away and crawls into my lap, straddling me. This isn't the time for my cock to wake up, but I don't have control over it. I bite back a groan when she leans close, her breath ghosting across the shell of my ear.

"They're mine. All of them. I didn't realize until now. Grace and Rylie are common enough names. The ones from the bonfire are from so long ago I didn't even remember. But Rune? Kol? Those aren't ones you hear all the time. They stick out in your mind and you remember them. I'm intentional when I choose names for them."

"I don't understand what you're saying." It kills me to admit it. I wish I could follow what goes on in her head. If I could reach in and read her mind, she wouldn't have to explain anything.

"They're mine, Emmett. All of them are my..." She leans back, pressing her lips together as her brows pull low. She swallows hard, shaking her head and peering at the forest.

"They're my characters."

Chapter Thirty
Maddie

As soon as I speak the words out loud, a gust blasts through the woods, sending the trees swaying. I bury my head into Emmett's chest, clinging to him in anticipation. The wind dies before it reaches us, and a low murmur rises in the sudden silence.

Slowly, I lift my head and stare at Emmett. His face is a blank mask, shutting me out completely. Unless he's just as shocked as I am. I duck my head again, not ready to find out which one it is.

"Uh, Maddie. How many characters do you think you have?" The rumble from his chest rolls through me, easing some of the anxiety.

"I'm not sure. I've got at least thirty stories and they all have at least two main characters. Plus, there's several that have more than one love interest."

He sighs, then drops a kiss to the top of my head. "More than one, huh?"

I snort. "Why choose? Some of them need more than one."

"Well, I hope you're ready for more than one character."

"Of course there's more than one. Grace, Rylie, Andie and Sebastian, Bailey and Beckett, Harper and Devin, Kaylee and Jordan, and Noelle and Austin. Plus, there is McKenna and the fae lady. She was the one fucking with you in the woods. Then there's the others I probably didn't even notice, which doesn't bode well for those stories," I mutter.

He cups my cheeks, forcing me to meet his gaze. "None of that. From what I've seen, you've got a shitload of information in your head. Why would you think you could remember all of them? And it's not like it's normal for characters to just waltz out of thin air. I know you said they were like actual people to you, but I'm pretty sure you didn't mean like this."

He nods toward the forest, dropping his hands to my neck, his thumbs brushing over my throat. My muscles tense as he guides my head to the side. Gasping, I seize his wrists, needing something to ground me to the present.

Dozens of people linger around the yard, mingling with one another. I don't even recognize half of them, they blend together so seamlessly. As if they've always known of each other and they're merely here for a reunion.

I never thought about them occupying the same space in my brain before. I kept them contained within their respective areas in my mind, bringing them to the forefront one by one as I wrote their stories. More step between the trees, craning their necks as if they're searching for someone.

"I think that guy is lost. Are you sure you wrote him a love interest?" Emmett mutters like he's worried he'll be overheard.

A flash from him has me squinting, and I grin. "That's Ezio. He's a vampire. Probably looking for Ella. I doubt he'd look for Dray. He's a wolf shifter, so they don't exactly get along except for Ella's sake. Fated mates can be so freaking frustrating."

"I'm sure," he murmurs.

I scramble off him and race for the sliding door. "We really need stairs on this thing. You should get on that."

Once I reach the front door, I stutter to a stop and rest my hands against the wood. It's one thing to hover above them, even on the deck. It's entirely different to step outside—to be among them. That move will make everything real. My chest tightens as I worry if they'll be there when I turn the knob. Another part of me hopes they've disappeared.

Emmett's warmth seeps into my back, and I lean into him. "It's okay to be scared."

"I'm not terrified."

His arms circle around me, holding me close. "I didn't say terrified. I said scared."

"Well, I'm neither," I say with conviction. Neither of us are convinced.

"Do you want me to go out there first?"

"I need to do this. I need to talk to them and find out what they want."

"Sounds like Kol wants to watch us fuck." He chuckles and I jab him with my elbow.

"To be fair, I'm sure he wouldn't mind. Then again, I think he reserves that for his own relationships." I pull in a deep breath.

My mind races, different threads weaving together. If I tug on the wrong one, I fear the whole thing will unravel, leaving me in the same position I was before they showed up. It's a delicate balance I'm not entirely ready to tackle. Emmett's scent washes over me as he brushes his lips across my neck. His presence calms the raging turmoil inside of me.

"You don't have to go out there right away." His fingers skim along the strip of skin above my waistband.

There it is. The out I desperately needed to hear. Even though I'll never take it. Knowing I have a choice makes all the difference. I'm sure he has no idea how much it means to me.

"How long has it been?" I murmur, leaning into him and borrowing his strength.

"Month and a half. Feels longer, doesn't it?"

"Feels like fate," I mumble under my breath, then clear my throat. "I'm ready. Just don't...don't throw me over your shoulder when you meet some of them. A couple of my characters are a bit scary."

"I'm sure I can handle it. It's not like they're real. Unless they are." He exhales as I turn to face him and fight a grin when deep grooves form between his eyes. "I wonder if I'd die if one of them shot me. Do any of them have guns?"

I open my mouth to drop a witty remark to lighten the mood, then snap it shut when his words sink in. Are they real since they came from my head?

Grace felt real when she hugged me. Rylie's hand didn't disappear when we made proper introductions. And every time I brushed against someone at the bonfire, they were solid. But Kol didn't have wings when he was shouting at me for not finishing their story.

"Some of them are from this world, but others aren't." I wince, not entirely sure how to explain the different subgenres I write in. "I mean, some of their stories take place in like the fae realm or Hell."

"Hell. Let me guess. The man who wants to watch us is from Hell. Because that tracks, honestly. Did you notice his tattoos?"

"Yeah, he walks through shadows, so his tattoos kind of live in that space. You're taking all of this surprisingly well."

He smirks, squeezing his eyes shut before gazing at me. "At this point, I'm just glad I'm not blacking out. Maybe it's shock. You're not running around like a chicken with your head cut off, either."

"Yeah, we're going with shock. It'll hit us later and we can deal with that together."

"Together," he breathes, running his hand through his hair.

"Unless this is too much. Obviously, this is a lot to take in. And completely out of left field. I wouldn't fault you if you left." I'm babbling, but I can't stop. I was so overwhelmed, then excited, I never questioned whether he'd accept this. "I know the car isn't working, but we can get you into town."

Am I offering up a ride I don't have? Yes. Do I even know if the people outside have transportation? No. Maybe they vanish like the fae woman in the woods. I should really name her. I have a sticky note with a list of possible choices, but then I hit writer's block and couldn't be bothered. Which is exactly why there's a crowd standing on the lawn waiting to yell at me. I doubt they're here to help.

I swallow hard, still worried if I've shoved Emmett into a situation he isn't prepared for. How I could possibly prepare him for something like this, I don't know. Still, he doesn't deserve to be put in the middle of my problems. My breath stalls in my lungs and I shuffle away until my back hits the door. Dealing with this on my own won't be easy.

"I'm sorry. I'd leave, but with the car not working, I don't have that option. I can help you pack if you want." I step to the side, hoping he won't make this a big deal. My chin quivers and I bite my tongue to stop the tears. It doesn't work—mostly because it hurts.

"Maddie, stop." He halts me with his hands on my shoulders. "You're spiraling. Just calm down."

A hysterical bubble of laughter escapes me. "When has telling someone to calm down ever fucking worked?"

He doesn't join in, giving me a stern look. "First of all, I'm not leaving. The idea that I'd run out on you is laughable. If you start packing my shit, we're going to have problems."

"It's not running out. You don't owe me anything, and I realize you're a good guy, so you'll feel like you have to stick around. But I promise I can handle this. I'm a grown-ass woman."

His brows pull low, and he shakes his head. "I have no doubt you can handle this alone, but you don't have to. I'm well aware of how much of an amazingly strong woman you are."

My heart skips a beat as his words sink into me. "Okay. Doesn't mean—"

"No. You're going to listen to me now. You didn't plan for this any more than I did. When I came here, I thought I'd be spending the next four months alone. And when you fell into my arms, literally, my entire world changed. I don't know what the hell is going on out there, but frankly, I don't care. They don't matter to me other than the fact that they're a part of you."

My eyes dart around, never fully settling on him. I'm afraid of what I'll find. "I just wanted to—"

"You wanted to give me an out. I don't need one. I don't *want* one. This is the reason we were thrown together. I'm here to help you—to be here with you while you're dealing with your characters."

No one has ever stated so plainly their support of me. Chloe may be in my corner, endlessly guarding me from everyone, including myself. She wants me to succeed, but she has her own life to live. She never needed an out. She knew going in what it entailed to be my friend and vice versa. It's completely different with Emmett. I'm not falling in love with Chloe. I swallow hard, not sure what to say, especially after my emotions drop that bomb on me.

"I feel like that's a little lopsided. You shouldn't exist solely to help me with this shitshow."

"Well, when we're done with this, I'll find some issue you can help me through. Besides, I like taking care of you. Maybe that's my purpose."

I snort, finally meeting his gaze. "Your purpose in life is to feed me and protect me from monsters under the bed?"

He grins, sliding his hand to the back of my neck and tugging me closer. "Unless you have someone milling about out there who actually hides under someone's bed."

My eyes glaze over, an idea taking hold. The world falls away as my lids flutter shut. What if there was a stalker who hid under their prey's bed? Or maybe one of them is a demon or a creature who travels through a portal under her bed.

"And it only opens when she comes," I whisper, then giggle.

"Uh, what?" Emmett's question catapults me from my musings.

"Sorry, nothing. I can't add another WIP to my list, so you need to keep those kinds of ideas to yourself."

He doesn't seem to understand, but that's fine. He could move in a certain way and a story could hit me. I pull in a deep breath, bracing myself for the real issue I need to tackle. Finding Grace is my first move. She showed up first and clearly knew more than the others. Her shoving Kol back into the forest showed she's in charge. The rest will have to wait until I can wrap my head around everything.

"Do you need me to feed you before facing the music?" Emmett asks, resting his forehead against mine.

"I'll survive." I push onto my toes and brush my lips over his, then sink back to the floor. "Oh shit. What if we have to feed them?"

Chapter Thirty-One

Emmett

Pins and needles work their way along my skin, and I cross my arms before leaning against the porch. Being around all these people who aren't really people gives me the eebie-jeebies.

I keep expecting one of them to walk through me like a ghost. None of them do, of course. They're avoiding me like I have the plague or something. Or they're afraid I'll punch them. To be fair, I might.

Not many of them were too happy when I made my announcement yesterday. All of them wanted a piece of Maddie, and I shot them down. She might have been excited to meet everyone, but her emotions were all over the place. I forced her to shower, then spend the rest of the night ignoring them. It did nothing for her anxiety, yet I don't regret taking control.

Half of these characters are eyeing me like they want to shoot me. One of them reached for a gun. Not that he had one, but I recognized the move. I can't remember where I've seen it before, though. The memory sits just out of reach, hiding in the corners of my mind.

"Sorry about this," Grace murmurs as she leans next to me.

"What exactly are you apologizing for?" The question comes out sharper than I intended, but she smiles softly.

"I didn't want her to be blindsided. I thought she'd get there on her own." She sighs and her head thumps against the wood.

"Not me you should be apologizing to. If you ask me, this was the better way. I tried to throw her ass in the car to get away from what I thought was a possessed forest."

She gives me a strange look, then wrinkles her nose. "Why would the forest be possessed?"

"Maddie and Rylie saw a portal. And there was a woman. Maddie said they were fae, but I don't know what that means. The woman apparently doesn't like humans." I track Maddie's movements as she listens intently to a woman with sharp cheekbones who keeps glaring at a man in a suit standing ten feet away.

"Oof, yeah. The fantasy characters are a little hard to deal with. They operate with the rules of their world, which don't always translate to ours."

Magic. She's talking about magic. When Maddie brought it up the other night, I didn't think much of it. I thought it was one of those things you throw out there when you can't explain shit. Like poltergeists or creatures lurking within the inhospitable places tucked away in the trees.

Until I came here, I led a boring life devoid of such things. Nothing went bump in the night. My cupboards stayed firmly shut. Mythical beings were relegated to the fairy tales I barely remember my mother reading to me when I was young. Those stories never touched my world as an adult.

Grace clears her throat and I glance at her. "How are you not halfway to town by now?"

"I told her I'd stay for her. She's going to need something normal in her life." I'm not about to explain our relationship to someone like Grace. I doubt she'd understand.

"You're really not a character? I thought she'd written you into existence. The perfect book boyfriend who made her food and—" She blushes, wrapping her arms around her middle.

"Slept with her?" I chuckle and grip the back of my neck. "If she wrote me, she did it long before I came here. She hasn't written since she got here despite my best attempts. I also don't randomly disappear when she's not around. Pretty sure I'm not a character."

"You don't have to convince me. I thought you'd want to know, though. I was talking to Devin, and he mentioned your conversation the other night. He was a bit thrown by your responses."

"The fact he's a character Maddie dreamed up *and* he thought I was one too helps it make more sense." My eyes find Maddie once more. "I don't know what led me here other than a job, but maybe fate exists. And I'm not going to fight against my destiny. Especially if it includes Maddie."

She bounces from one foot to the other. A man stalks toward her and she wrings her hands together. The urge to step in front of her, stop him in his tracks, takes over. She waves me off when I shuffle closer.

"It's fine. Samuel isn't...it's fine," Grace says. "I just want to say, maybe find a purpose here. Beyond Maddie. It's not bad to support her and everything, but she'll go back to her own life before you know it. I'm not saying she'll leave you behind. Just find who you are, too. Because you can't only live for her. No matter how much you love her."

My spine snaps as I tense. I don't bother to correct her. Is this love—this thing between us? I don't know.

Grace is pulled away by Samuel, who keeps glancing over his shoulder at me. I doubt he's jealous and if he is, he won't do shit about it. It's more likely he's pissed at Maddie yet can't take it out on her. I'll probably have to stand between Maddie and her characters a lot in the coming days.

Pushing from the porch, I brace myself. Others will wonder what I'm doing here—why I'm staying when I'm clearly not one of them. They're all looking for their happily ever afters. My own will be put on the back burner until she writes again. I don't know if it's love, and I'm not ready to even decipher my feelings for her. Clearly, there's something there.

I slip my arm around Maddie's waist, not wanting to interrupt her conversation. The man she's talking to looks so out of place in his three-piece suit. She sags into me, her exhaustion apparent. I tighten my grip on her and she sighs.

"I understand you don't want to be here, but I'm not the one who *brought* you here," she says with more patience than I would have.

He throws up his hands. "Who the fuck do I need to talk to then? Because I have a goddamn venue to run. I'm supposed to have three weddings this week alone."

"Didn't realize you could get a divorce that quickly," I mutter, and he snaps his mouth shut. Maddie's lips twitch, but she keeps her amusement to herself.

"Tate here runs a destination wedding venue on his family's vineyard." Maddie pulls in a calming breath. "And his sister is perfectly capable of running things while he is here. Although, I don't even know if that's needed. Time might stand still while you're...gone."

"But you don't know for sure," he growls, then points to a woman loitering nearby. "And why the hell is *she* here? You can't honestly think I'd fall for anyone, much less her. For fuck's sake, she's engaged to someone else. And I don't see that freeloader here."

Maddie presses her lips together and her body tenses. If this is the shit she's been dealing with, no wonder she looks so exhausted. Getting her away from this asshat is my first order of business.

"Sounds like you could use with a little time...away. Why don't you go check out the lake. Take a walk." The words are a suggestion, but my tone says he doesn't have an option.

He huffs like he'll argue, then thinks better of it and stalks away. The woman lingers, her body swaying between us and going after him.

"I should talk to her," Maddie murmurs, resting her head against my chest.

"No. You're going to come inside and eat. You need a break." Gently, I steer her around and guide her toward the cabin.

My surly face keeps everyone at bay until we reach the stairs. We're met with a wall of men, wearing matching dark expressions as they block our way. Half of them are in suits, the others dressed more casually, but they're all in black. And scary as hell.

"Well, shit." Maddie's feet stutter to a stop. "Listen, guys. I understand this isn't what you're used to, but if you don't get the fuck out of my way, I'll turn you all into heroes and make you save the damsels in distress."

One of them snorts, rolling his eyes. "As if Sage needs saving."

A wicked grin spreads across her face. "Then I'll write her out of your story and she'll find other men to play with rather than you four."

His lip curls, yet there's an edge of fear in his eyes. He shakes his head as he stomps away, disappearing into the forest. The others men in suits follow, and I wonder if they'll be back. Maddie glares at those left, and they hurry away without a word.

"Two different stories?" I ask and she nods.

Maddie deflates and I lead her inside. Usually, she'd sit at the island to watch me cook. Instead, she collapses onto the couch with a groan. By the time I'm done making her a sandwich, she's asleep. I don't have the heart to wake her, so I stick the plate in the fridge.

I'm covering her with a blanket when there's a tentative knock on the door. The last thing I want to do is deal with anyone. I doubt they'll go away, though. I glance at Maddie one last time before going to the door. They knock again and I bite back a growl. If they wake up Maddie, I'm going to end up throwing them off the porch.

Snarling, I rip open the door, ready to blast them. I stop short when I meet a woman's wide eyes.

"She's sleeping. You'll have to come back later." I soften my voice so I don't scare the poor kid. She's an adult, but she looks at least ten years younger than me.

"Oh, I didn't need her. I was actually hoping I could talk to you."

"Why the hell do you want to talk to me?" I run my fingers through my hair and then it hits me. "I'm not going to put in a good word for you."

I go to shut the door and her hand shoots out, slapping against the wood. "Shit. Sorry. I just need some advice."

I raise an eyebrow, waiting for her to speak. She doesn't. "What do you need?"

"Okay, so I'm Peyton. I kind of got tricked into—it doesn't matter. You see those guys over there?" She points to three guys throwing a football around with a couple others.

"The football players?"

She snorts, fighting a grin. "They're hockey players. Not that you'd know that. The thing is, they're really nice and fun and pretty."

"This sounds like a conversation you should have with Maddie."

She winces, shaking her head. "I got off track. The thing is, I'm pretty sure they only see me as a friend. Half the time when I see them around campus, they completely ignore me. And others picked up on that, and I'm really to the point where I don't think they want to be seen associating with me. How do I...I don't even know what I'm asking."

"You're asking how to get out of the semi-friendzone. Which isn't hard when it's guys."

She rolls her eyes. "I don't just want to sleep with them. I don't know how to ask what's wrong with me. Or what is it about me that makes them treat me like I'm invisible? Even if they don't want to be with me, fine. I can handle that."

"Can you?" I have a feeling she's in much deeper than she's letting on. If this is their story, though, they should all know they'll get a happy ending.

"Of course I can. I'm not attached or anything. I just thought college would be my fresh start, ya know? And then I met them, and it felt like—"

"Fate," I murmur.

I catch Grace's eye and jerk my head. Her gaze bounces between Peyton and me as she heads toward us.

"I just figured if someone could tell me what I need to work on, maybe I could avoid this in the future." She pinches the skin on her arm, glancing at the guys who are completely oblivious to her anxiety.

"Hey, Peyton. You okay?" Grace asks, resting her hand on the woman's lower back.

"What? Oh, yeah. Sorry to bother you." She smiles, but it looks more like a grimace.

She shuffles down the steps, and I realize I didn't give her any helpful advice. "Peyton," I call and she turns. "Just be yourself. And maybe call their asses out on it. Not going to be easy, but it might be what they need."

She nods, then skips over to the others. She plasters a grin on her face, not that any of them can tell it's fake. Grace sighs and I gesture her closer.

"Do they know?" I ask quietly, and she raises an eyebrow. "Do they know Maddie writes romance? That they'll be falling for each other?"

"Some of them do. Like Tate, the wedding guy." Her wide eyes find mine. "Don't call him that. At least not to his face. For others, they're still in the dark. Maddie hasn't gotten far enough in their stories for them to realize. They'll get there. Especially if they can help her along."

"I'm going to be honest, Grace. I don't know how much this is going to help. She's exhausted and overwhelmed."

"I'll see what I can do. I'm not an expert in this, just the first to show up."

My fingers dig into my palms as frustration rolls through me. "Better figure it out quick or I'm getting her the hell out of here one way or another."

Chapter Thirty-Two
Maddie

My lids flutter open, revealing a man's face, and I scream. My fist swings around out of instinct, yet it never connects. He moves too quickly for me to track, his cold hand enveloping mine.

"Ah, ah, little writer. None of that now. We merely have a few questions we'd like to ask." He tilts his head and a shiver rolls through me. "If I release you, will you try to hit me again?"

I shake my head, swallowing hard as he lets go and steps back. The shadows around the room don't even touch him, and I realize who he is. Most of my characters don't scare me. They're a product of my own imaginations and shouldn't be able to hurt me.

Then again, this man is a vampire. And an asshole. I have no idea how much the rules of their stories translate into this world. I push myself upright, hoping the new view will give me more leverage. As if I have any advantage over an immortal.

"Dray? Perhaps you'd like to ask since I put humans on edge," Ezio murmurs, never taking his eyes from me. My gaze darts to the other man lounging on the opposite couch.

Dray sighs as his foot drops to the ground and he rests his elbows on his knees. "If you weren't creeping up on her while she was sleeping, maybe she wouldn't be scared of you."

"She was sleeping too long." Ezio tucks his hands in his pockets, feigning nonchalance.

"Sorry, I was exhausted and overwhelmed by six dozen people showing up randomly and finding out they were products of my mind come to life and just needed to fucking sleep." All the frustration and turmoil bubble out until I can't take it anymore.

I don't want to talk to them. I don't want to deal with any of this. I don't want to even think about writing. It's too much and not enough, and there's nothing I can do about any of it. My emotions ping-pong around my chest, threatening to suffocate me. I was so excited once I got over the shock. Now I realize I didn't know what shock was.

"If you wanna take it out on Ezio, just let me know. I gotta find my phone first. And Ella. She'd find this shit hysterical." Dray grins, glancing between us.

"There will be no such happenings," the vampire says, baring his fangs. They barely slip below his bottom lip. Thank fuck he's not looking at me.

"Who the hell uses the word 'happenings' anymore? For fuck's sake. Step into the next century. I'm fucking begging you."

His lip curls as he eyes the shifter. "There's only one person I need to beg, and it certainly isn't you."

Dray coughs, sitting back as he buries his face in his elbow. I sigh before tucking my feet underneath me. I stash the little piece of information Ezio unknowingly revealed in the recesses of my mind. I have very little to go off of when it comes to him, and it drives me nuts. Beyond the fact that he's a vampire who may or may not be several centuries old, he's also obsessed with Ella. Part of me wonders if he'll warm up to Dray. Those two have the perfect setup for enemies-to-lovers. The hardest part would be getting Ezio past his prejudices against...well, everyone.

Glancing around, I try to spot Emmett, but he's nowhere to be found. He can't have gone far. The sun has barely set, and he wouldn't leave me alone. Especially not with these two. Even if he couldn't figure out that they weren't entirely human, he'd sense they were something supernatural. Emmett doesn't seem comfortable around any of my characters—particularly the fantasy ones.

"Anyways." I pull the word out and my muscles tense as their gazes swing to me. "What questions did you have?"

"I thought you were too overwhelmed and exhausted to engage," Ezio quips, and I glare at him.

"You forget I hold your fate in my hands, Ezio. You'd do well to not antagonize me."

He grimaces, nodding his head in defeat. Fucker. He's going to be a little bitch the entire time I'm writing him. I just know it. Some characters bounce around my mind, always ready and willing to help move their story forward. Others sulk in the background, too busy with their own thoughts to be bothered.

And then there's the ones like Ezio who think he knows better than me. Usually, I let him do his own thing, but this one's such a pillock. Which is exactly why I couldn't move forward with their story. Ezio kept interrupting, trying to force Dray out. Ella needs both of them, whether Ezio likes it or not, and everyone's just going to have to deal.

Dray clears his throat and I focus on him. "Here's the deal. We've obviously got some shit to work out, but we'd really appreciate if you focused on our story. Mostly because we can't find Ella and that's setting both of us on edge."

I shoot to my feet, the blanket pooling at my feet. "What do you mean, Ella isn't here?"

Not waiting for their response, I race for the deck. It's closer than the front door. Ezio steps to the side as I barrel past him and fling open the sliding door. I don't know all the rules of what's happening. I assumed all my characters from my WIPs were here. It's not like I counted them, though. Maybe I should have written them all down, but I didn't have them all named either. It's another thing to add to the list.

I scan the yard, but there aren't nearly as many people as there were earlier. Fire flickers through the brush where Emmett and I went to the bonfire. The groomsmen are probably hanging out. I wonder if others joined them. Laughter floats through the air, mingling with sounds from the insects and owls.

"We've looked for her everywhere. The lake, the shoreline, the yard," Dray mumbles from behind me.

"Did you look in the forest?" I glance over my shoulder when he doesn't answer.

A wordless conversation flows between them and Dray rushes for the door. Ezio watches before he launches over the couch, then turns to me.

"Please inform us if she appears."

I nod, and he grabs the railing before jumping over the edge. He lands cleanly fifteen feet below, and his image blurs as he races toward the woods. Kol whips his head around, following the vampire's progress. The demon turns slowly and meets my gaze. He glances around, then his shoulders curl slightly as dark wings materialize from his back.

I step away from the railing and wait for Kol to land in front of me. As he does, a crash from inside the cabin distracts me. Emmett's wide eyes flash, a glass shattered at his feet. My body sways toward him, but he shakes his head, shooing me back to the inevitable conversation with Kol.

"Didn't mean to startle him," Kol mutters as his wings vanish.

"I didn't think you could bring those out while here." I kick myself as soon as the words are out. Fuck. I feel like every interaction I have with them devolves into awkwardness delivered by yours truly.

"I didn't either." He grins, then winks, and I wrinkle my nose.

"Don't wink at me. It's creepy."

"Duly noted. Hate to be the bitch, but you need to get going. We're a restless bunch and the sooner you get your head out of your ass, the sooner we'll go away. Might I suggest you write ours first?"

"Everyone wants their book first. I can't write thirty stories at once." They don't seem to understand. I can't blame them. I essentially abandoned them all.

He runs his fingers through his ash blond hair as he glances over his shoulder. "Thing is, Nix is about to lose his shit. I don't know if he could start a forest fire, but I don't think you want to test that theory."

I find Nix lurking on the edge of the forest, Rune not far away, though they're not talking. Even from here and with the dying light, I can tell he's wound tight. Rune is tense too, but he's better at hiding it.

"I'll figure it out. It'll be fine," I murmur.

"Will it? Because we're all here for you. Maybe...Never mind. Just write." He shuffles toward the railing as if he'll tip right over to get away from me.

My hand shoots out, then drops before I reach him. He shies away from my touch, and I take a giant step back. Dealing with the characters and their quirks and traumas and back stories is usually easy because I'm only focused on one story at a time. Now that they're all in one place, it's hard to keep them straight. With someone like Kol, my mistakes could be costly.

"What were you going to say? Because I could use all the help I can get."

He doesn't look convinced as he bounces on the balls of his feet. "Break it into smaller groups. One massive one like this afternoon is not great. Maybe a dinner or head down to that fire that Nix is itching to get to. See how everyone interacts and see if it sparks something. Invite us first, though, since we need to find Evalie."

"You'll find her." The words slip out and I bite my lip.

He narrows his eyes, leaning closer. "You know where she is? Because if you know and you're not telling us..."

The threat hangs in the air between us. Being a brat to him like I was with Ezio will not end well for me. The problem is, I *do* know where she is. But if he blasts in there right now, the whole story will unravel, and they'll never get their happily ever after. I can't risk that happening. Especially since they're flesh and blood now.

"Time for you to go, Kol," Emmett growls from the doorway.

The demon jolts, glaring at Emmett, then me. With a huff, Kol spins and jumps over the side just like Ezio did. Emmett's hand envelops mine and tugs me into the cabin. Exhaustion swamps me once more.

"Are you okay? Do you want to eat?" He guides me into the kitchen and settles me on the stool.

I scrub my hands over my face, attempting to wipe away the anxiety swirling in my gut. Or at least the physical evidence of it. As he sets a plate in front of me, the glass clatters on the island. I should eat, even though it doesn't look appetizing at all. I doubt Emmett would let me get away without at least trying to force some of it down.

As I reach for the sandwich, he swoops in and snatches it away.

"Hey, I was going to eat that."

"No. You were going to force it down. I'll heat you up something else."

If I had it in me, I'd argue with him, even though he's right. The sandwich goes back in the fridge, and he pulls other stuff out. I lay my head on my arms, letting my mind wander as the sounds of his cooking fill the space. Kol's idea isn't a bad one. If I was able to talk to them in smaller groups, I wouldn't have to feel the weight of the gazes. It might not matter, though.

"Maddie, we need to talk."

I tense, not wanting to lift my head. His tone doesn't bode well for me. I imagine he finally hit the spiraling part, and he's changed his mind. His words from earlier were exactly what I needed at the time. They flowed from him without thought. Which is exactly the problem. If he was able to say them without second-guessing himself for even a second, what chance do I have that they were sincere? I'm sure he meant them at the time, but after the shock wore off...

"I can get someone to look at the car. I'm sure one of them knows how to fix it. I'd have to think about it." My voice is muffled by my arm, and I refuse to look at him. The last thing I want to do is have him seeing the devastation in my eyes.

I honestly thought this was it. Which is silly, considering it hasn't been that long since we met. He understands me, anticipates my desires, is fantastic in bed, and he actually wanted me. I don't know what he saw in me, but clearly the rose-colored glasses have been knocked off. If I could, I'd snatch them up and glue them to his face. The thought makes me snort.

"I'm not worried about the car," he says, and I peek at his back. "This isn't going to work."

My heart skips a beat and not in the way I want. I swallow hard before lifting my head, ready to face the end of what we started.

Chapter Thirty-Three

Emmett

As soon as I spot Maddie's face, I know I fucked up. I run through our conversation again and sigh.

"I didn't mean it like that. We need to talk about how you're going to navigate this situation. You can't throw yourself into the midst of chaos and expect everything to change."

Her eyes narrow even as the heartbreak in her eyes fades. Not completely, but enough that I know she's listening. We're clearly not on the same page. Or she doesn't believe me when I say I want to be here.

Both discussions are important, and I don't know which one to have first. Dealing with her character issue and proving to her I'm not going to run will hopefully happen all at once. My actions will have to speak for themselves, since she doesn't seem to trust my words.

She clears her throat, eyes fixing over my shoulder. "I don't know if I can do this right now."

"Apparently whatever I say you won't believe, anyway," I mutter, turning back to the stove.

"What's that supposed to mean?"

I dish up the pasta and drop it in front of her. "Eat. Then we'll see if you're ready to talk."

Usually, I'd sit next to her, but I can't bring myself to. I lean against the counter, focusing on my own bowl. No way am I putting myself in the line of fire when she's hungry. I shouldn't have brought this up until after she ate.

Only the scraping of our forks fills the room, setting my teeth on edge. I brace myself when she's done, waiting for another round of misunderstandings.

"Kol had the idea to break them up into smaller groups. Might be easier to figure out where to go." Her eyes droop just before she drops her head onto her folded arms.

I sigh, setting my bowl down and making my way toward her. Pressing my chest against her back, I cover her body with mine.

"You don't have to have a plan tonight, Maddie. You're not going to be able to go from not writing to churning out a thousand words."

She snorts, then her shoulders shake. Straightening, I slide onto the stool next to her, rubbing her back. I didn't mean to make her break down. I should have waited until tomorrow.

She lifts her head, a grin spread across her face, and I jolt.

"You're not crying."

"Nope. I forget most people don't know. A thousand words isn't all that much. It's not even a chapter. Unless you do that on purpose. If I want to finish a fraction of the stories, I'll have to write hundreds of thousands of words." She sobers, the corner of her mouth twitching. "Which is exactly the problem. I don't have the time, even if I had the creativity and stamina."

"You were excited when they first showed up. Which one do you want to start with? Because it's not about finishing them all. You just need one, right?"

"I suppose. I just have so many," she whines as she covers her face.

"None of this has to be sorted tonight. Why don't you go take a shower, then go to bed. We'll deal with it in the morning."

She nods, sliding from the stool and wobbling. I steady her before standing and lifting her into my arms, fitting my fingers underneath her ass. My cock hardens as she wraps her legs around my waist. When she nuzzles her face into my neck, I swallow a groan. She's going to be the death of me if she keeps it up. I won't deny her whatever support I can lend her. I grit my teeth as I carry her to the bedroom.

When we get there, I try to put her down, but she clings to me. "Gorgeous, you're still dressed. At least let me get your pajamas on."

All the tension in her body fades away as she unwinds her limbs from me. She hits the mattress, her entire being melting into a puddle, and I smile. Her eyes flutter closed as I tug her pants off, then struggle with her shirt since she's barely helping. I tug her upright and drop to my knees. Her forehead hits my shoulder and I loop my arms around her.

"Remind me," she breathes, her fingers curling in my shirt.

"Of what?" I whisper into her temple.

"Who I am. I've lived through my characters, tucked away in so many worlds, I think I forgot who *I* was. When I came here, I felt...alive. For the first time in a long time, I felt like I was me again. You reminded me of who I was deep down. I need that again. I know I shouldn't put that on you—"

I shush her as I run my fingers through her hair. I'm sick of her thinking I need an out or apologizing for something I freely gave to her. I wouldn't be here if I didn't want to be. Grace told me to find a purpose beyond her, but I think this is why we crossed paths. Being there for her might help me find who I'm supposed to be. And if all my life amounts to is reminding her how strong and capable she is, so be it.

She sits back, her hands falling to her lap. Exhaustion lines her eyes and I strip off her shirt. I don't know how to remind her of how tough she is, with or without me. But I can stay with her while she falls asleep. I pull off my own shirt and tug it over her head. She gathers the hem, bunching it in her fists, then buries her nose in the fabric.

Tossing back the comforter, I gesture for her to crawl between the sheets. I cover her, intending to slide in next to her, but she stops me.

"Just tell me I'm making the right decisions." She blinks at me, indecision swimming in her eyes.

I brush my lips against her forehead and breathe in her scent, letting it ground me to the present. "I can't promise you that. As long as you trust who you are, you'll make the right decisions for you."

"I don't know who I am."

I pull back, meeting her hooded gaze. "You're sweet and strong. You're capable and independent."

She snorts as a smile pulls at the edge of her lips. "Except I haven't made a single meal since I've been here. You even dressed me tonight."

"To be fair, most of the time I'm undressing you," I say, and she grins. "You're an amazing writer, Maddie."

"How would you know? You've never read any of my books."

"Do you honestly think all your characters would defy the laws of our universe to manifest into existence if you weren't?" I don't know if that's how this works. I'm hoping she buys it, though.

She sighs, cuddling farther under the covers. "Maybe. Guess we'll see how good I am when I start writing again."

I don't point out her use of the word "when" instead of "if." She's not in the right headspace for that. It doesn't matter anyway. She'll get there, eventually. If I have to keep reminding her how amazing she is, then I will. I wait until she falls asleep, her light breaths filling the room.

As the minutes tick by, I can't help the anger growing in my gut. They showed up without a word of warning and ambushed her. They sent her into a tailspin, defeating the purpose of them showing up in the first place. While the guilt might not solely rest on any one character's shoulders, I know who I'm going to blame.

"Grace," I bellow as I step onto the porch.

There are only a few people milling about the yard now. Their gazes follow me as I stomp down the stairs. Grace appears around the corner, and I wonder where she wandered off to. In fact, I have no idea where they'll go at night.

Do I need to get more tents? Is the lawn going to look like a campsite? If they burn the grass, I'm going to fucking lose it. I'm not a goddamn landscaper. Shit. I have to ask Grace about feeding them, too.

"I'm not a fucking dog, Emmett. Please don't call for me like I am." Gone is the meek woman who was hesitant of any missteps. It's as if as soon as her secret was revealed, she was able to shed the facade.

"I don't know what the fuck you all are doing, but it needs to stop. Maddie won't survive if everyone keeps bombarding her like this. And where are they going to sleep? How about eat? It's like no one thought about basic human necessities." My chest heaves as my heart pounds in my chest.

"Shit," a man mutters as he stomps up to us, glaring at Grace. "Sit down before you pass out."

His hand hits my shoulder, shoving me toward the ground. My ass hits the dewy grass, and he pushes my head between my legs.

"I have this handled, Samuel," she says through gritted teeth.

"Looks like it. Why don't you just go and read a book or something? And it's Sam," he growls as he crouches in front of me.

My vision blurs and I clamp my mouth shut so I don't puke on him. If I wasn't fighting for air, I'd tell him off for snapping at her. Guilt floods me when I realize I did the same thing. And I didn't just snap at her—I full-on yelled. Most of my tirade wasn't about her, but I sure directed it at her. I let my emotions get the better of me in my haste to protect Maddie.

"Don't you patronize me." She shoves him out of the way and takes his place in front of me. "Emmett, I understand. You're worried about Maddie, and I understand."

"I'm sorry," I mutter.

"You're fine. Contrary to popular belief, I can handle it. And I know you're not upset with me."

A rumbling from Sam has Grace glaring at him again. He's too busy shooting daggers at me to notice, though.

He steps closer, nostrils flaring. "Why are you apologizing? What did you do?"

"Oh my God. You can't be an ass to me, then turn around and defend me. Either stand next to me or get the hell out of my way," Grace hisses.

Sam throws up his hands and stomps away, mumbling about her wishy-washy behavior. The tightness in my lungs eases and I pull in steady breaths. I don't think it was a panic attack, but I'm not ruling anything out.

"That your happily ever after?"

"Honestly, I'm starting to question Maddie's judgement. Perhaps her writer's block jumbled up the stories and she plopped Mister Asshat in mine on accident." She sighs, dropping and crossing her legs. "What's she doing?"

"Sleeping. Where are all these people going to go?"

"Well, as you probably noticed, a lot of them have dispersed. They disappeared into the forest, but they'll be back tomorrow. I have a feeling the groomsmen will camp out by the lake." She gestures toward the bonfire that's barely visible.

"The groomsmen?"

She waves away my question, glancing toward the trees. "You don't need to feed us. I mean, we can eat, but it's as if we can go a long time without. Same with the bathroom." She grins and the rest of my anxiety seeps into the ground.

"Well, I'm glad I don't have to buy a bunch of buckets."

She gasps, pressing her hand against her chest. "How dare you, sir. I do not pee in a bucket. I'm a goddamn lady. I'd do it if the alternative was a men's locker room, though. Hands down—every time."

"You spend a lot of time in guy's locker rooms?"

She shakes her head, a secret hiding within her smile. "Another story for another time. Hopefully, one Maddie will be able to finish."

"She's struggling, Grace. And I don't know how to help her." I drop my head in my hands. "It hasn't even been a day and she's overwhelmed. She went from one end of the spectrum to the other."

"You're right. It's only been a day. She'll figure it out. It's what she does."

"I don't know what that means. I can't even wrap my head around all of you living in her mind to begin with."

She laughs lightly, tucking a strand of hair behind her ear. "Us mere mortals will never understand the way a writer's mind works. We'd hurt ourselves if we tried."

I glace up, shooting her a skeptical look. "Are you even mortal?"

"No idea. I feel like I am, but I'm probably not the best judge."

"I just want to help her. And I heard you earlier when you said I needed purpose. But what if this *is* my purpose? At least right now."

She gives me the courtesy of thinking it over instead of scolding me right off the bat. After a minute, though, my stomach begins to twist itself into knots. I feel like I'm missing something—some secret Grace is hiding from me.

"When you're around Maddie, do you worry about those things?" she finally asks.

"No."

"So she quiets the parts of your mind that question who you are? Or what you should be doing with your life?"

"Yeah. She does," I breathe, the realization wrapping around me like a soft blanket.

"Then I suppose you have your answer."

Chapter Thirty-Four
Maddie

"I promise I'm full, Emmett," I say with a laugh. He's been trying to force one more pastry on me for the last ten minutes.

"You didn't eat lunch yesterday," he grumbles, dropping it onto the plate on the dining table.

"You've been feeding me every meal. Missing one won't matter. Besides, I need to come up with a plan today. Those bitches have been wallowing in limbo for a week since they got here. I'm going to organize my WIPs and figure out which characters I need to invite to lunch. And no, you're not cooking." I grab my plate and take it into the kitchen. I'm not used to cooking for large groups of people, but I'm not about to make Emmett take that on.

He follows me and transfers the pastries I forgot the names of into a container. I'm pretty sure he woke up early to bake them, though there's no evidence of that on the counter. My mind wanders back to the scones at the bed-and-breakfast. I wonder if Emmett could recreate them.

"You can't tell me I'm not allowed to cook. I like it. Gives me something to do. Plus, you have more important things to worry about than a menu."

My eyes glaze over, not really seeing the counter in front of me. The tip of my tongue slips between my teeth as my mind spins, sorting through my memories. The bed-and-breakfast I stayed when I was on the way up here felt off, like it wasn't reality. I assumed it was merely because there aren't many places this far north. Questions roll through my head, piling up and blocking out the real world.

"Chloe made the reservation. She's not a character, though. Unless I made her up. No, that doesn't make sense." I pinch the bridge of my nose, trying to ease the headache forming.

"Hey there," Emmett murmurs, his hands grabbing my waist and tugging me toward him. "What's going on?"

"I'm just trying to figure out how much of my life I made up in my head and what's real."

"Wouldn't it be real whether it was in your head or not?"

I scowl, narrowing my gaze. "You know what I mean."

"Not really. I'm just a supporting character in your story, gorgeous." He grins and I roll my eyes.

"It's called a side character, but whatever. I still have to do some planning and I hate it."

I'm whining and not making any sense, but I think I deserve it. This entire situation isn't how I expected my vacation to go. Then again, it wasn't supposed to be a vacation at all. Maybe a working vacation. Chloe would be kicking my ass up and down the shoreline if she knew how much I've procrastinated.

"I hate to tell you this, Maddie, but you already organized your files." He shakes me a little and my eyes find his. "What else are you worried about?"

"You don't think Chloe is a character, right?" I've already convinced myself she isn't, but I need outside confirmation.

"Well, did she just show up one day out of the blue?"

I squeeze my eyes shut. "Yes. She used to go to private school and then she randomly showed up in class."

"And were you the first one to talk to her?"

My brows pull low, both at his question and trying to recall the memory from the deep recesses of my mind. I don't understand why he's asking, though.

"I don't think so. I remember when the teacher introduced her, I was jealous because I wanted her name. So, the teacher talked to her first. Why?"

"Didn't you notice that none of your characters talked to me until you did? They were too focused on you to notice anyone else. Plus, have you ever written her?"

I let out a heavy breath, mentally letting go of the anxiety riding me. "Okay. Fine. Real people in my life: Chloe, my family, and you. Everyone else is suspicious."

He laughs as he drops his hands and returns to putting away the food. I grab my computer and take it into the dining room, making a hard right before I set it on the table. That surface is nothing but a distraction in the making. Every time I close my eyes, I see Emmett standing over me, telling me to come for him. Maybe I'll use that to my advantage when I write a spicy scene.

The thought pulls me up short, and I hover by one of the couches. I have no idea how much control I have over my characters. Usually, it doesn't matter since they're stuck in my head. Now that they're roaming around, I don't know what they'll do. If they seize my plot and go off on a tangent, I don't worry about it. I can either fix it in editing or let them do their thing. Now that they're out in the wild, I wonder if they're going to start ripping off their clothes in the middle of the lake. Will the others form a ring around them while they fight? Will they stalk each other through the trees?

"Maddie?" Emmett's voice breaks through the haze. He grabs the computer and sets it on the coffee table.

"I don't want to second-guess what I'm writing. I don't want them whispering in my ear, trying to convince me to go a different way." My gaze collides with his as my thoughts tumble together.

"Aren't they whispering in your ear, anyway? At least this gives you a little separation."

I bite my lip, gnawing while I consider his words. His thumb pulls the flesh from between my teeth. My lids flutter, anticipating his kiss, but it never comes.

His hand drops from my face and he's halfway across the house before I come to my senses. A sound echoes in the back of my throat and he throws a smirk over his shoulder. Bastard did that on purpose.

"Two can play at that game, sir."

His feet stutter to a stop, and he slowly turns to face me. "Sir?"

"Problem?"

Desire flares in his eyes as he scans me up and down, and heat settles between my legs. My body sways toward him yet doesn't take the bait. He merely pivots on his heel and prowls to the door.

Collapsing on the couch, I shudder. With just one look, he's reduced me to a puddle and thoroughly derailed my train of thought. Which isn't a bad thing since I was about to spiral again. I need to stop worrying about the what-ifs and get to work.

I grab my laptop and flip it open. While I wait for it to boot up, I rest against the back of the couch. I roll my head to the side and try to figure out who Emmett is talking to at the front door. He's blocking the way and they're speaking too softly for me to figure it out. I close my eyes, letting my mind wander.

Someone clears their throat and I jolt upright. "I apologize for disturbing you. I'm Gideon."

"Yup, I know. I kind of invented you." I don't know if that's the right way to put it. From the scowl on his face, he thinks it's shit, too.

"I overheard someone speaking of your...proclivities toward *feelings*." He utters it like it's a dirty word.

"If by feelings you mean making people express emotions, I suppose I have ...proclivities toward that."

"I'd like you to refrain from applying those to whatever story you've started with Charlette and myself. We're perfectly content with the way things are." He straightens the cuffs on his dark suit, nodding as if he doesn't need a response.

"Have you talked to Charlie about this?"

His head jerks up at my use of her nickname. From what I remember, he's a bit possessive of his little pet name for her. I smile sweetly at him as I tap my finger on my keyboard. He tucks his hands in his pockets, but not before I notice the slight trembling.

"We both are getting what we want out of our agreement. We'll be free to go our separate ways soon enough. No reason to fiddle with the story."

I suppose an arranged marriage would be classified as an agreement. Him tricking her into it, though, takes away some of the collaboration. And as hard as he fights against the plot, he doesn't want to leave her. I can't figure out if he's lying to himself or me. I hold up a finger when he opens his mouth. He snaps it shut, scowling again.

I pull up their story. There isn't much there since I had the idea right before I lost myself in complete writer's block. For a long while, I could start a book but would crash and burn by a certain point. Eventually, I couldn't even write. Poor Charlie never had a chance. At least I took some notes so I wouldn't lose it in the chaos of my mind. Reading through them, I don't find much to help.

"I'll see what I can do. However, no one wants to read a book where the two main characters just dissipate. I could branch out, though. Maybe turn it into a murder mystery?" I track the emotions playing in his dark eyes.

"I hardly have time to solve a murder. That'd be absurd."

"Oh, no. You misunderstand." I brace myself for the inevitable explosion he's about to have. "I was going to have *you* be the murderer. And of course you'd have to kill Charlie. I think that would be a good twist. Maybe I could steer the reader into thinking it was her."

His nostrils flare and his hands curl into fists in his pants. I know he won't hurt me. My muscles tense anyway. Gideon might be involved in some shady shit, but he doesn't hurt innocent people. It's how I write my characters—morally grey anti-heroes, ethics wrapped in shadows. At least when I'm in the mood. Sometimes I need a break from the darkness and write fluffy ones frolicking through the tulips. I always seem to come back to the shadows, though.

"What possible motive could I have for taking Charlette out?"

"Maybe she's a mole planted by a rival mafia family. Her father orchestrated the whole thing, manipulating you. Well, the entire Ashford family, actually. I could have Gabriel and Charlie hook up behind your back." The more I talk, the redder his face gets, and he yanks his hands from his pockets, then balls them by his sides.

"You wouldn't," he growls.

I drop the sweet smile. "I will if you don't back the fuck off."

He leans away, flustered more than I anticipated. I didn't expect him to be close to tears. I honestly think he'd break down if I did anything to Charlie. Even if I made her the villain of the story, he wouldn't be satisfied. For him, it's all or nothing for her. She either lives happily ever after or I'll hear the brunt of his tirades.

"Duly noted." He nods before spinning on his heel and stomping past a very confused Emmett and Rylie.

"Where the hell did he come from?" Rylie whispers from the corner of her mouth.

"No fucking clue," Emmett mutters, then focuses on me. "You good?"

"Of course. I was just putting Mr. Ashford in his place. I'm sure he'll be patient and grateful for whatever I write now." I grin, then turn back to my computer.

I pull up Rylie's file next, inserting her name now that I know where she belongs. I'm sure that's why she's here. More will come, expecting me to listen to their woes. They'll make demands, and I'll have to cater each response to their personality. It's exhausting when I think about it.

Rylie plops onto the other couch, considerably dressed down from the first time I saw her. She tucks her legs underneath her, showing off the holes in her knees.

She tugs at her tank top as she glances around the cabin. "This place is awkward. Like it can't figure out if it wants to be rustic or rich."

"Emmett is fixing some of the more rustic parts so no one dies from falling off the deck," I say as he settles next to me. He leaves just enough space between us to be noticeable.

"I already fixed the deck. And the porch. No one is dying," He stretches, setting his arm on the back of the couch behind me.

I roll my eyes as his fingers brush against my shoulder. "How are you not overheating in sweatpants, Rylie?"

"What?" Her gaze focuses on me. "Oh, I dunno. But I've been forced to wear pencil skirts and blouses for weeks now. I needed comfort in my life after dealing with my asshole of a boss who doesn't even know my name. By the way, should he be here? Got any idea what's up with that?"

"No? I don't even know how *you're* here, much less him. Has he...hold on."

I skim the last chapter I wrote in their story, realizing they haven't met in person yet. I forgot I pulled out the timeline. Aiden can't fire her unless he has permission from his brother, and Aiden's been putting off talking to him. Now I understand why he said he was coming to the cabin when I first met Rylie. At the end of this chapter, he's getting on a plane. I wonder if he's in limbo, getting more frustrated by the minute since the plane won't land. Or is he in a black hole of nothingness?

I read the last sentence again, tilting my head. Closing my eyes, my mind fills with words and images—Aiden on a plane, muttering to himself as he types out a scathing email to his brother. My lids flutter open, and my fingers move without thought, opening a new page. The rest of the world falls away as the story flows. Finally, the words come.

Chapter Thirty-Five

Emmett

I'm not trying to read what Maddie is typing, but it's hard. I keep glancing at Rylie, who looks like she has the same idea as I do—keeping as still and as quiet as possible. Moving might spook Maddie and kill her inspiration. My hand starts to cramp, though I'm loath to switch positions. My fingers tremble, barely touching her skin. Slowly, I ease them off her and she shivers, but she never stops typing.

Ten minutes later, Rylie and I are still playing the waiting game. A soft knock at the front door has Maddie's head twitching, and I tense. Rylie's wide eyes meet mine. Whoever it is might go away, but I'm not willing to risk it.

Easing my arm away, I hold my breath. When she doesn't react, I gently push myself from the couch. It isn't easy since the cushions sink in. Rylie gives me an indecipherable look, and I exhale gently. I've never focused more on not tripping than I am right now. The knocking doesn't stop and I shuffle faster.

Pulling the door open, I bite my tongue so I don't start yelling. One of the younger hockey players nervously runs his hand through his light hair. He glances at Peyton, who's hanging out with a group of others in the yard thirty feet away. Somehow, they've acquired a bunch of lawn chairs. The urge to yell at them to not build a firepit fills me and I glare at them.

"Uh, everything okay? You're not going to yell at them to get off your lawn or something, right?" He grins, laugh lines creating grooves around his mouth.

"Last thing we need is a forest fire."

"Oh, they won't do that. Actually, I don't even know if we can burn shit down." He holds his hands up. "Not that I'd do that. Honestly, I'm just here for some advice."

"What the fuck is up with everyone asking me for advice?" I mutter.

"So, I should...leave?" He takes a step back and I roll my eyes, then step outside.

I close the door softly, not wanting to disturb Maddie, and gesture for him to follow me around the house, away from the others. It's not exactly private with so many people still gathered. At least his friends won't overhear.

"What do you need?" I ask as I collapse onto one of the Adirondack chairs set up on the side porch.

He sits next to me, legs flailing as he slides to the back. "Kolby, by the way. My name. Uh, I saw you talking to Peyton yesterday."

"And you thought I'd tell you what we talked about? Not a fucking chance." I know enough about women to understand that would be a mistake.

"What? Hell no. I just thought maybe she told you what was going on with us. And you might have asked the writer about us. And maybe you could give me a little insight into what we have in store?" He holds his hands up again as if I'm going to punch him. "No details or anything. I'm just looking for vibes."

I eye his hopeful face. I don't often feel old, but staring at him, I definitely feel it. No grooves other than the laugh lines. No receding hairline or greying. His skin is pretty flawless, which I usually wouldn't notice. He just looks so young. Life hasn't beaten him down. He plays hockey, though, so maybe his knees creak when he stands. It'd make me feel better.

"Vibes, huh? You sure you're not searching for the ending?" I ask, and he shakes his head. "I'm not going to tell you anything. Unless you need something else, I can't help you."

He presses his lips together, wrestling with himself. He's got questions and I'm guessing they center around Peyton. I doubt he'll ask them. His fingers drum against the arm of the chair as he works through his issues.

"So, I can't ask you about the ending. Or the vibes. Or about your conversation with P."

"Nope. None of that."

"But I *can* ask about how to flirt. You seem like a guy who knows how to do that."

"I get the feeling you don't have problems with flirting."

He sighs, his brows pulling low, and he frowns. "Except not that kind of flirting. This is...important. The other shit is just for funsies. But how do you flirt with someone you actually want to be with?"

I don't know how to answer him. Now I'm the one with the questions I won't ask. It's none of my business if he's in love with Peyton or not. Bringing this to Maddie won't help. She's already worried about her stories being influenced by these people. Kolby's expectant face sits in front of me, begging me for a scrap of insight.

"Maybe instead of focusing on the flirting, you focus on her. Them. Whoever you're trying to be with. It's not about your game. It's about being there for them. Stop thinking you're the center of this." I have no idea if this advice is good or not. Kolby's nodding, but that doesn't mean I made any sense.

"Okay, so just be myself and focus on her. Got it." He pushes to his feet, then spins to face me. "What if I don't know how to be who I am?"

"You're young. You'll learn."

He laughs, tucking his hands in his pockets. "Guess I'll figure it out. I'll just have to get her to not see me as a friend."

"What? Fuck no. You want to be her friend. Be the best fucking friend you can be. Why is everyone so terrified of being friend-zoned? All you have to do is treat her respectfully. Why is that so fucking hard?" I drop my head in my hands.

"Listen, just tell her how you feel and be her friend. Don't wait around for her to figure it out."

"Yeah, okay. Listen, might not be my place, but you should probably talk to the writer."

"Maddie. Her name is Maddie. And I talk to her every day."

"Sure, but do you ever tell her how you feel? Seems like that little nugget was more for you than it was for me."

He waves awkwardly, then walks away. What a fucking asshole. For someone who doesn't know how to flirt, he sure seems to think he's pretty smart. The smirk he gave me as he delivered his advice was a little much. He doesn't understand Maddie's and my relationship. She's dealing with enough shit without me dropping a bomb on her. I'm perfectly content showing her how I'm feeling in the form of multiple orgasms.

I shove to my feet and follow him. When I round the corner, I find Kolby back with the group, forcing himself to laugh along with them. None of the others seem to notice. I watch them for another minute, debating whether I should join them. I open the front door instead, leaving them on their own.

Stepping inside, I blink rapidly to banish the black spots floating in my vision. Gently, I close the door, not wanting to interrupt Maddie's writing. I close my eyes and lean against the wood. I need a plan on how to support her, but I have no idea what that looks like.

"Oh, hey," Maddie calls from the kitchen and my lids flutter open. "I was thinking of making sandwiches for lunch. Do we have burgers? I wanted to do a cookout. Maybe not tonight, but soon. Oh, and I figured out I probably won't need to meet with all of them. They're an impatient bunch so they'll probably just pop up like Gideon did."

Rylie stops in front of me, raising an eyebrow. "You good?"

"I'm fine. How much did she write?"

She scowls, glancing over her shoulder. "Too fucking much, in my opinion. You know what she decided to do? Bring him here. She put him on a plane to come here. Who fucking does that?"

"The writer. You know what she writes, right?"

She waves away my question. "I was hoping she wouldn't make me fall for *him*. I kept thinking he was just a red herring. Then someone else would pop up and...she seems determined to shove Aiden—Mr. Sullivan and me together."

"Trust the process, Rylie. Not the first book she's written."

She nods, then shakes her head. "I need to get out of here."

I step to the side and let her slip out the door. She seems to hold herself separate from the others, hovering on the fringes. Aiden, Mr. Sullivan, whatever she wants to call him, coming here might alienate her even more.

"Maddie, do you think they can leave if you write it in the story like with Aiden?" I ask as I lean against the counter while she sits on the stool across from me.

"I don't think so. I've got a theory that they're stuck here until I finish their story. I won't know until I actually finish one. Which is exactly why I'm going to invite Andie and Sebastian to lunch. I assume their whole group will want to come too." She grins before shoving a croissant in her mouth. I don't know where she got them since I haven't been to the store in weeks.

"I think the cabin is keeping us here. The car breaking down. My truck going missing. More food showing up randomly. It doesn't make sense."

She laughs, more joy radiating from her than I've seen since we met. I caught glimpses of this woman, but she's never been this free. I'm hesitant to ask how many words she wrote. No matter how many, it's better than what she had before. And it clearly has taken some of the weight off her shoulders.

"Isn't it so random? I'm chalking it all up to magic. Mostly because if I think about it too hard, my brain will shut down. Plus, if I keep getting croissants, I'm not going to question things. Oh, and Jordan has experience with construction stuff, so I thought he could help you with the roof. Then I don't have to worry about you getting hurt." She slides her computer closer and wakes it up.

If she's not worried about the strange things happening here, then I won't be, either. I'm sure my mind will file away all the other things that crop up. I won't be able to stop myself from gathering up the information. Maddie might be able to ignore the signs of magic, but I can't. My truck is the thing that pisses me off the most. I don't know if that's magic or if someone stole it. Not that I was attached to it. I barely remember what it looks like.

"How many words did you get?" I ask as I turn to make myself a cup of coffee.

"Only five hundred. I'm out of practice, so while the words were coming, my mind was a little off track. As long as I don't fall down another rabbit hole of nothingness, it'll get better."

I spin to face her. "What do you mean, only five hundred? I was gone for like twenty minutes."

She glances up, smiling. "We've had this conversation before, Emmett. I'm just out of practice. If I can get back into the swing of things, I'll be fine. And I can finally finish these stories."

"All of them?" Alarm rolls through me, settling in my chest.

She only has two and a half months left at the cabin. And there's a lot of fucking characters here. I have no idea how long it takes to write a book. I'm sure it's different for everyone and Maddie seems fast, but I can't imagine she can finish all of them by the time autumn sets in.

The ache in my chest grows at the thought of her leaving. I don't know where I'll go after this. I doubt she'll want to stay here forever. Especially if this place allows her characters to randomly appear. She might not want to live like that. Following her back home seems desperate, though. Either way, we may not have a future. Pushing the panic aside, I struggle to ignore the pain.

"I can't write that much. Which, again, we've talked about. Although, not all of them are at the beginning like Rylie and Aiden's story is. Which is why I'm wanting Andie and Seb to come for lunch. Theirs is over halfway done. I just have to get over this little hump. Tack on an epilogue at their wedding and it's done."

I lean on the other side of the island, determined to focus on the present. "You gonna put what happens on the wedding night in there?"

She smirks, a slight blush dusting across her cheeks. "Maybe. I might need some inspiration. That something you could help me with?"

I open my mouth to tell her exactly how much I can help when someone knocks on the door. Maddie laughs as I drop my forehead to the counter, banging my head against the surface.

Her breath hits the shell of my ear and my cock twitches. "I'll get rid of them. You get ready to demonstrate your skills."

I groan as her footsteps fade. This woman is precisely what I need. A lot of people worry about their partner fitting into their life. It wasn't a fear of mine. It barely crossed my mind until Maddie tumbled into my world. I like taking care of her. I like helping her. I like having her by my side. And when the time comes, I don't know if I'll be able to let her go.

Chapter Thirty-Six

Maddie

I nod along as Austin blathers on about his work. A lot of times I pick a random job and keep the details vague. At least with my contemporary romances. The mafia and fantasy ones are easier. I'm pretty sure I made this guy an actuary. What the hell was I thinking? I'll have to change it, which pisses me off. Good thing I'm not too far into his story.

Grace tiptoes around the corner, and I send pleading eyes at her. She's been a godsend at distracting everyone while I get my shit together. I thought talking to my characters would jump-start something, but it's mostly been me avoiding them. Or getting excited, then blanking when I get in front of my computer.

My emotions have been on a rollercoaster for too long. I'm honestly getting nauseous at this point. After the high of writing a part of Aiden and Rylie's story, I thought I'd broken through some invisible barrier. I was quickly brought back down to earth when I blanked again for almost a week.

Grace winces, then shakes her head as she walks over.

"Austin? I need a favor. See, Maddie needs someone to look over her taxes. Is that something you could help us with?" Grace asks, widening her eyes at me.

"Well, I don't usually focus on the tax side of things, but I could probably have a look," he mutters, allowing Grace to lead him away.

I let out a sigh before turning to go back inside. Hopefully, Emmett is still waiting for me and didn't wander away. Maybe I should let him wander. He has other shit to get done. And so do I. Then again, a little inspiration never hurt anyone.

My hand hits the knob and someone calls my name. I knock my forehead against the wood and let out a groan. Straightening, I plaster on a smile. The door swings open and Emmett grabs my wrist, yanking me inside. I yelp as I fall into his arms, and he laughs as he kicks it shut.

"You looked like you needed saving," he says, and his fingers dig into the crease under my ass.

"I shouldn't have answered the door in the first place. The man kept trying to explain to me what an actuary was. I still don't really understand it. Something about numbers and risks. Now I have to change his occupation."

Emmett nuzzles my neck, lifting me onto my tiptoes. I wind my arms around his shoulders, and he swings me up. We're halfway through the kitchen, his teeth grazing against the sensitive skin, and I tell him to stop. His head jerks up, but he doesn't put me down.

"Sorry, I just need to write it down so I don't forget. Gotta change it before he corners me again."

He grins, setting me on the counter of the island, and I grab a pen and sticky note. As soon as I finish, he rips it from my hands and tosses it on the floor. Guess I'll find it later. I squeal when he picks me up again and tip my head back as he shuffles toward the bedroom. Gone are the days where we christened the cabin, I suppose. I wonder if I can give the characters a day pass. I doubt they'd be able to leave or some of them would have done it already.

Emmett drops me onto the bed, and I squeal, almost bouncing off the mattress. By the time I recover, he's already undressed and stroking his cock. Licking my lips, I stare as he hardens.

I don't usually have the urge to drop to my knees for a man. Sometimes I have issues with men going down on me, too. Right now, I'm imagining how dark his eyes would get if I did. Echoes of his inevitable groans fill my ears as I fantasize about swirling my tongue around his tip. The longer I picture it, the more I want to do it.

Nerves bubble in my stomach, but I ignore it as I slide from the bed to my knees. He sucks in a sharp breath, and I glance up at him. When my nails dig into his thighs, he grips my hair and tips my head back. A delicious burn spreads across my scalp, and I bite my lip.

I flick out my tongue and lick the tip. His breath becomes ragged as I draw the head into my mouth. When I take him deeper, his eyes flutter shut. I hum and he meets my gaze. While this might be something I'm doing for him, it's also for me. I want his attention on me, not wandering off.

My cheeks hollow as I suck hard, worried about whether I'm doing this right. From the flush on his face, I shouldn't be concerned. I swirl my tongue around the tip and his thighs clench under my hands. His fingers flex, gripping my hair, and I take him deeper.

His hips jolt forward, and his cock hits the back of my throat. I swallow instinctively and his breath hitches. He pulls out slowly, then plunges back in. I wrap one hand around his base and my lips crash into the makeshift barrier I've created. I may not have the urge to gag yet, but I'd rather it not happen at all. He moans as he thrusts over and over, his gaze fixed on me. I drop my hand just as he buries his cock deep.

"Fuck," he grunts, forcing my head back, and he slips from my mouth.

I lick my lips and swallow several times. He shakes his head when I open my mouth again and I pout.

"But I—"

"I know what you want, gorgeous, but I'm not coming down your throat."

"Why not?" I whine.

His thumb brushes across my cheek. "Because I refuse to come before you do. Understood?" He waits until I nod before releasing me. "Clothes off. On the bed."

"Yes, sir," I say coyly and he growls.

I scramble to obey him, flinging my shirt and shorts aside and dropping onto my back on the comforter. He smirks, and my body thrums in anticipation. A yelp leaves me when he drags me to the edge of the mattress.

"Emmett," I gasp as he sinks to his knees. "You don't have to."

He glares at me. "There is no *have to* when it comes to savoring your pussy, gorgeous. I *want to*. Every fucking day of my goddamn life if I have a choice."

I open my mouth to argue and a moan slips out instead as his tongue flicks at my clit. My mind checks out the longer he spends between my thighs. My fingers dive into his hair, gripping the strands. I tug him closer and he growls, the sound vibrating through me. Pleasure overwhelms my senses and I push him away, all while snapping my legs close to keep him right where he is.

He hums, sending shockwaves through me. My legs buck and his large hands wrap around my thighs. When his tongue flicks against my clit over and over, I tumble over the edge. My back arches and I gasp as stars sparkle across my vision. This is exactly what I've been missing—us together.

"Such a lovely sight," he murmurs into my skin.

My breath wheezes from me, my limbs jelly as they plop onto the mattress. I yelp as he sinks his teeth into my thigh. I prop myself onto an elbow and glare at him. He shoots me a cheeky grin before repeating the move. I squeal, shoving his head away from me while he chuckles.

"Come here," he commands as he stands and holds out a hand to me.

"Where are we going?" I ask, even as I weave our fingers together.

He tugs me up, then pulls me toward the door. "Fulfilling a fantasy of mine."

I peek around the cabin, slightly worried someone will pop in while I'm completely naked. Emmett doesn't seem to have the same concerns as he saunters alone, his ass flexing with each step. My mouth waters and the urge to bite him overtakes me.

He glances over his shoulder as he drops my hand. "Stay there while I get these couches out of the way. And stop looking at me like that."

"Like what?" I ask innocently.

"Like you're going to beg me to fuck your face again."

I pout, but he's already turned away. We don't use the small sitting area right off the bedroom. I don't even know why they have it here or why they stuffed three couches around the fireplace. In the winter, it might be nice, I suppose.

Emmett grabs a thick blanket and spreads it out in a flourish, then points at me. "You here. On your hands and knees."

"This is your fantasy? To fuck me in front of a fireplace?" Again, in the winter months with a roaring fire it would be nice, but it's the middle of summer and the grate is cold.

"Actually, it's to fuck you in front of the window as the sun sets. Or rises. Or the moon shines down on your beautiful skin. But I'd rather the others not watch you come on my cock."

I settle on my hands and knees and glance back at him. "You won't be able to see me come if I'm like this."

"I wouldn't be so sure of that." He tips his chin toward the bedroom and I face forward.

He's propped the mirror previously hanging on the wall on the floor and my eyes meet his in the reflection. He smirks and I wonder how long he's planned this fantasy of his. Excitement rolls through me. Tonight is definitely going to be one to remember.

Emmett sets my laptop on my lap, and I yelp as it scrapes across my nipple. I don't know what he was thinking, but he snatches the computer back. The bed bounces as I scoot to the side. I rub the injury, whining as his eyes glaze over.

"They're not going to talk to you," I mutter as I cross my arms over my chest.

He shakes his head, then runs his tongue across his lips. "I bet I could persuade them to find their voice."

I roll my eyes and grab Emmett's shirt off the side of the bed. Pulling it over my head, he groans in mock complaint. He sets my computer on my lap again, and I flip it open. One of these days, I'm going to have to get on a schedule. But today is not that day. The rest of today is for bedroom activities and writing.

My fingers hover over the keys as I stare at the screen. My muscles tense and my hands begin to shake the longer the words escape me. They're stuck behind a wall erected in my mind. My lids flutter shut, and I throw my head back against the headboard. The mattress dips as Emmett slides in next to me.

"Do I need to motivate you?" he murmurs, and I let out a startled laugh.

"They were there before. Rylie started talking and it just happened. The itch was back and I thought, *this is it.* I didn't have to worry anymore." My fears tumble out of me, one after another. I snap my mouth shut, cutting off the deluge of thoughts.

"Don't do that," he whispers, brushing my hair over my shoulder. "Tell me what's going on in that pretty little head of yours."

"I didn't realize men actually said shit like that."

"Because you weren't dating the right kind of men." He smirks, then presses a kiss on my temple.

My mind latches onto one word—*dating.* We've never talked about where we were in this relationship. I don't even know if I should call it a relationship. Being here together, essentially trapped, makes it difficult to have those conversations. Future isn't in our vocabulary. Not yet, anyway. I've been shoving my feelings down deep, hoping when he brings it up, I'll know how to respond. Now that he has, my tongue is tied and I'm holding my breath, waiting for him to continue.

"Tell me about one of your stories," he says, pulling me back to the present.

I pull up my master list of works in progress and scan the folders. My bottom lip slips between my teeth as I wait for one of them to pop out at me. When it doesn't happen, I just pick one randomly.

I smother a grimace when I realize the one I chose is a dark romance. My main character hasn't had a very good childhood. Now she channels that trauma into making assholes pay for their misdeeds. Plus, she has four love interests with dark backstories of their own.

He nudges me with his elbow, and I begin. The longer I talk, the easier it becomes. I forgot how much I enjoy just telling someone about the books I'm writing, the ideas I have, and how I want to wrap everything up. Most people zone out after a couple minutes. A few will stick around until I get to the point where my words taper off because of the glaze over their eyes.

Emmett, of course, does none of these things. Instead, he keeps up a steady stream of questions I'm forced to answer. All the information is there, hanging out of reach until he coaxes it forward.

Chloe tries to help when she can, but I know it's hard for her. She often can't follow my train of thought and we both end up frustrated. Which isn't that big of a deal. Usually, I have my author friends who go on about their books just as much as me. Being cut off from them hasn't been easy, even with me shoving all the loneliness aside.

"If you only have those last couple chapters and the epilogue, why are you set on finishing Andie and Sebastian's story?" His fingers brush along every inch of exposed skin he can find.

"I figured it would be easier to write their story. It's small-town contemporary. No one is trying to kill each other. I don't have to write a battle scene, which isn't that different than writing a spicy one, but there it is. I have to fix the dark ones so they're in a place where they can fall in love. It's a lot harder than you'd think—to force them to admit their feelings for one another, especially when they've lived lives where hiding emotions is the only way to survive." I don't know how else to describe what it's like.

"You feel that, don't you?"

"Their emotions?" I ask, and he nods. "I suppose I do. To me they're real, so of course they have real feelings."

"Isn't it exhausting?"

"Clearly, since I haven't written in effing months." I laugh, but the sound is hollow.

Once I got over the shock of my characters showing up, I thought everything would magically fix itself. I suppose I'll have to do it the old fashion way and just write. As long as I don't let myself get overwhelmed yet again, I'll be fine. Everything will be fine.

Chapter Thirty-Seven

Emmett

"So, you're telling me that she can just write whatever the fuck she wants, and we're just supposed to go along with it? These are our lives she's playing with," Tate growls, slamming his hands on the table I hauled up from the lower level. If he wiggles in that chair much more, the legs are going to break and spill him onto the lawn. After all his bitching, I'd laugh.

"She's the only reason you exist, fucker. Why don't you show a little respect?" I snap, and he has the good sense to look away.

Aiden, Rylie's love interest, rolls his eyes, but I let it slide. He showed up a couple hours ago, all bluster and cockiness. Asshole pulled up in a limo which vanished as it sped off down the dirt driveway. I don't think anyone else noticed. Rylie disappeared shortly after, pretending she didn't see him arrive.

Time seems to warp here—at least when it comes to the characters. It took Aiden ten days to show up from when Maddie wrote about him. I don't know how it all works and apparently neither does Grace. If she does, she hasn't told me.

Grace clears her throat, gaining his attention. "Tate, she's not playing with anything. And she just found out we're...corporeal, for lack of a better word. We're all going to encourage Maddie to keep writing so we can go on with our lives instead of wasting away in this in-between space like we have for months."

"What I don't understand is why now? Surely she's not the first who has gone through this. Why were *we* the ones chosen?" Juliette says, placing her hand on Tate's arm when he looks like he'll argue with Grace. He shakes Juliette off and she sighs, glancing away.

"I don't have all the answers. And even if I did, I don't know if I'd tell anyone. Might eff with the time continuum," Grace mutters. "We're just going to have to get through this together. But bitching about the circumstances isn't going to help. And neither is fighting against fate."

"You're not seriously suggesting that, that...that *writer*"—Aiden spits out her title as if it's a dirty word—"is actually fate. How the fuck do you even believe in that bullshit? Next, you're going to start spouting how karma is real."

The table falls silent. In fact, the entire crowd gathered on the fringes of our little group turn to stare at him. Aiden's eyes widen as he glances around. The struggle to find a way to backtrack is written all over his face. I smother a grin behind my hand and catch Grace's eye. She sighs, then presses her lips together.

"Strange how you can totally believe magic is real, but not fate or karma. I suggest you adjust your way of thinking before either one of them put you in your place," Sage murmurs as she picks at her nails with a wicked-looking dagger. Most of the others turn away, going back to their own conversations after her admonishment.

Sage slipped onto the property a while ago without anyone trailing her. Grace said not to worry about it—her love interests will show back up, eventually. Finding her men doesn't seem like the biggest problem we have since she has about a dozen weapons strapped to her body. Thankfully, she's kept to herself and doesn't seem to care about anyone else. She doesn't seem to care about anything. My plan is to stay out of her way.

"What if we don't want what she wants?" Peyton asks softly, her eyes flicking toward her roommates, who are too busy wrestling to pay attention.

"You just have to trust the process," Grace says delicately.

This whole thing would be a lot easier if everyone knew the types of books Maddie writes. When I suggested we tell them, Grace was adamant it would send the whole world tumbling down around us. She suggested this meeting instead, but I didn't think it would turn into a therapy session. I'm not equipped to deal with all this. I'm not one of them.

"Maybe Emmett can help ease your mind." Grace nudges me and I glance at her. She nods encouragingly, as if that'll make a difference.

I swallow hard as everyone turns to me. "Uh, well, she's writing. Which is more than she was doing before."

"What exactly was she doing before?" Kol's voice, full of laughter, comes from behind me and my muscles tense.

He's not a bad guy, but he sets me on edge. I don't know when he's going to be smiling or scowling. And the way his switch flipped when he thought Maddie was harboring Evalie…it was a step too far for me.

"None of your fucking business, butterfly," I snarl as he sits in the empty seat next to me.

Peyton leans over to Grace, attempting to whisper and failing miserably as she asks, "What's with butterfly?"

Kol laughs, though it feels forced. His hand lands on my shoulder and his fingers dig into my skin. I swear they're tipped in claws, they're so sharp.

"Take a walk with me, Emmett. I need to pick your brain about something." It's not a suggestion.

I shake off his grip, though it was probably more him letting go than anything I did. "Perfect. I have a few things to say myself."

Grace's eyes dart between us, opening her mouth as if she'll protest. Peyton pulls her attention away, and I take the opportunity to stand and make my way toward the beach. Weaving through what feels like a crowd, I suppress a shiver at the heat coming off Kol. When I can't take it anymore, I glance over my shoulder and find him a good five feet behind me. If we were on better terms, I'd ask him what the hell is up with him, but we're not.

We finally reach the lake and I spin to face him, crossing my arms. It takes everything in me to keep myself from reacting when I realize several others have joined him. They mirror my stance as they fan out in front of me. Part of me hopes Maddie is writing their story as we speak, and they'll vanish before they get a chance to confront me.

"This is Rune, Dez, and Nix. Part of the same world and all that," Kol says, waving his hand at the others. "First up—butterfly?"

My lips twitch as I bite my tongue. "Those wings you hide so expertly are a little iridescent."

"Butterfly wings aren't truly iridescent," Nix says, his deep voice reverberating in my chest.

I shake my head. "I don't even know how to respond to that."

"I could go through the science on it, but I doubt you'd care," he says.

Kol runs his hands through his hair, annoyance stamped across his face as he glares at Nix. I wonder if they go through this a lot. From the looks of it, this is a typical occurrence with them. I'm guessing Kol doesn't want to talk to me about butterflies and wings, but he also doesn't seem very keen on getting the actual discussion started.

"What do you want, Kol?" I grumble.

"Why don't you start?" He smirks, raising an eyebrow.

Fucking bastard. "Stop hanging out on the deck. Maddie doesn't like it."

"Throwing your girl under the bus isn't very nice," Dez mutters.

"I don't fucking care what your kinks are, Kol. Her consent matters, and I'm not about to let you see her walk around naked or watch me fuck her." All four of them step back in unison while Kol's skin darkens. "What the hell are you guys, anyways?"

"First of all, I wasn't going on the deck to spy on you while you two were fucking. I'm not the only one who can see into those windows, though. Perhaps you should hang up some goddamn curtains. And second of all"—his face splits into a wolfish grin—"we're demons. Straight from Hell. Would you like proof?"

Shadows swirl around his body, the ghost of his wings wisping from his back. I'm not surprised since I knew they were some type of fantasy creature. The wings alone gave them away.

I keep waiting for the terror to grip me, but it never comes. If I was a part of their world, I'd probably be terrified. Instead, I'm indifferent to his obvious intimidation tactics. Then I remember Maddie already told me they were from Hell. I guess I subconsciously internalized that fact and discarded it as non-threatening.

"Just stay the hell away from the house. And if you come at Maddie again, we're going to have problems—demon or not."

Rune, who hasn't said a goddamn word yet, rounds on Kol. "You went after her?"

Kol scowls at me, then turns to Rune. "My emotions got away from me in the moment. She knows where Eva is, yet refused to tell us."

"So you what? Threatened her?" Dez cuts off whatever Rune was about to say.

"Of fucking course I didn't. Shit just got away from me." Kol faces me again. "Won't happen again, but she needs to get going. Evalie doesn't have the time to wait around. She's gotten herself into some heavy shit and she won't survive without us."

I grind my teeth, glancing toward the cabin. Maddie leans against the deck railing, watching us with a slight smile on her face. What I wouldn't give to abandon these guys and go to her. Every time I catch a glimpse of her, heat fills my veins and my chest tightens. I want to lock her up in the house and worship her for another two months.

"If you're done ogling her, perhaps we could get back to the topic at hand," Nix says.

"Maddie will deal with things as she sees fit. And you'll just have to deal. You have to trust she knows what she's doing. And if you can't, then you're better off staying away from her." I brace myself for their reaction. I'm not used to issuing orders to demons.

Instantly, Nix and Dez vanish in a puff of smoke. I glance around, but they're gone. Rune chuckles, then fades away. Kol sighs, running his hands through his hair.

"They won't admit it, but they're worried too. She disappeared, man. Out of thin air. She was just...gone. We can't lose her. Hell will crumble. The mortal plane will devolve into chaos. I can't even express how fucking terrible it would be if she—" His mouth snaps shut, refusing to finish his sentence.

"You should talk to Grace."

"Because you refuse to go against *her*," he sneers, gesturing at Maddie.

"Watch it," I snap, and he sucks in a deep breath. "I don't know how much clearer I can be about this, Kol. Maddie is the author. She decides what's going to happen. She isn't going to do anything for shock value."

"How do you know?" He holds up his hands when I growl at him. "I'm just wondering how much you know about her and what she does. The only thing she's done is nod. She doesn't say anything."

I can't reassure him like he wants. Lying to him won't work. He probably can smell that shit from a mile off. I glance at Maddie once more before settling my gaze on him.

"You're right. I haven't read your story," I say, wanting to wipe the triumphant look from his face. "However, I know Maddie. I'm more qualified to assess whether she'd needlessly off a character for shits and giggles."

He shakes his head, not fully convinced. I doubt he will be until she finishes their story and Evalie is safe and sound. Then again, I have no idea what their story is about. Maybe Maddie does have every intention of killing her off. I assume romance books aren't like that, though. A happily ever after only happens when everyone lives, right? Then again, they're from Hell, so maybe if she dies, they can still be in love. I could ask Kol, but he's teetering on the edge already, and I like all my limbs attached to my body.

"Is that what you wanted to talk about? Your story?" I ask, eager to get this over with.

Kol's face falls, despair lining his eyes. He shakes his head, then sighs once more before disappearing into thin air. I fucking hate when they do that. From what Grace said, none of them can leave. Where they're vanishing to, I have no idea. I doubt they do either. Maybe it's just some void they can wallow in.

Maddie waves to me, her smile still firmly in place. She'll ask me what they wanted. She'll ask about the little gathering we had before, too. She'll want to know everything. I won't stress her out, though. Everyone here wants their story finished. They want to go back to their lives, regardless of Maddie's involvement.

Everything hinges on her ability to write. I wonder if this pressure is normal for her. Does she live with this in her head all the time? Characters screaming at her, arguing with the plot, blaming her when their lives go off the rails. If that's what she deals with, maybe having them out of her head will be a blessing in disguise.

Chapter Thirty-Eight
Maddie

I fucked up. Again.

My first mistake was making one of my characters an actuary without knowing what that was. The next one was opening the door whenever someone knocked. This time around, though, I think I might truly hate one of my characters.

He's a pompous ass who doesn't seem to care about anything or anyone but himself. Which, granted, I've dealt with before. But they had one redeeming quality. This fuckwad doesn't. I've searched and searched and I'm coming up empty-handed. He has to have one, but I can't find it.

Rylie glares at me from the other side of the deck while Aiden rants at me. He's going on about the ridiculousness of his story. He doesn't understand that Rylie is his love interest. It's on the tip of my tongue to just blast him with that little tidbit. I won't throw Rylie under the bus, though. She doesn't deserve to deal with his wrath.

"Please tell me why the hell I'm here," he demands through gritted teeth.

"Because you're one of my characters. I don't know how else to explain that to you." I smile tightly, hoping he'll finally accept the answer.

"What kind of book is it? Because if I'm about to lose my company—"

"You're not going to lose your company," I say, then mutter, "unless you keep badgering me."

"You should speak up if you have something to say, miss. No one gets anywhere in life by being a timid little—"

Emmett slips between us, and I jerk away. I didn't realize he was hovering so close. He crosses his arms as I lean around him.

"Finish the sentence," Emmett growls.

Aiden smirks, mirroring Emmett's stance. "mouse. A timid little mouse. I may be an asshole, but I'm not misogynistic."

"That's true," I whisper to Emmett. "I only make my villains misogynistic. Being an asshole is a toss-up, though."

Emmett closes his eyes, his jaw flexing as he grinds his teeth. Obviously, he wasn't expecting me to agree with Aiden. I wonder if I wasn't supposed to. Am I required to take Emmett's side against my characters? I don't know what the protocol is in this situation. I wave Rylie over, hoping she can save me from whatever pissing contest these two are about to engage in.

Her eyes widen and she stumbles back. I don't even think Aiden has noticed her. I swear she hid when he showed up. Emmett said she was nowhere to be found when they had their little gathering where Aiden shoved his foot in his mouth. Aiden glances over his shoulder, and she ducks behind Ezio. I wonder if she knows she's hiding behind a vampire.

"Now that we have that settled, I'll need you to get back to it. Write me back in my mansion and I'll be out of your hair. Also, someone needs to find my assistant. I have her notice." Aiden glances around, searching for Rylie.

I bite my cheek, then sigh. "You're not allowed to fire her. It's in the contract. So, unless that notice has your brother's signature, you're better off dropping it in the fire rather than handing it to her."

He throws up his hands and stalks away. Rylie pushes farther into the corner, but he doesn't notice as he makes his way through the sliding door. Maybe I shouldn't have put out an open invitation for people to mingle. I thought it would help, but this has been a bit of a disaster. I've been desperately trying to find a breakthrough in the last two and a half weeks.

"This was a bad idea. We should have gone with the small lunch like you said. Or at the very least, done this down at the beach," Emmett mutters as he spins around and wraps his arms around me.

"Too late now," I say, burying my face in his chest.

"It's not." Emmett turns us, keeping me hidden from the others. "Party's over. Everyone out."

His voice echoes over the crowd and immediately footsteps shuffle toward the door. I peek from the corner of my eye as they leave. Rylie glances back and I pinch Emmett's side. Somehow, he knows what I need and waves Rylie over to us. She hovers several feet from us until the others are gone.

"I'm sorry," Rylie whispers.

I untangle myself from Emmett. "I'm pretty sure I should be apologizing to you, Rylie. Not the other way around. I'm the one who invented him."

"Honestly, I don't think that's how it works," Emmett interrupts Rylie before sitting on one of the chairs and pulling me onto his lap.

Rylie collapses onto the other one. "What's that supposed to mean? She wrote us and here we are. Pretty sure that means she invented us."

Emmett's hand runs across my back, easing away the tension of the afternoon. "What about when they were kids? It's not like Maddie is writing their entire childhood. Sure the bigger things get worked out, but she doesn't write every memory they have."

I close my eyes, content to let them argue the finer details. It doesn't matter either way to me. Whether I invented them or not won't change the present or their future. Besides, in my mind, once the story is done, it's done. My part is finished, and it's up to them now to make it last. I'm not a part of their happily ever after. Their pasts only play into the story because they shaped who the characters are today.

"Just because she didn't write about their childhoods doesn't mean she doesn't know about them. Maybe she's just making them up in her head and that's where they are born or invented or whatever. Like Aphrodite," Rylie says smugly.

I swallow down a laugh while Emmett squeezes my side. "I think you mean Athena."

"Wait, what? No, Aphrodite is the goddess of love and all that, right?"

"She is, but Athena was born out of Zeus's forehead without a mother. There's an alternate version, but that's the one most people know. Nothing to do with the goddess of love, which is a very underwhelming way to describe Aphrodite, but I don't think you want to get into that."

"Greek mythology was never my strong suit," Rylie mutters, dropping her head back.

"Rylie, you realize you're going to have to interact with Aiden, right? He's not going to be able to leave now that I brought him here." I grimace when she makes a face.

"Why exactly did you make him come? He was perfectly fine...away from here. He's clearly busy with his business, which you know since you *gave* him the job. Or family, I suppose." Bitterness seeps into her tone.

I glance at Emmett, who subtly shakes his head. Apparently, he's only my knight in shining armor when men are being assholes. Dealing with the consequences of my own actions was not on my to-do list today.

"I need him here to finish the story," I mutter, hoping she'll drop it.

Emmett holds up his hand when Rylie looks like she'll push the issue. "Shit will happen the way it's supposed to. Don't ask her what it's about. And don't go sneaking around asking Grace."

Rylie blushes, plucking at her sweatpants. "I don't like it when you two gang up on me. Fine. I'll go along with whatever you've got cooked up, but I refuse to wear those effing pencil skirts anymore."

She shoves to her feet, huffing as she wipes her palms along her legs. With one last withering look that doesn't have any heat behind it, she flounces off through the cabin. I cuddle closer, wishing I could spend the rest of the day curled up with Emmett. We're both behind on the things we need to do. And he won't let me use him as a distraction from my writing anymore.

"Alright. I'm grabbing your computer, then getting going on finishing the bathroom." He sets me on Rylie's vacated seat as I pout.

"I'm making dinner tonight," I say when he stands, and he plops back down.

"Listen, I know you're hell-bent on being involved with cooking, but I don't want you to." He pins me with a glare. "And you don't want to, either."

I puff out my cheeks, contemplating how far I want to push this. He's right. I don't want to cook. By the time I get done, I no longer want whatever I've made. Emmett has a sixth sense about what I'm craving, and I never have a complaint. If I was writing a book boyfriend for myself, he's who I'd pick. I grin as I run my gaze down his body. Definitely made for me.

"Fine. But I don't want to take advantage of you. You're here to do a job—"

"Which includes feeding you. Now, get comfortable." He pushes to his feet again and trails his fingers along my neck before disappearing from view.

I've become so used to the silence, the low mumble and occasional burst of laughter is jarring. Part of me loves that there are people here. The other misses the quiet. Not that it was doing much to help me.

My mind wanders as I wonder what Chloe is up to. I don't even know what day it is. Not that she leads a normal life. Before I left, she talked about volunteering for some foundation. Maybe I should have stayed a bit longer. She tried to hide the sadness in her eyes when I left, but I could tell. She never would have let me stay, though. She would have thrown me in the car and driven me here herself. Then I'd be without a car. I suppose I'm without a vehicle either way.

Emmett reappears, a tray and my computer tucked under his arm. He doesn't wait for me to straighten, just sets them on my lap, and turns to go back inside.

I bite my cheek, resisting the urge to call for him. I crane my neck to watch him walk away. His jeans stretch across his ass, and I squeeze my thighs together, licking my lips. An ache sprouts in my chest.

I open my computer, searching for Rylie and Aiden's story. I wish I could have told her how I was writing their romance, but I'm pretty sure she would have thrown me off the deck.

I get seven words in ten minutes before I give up. One by one, I pull up the various WIPs. It's strange having an actual person instead of an image of my characters in my head. Getting to know them should help with translating their personalities onto the page.

Someone clears their throat next to me and I jolt, almost spilling my computer on the deck. She snorts as she drapes herself across Emmett's chair. My mind flips through the pictures of my characters until I settle on one.

"Sage. What can I do for you?" I murmur, busying myself with my computer.

I've only written a couple chapters of her story—one of which is a spicy scene. I wonder what happens to them when I write out of order. Since one action flows into another, I don't do it often. I peek at her from the corner of my eye, then snort. I cover the sound with a cough. It's not like she's going to have sex hair or something.

"Trying to figure out if I'm going to stab you?" she asks with no inflection in her voice. It's disconcerting to say the least.

"No. You know, if you stab me, you'll be sitting in limbo forever. And we both know you won't survive that."

"Maybe that's my goal? I could do with a break from life." She glances out over the lake, a blank expression on her face. "Just for a little while."

I follow her line of sight. Not that I can find what she's looking for. "Life hasn't been kind to you. Doesn't mean you don't deserve more."

She slowly turns to face me. Something flickers within her green eyes, yet she blinks and it's gone. The corner of her mouth twitches before she sighs. I wonder what's going on inside her head. I've had some characters keep shit to themselves—their quirks, their kinks, their motives. I've dealt with it all despite how hard it made things for me.

Sage is a whole other can of worms. Vague. It's the only way to describe her. She protects what's left of her by hiding, even from herself. I didn't lie. She deserves to find more. And I know she'll find whatever she's looking for in the men she's so desperately pushing away. Discovering who she is while writing her story will be harder than most. It's why I've put off working on their book.

"I'm only here to make sure you get your shit together. Everyone is a little on edge." Her head drops back, resting against the chair, and her eyes flutter closed.

Bothering her might end up with the pointy end of a knife sticking from my leg. From what I remember, Sage has an affinity for aiming for the meaty part of the thigh. I've never been stabbed, but I've researched enough to know it's painful. I wonder if I could convince her to show me how to throw a blade.

Without opening her eyes, she mutters, "Stop staring at me and get to work. I'm sick of listening to the others bitch. I doubt I'll be getting out of this hellhole anytime soon, so the less people around, the better."

I concentrate on the screen in front of me. I didn't even think about what happens when I finish one of their stories. Will they disappear as quickly as they came? Will they hang around, waiting to see how the others fare? Hopefully if they go back to their own worlds, the sudden silence won't be as jarring. I don't know how I'm going to get this all done, regardless of Sage's subtle threats.

Chapter Thirty-Nine

Emmett

"No, Axel. I don't know what slashing is. I don't follow hockey," I say, trying to keep the exasperation from my voice.

He's been talking my ear off for the last hour while I try to install the new sink in the half bath. I thought about asking him for help, but this is a one-person job. Axel doesn't seem to care that this room is the size of a shoebox, and I keep accidentally kicking him. I thought he'd get the hint when I didn't respond to his prattling. Instead, he plopped himself on the toilet and kept up most of the conversation.

He leans on the sink, ducking to catch my eye. "Well, you should. It's better to go to a game, but it's fun either way. I'd invite you to one of mine, but I doubt that would work. You think your writer could make that happen?"

"Doubt it. I'm just a regular person. Can't exactly be written into a story."

Maddie tried to put herself into one of the scenes and it didn't work. My experience wouldn't be any different. I glance at Axel, wondering if he'll try to go around me about this. Most of the men have taken to coming to me instead of going to Maddie. And I'll never tell her. She'll either be grateful they aren't bugging her, or she'll be pissed they think she needs a bodyguard. Probably the latter rather than the former.

"Evie said you were a book boyfriend. I don't know what that means," he mutters.

"Pretty self-explanatory. Not that I agree."

He rolls his eyes, rapping his knuckles on the counter. "Couple of the guys are taking notes. Thought you should know, so you don't blow it."

What. The. Fuck.

"I'm not worried about what those assholes think. As long as I focus on Maddie, give her what she needs, shit won't go sideways."

"Is that what a healthy relationship looks like?"

I glance at him, tilting my head to see him around the pipe I've been tightening. He grins, but it's forced. I merely stare at him until he sits back, hiding from view. Sighing, I resign myself to finally dealing with him. Shoving from under the sink, I take care to not bash my head on anything. I've already done it twice, resulting in a goose egg on my temple.

"Spill," I say, leaning against the wall so I can face him.

He laughs awkwardly, avoiding my gaze. "What?"

"You haven't been hanging out in a tiny-ass bathroom just to talk hockey."

He runs his hand through his hair, the curls flopping back into place. "Guess that's true. You seem like you have enough on your plate without worrying about the rest of us. Problem is, we only have each other to talk to and it's a little weird to talk to the others."

It's my turn to laugh awkwardly and avoid his gaze. "What?"

"I'm just saying you didn't exactly sign up for this. At least where I'm from, this shit isn't normal. I'm pretty sure it's not for you either. The thing is, we're all just here and we're all a part of this thing. But *you* aren't. There's a layer between the situation and you, which helps, I suppose."

"Helps what, exactly?" I need him to say it. If he won't admit out loud that they can't talk to Maddie, she'll never get anywhere. She's still struggling to figure out where to go from here.

"Work through shit? Figure out where our lives are supposed to go? Decide if we're real or fake and if all this is worth it?" He winces, running his hand through his hair again. "Plus, it's real fucking hard to talk about all the other shit with a woman you don't know."

I sigh and my head thumps back against the tile, adding to my already raging headache. "You realize just because I'm five-ish years older doesn't mean I know more about sex than you. Or relationships."

"But you and the writer—"

"Maddie and I have only known each other a few months."

It isn't until the shock spreads across his face that I remember we're supposed to be pretending we're married. I never thought keeping up a fake relationship while cultivating an actual relationship would be that difficult. When it was only one or two people, it wasn't that hard. With over sixty people around now, it's harder. Probably would help if I remembered she's supposed to be my wife.

Axel leans his elbows on his knees. "Are you telling me you two got married after only a couple weeks? How'd you know she was the one?"

I could continue this farce or end it now. Axel seems like the kind of guy who likes to spread gossip, though I'm sure he'd keep shit to himself if I asked. At least I hope he would. I wish I could talk to Maddie about this before answering.

I open my mouth, still unsure what's going to come out when there's a knock on the door. Relief floods through me, followed closely by guilt. Axel reaches over and slides the pocket door open.

"What if they're twins?" Maddie says, her eyes fixed on the legal pad in her hand. She taps a pen against her lips, drawing my gaze to her mouth. "They could be identical and *that's* why she doesn't notice when he's at the altar instead of his twin that she met at dinner."

Her smile fades when she glances up and notices Axel grinning at her. She hides the notepad against her chest as if he'll jump up and snatch it from her. I don't mind her interrupting my day like this. She's been doing it more and more as she adds to her WIPs. Sometimes she just wants me to listen, but more often than not I ask questions. I don't know if it helps—seems like it does when she suddenly shushes me and grabs her computer.

"I think twins is a great idea. They'll have to have something that sets them apart from one another, though. A mole or something," I say, attempting to ignore Axel as his gaze bounces between us. "Which book is this?"

She wrinkles her nose and I wonder if she'll answer. "The arranged marriage one."

I smirk, glancing away. Now I understand why she was hesitant to say. "The twin isn't here, right? So, is he a villain or a side character?"

Panic washes across her face. "Why the hell would you ask me that? This is a goddamn standalone." She stomps away and I wince.

"Uh, what the hell was that? Can it not be a standalone if he's a villain? Or a side character? Or because he's here...or not here?" Axel grimaces and I drop my head in my hands.

"I have no idea. Don't tell anyone about her book, though. She doesn't want the others to know about her writing." I push to my feet and my knee smacks against the vanity.

Axel scrambles out of the bathroom, then spins and blocks the doorway. "I wouldn't tell just anyone. But can I talk to Eve about it? She won't say anything, but I'm sure she'll ask and I'm not great at lying to her."

"You two friends?"

His face drops, a mask falling over his features, and I catch a glimpse of the man he probably is on the ice. I almost forgot he's a hockey player. He certainly looks like he'd be able to smash me into the boards right about now. Maybe I should have paid more attention while he was chatting my ear off.

"No. We're not friends. Just roommates. Forget it. I won't say anything. And neither should you." With those final words, he pivots and stomps from view.

I jolt when the front door slams, making a mental note to ask Maddie what the deal is there. Maybe she could make them friends who fall for each other. I'm halfway to the deck before my feet stutter to a stop. When did I go from letting her come to me with her ideas to seeking her out with my own? It's not that I mind, but the shift is throwing me off.

"Emmett?" Maddie calls from the deck and I glance up. "I'm sorry I yelled at you."

"What? I don't fucking care about that. I'm a little confused, but you weren't mad at me. But also, I have thoughts about Axel's story."

Her eyebrow lifts, then she nods once before going back onto the deck. I follow her, settling in what I've come to think of as my chair. She sets her computer on her lap, clicking around a bit before she gives me an expectant look.

"Well?"

"Now? I thought you were working on the arranged marriage one?" I grip the back of my neck.

"You talked to Axel and came out of it with ideas. I want to know. Now start talking."

"Most of the shit he was talking about centered on hockey. He'd drop hints about Eve every once in a while. Don't think he realizes they'll fall in love. They *are* falling in love, right?"

She gives me a look. "Of course they're falling in love. I just haven't figured out how they'll get together. Or what the conflict is. Or why they want to be together."

With each statement, she becomes more morose as her eyes dart across the screen. I wait, knowing her need to work through this shit by herself. If I start throwing questions at her, she'll shut down. That move might get me laid, but it won't help her. Then again, she's wearing those itty-bitty pajama shorts I like. Plus, her tank top pushes her breasts up. Whiling away my time staring at her chest is certainly entertaining. Even if it leaves me with my cock so hard, it's about to rip my jeans.

"Okay, I can't worry about all those things right now. What's your suggestion?" She glances at me when I don't immediately answer, and I avert my eyes. "Were you just staring at my boobs? You know they don't have any grand insights, right?"

"Pretty fucking insightful if you ask me," I mutter, stealing another glance.

"Oh yeah?" Her arms squeeze her breasts together until they're practically spilling from her shirt. "What amazing wisdom do they have to impart?"

My mouth goes dry, and I try to swallow once, then twice. It doesn't help. I wish I had a witty comeback, but I'm not the creative one in this relationship. I've got a corner on the dirty talk, but that's about it.

"They're—" I clear my throat and her shoulders shake. "I've got nothing. I thought I could pull it off, but nope. They've rendered me speechless."

Her peals of laughter ring through the air, warming my chest. The last three weeks have been a whirlwind of one shock after another. She hasn't had enough breath to laugh. I wish I could have known her earlier, to understand how important this moment truly is. My mind fills with questions I want to ask about her past. I shut them down one by one. I'll deal with them later when I won't be interrupting her joy.

"Would you pass out if I flashed you?"

"Won't know until you try it." I smirk, then lick my lips as she leans forward.

She plays with the hem of her tank top, swaying as she teases me. My eyes fix on the strip of skin she reveals. My cock hardens and I grip the arms of the chair. When she pauses, I glance around to make sure no one's spying on us. The constant murmur from the others has died without my noticing.

"I suppose I can just put these away if you're distracted."

My eyes snap to her chest, not that she's moved at all. "Distracted? No. Hypervigilant? Yes. Unless you'd like an audience as you put on this little show."

Confusion spreads across her face, then morphs as she realizes what I'm implying. She cranes her neck as she attempts to peek over the railing. I chuckle when she turns to check the roof until I remember some of her characters have wings. I only know about Kol and his friends, which doesn't mean much. They usually keep them hidden, so it's entirely possible others are doing the same.

"Perhaps we should take this inside." She giggles, gripping the edge of her computer when it starts to slide off her lap.

I push to my feet and bend down to kiss her swiftly. "Nope. You have writing to do. And I have a cold shower calling my name."

"Wait," she calls as I reach the door. "What was your suggestion for Eve and Axel?"

I rap my knuckles on the frame, contemplating the ramifications of putting my own ideas into her story. They should wholly be hers, not influenced by someone like me.

"Make them friends. Whatever happens after, okay, but make them friends."

Chapter Forty
Maddie

I don't know how it happened, but somehow Emmett's words opened a floodgate in me. Two weeks later and it takes everything in me to pull myself away from my computer. It's been so long since the only thing I've had to worry about is writing and I forgot how much I enjoy it. I forgot how amazing it feels to finish a chapter, to get through that one scene, to write a confession. This is what I've been missing for the last six months that I've been in the throes of writer's block.

"I don't want to break your concentration, but I need you to come eat, gorgeous. You're going to waste away to nothing if you keep this up," Emmett says softly.

He learned pretty quickly how to deal with me. I didn't want to keep biting his head off just for wanting to feed me. The irritation the first time must have been stamped on my face, though. He'd backed away so quickly he tripped over one of the stools. It broke the tension enough, and he didn't do it again. I didn't want him to have to tiptoe around the cabin just because I was writing. I'm capable of blocking him out.

"I just need to finish this chapter," I mutter, but I'm not typing.

"How much more do you need?" His lips brush across my neck and I tilt my head, my eyes fluttering closed.

I don't know if he's talking about time or words. Either way, I need to eat before I pass out. My stomach gurgles, making Emmett chuckle.

He brushes my hair behind my ear and whispers, "I win."

Sighing, I push to my feet. I've tried to find the right workspace while here. The dining table doesn't have the right vibe. The bedroom is too comfortable. The deck isn't bad unless my characters are out there throwing a party, which seems to happen every other day. I don't know how to feel about them getting along like they are.

Sometimes I hide on the deck and spy on them. It's strange to see their interactions with their significant others. Especially when I'm actively writing them. Axel and Eve have become friends, laughing and pranking the hockey players. Peyton thinks it's hilarious, sometimes joining in.

Emmett sets a bowl of cheese-filled pasta in front of me, then slides onto the stool next to me. I plop down, sighing as another storyline pops into my head. I haven't been able to stick to one story, and it's fucking with my brain. If I could just finish one of them, I'd feel like I was accomplishing something. Words are great unless they're not getting me anywhere.

"Slow down," Emmett murmurs, his hand covering mine, and I realize I've eaten half the bowl without noticing.

"What if I can't finish them?"

The spoon clatters against the dish as I finally give voice to my greatest fear—when my mind lags, unable to find the words. When my fingers stall, unable to finish a sentence. When my body shuts down, unable to keep writing. Those are the times the doubt creeps in. Sure, I'm doing what Chloe sent me up here to do, but at what cost? What am I really achieving if I can't end things?

"Why are you worried about the ending when you haven't gotten there yet? No use borrowing tomorrow's problems for today."

Emmett goes back to his food as if he didn't just drop another bomb on me. He's been doing that a lot lately. I don't know if where he picks up these random pieces of advice.

"Because if I anticipate the issue now, maybe I'll..." I bite my lip and stare at the pasta.

"Maybe you'll what? Be able to fix it? Because from where I'm sitting, doesn't seem like that's an option."

"What do you mean?"

Panic floods my system and my stomach flips, threatening to upend its contents. He went from giving great advice to confirming my worst fears. I can't fix my writer's block if I can't finish a fucking story.

He sighs, spinning to face me. "You can't fix something that isn't a problem. And it's not an option to be worried about it because it hasn't happened. Besides, I'm pretty sure you're incapable of failing."

He gives me a small smile before turning back to his pasta. I don't want to disturb him. And I certainly don't know how to respond. I stuff another forkful in my mouth. It probably tastes amazing, but it's like sawdust in my mouth. Letting his hard work go to waste would be, well, wasteful.

"Talk," he grunts.

"I already failed. I wrote that book—"

"And it was fine. Sure, it wasn't a masterpiece, but it was a good book. You're too hard on yourself. You've written some real good stuff."

"You haven't even read my stuff."

He gives me an indecipherable look. "Instead of focusing on the one book that was okay, why don't you remember the other ones? The ones that touched people. The ones that changed their lives. *Those* are the ones you should remember when you feel like this. When exactly did you decide that your career hinged on one book?"

"I-I don't...That's not what I was..."

He raises his eyebrow, then grins before shoving the last piece of pasta in his mouth. For someone who doesn't understand the publishing world, he certainly seems to have a grasp on the thoughts plaguing me.

I let the success, or lack thereof, of one book define my entire career. My author friends tried to get through to me. Chloe and Ryland both said something similar. My mother—she doesn't count. She barely sees what I do as a viable option as a job. My father doesn't care either way. I could be a burlesque dancer for real, and it wouldn't matter.

"How do you know if it was an okay book or not, anyways?" I mutter, dropping my elbows on the counter and propping my chin in my hands.

"I read it. Which book are you almost done with?" He grabs our bowls and slides around the island.

"Um, I don't know. What do you mean, you read it?" I didn't bring any copies of my books here. And the internet is spotty as fuck.

He runs his hand through his hair and gives me a sheepish grin. "I bought them when I went into town before we were stuck here."

"When the hell did you read them? You've been with me most of the time. Or working on the cabin."

"Yeah, well, you sleep late. I'm up by like six every morning."

"But you're there when I wake up." I don't exactly know how I feel about him reading my books. "Don't tell me you're sitting there in bed, reading while I sleep, and then, what? You hide your phone when I wake up?"

He chuckles, turning to rinse the bowls. "No. I go sit on the deck. Then come back in after a few hours. Most of the time, I fall back asleep. I like waking up next to you, even if it is a few hours after I've already woken up."

I smile as I duck my head. Emmett has a way about him. I've seen it when he interacts with others, but mostly with me. My mind does me dirty, spiraling into a dark abyss of depressive thoughts. Then Emmett comes in, distracting me from them—easing my worries. Just minutes ago, I was terrified I wouldn't finish any of my stories. Now I want to know what he thinks of my work. I wouldn't have been able to handle this turn of events without him. I don't know how I'll survive when I'm forced back to society.

"Oh, shit," I cry, dropping my head in my hands. "We were supposed to be pretending we're married, and I completely forgot. Shit, I'm bad at this. How the hell do other people remember all this?"

He chuckles, his knuckle tucking under my chin and forcing me to meet his gaze. "Axel thinks we dated for a few weeks, then got married. I'm pretty sure he'll spread the word for us."

"I'm going to be honest, I don't know how to pretend to be married." I bite my lip and his thumb reaches up, pulling the flesh from between my teeth.

"That makes two of us. I'm pretty sure it's not much different than what we've been doing. But if you want to tell the few people who already know to spread something else, be my guest." He drops his grip on me and spins back to the sink.

There was something in his eyes before he turned. I wish I had just a few more seconds to decipher what it was. Pretending I was married to him was only supposed to protect me from Grace. It morphed into something else when more people showed up. I could come clean, but what if they don't trust me afterward? What if I've fucked myself over with what I thought was an innocent fabrication?

"Whoa, what's wrong?" Emmett's voice jolts me from my thoughts.

"Nothing. I just didn't think this through. I should tell them, regardless of what they'll think of me. It's not fair to you."

"Not fair...Maddie, I don't give two shits what they think of me. No one would fault you for telling a random person who showed up in the middle of the night that you were married. And I certainly don't have a problem with you claiming me. Stop worrying so much about what they think. They're essentially *you,* anyway."

"But they're not me. And I need them to trust me. How can I ask them to trust me when I lie to them?" My forehead thunks against the counter and I groan. I'll deal with the tingling sensation in my chest over his talk about claiming him later.

Emmett's fingers run through my hair, brushing the strands away from my face. My muscles relax as he continues to rake his hand over my head. His movements don't stop the thoughts, though. I've seen what healthy marriages look like, and this isn't one of them. Emmett takes care of most of my needs, and every time we talk, it's centered on me—on my work. That isn't healthy. I've taken over everything.

"I'm sorry," I whisper, and his touch leaves me.

His body covers mine as he presses his chest to my back. "For what?"

"I feel like all I do is take. I don't give anything back. It's not fair. It's why I gave you an out. I'm just shit at this whole thing."

"What whole thing? A relationship?" There's an edge of glee in his voice, which only makes me feel worse.

"If that's what we're calling this," I mumble, half hoping he doesn't hear me.

He chuckles, the deep sound resonating through my body. "Well, seeing as how we're married, I'd call it a relationship."

"You're not helping."

"Because you're being ridiculous. If I didn't sign up for this, do you think I'd still be here? I could have left long ago or exposed your little white lie. I could have run when the portal opened up. Or the lady tried to kill me."

"She wouldn't have killed you."

He presses his lips to the sensitive spot behind my ear. "Regardless, when I wanted to leave, I tried to take you with me. Did you forget that?"

"We're still talking about me instead of you. You're only focused on me, and that's not healthy."

He sighs, then pulls me upright. I don't want to face him. If I look into his eyes, I'll lose my nerve. I'll let him stuff me with food and seduce me with his touch, and we'll never finish talking about this. He'll distract me without caring about himself. I don't know why he thinks he isn't worth more than merely being there for me. He has a life beyond me.

When I won't turn around, he wraps his arms around me, resting his chin on my shoulder. "We talked about this. And I'll keep telling you as much as you need, but at some point, you need to let this go. It's only a problem because you're making it one."

"You can't honestly tell me only focusing on me and all my problems is healthy. Or that you won't resent me later because of it."

"I can one hundred percent say I won't. You're worth any sacrifice you imagine I'm making." His fingers play with the hem of my shirt, and they skim across my flesh. "We'll figure this out. We'll get through it together."

For now.

I keep the words to myself like a coward. Facing the future will wait for another day.

Chapter Forty-One

Emmett

Jordan appears over the edge of the roof, lugging a bundle of shingles over his shoulder. "Listen, I'm thinking we need another hand up here. Otherwise, it's going to take all day to get this done, and I don't exactly want to be out here in this heat that long."

"Well, if you want to ask someone else to help, be my guest. But they can't dick around. I'm not going to tell Maddie one of her characters killed themselves by falling off the roof because they fucked around and found out," I say as he drops the bundle next to me.

"Don't worry. I won't pick the assholes. Or Beckett. He's one of my best friends, but he has a hard time focusing. Except when Bailey is around, but we're not allowed to talk about that."

He disappears down the ladder before I can respond. I don't know why he's not allowed to talk about Bailey. Unless he's talking about Beckett and Bailey interacting. Maybe there's something going on between them and that's what he's alluding to. I shouldn't get involved. I think I've done a good job keeping everyone at bay for the last several weeks while Maddie has been writing. The amount of people knocking on our door has diminished to a trickle and usually it's Rylie hiding from Aiden.

As the *pfft* of the nail gun surrounds me, my mind wanders back to Maddie. She's been writing more and more every day. Yesterday I had to force her to stop to eat, but she didn't actually stop. She brought her notepad to the table and ate with one hand while she took notes. A couple times she froze with the sandwich halfway to her mouth, staring into space while she worked something out in her head.

The deeper she falls into her stories, the more time I have to finish the projects I've been putting off. I hate it and love it all at the same time. When I ask her at the end of the day how her books are coming, she gets a little grin and she giggles. I can handle the lost hours with her if she's so happy, but part of me wishes we could go back to being holed up alone in the cabin exploring this new relationship.

The thought has me dropping my chin to my chest. She hasn't brought up me leaving again, thank fuck. Every once in a while, I catch her watching me with a wary expression. Or maybe it's wistful. She always turns away too quickly for me to really read her. I understand her reservations since I had the same ones. I don't want her worrying about me, though.

Focusing on the roof helps to keep me from falling down a rabbit hole. Eventually, we need to talk about our future. I'd like to push aside my fear of her leaving and just enjoy the here and now. My brain has other ideas. It crops up in the quiet parts of my day. Which is part of the reason I gave in so easily when Jordan told me we needed help. If others are around, I'll have to make sure they don't hurt themselves, leaving no room for anything else but the project in front of me.

"No, Harper, I'm not going to push your husband off the roof. But if you keep shadowing him, I'm going to put you to work too," Jordan yells, then grunts, and I'm pretty sure someone smacked him. He laughs and the ladder rattles as he makes his way up. "Alright, boss. I got backup. I tried to limit who came, but everyone was a little bored."

At least half a dozen people clamber up behind him, and I bite back a groan. I recognize all of them, even if I don't know their names. I've been forgetting more as the days bleed together. Not remembering names is one thing, since there are so many of them. Blanking on how to make coffee is something else. I blame the heat.

"Any of you have experience?" Most of them nod their heads and I let out a sigh of relief.

"We don't have enough nail guns to go around, so I need someone putting down the new layer and another coming up behind and nailing it in place. Whoever knows how to fix holes can get going on that. If you don't know how to use this"—I lift the tool in my hand—"stay the fuck away from it. I doubt you need tetanus shots, but I'm not risking it. Understood?"

They all nod, and one of the women grabs a gun. She hefts it in her hands, smirking as the nails jingle. I grimace, wondering if I should have been more clear about where they point the things.

"Don't shoot us, Sage. We don't have insurance," one of the men says. I think his name is Ryder.

Her face blanks and he laughs nervously, then turns to grab some shingles. We work for an hour with only hammers and the occasional curse piercing the silence. It doesn't bother me now that I have others around. My mind fixates on the task in front of me and I work until my hands are numb.

"Emmett?" Maddie's voice is a balm to my soul, and I close my eyes, praying she'll call for me again. "Emmett, it's lunchtime."

It's not. We've only been up here a few hours, but she woke up early today. I grin, shaking my head when I hear her huff.

"Don't make me come up there, Emmett," she yells.

"Hold your horses, woman. I'll be down in a second," I yell back, and every head swivels toward me.

"Buy me a horse and maybe I'll think about it."

"I'll buy you a horse when you can prove to me you can take care of it."

Kolby chuckles under his breath, and I glare at him. He holds up his hands, mirth dancing across his face. Fucker doesn't look the least bit ashamed of himself. The urge to throw my nail gun at his head is strong. Instead, I set it down gently and make my way down the ladder. When I reach the bottom, I find Maddie with her arms crossed, an annoyed expression pulling her lips into a frown.

"Don't be like that," I murmur as I pull her body against mine. "You know you don't know how to take care of a horse."

"I could learn," she cries, fighting a smile.

"I'm sure you could." I cover her mouth with mine, and the world falls away.

She opens for me, and I sweep my tongue along hers. A whimper leaves her, urging me on. I slip my fingers into her hair and tilt her head, deepening the kiss. We should stop. We should go inside. We should do a lot of things. I can't pull away from her. Her scent consumes me. Her essence fills the dark holes in my soul, the absent spaces within my mind.

The sounds of whooping and clapping fill the air, and I rip my lips from hers. She giggles, ducking her head into my chest. Glancing around, I groan at the crowd focused on us.

"Are they still watching?" she whispers.

"Oh yeah. Most of them are smiling, though that one dude looks like he wants to murder me. You didn't try to write yourself into any of these books again, did you?"

Her head snaps up, almost clipping my chin. "What?"

"Just making sure he's not going to try to fight me for you. I don't know how much skill you gave him with a knife, but I don't really want to kill one of your characters." I smirk so she knows I'm not serious. "Wait, you don't actually put any of yourself in the books, right? Is that why they all showed up?"

"Not here," she mutters, pulling me inside. She waves at Grace, who whistles as we pass her.

As soon as the door shuts behind me, she spins around. "First of all, I don't think they showed up because of me. I mean, they did, but you know what I mean. Self-insert is a touchy subject. I don't intentionally put myself into my characters, but I can't completely remove all traces of me. They steal quirks or traumas or random things. I don't do it on purpose."

My hands cover hers, stopping her from wringing them. "What's wrong with putting yourself in the stories?"

She recoils, her eyes widening. "I don't belong in a story. And making myself a part of them would be weird. There's a time and place for that, but it's not what I write. I can't stop when my characters steal shit and I definitely pull from my own life experiences. It's just not something I do purposefully."

"Okay, but that dude really looked like he was going to stab me," I say, trying to lighten the mood.

"Which one?"

I step around her, and she spins. Placing a hand on her lower back, I guide her toward the deck. As we step outside, she shivers. I'm not entirely sure it's from the temperature change. We've settled into a routine lately and I worry we've lost the spark of newness. The deeper she buries herself in her work, the more I nervous I become.

I want her to succeed—to finish her stories and publish them. I want her to prove to herself she's more than just one book. Yet I'm afraid of what's to come when she reaches her goal. I've been avoiding the future, but I still fear it.

We reach the railing and I search for the man who was glaring. I finally find him hovering at the edge of the forest, anxiously glancing at the woman chatting with Peyton. I tip my chin toward him and Maddie squints, searching the masses. Sighing, I point, attempting to be subtle. He catches me anyway and I drop my arm.

"Axel? You called him *that one dude.*"

"Axel, right." My head throbs and I press my thumbs against my temples. Pain slices through me, settling into my chest, and I suck in a sharp breath.

"Emmett, are you okay?" Her voice reaches me after a beat, and I close my eyes. The ache slowly recedes, leaving an echo of something I can't define in its place.

"Fine. Just a headache. I'm going to get some water, then get back to work."

I weave around the furniture and almost run into the sliding door. My foot connects with the glass, and I jolt to a stop. When I lift my trembling hand, I swallow hard. I need to get a fucking grip on myself before I fall apart. And I don't have that option. Maddie won't survive without me.

As soon as I step into the living room, cool air flows around me. My muscles ease and the last of the pain ebbs away. The cold isn't as good as having Maddie in my arms, but I'll take whatever I can get at this point. Maybe I shouldn't have gotten on the roof in the middle of a heatwave. A lot of the others have taken to the lake, letting the water cool them off. I doubt any of them can get heatstroke like I can.

"I heated up the chicken you made last night. It's in the oven."

I lift my hand without turning around and head for the kitchen. Filling my stomach and drinking water will hopefully set me back on track.

A thumping from above pulls my eyes up and I realize the others are still working. I feel like I should feed them, but Maddie pushes me toward the stool. I should be out there with them. Jordan may know what he's doing, but it's not his responsibility. And if someone gets hurt, I'll never forgive myself. Even if they won't die when they fall off the roof, I still won't be okay.

"Turn your brain off. They're fine," Maddie says, breaking into my thoughts.

She sets a plate full of food in front of me, and I resign myself to eating instead of hurrying back out there. Maddie will probably stop me if I don't.

When she sits next to me, her scent washes over me, and my muscles relax bit by bit. By the time we're done, I'm feeling more centered—more myself.

Whatever happens, I realize I can't live without her. I'll merely exist in a world not meant for me, and I refuse to survive like that. I refuse to accept that all we'll have is this short time together. Unless she tells me to, I refuse to let her go.

Chapter Forty-Two
Maddie

I'm avoiding finishing. I've known it for a while now. Emmett brought it up. Grace mentioned it in a roundabout way. Even Rylie called me out on it, probably expecting some sort of reaction. I avoided them all. Not physically, since none of us can leave this place, but changing the subject usually does the trick. I thought they dropped it, trusting me to do my job.

Then Sage showed up. She didn't even have to say anything for me to know why she was here. She's a lot harder to ignore than the others. Especially when she perches on the railing of the deck, amusing herself by giving me a mini heart attack every time she sways. After thirty minutes, I've had enough.

"Is there a reason you're here?" I snap, my fingers hovering over the keys of my computer.

"There a reason you're avoiding shit?" She doesn't even bother to look up from her book. Where the hell she got it, I have no idea and I'm not about to ask.

"I'm literally writing. I've been writing nonstop for like a month—all day, every day. What else would you have me do?" I wince when the question pops out.

"Finish a fucking story." She'd probably snap back if she allowed herself to access her emotions.

I mumble something incoherent, hoping she doesn't bother asking me about it. I wouldn't be able to answer her, anyway. Focusing on my screen, I resist the urge to sigh. My eyes keep darting to her with every twitch. It's distracting as hell.

"I can see my presence isn't helping. Suggestion—" She waits until our gazes meet. "Let me make a teensy little change to your evening."

"I don't need a horse's head in my bed," I mutter.

She chuckles under her breath. It's just enough to give her some humanity. I tuck away the information for later when I bring myself to write her story.

"Don't," she whispers, and I wonder what my face is doing. She clears her throat. "I'll run it by your...husband first to make you feel better."

I bite my tongue, resisting the urge to question her as she slinks through the door. Emmett and I decided to leave it be. We won't talk about our fake marriage unless it becomes a problem.

Once my characters go back to their own worlds, they won't remember what my relationship status is. They probably won't even remember me. The revelation hits me harder than I thought it would.

Tipping my head back, I close my eyes. When I finish and they go back to their own lives, will they remember who I am? Will they recall their time here in my world? Or will it be a seamless transition for them—like no time has passed? The questions pile up, pushing the plots and storylines to the back of my mind. My stomach twists when the scenarios take a dark turn.

"Maddie?" Emmett's voice cuts through me and my eyes fly open.

"If they just showed up and they live in the stories, then is their world the real one or is ours? Or are both of them legit? And if that's true, then there has to be writers in their world. So, whose stories are *they* writing? I wonder if there's a million different places, and a million different stories, and a million different people, and they're all waiting for their happily ever afters."

Emmett crouches in front of me, a slight smile on his face. "Fell down the meta hole, huh? No use going down that path. You won't get anywhere and all you'll end up with is a headache."

My eyes fall closed again. "Let me guess, you've already done this little thought experiment."

"Bingo. Been down that road and drove straight into the ditch when I couldn't wrap my head around it. Now might not be the time to think about it unless it's going to help you write."

I snort, peek at him. "Did Sage talk to you?"

"She did. Which was fucking terrifying. Don't worry about it. We've got everything under control. You focus on writing."

He pushes to his feet and makes his way back inside. Resigning myself to getting back to work, I focus on my computer. It takes me all of ten seconds to pull up Sage's file and immediately close it. I'm not mentally ready to take on her emotional rollercoaster of a story. Instead, I open the one document I've been avoiding.

Scanning the last chapter I wrote, my mind sinks into the story. Hope and Zayne have been waiting long enough. They deserve to experience a happily ever after. Drawing in a deep breath, a small smile pulls at my lips.

Four hours later, the world comes back into view. The fog I'm in while writing lifts and color returns to my surroundings. I glance around, trying to figure out where I am.

As much as I love diving into my stories, it's disorienting to come back to reality. Especially since the lines are blurred now. I don't know how the others handle the blending so well. Even the ones who struggle to be around people seem to like the mingling. Maybe I'm the only one who finds it exhausting.

"How many words did you get?" Sage asks, and I yelp.

"Stop fucking sneaking up on me," I snarl, slamming my computer closed so she doesn't peek.

"Stop freaking the fuck out whenever someone asks you a question." She plops into the other chair. "Words."

My nose wrinkles at her demand, but I mumble, "Almost five."

"Five words? Or five hundred?"

"Thousand. I've been working for four hours. I'd be in deep shit if I only got five words."

She taps her finger against her lips, then turns to face me, determination in her eyes. "I always wanted to paint."

I struggle to keep my face neutral. "You could paint now."

She shakes her head, glancing out over the lake. "Frivolous. I thought about painting with blood, but that seems like it'd be a bit too far. Even for me."

The scuffle of a shoe from below has both of us trying to peer between the slats of the wood. A shadow detaches from near the wall, and we scramble toward the railing.

"You see anyone?" I whisper after a good thirty seconds.

"Nope. Damn rules."

Sage makes her way back to her seat, and I follow.

"What rules?" I ask, sinking into my chair.

"There's obviously rules to this place. We're confined to this area. We can eat, but don't have to. Some people can disappear while others are stuck no matter what they do. Not to mention the fading."

"Fading? No one is fading."

She snorts, giving me a look. "Dude, yes they are. Not surprised you haven't noticed since you're clearly avoiding everyone. Mostly it happens when we go into the woods."

"I have no idea what you're talking about." I'm not ready to admit she's right about me ignoring them. Acknowledging how awkward I feel when I'm around them would break what little trust they have in me.

"I'm going to assume you mean the woods part and not the other thing. Whenever one of us stomps off through the trees, we get to a certain point and the world just evaporates. Sometimes we're deposited right back where we started on the edge of the forest. Once in a while, hours or even days have passed. It's a bit disorienting. Personally, I've done it just to get away from them." She pulls out a book from nowhere and I scowl.

"Who the hell gave you my book?"

She smirks, waving the paperback between us. "This thing? None of your goddamn business."

I grit my teeth, resisting the urge to rip it from her hands. I don't like the idea of any of them reading my stuff. Especially the one she's reading. It's not my worst one. It's also not my best.

Small mercy, it's not *that* book. My palms itch to open my computer and start fixing the manuscript that sent me into this alternate universe. If I rewrite it, maybe I'll be thrown back in time to when I released it and none of this would have happened.

The sound of glass shattering inside the cabin yanks me from my deliberations and I shoot to my feet. Emmett stands in the middle of the living room, the remnants of a mug scattered at his feet. Slowly, he lifts his head, confusion stamped across his face.

"Is he okay?" Sage asks from behind me.

"I don't know. But I'm gonna find out."

Her hand lands on my arm, and I freeze. I may not know much about Sage, but the one thing I do know is she never touches people unless she's hurting them. I glance back at her, and she drops her hold on me.

"Go easy on him. I have a feeling he's a bit on edge." Indecision dances in her eyes until she opens her mouth once more. "I'm not one to give *relationship* advice, but maybe talk about the future."

"Future? I can't even think beyond today. Not only that, but Emmett and I are married—"

"Bullshit. You may be able to dupe the others, but I'm not a fool. If you two are married, I'm a ray of fucking sunshine with a pet unicorn." She skips to the railing, then shimmies down one of the posts. Emmett and I might have to have another conversation.

I bite my lip as I make my way through the door. Emmett hasn't moved, which is more concerning than anything else. He's been acting strange the last few days. He blames the heat, but I'm starting to think it's something more.

As I approach, he throws up his hands. "Don't come any closer. I don't want you to get glass in your foot."

"I'm going to grab the broom. Why don't you sit down?"

He scoffs, then pivots just to stumble his way up the stairs. He grabs the broom and vacuum from the small closet in the hallway. I'm not surprised he didn't listen to me. He seems to take on all the responsibilities, thinking he has to take care of me. It's another conversation we'll have to revisit. All our discussions are piling up, being pushed under the rug.

Dammit. Sage was right.

"Emmett, we should...what happened?" I wince as I chicken out. Emmett doesn't stop cleaning up the mess. I don't even think he heard me.

"Move," he grunts, and I shuffle back a few steps.

"We need to..." I can't force the words out. He's clearly going through something that's more important than our future.

He finishes cleaning and dumps the remains of the mug into the trash. I press my lips together, keeping everything inside. I should go back to writing and leave him be. I can't force him into anything, and I wouldn't want to either. He'll come to me when he's ready. At least I hope he will. We've never been in this situation. It feels so normal compared to the rest of our experiences—attempting to navigate a relationship.

I turn, intent on retreating to the deck and my computer. I can lose myself in the story again, forgetting the outside world. Our future, his purpose, the fake marriage—issues for just Maddie. Writer Maddie takes over and allows me to live vicariously through my characters.

I'm struggling enough to reconcile them being here. It's hard to drop myself into their stories completely because only an echo of them remains. I can't send them all to a remote cabin in the north, though. They might be meshing while they're here, but their stories won't.

"Don't go," Emmett whispers harshly and I turn.

He stares at his palms, then slowly lifts his head to meet my gaze. Lost. It's the only way I describe him.

"We don't have to talk about anything yet."

"Come here," he rasps. "Now."

A shiver rolls down my spine and my feet respond before my mind catches up until I'm standing in front of him. His hands tremble as they land on my hips and tug me closer. My heart skips a beat as his eyes find mine. I lose myself in his gaze and the world falls away. Maybe it's not just writing—maybe it's him. He allows me to forget everything else. He's my safe space when I only had words before.

My eyes flutter closed, and I rest my forehead on his chest. When his arms circle around me, a missing piece deep within me slots into place. If I never leave this place, I'll be fine as long as Emmett stays, too.

Chapter Forty-Three

Emmett

I slide my fingers into Maddie's hair, gripping the strands to keep her close. I want to speak up, tell her what happened earlier. The words have fled, though. They're right there, sitting on the tip of my tongue. Without knowing how she'll react, my nerves override my attempts to tell her how much she means to me.

"We need to talk," she murmurs.

"You won't be doing anything other than what I tell you to," I growl.

Her muscles relax, and her nails dig into my sides. A primal sound rumbles in my chest. I slide my hands down to her ass and pick her up. She gasps and her arms slide around my neck. I should take her to the bedroom, especially with the others just randomly popping up. I can't wait to be inside her. Not after what happened.

"Emmett," she pants when my teeth sink into her neck.

Her ass hits the dining table and I force her hands behind her back onto the cool wood. When I'm sure she'll leave them there, I straighten. My breath saws in and out of my lungs and spots dance in my vision.

"Up," I command, gripping her waistband.

I rip her shorts from her body when she obeys. She reaches for my belt and I growl, grabbing her wrists. I guide her onto her back, forcing her arms above her head.

"Don't fucking move." I raise an eyebrow and she licks her lips, then nods.

Trailing my fingers down her body, she shivers and her back arches. When I reach her knees, I grip them hard and shove them apart, sinking as my heart hammers. Her scent washes over me and I bury my nose in her dripping pussy as she whimpers. I can't resist tasting her, but I stay away from her clit. I need to watch her come. It's the only thing that will settle the ache in my chest.

I taste her one last time before pushing to my feet, and I free my cock. She licks her lips again, eyes fixed on my length as I grip myself. My hand is a poor substitute for her pussy, though.

"Eyes on me, gorgeous," I grunt.

As soon as our gazes collide, I slam into her, groaning as her heat envelops me. Her back leaves the table again, forcing me deeper. Her legs wind around my waist, holding me in place. She wiggles, trying to force me to move, but I'm not ready. I want to bask in the glow of her pleasure.

Gripping her hips, I stop her, refusing to move. "You're not listening very well."

"Just move," she wheezes, and her hands twitch as if she'll drop them.

"You'll take what I give you." I don't know what it is about her that brings out my primal side, but the need to dominate her sends a bolt of desire straight to my cock.

Her body goes pliant in my grasp, and a possessive need rushes through my veins. I fight the urge to plunge into her hard and fast. As much as I want to claim her, body and soul, I don't want to hurt her.

Her heel digs into my lower back and my eyes snap open. I didn't even realize I'd closed them. Fire burns in her gaze and she grits her teeth.

"Don't you fucking dare."

I lean over her, brushing my lips against hers, and she chases my touch. "I'll do whatever I damn well please. And you'll be a good girl and thank me for whatever I give you."

"Yes, sir," she breathes, and I groan.

"You're playing with fire, gorgeous."

I straighten and she grins. She knows exactly what she's asking of me. I tuck my chin to my chest and roll my hips, relishing the sounds I'm able to pull from her.

I could take this slow, coaxing the pleasure from her until she's writhing underneath me. Or I can fall back into the emotions floating just beneath the surface, the ones that spur me on to mark her completely. She needs to know who she belongs to, regardless of what she decides later. Whether she stays or goes, I want her to remember.

As I pull out slowly, she sucks in a deep breath, then I thrust into her. Her fingers scrape against the wood, straining to gain purchase. Her arms drop by her sides, and she latches onto the edge of the table as I continue to plunge into her. Her pussy spasms, gripping my cock as if to keep me deep within her.

Her fingers wrap around my wrists, digging into the soft skin. The bite of pain spurs me on, and my thrusts become erratic. Her back arches as she pulses around my cock, sailing over the edge. It's the most beautiful sight. I could spend the rest of my life watching ecstasy wash across her body.

I groan as I follow her into oblivion. My eyes roll back in my head as a weightlessness overtakes me. I tug her upright, fusing our bodies together. As she trembles against me, I run my hands under her shirt. Holding her close, the final remnant of my episode flees. If all we have is this, I hope it will be enough.

Several hours later, I can't keep my eyes off Maddie. Sage pushed me to finally act on Kol's suggestion. It wasn't hard to convince me, both because I wanted to do it when it was first mentioned, but also because Sage still puts me on edge.

She's never done anything, yet the sheer number of weapons she keeps on full display definitely helps her image.

"Are your palms itchy?" Maddie asks as she sidles up next to me.

"What? No." I tuck my hands in my pockets.

"Sure they aren't. Nervous?" She grins, knocking her shoulder into me.

My eyes dart to the kitchen, then toward the deck. "Not nervous. I'd rather be in there, though. Is there a reason I couldn't just cook for this dinner party?"

She chuckles and I wrap my arm around her waist. The calmness always surrounding her seeps into me. I wish we could kick all these people out and finish all the conversations we started. I need to know where she stands—what her plans are. And I need to tell her what I want.

My gaze flits to the dining table and the image of her from earlier flashes through my mind. Subtly, I try to adjust my growing erection, and Maddie giggles.

I lean down, my lips brushing the shell of her ear. "Knock it off or I'll throw you over my shoulder and fuck you in our bedroom while all these people listen."

She snorts and lifts her face. "You wouldn't dare."

"Wouldn't I?" This exchange does nothing but make me harder, yet I can't stop.

The smug look she gives me has me second-guessing myself. "Nope. Not even a little bit. You don't want other people to hear me when I come."

I grit my teeth, my nostrils flaring as I attempt to get my shit together. "Stop talking or I'll kick them all out."

"Dinner's ready!" Grace calls from the kitchen.

I jolt, scanning the small group. I spot Sam, Grace's love interest, on the deck, a beer in hand, talking to someone I haven't met. Pretty sure it's Ryder, the newcomer's man. Neither of them moves, though Ryder glances through the window.

"I should have talked to them instead of flirting with you," Maddie mumbles, and I pull my gaze away.

"Nope. You don't owe them anything." Empty words. We both know she's responsible for their lives—for their very existence.

She sighs, shaking her head, then pulls away from my grasp. Not before I catch the small smile gracing her lips, though.

Grace places a covered dish on the dining table as the others take their seats. Maddie slips into one, chatting with Sophie. The woman doesn't understand why she's here. Maddie said she hasn't really started their story, which makes for some awkward interactions with Sophie and Ryder. At least they both understand they're characters. I can't even imagine what it would feel like if I was dropped into the middle of nowhere with no idea how I got there.

"Emmett," Maddie hisses, and I make my way to her as Ryder sits across from Sophie, smiling awkwardly at her.

Halfway there, I pivot and stomp onto the deck. It'd be one thing if Sam refused to come inside, content to make Grace's life even harder. Instead, Tate has joined him, though where the hell he came from, I couldn't say. Grace and Sam are still waffling between whether they're a thing or not, despite Maddie spending a good chunk of her time writing their story. She keeps hoping she'll get them over the hump, as she puts it.

"Hey, assholes. Sam, get the fuck inside. Now. Go to hell, Tate." I cross my arms, waiting for one of them to move.

Sam has the good sense to look ashamed. Tate, not so much. His jaw ticks as he mirrors my stance. Sam's gaze jumps between us. He makes the right decision, hustling inside. Tate isn't worth my time. I should follow Sam and forget about him. My feet stay glued to the wood, waiting for him to make a move.

"I'm not leaving until I get some answers," Tate snarls when he can't take the silence anymore.

"You'll be leaving either way." I let the threat hang between us for a beat. "But since I'm feeling generous, tell me your questions."

"As if I'd talk to you. I'm going straight to the source." Regardless of his words, he doesn't move.

"You go within five feet of my woman, I will rip your limbs from your body and beat you with them."

His face twists and he opens his mouth. Then disappears. It takes a minute for me to register he's gone. The others are gathered at the lake for the most part. No chance I'd be able to find him again. Not that I want to. As long as he understands how serious I am and stays away from Maddie, I have nothing more to say to him.

Chapter Forty-Four
Maddie

"Is Emmett okay?" Sophie whispers.

I glance out the window and find Emmett standing alone, looking a little lost. My stomach flips, worry worming its way through me. I don't have an answer for Sophie, but I should go check on him. I'm still dithering when he swings around and makes his way inside. I bite my tongue, keeping the questions at bay.

Tate is an asshole I haven't had a chance to fix yet. I don't even *know* if I can fix him. Sam and Grace haven't seemed to progress in their relationship despite the chapters I've added to their story. I keep waiting for one of them to break. It's one thing to write a declaration of love. Witnessing one would be...amazing. On another level. I steal a glance at Sam, but he's as surly as he was last week.

Emmett slides into the chair next to me and his hand lands on my thigh. His fingers flex over and over as he attempts to get himself under control. I wish I could ask him about what happened. This isn't the time. Grace clinks her fork against her glass and the low murmur of conversation dies out.

"Thanks for coming tonight. I know this whole situation is a little unconventional, but I think we're all adjusting as well as..." She glances at Sam, then drops her eyes to the dishes. "Well, you know what I mean. Anyways. I cooked...this."

She lifts the lid with a flourish. A lemony aroma fills the air, steam wafting around us. Mashed potatoes, steamed vegetables, and a corn casserole surround the main dish of—

"Fucking fish," Sam growls.

"What?" Grace sets the lid down, confusion stamped across her face.

"I said—" He pushes to his feet, his fists planted on the table. "Fucking. Fish."

"What's wrong with fish? It's not even salmon."

He lets out a sharp laugh, a wild look in his brown eyes. "Every goddamn time it's fucking fish. I am so fucking sick of fish."

"Well, if you are *so fucking sick of fish,* then maybe you should get off your ass and cook a goddamn meal every once in a while," she snaps, rising to her feet as well.

"I did," he cries and throws up his hands. "I grilled, and you said it was dry. As if you weren't the one who kept pulling me inside and distracting me with silly shit that could have waited."

"Silly shit? Silly shit?" Her voice becoming shriller as she repeats the question twice more.

With a final cry of frustration, she picks up a roll and flings it at his head. His mouth drops open as he stares at the bun lying innocently on his plate. She bares her teeth at him, a clear challenge on her face.

None of us dare to move. Personally, I want to see how this plays out. Emmett leans closer and I shush him before he can interrupt the show.

"What the fuck is wrong with you?" Sam growls.

Her chin quivers and I wonder if she's going to cry. "What's wrong with me? Me? You asshole." She grabs another roll and cocks her arm back.

"Don't you dare."

She grins manically and chucks it at him, hitting him square in the forehead. Ryder smothers a snort behind his hand. It's a standoff—a breaking point for both of them. I fight a grin as Sophie's wide eyes find mine. She's so quiet, I almost forgot she was here.

"For fuck's sake, Grace. Stop throwing bread at me."

"You want me to stop?"

Grace snatches up the basket and rounds the table. She yells insults and questions at him as she empties the container, one roll at a time. I can barely hear her over his shouts as he lifts his hands and scrambles to get away from her.

"I thought you could catch, Samuel Ash. Show everyone your *amazing* skills," she shrieks.

When she's out of ammo, he straightens, and she freezes as the realization of what she's done crashes over her. Sam growls, the sound ringing through the sudden silence. Grace squeaks, spinning to take off around the table.

Sam goes the opposite way, skirting by Sophie's chair, and catches Grace. He tips her over his shoulder and she yelps. It doesn't take long before she's pounding on his back and yelling at him to put her down. Just before he reaches the hallway, he smacks her ass. The front door slams shut, cutting off her cussing him out.

The silence stretches once more. Ryder's the first to move, reaching for the spoon stuck in the mashed potatoes.

"What are you doing?" Sophie hisses, leaning forward.

"Eating. Didn't realize this was dinner and a show, but since the show is over—onto the dinner." He drops a generous dollop on her plate, then gets another spoonful for himself.

"Should we...check on them?" Sophie asks, and Ryder snorts.

"The last thing you want to do is go find out what they're doing, Ace."

Sophie's eyes widen, a curious expression on her face. She watches quietly as he dishes out the rest of the food to her, then himself. Emmett squeezes my thigh, and I glance at him. He clears his throat and murmurs a thank you to Ryder when he hands him the bowls with vegetables. When Ryder's done, he picks up his plate and moves to the other side of the table next to Sophie. He doesn't acknowledge her as she stares at him.

Emmett nudges me with his elbow, and I straighten, pulling my gaze away from them. I feel like I'm intruding on the beginning of something new. I have no idea where their story is going. Hell, I don't even think he noticed he served her before himself. My mind races as I focus on the food until I have a better idea of who Ryder is. Sophie is harder to read as she quietly picks apart her food.

"Don't like fish?" Ryder asks, and Sophie's fork clatters on the table.

"No, I do. But even if I didn't, I don't know if I'd say anything. I'm slightly terrified Grace will bust back in here and start throwing rolls at my head," she mutters.

Ryder chuckles, pointing his knife at her plate. "Better get to eating before she catches you, then."

"Would be better with a bun," she murmurs under her breath as she ducks her head and starts eating again.

Ryder silently grabs the bread from Sam's abandoned plate and cuts it open. Emmett's elbow jabs into my side and I wave him away. I need to know whether he's going to give it to her or keep it for himself. Emmett may not understand how important this interaction is, but I do. With the way my writing has been going, I need all the help I can get.

Ryder plops the bun on Sophie's plate without a word, and I grin. I swear Emmett's going to knock me out of my chair if he keeps poking me. My nostrils flare as I suppress the snarky words I want to throw at him. Instead, I shove some food in my mouth.

Five minutes later, Emmett clears his throat. "So, what do you do, Ryder?"

Ryder sets his fork down, giving his full attention to Emmett. "College, sir. Got a full ride, so I'm taking advantage of that."

"First of all, don't call me sir. Second, what's the scholarship for? Academics or sports?"

He clears his throat, his eyes darting to Sophie, then back to Emmett. "Football. Wide receiver."

"Which is why I invited him to dinner," I cut in. "Sam coaches football. It's high school, but he was at the college level for a while."

I press my lips together, not wanting to give away Grace's connection to the sport. She has enough issues in her world without me outing her. Even if Ryder has no idea who her father is, he'll understand the implications. She doesn't need to be bombarded with a bunch of questions. Unless they're not from the same world. I haven't figured that out yet.

Sophie's head snaps up. "Do you think they're having sex? *Can* we have sex here? It seems as if everyone is confined to their stories for certain aspects, but could a person from one story have relations with someone else? Someone they're not connected to?"

Ryder scowls and tucks his chin to his chest. He's not a prude, thinking her questions are inappropriate for the dinner table. He doesn't understand she's his love interest, so he can't be jealous. They haven't met in the story. I have three lines written. The rest is stuck in my head, waiting to form into some semblance of a plot.

I clear my throat, focusing on the discussion in front of me. "Even if you could, which I don't know if you can, I wouldn't advise it. Most of the people here have specific reasons for being here. The characters in their respective worlds play a crucial part. If you mess with that, you might end up messing up the story. And I have no idea what happens then. The world might blow up or something."

I hate that I don't have answers. Maybe they'd take me a little bit more seriously if I did.

"I wasn't saying I *would*. I was asking if we *could*. I'm assuming those two are a couple? If not, they should be."

"She threw rolls at him. They're just fucking," Ryder mutters.

"What the hell does that have to do with anything? They clearly have chemistry. Plus, they've eaten meals together. That's not a thing fuck buddies do." Sophie stuffs the buttered bun in her mouth as if her reasoning settles things.

"Those two are not fuck buddies. Possibly friends with benefits or one of those circumstances where they just can't help themselves."

Sophie waves her bread in a blasé fashion. "Either way, they cook together. Especially to the point where she'd know whether or not he liked salmon."

Ryder abandons his meal, turning in his chair to face Sophie. I grab Emmett's wrist, digging my nails into his skin. He pauses, his fork halfway to his mouth, and glances at me from the corner of his eye. I'm practically vibrating in my seat and my hold on Emmett is the only thing grounding me to the present. Otherwise, I'll drop straight into one of my stories, and I don't know when I'll resurface.

"Chemistry doesn't mean anything in this instance. Those two are in a spiral. They're fuck buddies who thrive off the emotions building in them. They'll never make it long term."

Sophie's face reddens and spins to face him as well. "What qualifies you to be the judge in their relationship?"

"Relationship? That wasn't a relationship, Ace. That was a disaster waiting to happen."

"If by disaster you mean an explosion of raw emotion, then I'd agree."

He rolls his eyes. "Unless they're capable of articulating those emotions and it goes beyond sex, then sure. But those two? They're too far gone to be able to find their way back to each other."

"Maybe they haven't even been there in the first place. They just need to find home."

Ryder rears back, confusion with a mix of denial flitting across his face. "What the hell is that supposed to mean?"

Sophie lets out a long-suffering sigh. "Most people are merely searching for home. Which isn't a place, contrary to popular belief. Home can be a million different places, but it resides within others."

"Let me get this straight. You think the only way to truly belong somewhere is if you're in a relationship? That's bullshit."

She grits her teeth and I hold my breath. She's about to eviscerate him. Romance novels, at their core, have an element of finding where the characters belong. They're searching for a place beyond themselves. And while Sophie might not know she's smack dab in the middle of her own love story, she apparently understands the importance of finding her safe space.

"It's not always about a romantic relationship. Some people don't *want* that, which is a perfectly fine way to live. It's valid. But a location in and of itself does not a home make. It's whoever you surround yourself with. And if you want to find a home, you have to find your people. If that includes a partner? Great. But home is more than four walls. It's more than a city or town or province. It's more than a major in college or an occupation. Those things come and go. Once you find your home, though...well, that's magical."

Ryder's mouth parts, and I slowly exhale, not wanting to distract him from the epiphany he's going through. Emmett tangles his fingers with mine and squeezes. I don't think he's trying to distract me, but I don't want to read too much into it. I'm afraid of admitting he might be my person—my home. If I put myself out there, say the words out loud, and he doesn't feel the same...I might never recover.

"People come and go, too. Sometimes before you're ready," Ryder murmurs, a tinge of anguish coloring his words.

Sophie rests her hand on his arm, and he jerks away. She clears her throat, turning back to her plate. "I suppose when they do, it merely means your home has to change. Even if you're not prepared to face it quite yet."

My eyes blur as my writer brain takes over. This is why I put off this dinner. After Kol suggested it, and Emmett brought it up, and Sage didn't even bother talking to me—I avoided it at all costs. I was terrified of finishing. I'm still scared of the ending, but an electric energy weaves its way around my fear.

Ryder turns back to his own meal, mumbling under his breath. "Regardless, Grace and Sam clearly have some shit to work out before they can figure out whether they belong together."

"That they do. Someone's gonna have to give in if they want to find home."

I rip my hand from Emmett's and jump up. Emmett calls to me as I race to the bedroom for my laptop. I shove away the thoughts of Sophie and Ryder's story as I plop onto the floor and open the document. A grin splits my lips as I finally start the beginning of the end.

Chapter Forty-Five

Emmett

"Should you go after her?" Ryder asks as he sits back in his chair.

"Nope." I dish up another piece of fish. Sam may be sick of it, but Grace really outdid herself. I've had four fillets already.

"She did look distressed," Sophie murmurs.

A spoonful of corn casserole hits my plate. "Yup."

Ryder scoffs, shaking his head. "Stands to reason you should check on her, then. Isn't that what a good husband does?"

I sigh, setting my fork down and peering at him. "You don't know the first thing about being a husband, good or bad. So I suggest you keep your shitty advice to yourself. Maddie is perfectly fine."

Sophie doesn't look convinced. Neither does Ryder, but he's acting like an asshat.

"How do you know she's fine?" Ryder lifts his hands when I glare at him. "No offense. Just wondering."

"Because she gets like this sometimes. She doesn't get to choose when inspiration or whatever hits. If she doesn't seize it, though, it'll float away. And do you really want her ignoring it? Your story depends on her being able to write. Didn't peg you as someone who wanted to float around in the void forever."

I focus on my food, trying to dissect what spices Grace used on the fish and whether I'd be able to recreate it. I could ask her, but she's probably a little busy right now.

"She's not…Is she writing my story?" Sophie whispers.

My head snaps up, an admission on the tip of my tongue. If I reveal anything about her manuscripts, I might fuck up the time continuum, just like Grace said. It's really a toss-up on what Maddie is working on. Bugging her to ask would be disastrous. And it wouldn't help Sophie, anyway.

"Hard to say." With each question, my appetite diminishes.

"Pull up, Soph," Ryder mutters. "You're on a collision course."

Sophie whips her head toward him, snarling, "Don't call me that."

"If you'll excuse me." I shove away from the table, leaving Ryder to fend for himself.

Slowly, I open the bedroom door and scan the space. I glance behind me, craning my neck to peer at the dark deck. She's not out there.

I turn back and find her tucked between the wall and the bed. I clear my throat and her head twitches, but her fingers don't stop. They're flying across the keys when her eyes dart to me, then back to the screen.

"Stop hovering and spit it out."

I open my mouth, then close it, smiling slightly. Watching her in her element is a thing of wonder. I've mostly avoided her whenever she's writing. I don't want to disturb her, afraid I'll break her concentration. Unless she needs to eat, that is. She doesn't take care of herself when she's in so deep. I should have made her eat dinner before rushing off.

"I'm bringing you some food. Try to eat it." I close the door and make my way back to the dining room.

Ryder and Sophie are studiously ignoring each other as they finish their meals. Ryder keeps glancing at her, though. He seems to have worked out who his love interest is at least. I doubt Sophie's caught up to him. I grab one of Maddie's sticky notes and scribble on it, then tuck it in my pocket. Neither one of them needs to figure out I'm telling Maddie about them.

Ryder shoots to his feet, almost knocking his chair over. He grabs his plate and brings it to the kitchen. I expect him to leave, but he returns to the table and gathers up more dishes. It's almost like he's on autopilot, going from one room to the other.

Sophie may pretend like she's not tracking him, but after three trips, she gets up and clears her plate as well. They work in silence until the table is empty. I sink onto the couch as they move around each other like they're linked together in a dance, one gliding around the other. I never imagined something as simple as cleaning could be so elegant.

I should help, but I don't want to disturb them. When Ryder turns on the water to wash the dishes, I take it as my cue to leave. I stop by the bedroom and drop my note on the bed. Maddie doesn't even seem to notice my presence.

"Wait," she calls, and I poke my head inside. "Where are they? I need them."

"Uh, who?"

"The bread bandits." She chuckles at her terrible joke.

"I'll find them."

I close the door gently and tiptoe through the kitchen. Ryder and Sophie don't notice, working in silence on the dishes. Why they're doing them by hand, I have no idea. It feels like a canon event I shouldn't interrupt.

The hot night air hits me when I step outside. When I was a kid, summers were spent collecting fireflies and camping out under the stars. With all the characters here, I'm thrown into my past. Bursts of laughter float along the breeze, and I stroll toward the lake. I don't think Sam and Grace came down here, but I'll give them all the time I can to finish whatever they've started.

Several small groups have gathered by the lake—bonfires, talking, and even spin the bottle. At least I think that's what they're playing. A few people notice me, and I hurry away. The last thing I need is to get pulled into a conversation with one of them. There's another group at the fire pit Maddie and I went to before we knew any of them were characters.

My stomach jumps as I get closer to the forest. I can't keep my eyes from searching for any of the random shit I saw in there. The portal doesn't worry me. If it pops up again, I just won't go into it. I doubt the magic would take me anywhere. It would probably dump me out on the other side of the yard or something.

The fae woman, though—she's what keeps me up at night. I still have dreams about her. I wake up in a sweat, wondering if she's perched in the corner of the room as she watches me sleep. I shouldn't care about her anymore. She hasn't been seen since that day and everyone stays out of that area.

"Emmett!" Beckett yells. "Get this man a drink. He deserves it."

"No, I'm good. I have to get back."

"What are you looking for?" Bailey, his love interest, slides next to me and I jolt.

"Uh, Grace. Maddie needs to talk to her."

Bailey smiles, grabbing my arm to pull me back toward the cabin. She glances over her shoulder when Beckett makes a noise in the back of his throat. She waves him off, then leads me on. Once we're out of his sight, she drops her hand. I really hope she wasn't using me to make him jealous.

"Sorry about him. For some reason, he thinks I need a keeper."

"*Do* you need a keeper?"

She laughs lightly, shaking her head as we climb the hill. "I'm not clumsy or anything. He just thinks I'm a bit too trusting. Especially when it comes to men. You don't count, though."

"That's a compliment, right?"

"Of course it is. You're not going to take advantage of me. You're completely dedicated to Maddie." She presses her lips together as if she's holding something back. "It's nice to see. Not many people are as committed as you are."

I don't know how to respond. I'm not about to ask her what she means. Mostly because I already know. Some wounds are deeper than others. My childhood was a mix of happy moments and distressing memories. They weave together, forming who I am today. They're the foundation of my existence.

"You should talk to Maddie," I say gruffly. "She might be able to help."

I'm not equipped to deal with someone else's trauma. Especially when it comes to cheating, which is what I suspect she's alluding to. I may have had a front row seat to the aftermath of an affair, but I watched it through the eyes of a child. Which is different than experiencing it myself.

"Oh, I wouldn't bother her with all that. I'm fine. And I know I'll heal, eventually. I'm assuming with Beckett's help." She smiles as we round the cabin.

I glance away, not willing to confirm or deny her suspicions. She stops by the front porch, biting her lip as she stares into the dark.

"Are we waiting for them to wander over? Because this is where I started."

She leans closer, whispering, "They're over by the car. I saw them earlier when I was making my way down to the bonfire. They were...preoccupied. I'd rather not walk up on them if they're busy."

She waves, then pivots and disappears into the night. I sigh, wishing I could avoid this interaction.

"Grace," I call as I take a few steps toward Maddie's broken-down car. "I really don't want to come over there."

Grace emerges from the shadows, straightening her dress. I smother a smirk when I spot her smeared lipstick. Ryder seems to have at least been partly right. Sam stumbles after her, his shirt buttoned wrong. As he steps into the porch light, I catch a flash of red on his neck. It's either a hickey or Grace's lipstick. I swallow down the laugh begging to escape.

Grace skids to a stop. "Sorry, what's up? Is everything okay?"

Sam saunters up next to her and spots her mussed up makeup. His shoulder brushes hers and he subtly swipes his thumb across his cheek. She widens her eyes, giving him a questioning look. I tuck my chin to my chest, trying not to bust into laughter.

"You have—" Sam shakes his head. "Oh fuck it. Come here."

I half expect him to lick his thumb and scrub at her face, but he's gentle, cupping her face as he cleans her up. Her face softens and I feel like I'm intruding on something special. She's looking at him like she's in love. And he's looking at her like she's home.

My vision dims and I blink rapidly. Their bodies blur, the edges of the world smudging. They don't seem to notice, too enamored with each other. I could blame it on the moonless night or the heat. My chest tightens and I struggle to pull in a full breath.

The front door slams open, and the two jump apart, their outlines solidifying. My head swims and I squeeze my eyes shut. I sway as nausea creeps up my throat. I'd love to blame the heat, but maybe I overate.

"Are you ready?" Maddie hollers.

I turn, finding her clutching her open computer in her arms. Even from here I can tell her eyes are shining with unshed tears. She plops onto the top stair and waves me over. The closer I get, the clearer my head becomes. By the time I sit next to her and the heat from her seeps into my side, it's as if I imagined all my symptoms. The world comes back into focus, and I breathe a sigh of relief.

"What are we getting ready for?" Grace asks as she stops a few feet in front of us, Sam trailing her.

Maddie smiles as she bounces in anticipation. "The end. I only have a few more lines and your story will be finished."

Grace's face falls even as she attempts to hide it. "That's...great. Did you hear that, Sam? We're about to get out of here."

He steps next to her, and his hand rests on her lower back. She leans into him as if borrowing his strength. She presses her lips together as she glances around. Not that she can see much in the dark. One of the groups down by the lake cheer, their laughter filling the air.

"You might not even remember this place," Maddie murmurs. "Or you might stick around. Maybe you'll be the first and the last."

Grace lets out a humorless laugh. "You and I both know that's not how it works. We're not that lucky."

"Guess not. We're a helluva lot of things, but lucky is not one of them."

Sam catches my eye, something dangerously close to respect hanging in his gaze. He nods and I return the gesture. Now that we're at the end, I wish I would have talked to him more, figured out where his head was at. He was clearly struggling. Mostly with his feelings toward Grace. And I ignored it all, too afraid to get involved. If he really does disappear, I promise myself I'll do better with the others. I don't want to walk away from this experience with regret.

"Are you ready?" Maddie asks, pulling my gaze to her.

Grace bites her lips, tucking a strand of hair behind her ear. "Maddie, remember. Sometimes you just need a little help to finish the story."

"Maybe I'll see you in the spin-off," Maddie whispers. She lowers her gaze to her computer and slowly types the last few words.

Chapter Forty-Six
Maddie

Tears obscure my vision as I write the last sentence in Grace and Sam's story. I don't typically type *The End*, but it feels more appropriate now. I glance up and a sob catches in my throat. Their figures are hazy, blurring around the edges.

Grace mouths her goodbye, pride shining in her eyes as I finish, and they fade away. I stare at the spot they once stood and my heart aches. When Emmett wraps his arms around me, I lose it, sobbing into his chest.

Usually, I don't get emotional when I finish a story. This time is different. I knew it would be. It's why I put off finishing. Because I knew once they no longer had a reason to be here, they'd disappear as quickly as they came. I just didn't expect it to hurt this much.

"It's okay. You'll be alright," Emmett murmurs into my hair.

He kisses my temple, and the weight of my computer leaves my legs. Before I fully comprehend what's happening, I'm in his lap and he sways back and forth. He's whispering words I can't make out. I wish he could rip the pain away, leaving only the sense of accomplishment behind. I've been emotional before, but nothing compared to this.

"Remember, they're in their story now, living your words. I'm so proud of you."

"I feel like I abandoned them."

He pulls back, holding me by the shoulders. "How did you possibly come to that conclusion?"

I shrug, but he glares at me, not accepting my half-ass attempt to brush it off. "They were here, helping me get over my block. Especially Grace. She jump-started everything. She was—" I stop, unwilling to admit anything else.

"She was your friend. Hard to separate the character from the person when they're standing right in front of you. But she deserves what you gave her. And who knows, maybe she will remember. Maybe some remnant of her time here will be lodged in her psyche. At the very least, you're connected through the story."

"How do you always know the right thing to say?" I ask, sniffling as I snuggle closer.

"It's my superpower. Now, let's get you inside so you can finally eat."

Despite his words, he doesn't move, content to hold me a bit longer. It might be pathetic, but Grace *is* my friend. She has the parts of me I actually like. My job is isolating, leaving large swaths of time I'm completely alone. Other than Chloe, my characters are the closest thing I have to a connection. They're a part of me, yet completely their own entities. Having them here, in the flesh, makes it harder to distinguish what's real and what's fantasy.

"They're all going to disappear," I murmur.

"I'm not going to be sad when a few of them vanish." He chuckles and I join in. "When it comes down to it, you're giving them their lives back. Not to sound like a broken record, but they deserve more than what they found here."

"I know. Doesn't make it any easier to deal with."

"No, I suppose it doesn't. As long as you don't let this derail you. Tonight, though, let yourself be sad." His hand runs across my back, then freezes. "Vacation."

I pull back to study his face. "This isn't a vacation. We're both supposed to be working."

"We *are* working. You more than me. But what if *they're* on vacation? What if in their memories this was a vacation, and they'll remember? You wouldn't even have to put it in the stories. You'd know and that could be enough." His fingers slip underneath my shirt and goosebumps scatter across my skin.

"I'm hungry." I need to focus on something other than Grace being gone. "Please tell me Ryder and Sophie left. I don't know if I can deal with another character tonight."

"Let's go check. And if they haven't, I'll kick their asses out. They've got some energy between them, but I don't think they realize. Oh, and she doesn't like being called Soph. I left you a note in case I forgot." He sets me on my feet, then leads me inside.

Thankfully, it's just us now. Emmett guides me to the clean dining table and sets my computer next to me. The need to open it and start writing again sends a bolt of anxiety through me.

Despite the stories I've finished, I don't have time to slow down. I've always struggled with deadlines, but I'd never get anything done without them. I wish I was like other authors who don't have to worry about these things. If I was just a little less *me*, maybe I never would have spiraled. Tears spring to my eyes and I wipe them away.

Emmett places a plate of Grace's food in front of me, and I bite my tongue.

"She's living her life. Remember that," he murmurs.

"No, it's not that. I mean, it is, but no. I just wish my brain wouldn't do shit like this. I wish I could change the way I operate. If I can just do things differently—"

"Then you wouldn't be you. You'd be someone else. And if you were someone else, then your stories wouldn't be yours." He sits across from me and gestures for me to eat.

"Why do you get ice cream and I don't?" I glare at his bowl as he picks up a spoon.

"Because I ate my dinner. You haven't yet. And don't change the subject."

I scowl, picking up my fork and stabbing a piece of fish. The citrusy flavor explodes across my tongue and my eyes flutter closed. I can't hold back a moan and kick myself for rushing away from the table earlier. I take another bite, almost whimpering at how delicious it is. Grace did not get her cooking skills from me, that's for damn sure.

"You're really going to have to stop that."

My head snaps up and I meet Emmett's blue-green eyes. "Have you tried this? It's amazing."

"I have, but if you keep making those noises, you're going to end up bent over this table."

"You say that like it'll deter me." I smirk, then stuff another piece in my mouth.

"You're derailing the conversation, Maddie. Talk."

I sigh, suddenly not wanting to say anything. "It's just imposter syndrome. The constant fear of not being enough or producing something no one likes. It's what sent me into a tailspin before. I convinced myself I was a hack. I have readers who have been with me from the beginning and sometimes they were the only reason I kept going. I finish books and series for them. And I constantly felt like I was doing them a disservice."

"Did they tell you that?" The heat in his voice has me huffing out a laugh.

"No. They're all amazingly supportive. Even if they did think I was failing, I'd never know. Not knowing is a blessing and a curse. I don't read my reviews for a reason. Hard to get away from them when they're splashed everywhere, though. I couldn't avoid them and still market my books. Can't get new readers if you don't talk about your stuff. And then I started looking at everyone around me and what they were doing."

"Which I'm guessing didn't help."

"Not even a little bit. It's hard being an author. Dealing with jealousy, but also being excited for other authors and their success. The constant fear of your latest book flopping. Or making it." My chest tightens the more I reveal.

"Isn't that a good thing? Your book making it? Then you wouldn't have to worry as much. You could hire someone to do all the other things."

"Of course. But it's also terrifying. The highs are higher. And the lows are in the fucking gutter. The expectation to repeat the success is overwhelming. My first book in the trilogy was a hit, and I knew I'd have to do it again if I wanted to keep going. When everyone loved the second book just as much, if not more, than the first, I was ecstatic. I thought I'd conquered my imposter syndrome. And then I crashed and burned at the finish line." I sigh, setting my fork down as my appetite vanishes.

"Sounds like you forgot to celebrate your successes. You started judging yourself by other people's standards. But you're not them." He nudges my plate, urging me to keep eating.

"I'm not, but it's still hard. Usually, I try to ignore comparing myself to others. I hole up and focus on the stories. This time around, I didn't have the escape because I wasn't writing. Most of the time, I take a break after a release, then get back into it. I couldn't. I just couldn't get back to where I needed to be."

He rounds the table and turns my chair to face him. I swallow down the tears when he drops to his knees. He wraps his arms around my waist and drops his head onto my lap. Burying my fingers in his hair, I close my eyes. We've talked about all this before, but never this in-depth. Never when I've finally ignited my spark.

"What if this is exactly where you needed to be?" His muffled voice reverberates through me.

What if?

I thought I'd go to bed, maybe convince Emmett to dick me down. Neither of those things happened, unfortunately. As soon as Emmett stood up, I reached for my computer. Three hours later, my eyes are drooping to the point where the words on the screen blur.

"You need sleep," Emmett murmurs, brushing my hair from my forehead.

"I just want to finish this paragraph." I blink rapidly, waiting for the words to come.

Emmett stands quietly next to me, and I do my best to ignore him. He's not reading over my shoulder, but his hovering might be a bit too much. After two minutes, I give up and cut my losses. I'll pick it up tomorrow. Peyton and her boys will be fine until then. Even if I am in the middle of a spicy scene.

I step straight into Emmett's arms, allowing the heat from his body to warm me. "I've never done a friends-with-benefits-to-lovers story. It's slightly terrifying."

"Whose is it?"

"Peyton and her guys. They have some shit they're going to go through, though. It won't be pretty. Gotta toughen her up so she can ream their asses." I glance up at him and gasp. Shoving away from him, I snarl, then slam my computer shut.

"Sorry," he says, chuckling. "I only caught a couple words."

I narrow my eyes at him. "Which ones?"

"Drag, needy, intoxicating..." He pulls out each word, a sensual edge to them. "Cock."

He grabs my hips and pulls me close to him. I shiver as he slides his hand along my body to my neck, threading his fingers into my hair. He tightens his grip and tugs my head back. My lips part in anticipation of his mouth crashing into mine. Yet it never comes. Instead, his teeth scrape along my jaw.

"Turn around and place your hands on the table," he growls. He steps away, dropping his hands from me.

I sag, my knees almost giving out completely, and I grab the back of the chair. "So bossy."

A dark chuckle rolls around me as he saunters away, turning off the lights one by one until only one remains over the oven in the kitchen. As he turns, I slap my hands on the table, wincing as the sound echoes through the room. Tucking my chin to my chest, I bite my lip as my muscles stiffen.

He kicks the chair aside and runs his hand down my arm. "You seem a little tense, gorgeous."

My lids flutter closed as he tugs something from his pocket. Fabric slides across my face, then settles on my eyes. I'm pretty sure it's a napkin, and he ties it, making sure my hair doesn't get caught. It's just another sign of how considerate he is. Even while he's giving me commands.

"I'd tie you up, but I'm not sure you're ready for that. Wouldn't really fit the scene either."

"Scene?" I whisper.

His breath on my neck has a bolt of desire skittering down my spine. "I may have caught more than a few words."

A shudder rolls through me, and my thighs clench. "If you did, then you'd know to tie my wrists together before fucking me on a desk."

"Have to get you naked before I do that. Plus, you'd have to wait until I build you a desk." The warmth from his body fades away as he steps back and I glance over my shoulder even if I can't see him.

"You're building me a desk?" A well of emotions rises in me and wetness seeps into the fabric. I drop my head again, hoping he didn't notice the tears in my voice.

"Don't cry, gorgeous."

"I'm not. Might be the sweetest thing anyone has done for me, but I'm not crying."

He slips his hands under my shirt, sliding the fabric up until my back is exposed. My breath catches as his lips brush across my skin. A soft moan leaves me when he reaches around and cups my breast, then rolls my nipple between his fingers.

"Emmett," I groan, wishing he would stop teasing me. I'm already soaked, the heat between my legs building with each passing moment.

He hums, keeping up the exquisite torture by moving to my other breast. "I'm merely distracting you with pleasure, Maddie. Be patient."

"I need you inside me." The confession slips from me without warning.

"All in due time."

I push my ass into him, attempting to entice him. He grunts, his fingers pinching my nipple.

"Perhaps I really will tie you to the bed. Then I can take all the time I want with you," he growls.

His hands drop to my waistband, and he strips off my leggings and underwear in one fell swoop. The fabric bunches around my calves and he frees one foot. I glance down, peeking from under the napkin, and my jaw drops.

"What the hell are you doing?" I demand as he grabs my ankle, then grins up at me.

"Best I can do until I get some proper restraints. Now stay still."

He uses my pants to tie me to the table leg. When he whips off his shirt and reaches for my other leg, I squeal, kicking out.

"None of that, gorgeous. You're going to be a good girl and let me do this. Then you'll take my cock in that pretty little pussy of yours."

Wetness drips down my thighs at his words, and I slide my other foot over until I'm spread wide for him. Anticipation thrums through my veins. I'm so wound up I'll probably come at the slightest touch from him.

He stands, running his fingers up my body and I drop my forehead to the table, a whimper escaping me.

"Such a needy, intoxicating creature you are. Don't worry, gorgeous. I'll take care of you. I promise."

Chapter Forty-Seven

Emmett

I thought with a little rest I'd be good as new. I've used the last week off to focus on Maddie and staying out of the heat. Instead, it's become a more regular occurrence for my head to swim. Mentioning the episodes to Maddie won't do anything other than make her worry. So I keep it all inside, hoping things will get better.

I swing the axe down, splitting the stump in two, and wipe my brow. I probably shouldn't be out here chopping wood even if the sun is setting. Then again, relaxing inside the air conditioning doesn't seem to be helping. Might as well get this done now rather than when the temperature really does drop. We're still at least a month from any type of colder weather, but I'd rather not be caught without it. The fact that I'm preparing for a winter in the north isn't lost on me.

"Emmett?" someone calls from behind me, and I spin. I don't recognize him, but I'm pretty sure he's one of Peyton's men.

"Can I help you?"

"Hoping so. Grey." He holds his hand out and I shake it.

"Is Grey your name or…"

He gives me a long-suffering smile. "Yeah, go ahead."

"Don't know what I'm going ahead with." I grab another chunk of wood and set it on the stump.

"Most people have some joke...never mind. I've got an idea for the writer. Thought I would bring it to you instead."

I swing the axe, splitting the log in two before asking, "Why's that?"

"Because I was by the deck when that vampire dude tried to interrupt her. She's got a mouth on her." He chuckles, running his hand through his blond hair. I wonder if he dyes it to get the strands so light.

I slam the blade into the stump and turn to face him, crossing my arms. "Maddie can speak however the fuck she wants. Especially to you lot."

His eyes widen, and he tucks his hands in his pockets. "Wasn't going to complain about it. Just an observation. Peyton has the mouth of a sailor, sometimes complete with the accent. Maybe I should have included the part where your woman shoved him over the railing. I mean, he's a vampire, so he landed on his feet. I wonder what would happen if she pushed me off the deck."

"I wouldn't advise testing that, in case of an unfortunate outcome. I'm guessing you play hockey," I say, and he nods. "Would you like to start the season with an injury?"

Horror spreads across his face. "Definitely not. The season starts in a couple weeks. I can't afford to not play. I'm on scholarship. Wait. We were in the middle of the season, but now it's summer." He shakes his head. "Either way, I can't get hurt."

"Unless Maddie writes it in, I'm sure you'll be fine. But maybe don't jump off the deck."

"Oh shit. She's not going to...maybe I should get her a gift," he mumbles, glancing at his feet.

His question sparks a memory. A plan forms in my mind and I grin. I'll need to interact with the characters if I'm going to pull this off. I doubt Grey could help me. He doesn't seem like he's dabbled in what I need. When I focus on him again, he still looks like he's trying to come up with a gift for Maddie.

"Don't give my woman gifts," I grumble.

"Uh, okay. It wouldn't be romantic," he mumbles, then smirks. "But she *is* my writer. So…"

I roll my eyes. "Why exactly did you need to talk to me?"

"Oh, yeah. I need to know what's going on with P. Something happened, but she won't tell any of us what. Thought I'd ask you about it."

"Something bad?"

He shuffles uncomfortably, no longer meeting my eye. "I don't know. With the way she avoids the subject, I think it is. She won't talk to the guys about what happens on campus."

"Why don't you ask her about it?"

His Adam's apple bobs, and he crosses his arms. "Her and I are not currently interacting. However, we'd like to know if she's being harassed."

"I'll talk to Maddie about it. But your best bet is to ask Peyton. And trust the process. Some things don't fully make sense until the whole story is told."

He nods, deep grooves forming between his eyes. Then he wanders away toward the forest. The leaves above him rustle before he fades away. I wonder how long he'll be in the void. The forest will eventually drop him right back into this world, but he seems to need the break.

Sighing, I drop my arms and make my way to the cabin. My plans for Maddie are on the back burner until I have a conversation with her. I've strived to stay out of her writer space. I don't want to influence her stories. Interacting with her characters doesn't seem to affect her writing, at least. I doubt they'd leave me alone unless Maddie threatened them.

"Maddie." I knock on the door frame of the sliding glass door, and she glances over her shoulder. "This a good time?"

"Sure. Saw you out there being all sweaty. By the way, don't come near me until you shower. I know in books the pheromones are supposed to make everyone go wild, but in reality, you're just stinky." She wrinkles her nose.

I stalk toward her and swoop down, capturing her lips with my own. She squeals and pushes me away as I laugh. Plopping into the chair next to her, I wait until she sets her computer aside and tucks her legs underneath her.

"Now that you're done attacking me with sloppy kisses, what's up?"

"You know who Grey is? One of Peyton's guys?" My stomach flips as she nods. I'm still not entirely sure I should be doing this. "He came to me wondering what was going on with her. He thinks she might be getting harassed on campus. I don't want to bog you down with this, but he seems real concerned."

She taps her pen against her lips, a faraway look in her eyes. "He's worried about her?"

"From the way he was acting, I'd say so."

"Thank fuck. He's so closed off all while playing at being open. It's all superficial shit, though. And he's been pulling away from Peyton. Girl is going through it right now. I just need to get them over the hump."

"The hump?"

She waves her hand, and I wonder if she'll answer. She never has before. "There's a point in every romance book where they have to get over themselves. They have to be willing to admit their feelings, even if it's just to themselves. Different for every story, but it always happens. Once they're over the hump, shit really gets going and they're able to find their way home."

I glance away to hide my smirk, remembering Sophie's words at the dinner party. I wonder if Maddie used it before and that's how Sophie knew. The connection between Maddie and the others sends my head into a spiral, so I avoid it as best I can.

"You going to tell me what happened with the vampire? Do I need to have a talk with him?"

She busts out laughing, then smothers it behind her hand. "Sorry. You should not do anything with him. In fact, stay far away from him. He's just pissy and has a stick up his ass. He shouldn't bother anyone again, though."

"What's he pissy about?"

Her head hits the back of the chair, and she closes her eyes. "He thinks Ella, his love interest, is disappearing. She's not. She's sneaking away with Dray, but if I told Ezio that, he'd be even more pissy. He's struggling with sharing."

"I wouldn't want to share you," I mumble.

"Good thing I'm not into that sort of thing. You know, he's not even jealous of Dray. He just wants more time with Ella. Ezio doesn't feel like he's enough for her. He hasn't figured out she's his fated mate yet. Actually, none of them know. Dray suspects, I think. Maybe Dray and Ezio are fated too." She stares into space for a minute, trying to figure out the plot. "Part of me wishes I could just tell them. Can't risk it, though."

We sit in silence for several minutes before she grabs her computer once more. Her typing fills the air and I close my eyes. As the sun fully sets, the sound of the others having another bonfire floats along the wind.

They're on a continuous vacation and treating it as such. Other than the demons. They're still on edge, frequently stalking into the woods. Nix keeps trying to leave. Yesterday he had a meltdown in the driveway when the magic kept plopping him back on the porch.

"Do you think I'm too harsh?" Maddie asks, and I glance at her.

"I don't know what that means."

Her brows pull low as she stares at her screen. "I give characters tragic backstories. I send them to hell and back. I put them through some terrible shit. All in the name of a good story. Watching them and who they are because of what I've written isn't easy. I wonder if I'm too harsh. Which is ironic, since I often worry I'm not putting them through enough. At least not to warrant their reactions to situations. And don't get me started on some of the shit I've already published."

"Would they be interesting if they didn't have bad shit happen to them? Book wouldn't be good if the characters were boring."

"But there's so much pain. Each of them has different kinds, but I'm able to deal with the emotions that come with it when I'm only writing one book at a time. Them all grouped together with their massive amounts of trauma is a bit overwhelming. Add in the side characters in the stories...makes me worried I'm too harsh on them."

"Think about it, though. This is reality. Even if they're fictional, their existence should be rooted in reality, right? No one has a perfect life."

"You're right. Of course, you're right." She almost sounds annoyed about it. "Life is messy and if I don't write them like they're real people, then no one will relate to them. And if no one relates to them, the book will bomb. Because no one was to read about perfect people."

She nods once, then again, determination in her gorgeous eyes. She writes a few more lines and her face contorts. I lean, trying to peek at her screen. Her screen is too dark, especially with dusk taking over the sky. I give up, content to watch her facial expressions as she types. I never noticed how much she moves while writing.

When she lifts her hand and waves her finger around, I bite back a smile. "What are you doing?"

She jolts as if she forgot I was here. A blush spreads across her cheeks and my cock twitches. "Sometimes it's hard to figure out where everyone is. Especially in fighting scenes."

"You realize you have a lot of people hanging around. You could direct them so you could figure out where they're standing or moving. I'm sure they'd love to reenact a battle scene for you."

Her eyes widen and her mouth drops open. "You are so fucking right. Why didn't I think of that?"

"Because you're so used to having them in your head. I'd suggest bringing in certain characters if you're struggling with a scene when they're arguing or something, but you'd probably have to tell them what they're fighting about."

Closing her eyes, she presses her lips together, fighting back laughter—or tears—I'm not sure which one. I lean forward, ready to comfort her if need be, when her shoulders shake.

"What the hell is happening?" I growl.

"Sorry," she gasps. "Those scenes usually end up with naked people. Which are the other ones I have to figure out how to block. Kol might be a voyeur, but I am not."

"I'd advise you to not go into the woods at night, then. Pretty sure there's more than a few of them working out their frustrations once the sun goes down."

Her peals of laughter overtake the night, warming my soul. I close my eyes, a smile playing on my lips as she starts typing again. These are the nights I cherish. I just hope we'll have more of them and I won't have to warm myself with mere memories in the future.

Chapter Forty-Eight
Maddie

I thought it would take me months to finish another story. Yet here I am, perched on the porch steps yet again with characters staring at me while I write another ending. This is the third release since Grace and Sam vanished. Thankfully, Emmett joins me most of the time.

He refused when I had to go near the woods once I told him I was finishing Hope and Zayne's story. They've kept to the woods, stalking between the trees. Apparently, Emmett saw them right before he met the fae lady, who I still haven't named yet. I really should get going on her retelling so Emmett won't be scared to go to the bonfires over there anymore. I'll get to it eventually.

"You ready?" Emmett whispers in my ear as he sits next to me.

"No. Then again, I doubt I ever will be. These guys have been in my head for a long time."

He loops his arm around my shoulder and tucks my body into his. "They'll still be there."

"Not really. Grace and Sam are gone. No voices, no scenes, no echoes. They live in their own world now. I finish their story and they're off living their best life. I don't hear them anymore." It's both amazing and depressing. I had to get used to not only Grace not being here in person, but in my head as well.

"What about Eve and Axel?"

"Gone. I'm happy for them, but it's still hard." I lay my head on his shoulder, and he presses a kiss to my hair.

"It'll get easier as you go. Plus, you're writing a lot. Look at all these people." He gestures to the group in front of us. "What did Grace call them?"

A smile tugs at my lips. "The Groomsmen."

"Why exactly?"

"They meet their love interests at the wedding of another one of the grooms-men. Although in Andie and Sebastian's case, they already knew each other from childhood, so they didn't exactly meet at Harper and Devin's wedding. It's a bit confusing since there's a lot of them."

"So, Harper and Devin's book is first in the series?"

I grimace, wondering if I should publish it that way instead of my original plan. "Andie and Sebastian's is first. But now I'm starting to think that's a bad idea."

"Are you going to publish them right away?"

I snort and my head rests on his shoulder again. "Abso-fucking-lutely not. These stories have a loooong way to go. I have to edit them all, then send them to my beta readers, then send them to my editor and go through that process. Then they'll go to my proofreader and finally to my advanced readers. It's nice to have a lot of these finished so I can focus on the shiny new ideas that will pop up, but I'll be in editing hell for fucking years after this."

"You don't sound too upset about that," he murmurs.

"Usually, I dread the process. Writing is the fun part. Creating new worlds and coming up with characters—there's something special that comes along with building something new. Editing is the exact opposite. It's tearing down and dissecting and slashing the unnecessary from the story. This time around, though, the writing was the hard part. I'm optimistic about the editing because the writing was so difficult." I close my eyes, letting the music of the night fill me up. It takes at least a minute for me to realize the Groomsmen have gone quiet.

Someone clears their throat, and my lids flutter open, not quite ready to give up the peace. "When we go back, will we all be together?"

I puff out my cheeks as I study Bailey. "I don't think so. You'll be wherever your story was when you got here."

She glances at Beckett, then back at me. "How do you know that if you can't talk to us when we're back in our own world?"

"Because I've written a lot of things lately that others would definitely notice. Plus, with the endings I've written, don't you think the relationships between people would change?"

Grooves form between her eyes. "What things would others notice?"

Beckett steps forward and grabs her arm gently. "Okay there. Probably best not to open that can of worms. Why don't we get this show on the road?"

"Good idea. I can't send all of you back at once since I can't write them all at once..."

"You could just end them all the same way," Sebastian cuts in. "Copy and paste would take less time. And it would tie the series together."

Emmett tenses and I peek at him from the corner of my eye. "Please don't give her any more ideas."

"It's fine. I have enough ideas I'm dealing with. I know what I'm going to do to finish and maybe the magic will drop you into your stories at the same time. You all ready?" I straighten, placing my fingers on the keys.

They all nod, and I focus on the screen, writing the last few lines of one document after another. Once I finally glance up, Noelle and Austin are the only ones left of the group. Slowly they fade, a grin on her face and a scowl on Austin's. I'm not surprised since he's still not sure why I paired him up with her. Relief floods my system when they wink out of existence.

"You okay?" Emmett murmurs, leaning close to me.

"You know, I really am. I started their stories ages ago. I needed to finish them. It's been a long time coming." Tears still fill my eyes as I remember when I got the idea for their books.

"How long?"

I close my laptop and stand. "Andie and Sebastian's story was the second book I wrote when I decided to publish. Other shiny ideas popped up and derailed the project, though. Plus, I wasn't ready to figure out if I was going to put sex in my books yet. Turns out that was a moot point."

He chuckles, resting his hand on my lower back to lead me inside. I have more to do tonight, but I need a break. I head straight for the deck, needing to be around people without actually being around them.

Emmett doesn't follow me, and I glance over my shoulder after I lean against the railing. He's in the kitchen, probably getting me a slice of cheesecake. The dessert showed up right after Grace vanished and has been replenishing itself ever since. Apparently, the magical force controlling everything around us no longer feels the need to hide. I'm not complaining when it gets me sweets.

"Who's next on the list?" Emmett hands me a plate and fork and posts up next to me with his own slice.

"You make it sound like a hit list."

"Well, you are kind of taking them out." He grins, then takes a bite, drawing my eyes to his mouth.

I roll my eyes, and we eat in silence. He takes the plate from me and sets them on the small table he built me. I still get a warm fuzzy feeling in my chest every time I see it. Followed closely by a healthy dose of guilt. He does so much for me and yet I give nothing back. Fucking him doesn't seem like enough. He's constantly saying he's right where he wants to be, yet I'm not convinced.

"Spill," he says, and I wonder if he can read my mind. "Who's next?"

My muscles relax, and I tuck my chin to my chest. I'd rather not admit how terrified I am of our future. I keep putting off talking about it in the hopes I can find a way to give back to him before he realizes how unbalanced we are.

"I'm close with a few, but the next one you probably don't want to watch."

He winces, gripping the back of his neck. "Don't tell me. It's one of those fantasy ones, isn't it?"

"Yup. The tree one. Not with the lady who tried to off you. The other one. I'm still a little worried about the ending, though. Maybe I should change it." I peer into the dark, catching a flash of blonde hair weaving through the trees by the lake. I wonder if she's actively hiding from her love interest. Or interests, if she's in a why choose romance. I squint, trying to make out who it is, but they disappear into the dark.

"Nope. You're not changing it. If it needs to be worked out in editing, then so be it. If you keep messing with it, you'll never finish."

"How do you know that?"

He loops his arm around my waist and tugs me close to his side. "Because you tried to do that with Eve and Axel. And you've been muttering about Juliette and Tate's ending for the past two days. Not to mention Rylie and Aiden's last chapter."

"To be fair, I've been putting off Rylie's because I know how horrible it will be when she leaves. She filled the space when Grace left, even if she does complain about Aiden and his asinine demands. I'm hoping changing his occupation will help once they're back, but he's still an asshole, so that's up in the air."

Maybe if I keep talking, I won't have to go to the forest tonight. He releases me and my plans go up in smoke. Every time I finish a story, I worry I'm rushing things now. Maybe if I slowed down, I'd be able to put in the care their stories need. I don't want to fall into the same issue I had before. It's a delicate balance I haven't fully figured out. I might never be able to find a harmony between the two.

"Why don't you ask Rylie to go with you to the woods? I'd feel better having her with you if I can't be." An edge of hostility creeps into his voice.

"You know I'm not stopping you from coming, right? I'd rather you were there."

He shakes his head and turns away from me. "You and I both know that'd be a terrible idea. Every time I get close, weird shit happens. I won't be the reason you don't finish a book and release them."

He stomps into the cabin before I can respond, and I sigh. He's right, even if neither of us like it. The last time he was down there, a storm popped up out of nowhere, complete with lightning flashing over the lake. As soon as he was back in the cabin with me over his shoulder, the sky cleared and birds started chirping again. I hate that he's being cut off from this, though. He's been there every other time I've finished. It'll be strange to not have him by my side.

I wander inside while I contemplate whether I can put this off until it's daylight. It wouldn't be fair to the characters, though. Emmett will just have to get over not being able to go. Besides, I might have to get used to doing this on my own. The thought sends a shiver down my spine and a stab of pain into my heart. Until he says something, I'll just continue to search for a way to support him as much as he's supported me.

"Better get going before it gets too late. You know a lot of them vanish the later it gets."

I tuck my computer under my arm and try to catch his eye as he puts the cheesecake away. "Are you going to be okay by yourself?"

"Course. I've been alone before, Maddie. Not like you're moving to the other side of the country." His shoulders tense as soon as the words are out, and I force out a laugh.

"Definitely not. I doubt I'd do well on either of the coasts. I'll stay right where I am, thanks."

He nods and I wait for him to take the bait. After a minute of silence, I shake my head and turn for the door. Slipping on my sandals, I attempt to quell my ever-growing tension.

"I'll be back in a few," I call, and he lifts his hand, not bothering to answer. As the door shuts behind me, I wonder if this is the beginning of the end for us.

Chapter Forty-Nine

Emmett

I swing the hammer down, missing the nail for the third time, and let out a curse. Should I be using tools while I'm distracted? No. Has that stopped me? Also no.

I can't seem to stop punishing myself, though. If I get hurt, so be it. I deserve it after the way I treated Maddie the other night. It's not her fault I wasn't able to go to the forest with her. It's not her fault I was useless to her.

No, not useless. Actively hindering her progress. Not being able to support her kills me. Then I made the mistake of not letting shit go by the time she came back. It only made it worse when she didn't blame me for my shitty attitude. I kept most of my emotions inside, but I only ended up hurting her with my silence.

I toss the hammer to the ground, giving up for now. Dray has been loitering on the fringes of my vision for the last twenty minutes. I've been trying to ignore him. Now that I don't have anything in my hands, he shuffles closer. He's not usually so skittish. I imagine being a werewolf gives him some big dick energy.

"What do you want, Dray?" I grumble, wiping my hands on my jeans.

"This might seem like I'm stalking you—"

"Not a great way to start," I mutter as I cross my arms.

"Probably not. Got a little magical nudge telling me you needed something made. Know anything about that?" Some of his swagger has returned, and I'm not entirely sure I'm okay with it.

"A magical nudge, huh?"

"Don't know if it's this place or my own magic, but yeah. What did you need?"

I drop onto the step of the front porch. I've been trying to fix one of the pillars with no luck. He comes closer, awkwardly looming over me. He wrinkles his nose as he grips the back of his neck. Even with him trying to appear unintimidating, he's doesn't succeed.

"Sit your ass down. I'm not going to stare up at you the entire time," I growl.

He plops next to me, a lopsided grin on his face. "What are we looking for, boss? Crossbow? Lance? Falchion? I've never made a morning star, but I'm sure I could figure it out."

"What the fuck is a morning star?"

"Basically a spiked club. Kind of like a mace, but deadlier. They were used around the fourteenth century. A variation of it came out around the sixteenth century. They called it the holy water sprinkler." He leans against the railing, turning his face to the sun.

"And a falchion?"

"Type of sword. Curved blade and single-edged. Good for both offense and defense."

"You got a thing for ancient weapons or something?"

He pierces me with a stare, and my spine straightens without thought. "For someone who hammers wood instead of a nail, I don't think you're in a position to bash someone's hobby. I enjoy the history of weapons and sometimes recreating them. Do you have a problem with that?"

I shake my head, glancing away. "I wasn't bashing you. Especially since I'm asking you for a favor."

"Glad to see we're on the same page."

A heavy silence stretches between us, and I clear my throat to ease the tension. "Do all werewolves make weapons? Is it like a family thing?"

He gives me a strange look, then his face breaks into a grin. "Werewolves aren't real. I'm a wolf shifter. Slightly different, but I'm sure your writer can fill you in. Now what do you need made?"

"A dull dagger."

His face falls, confusion taking over. "Why the fuck would you want a dagger that's dull? The point of a dagger is to be sharp in order to cut through things. Preferably skin and muscle. Possibly bone if it's serrated."

"Because I'd rather Maddie not accidentally stab herself. Or me," I mumble.

He tips his head back and cackles. The door behind us opens and I glance over my shoulder as he continues. Maddie's eyes, full of concern, dart back and forth before finally settling on me. She opens her mouth, then snaps it shut. She tries to smile, but it's more like a wince, and she shuts the door quickly.

"Something going on there, boss? You two aren't on the outs, are you?" Dray asks, cutting into my thoughts.

"We're fine. Worry about your own relationship. And get me that knife."

He stands and salutes before vanishing in a puff of smoke. I haven't seen anyone else other than the demons disappear like that. Usually, I'd ask Maddie about it, but we're clearly not on even footing anymore. And it's entirely my fault. Getting her a dagger might help, but it feels like I'm trying to buy her love. Nothing will be fixed with a gift, but it's a start, I hope.

I push to my feet, intent on mending things between us before it gets out of control—before I lose her. The cabin is quiet, the sounds from outside muted. Maddie isn't in the kitchen or at the table. The living room is empty, and I peek into the bedroom. She's not in there either.

When I search the deck, a lead weight drops into my stomach. She doesn't go into the lower level unless I'm down there. It's mostly unfinished, with one door to the outside that doesn't open easily with the humidity.

"Maddie?" I yell as I spin around.

Silence greets me, only adding to my anxiety. Stomping down the stairs, I squeeze my hands into fists, digging my nails into my palms. It doesn't help quell the apprehension. There's no reason to believe she's disappeared like the others have. She couldn't have gotten out of the house without my noticing unless she came down here. Most of my tools litter the floor and I make a mental note to clean up the space.

"Maddie, are you down here?"

I call for her several more times as I check the few rooms someone put up. The flimsy walls wouldn't stand up to a brisk fan. I've been meaning to at least tear them down to make it safer.

Finishing off the area properly would be best, but with the way I've been working, I doubt I'll have time. Unless I stay through the winter. Which entirely depends on Maddie. If she leaves, this place will be a graveyard for my memories, haunting me as I wonder what could have been.

I hold my breath as I try the door. The knob doesn't even move, the lock still firmly in place. I haven't found a key, and the deadbolt is on the inside, obviously. There's no way Maddie got out this way. I race back upstairs and throw open every door as I search for her. Slowing down, I make my way to the front hallway.

"No reason to think she's in trouble. This place is fucking magic. Characters manifested into existence straight from her brain. It's not a stretch to believe it magicked her someplace else. It's not like she can leave the area. There's plenty of people around to keep her safe. I shouldn't need her in my back pocket to keep my shit together."

I rip open the front door and press my lips together when I come face to face with Rylie. My gaze flashes to her hands as she wrings them, and all the calmness from my pep talk from a second ago vanishes.

"Where is she?" A rumble reverberates through my chest.

She bites her lip. "The forest. Where the portal was."

I take off, skipping the stairs and vaulting over the railing. I don't care if the forest doesn't like me. I don't care if the fae steal me away into a foreign land. I don't care if I'm breaking every rule I've silently given myself in order to not interfere with her work.

A frustrated scream echoes through the air, and I push myself faster. I skid to a stop by the cold fire pit and scan the area for Maddie. I push through the crowd when I spot her posted up next to the forest line, her back to me.

My bones ache the closer I get to her. The fae woman comes into view and her eyes snap to me. Her pupils disappear in a kaleidoscope of color. The predatory grin stretching across her face sends a shiver down my spine.

"Well hello there, mortal." She tilts her head. "What could a male possibly need from little ole me?"

I swallow hard, fighting back a groan. "Maddie."

Maddie glances at me, her brows pulled low. She shakes her head before turning back to the woman. I have no idea why Maddie came down here. The last I heard, she wasn't even close to finishing.

Rylie and Aiden's story was next, then Juliette and Tate's after. It's only been two days since the Groomsmen left, so I doubt she's made major changes to her schedule. Then again, she hasn't been forthcoming with her writing.

"Eyes on me, Belvina. You had a complaint, so spill. I'm not going to stand around all day while you harass the locals."

Belvina's face takes on a sour look as she focuses on Maddie. While I'm thankful I'm no longer the center of the woman's attention, I don't like Maddie being in the line of fire. Maddie hands off her computer to Nix, though when the demon showed up, I have no idea. Belvina's nose scrunches as her gaze drags over his body. He doesn't seem even a little bit fazed by her scrutiny.

Maddie clears her throat, and Belvina's eyes snap back to her. "You have two options right now. Tell me what your issue is, or I delete your story. You will cease to exist. Your world will vanish. No one will ever know to even remember your name. Choose wisely."

My cock hardens as she berates the woman. Is this the worst time to get a hard-on? Yes. I can't help it, though. I've never heard Maddie be so...forceful before. I wonder if I could push her to use it when we're alone.

"Get your shit together," Rylie rasps from next to me.

"Stop looking at my crotch and we won't have a problem," I mutter.

She makes a noise in the back of her throat, then steps back. I don't want to distract Maddie, but my palms itch to grab her. She's too close to Belvina. I wouldn't put it past the woman to snatch my wife and toss her through a portal. It takes me a minute to realize what I've called her. Even if it is in my head, I've never claimed her in that way. Warmth spreads through me the more it settles in my soul.

"Fine, human. Though you should know how difficult I can make your life should you cross me."

Maddie tips her head back, annoyance etched into every line of her body. "Just get to the fucking point."

"Send these heathens away, then we'll discuss things."

"Not a fucking chance," Maddie snaps.

Belvina's face twists, her jaw almost seeming to detach before she pulls herself together. "I find this world disturbing. Transform me. Now."

Maddie's mouth drops open. "You have got to be fucking kidding me. Request denied. Just keep to the forest and stop fucking with Emmett."

Belvina straightens, the lines of her body blurring. "Think wisely before you deny me, writer of words."

"Even if I could, which I can't, I wouldn't transform you. The last thing we need is a goddamn feline skulking around. Get back to your hideaway and stop messing with people, or I'll make good on my promise."

The woman vanishes in a flash of white light, temporarily blinding me. Once the spots clear from my vision, Maddie has disappeared and panic spears through me. I spin around only to find her halfway back to the cabin.

"You two have a fight or something? She's been surly the last couple of days," Rylie asks.

"We're fine," I grunt, and stomp after Maddie. "Thanks for coming to get me."

I rush after her, catching the front door as she tries to slam it closed after her. She doesn't even bother turning around to acknowledge me. I follow her all the way to the deck, waiting until she sits before I step in front of her and cross my arms.

"Are we going to talk about what just happened?"

She stares at her screen, attempting to look like she's busy. "I don't see the point. She's pissy. I dealt with it. You didn't need to come check on me."

My muscles tense as I attempt to keep my temper in check. "Rylie obviously thought I needed to be there."

"Which just proves how ready she is to go back to her own world," she mutters.

"Is this how it's going to be, then?"

"I don't know what you're talking about. Now, if you'll excuse me, I need to get going on this before I forget."

I walk away before I can make more of an ass of myself. We can't survive like this much longer. Without an idea of what to do, I go in search of someone—anyone—who can help me salvage what we have. I refuse to allow my shitty issues to prevent my own happily ever after.

Chapter Fifty
Maddie

"Why am I here instead of Emmett?" Rylie whispers, and I resist the urge to snap at her.

I strive to keep the edge from my voice as I say, "He's occupied trying to tear apart the basement. I'm not going to bother him or put this off. Does that satisfy your curiosity?"

"Please tell me you're not in your third act era. I don't think I can handle if Mom and Dad are fighting."

"So help me, if you start calling Emmett Daddy..." I let the threat hang between us while she blushes, refusing to meet my eyes. "What's that look for?"

"Nothing. Absolutely nothing." Her finger taps on her legs while I squint at my computer. "Do these two know they're about to get together?"

"Nope. They have no idea why they're here. I'm impressed none of you spilled the beans on what type of books I write."

Her eyes widen as she turns to face me. "Do you know how fucking hard it was? Those of us who knew or figured it out came up with code words. Which was better than wandering off in groups. We didn't want to leave anyone out."

A smile twitches my lips as an image of several of them sneaking out to the lake in the middle of the night. My heart clenches when it hits me how silent the world will be once I finish everything. I sigh, glancing toward the forest. A figure floats through the trees and I scowl. Belvina should be contained to the woods on the other side of the cabin.

I shove the computer into Rylie's hands and stand. "Hey! Get your ass back to your area!"

She slowly turns to face me, and my mind finally registers what she's wearing. The skirts from her white flowy dress swish back and forth gently. Tilting my head, I squint, but I can't make out her features. I have no idea who she is. I can't handle another WIP right now. Maybe that's why she's out of focus. I catch a ghost of a smile before she steps between two trunks and dissolves.

"Did you see that?" I ask Rylie as I sink onto the step.

"Oh, the ghost lady? Yeah, she's been hanging around for the last like week? Showed up when you yelled at Belvina the other day. No one can get close to her. She vanishes any time we try. We've just been leaving her be until you figure out who she is."

"Good thing I'm not seeing things. I don't need another idea, though. She'll have to wait until I get these done." I grab my computer and gaze at Sophie and Ryder, who are studiously ignoring each other. "Who's ready to go home?"

Sophie tentatively raises her hand, and Ryder rolls his eyes. He mutters something I can't hear, but Sophie apparently does since she scowls at him. When he glances away, she kicks dirt on his shoe. She pastes on an innocent expression as he glares at her.

"Oh, those two are going to have it bad for each other, aren't they?" Rylie whispers.

"I was trying my hand at grumpy sunshine. I think I did pretty well." I wave at them to get their attention. "You won't be able to come back here. Is there anyone you'd like to say goodbye to before I finish?"

"I already said what I needed to my friends. Thank you."

"Goody two-shoes," Ryder mumbles. "I'm good. Let's go. I'm ready to be gone."

I nod, then type the last line of their story and within seconds, they vanish. I'm surprised their story came so easily to me. I've been slowly working through them all, but Sophie and Ryder's was in its infancy when I got here.

Trying to finish one of the others wasn't doing me any good. I erased more words than I wrote. Finally, I resigned myself to writing their book and everything slotted into place. I really need to stop trying to force my brain into something it doesn't want to do. And now their story is done, and they're gone, just like the others.

A mix of emotions hits me, and I bite my lip to keep them inside. It's one thing to cry into Emmett's arms. Rylie would hug me, even if it would make her uncomfortable. It also would raise a lot of questions I'm not ready to answer, including why the hell Emmett isn't here.

"Seriously, what the fuck is going on between you two? Because Emmett has been stomping around being all growly."

"Nothing. We're fine," I say, and she glares at me. "We're just going through some growing pains."

"Growing pains. So you're hiding behind your stories instead of dealing with the problem."

"This is my job, Rylie. I'm a writer. I write. And if I don't write, I don't eat."

"Except Emmett feeds you. He is still feeding you, right?"

I roll my eyes, waving away her concerns. "You know what I mean. And yes, he's still feeding me. Everything will be fine."

I close my laptop and push to my feet. Ever since I had to go to the woods by myself, I've been off. I understand Emmett's reaction, but I didn't think he'd hold it against me. Rylie isn't the only one who's noticed his sullenness. I thought he'd get over it. I thought he'd talk to me about it. I thought he'd lean on me.

Yet he didn't. He shut me out and left me in the dark. He pushed me away when I finally found something I thought I could help him with. I'm still struggling to find a way to be there for him—to give back a little of what he's given me. And now he's closed off completely. I don't know how to fix this and it's killing me.

Instead of working on it, I've thrown myself into writing. I'm going to need to rework a lot of the endings. Plus, I forced Peyton and Xander into a fight. It wasn't very hard since Xander is kind of an asshole. When Peyton started pushing back, things got out of hand. And I know it's a direct result of what I'm going through with Emmett.

"Maddie," Rylie calls when I open the front door, and I pause. "Don't leave it too long. You know what happens when you do."

I nod before shoving into the cabin and closing the door behind me. Banging from the lower level streams up the stairs. At least he's taking some of his aggression out on something. I wish I could do the same. Maybe I could ask Sage to teach me how to throw a punch. Or Kol. I doubt I'd be able to take a hit from either of them, but especially not a demon.

Collapsing onto the couch, I close my eyes, clutching my computer to my chest. A scuffle of a shoe has me shooting upright. Gideon settles onto the sofa across from me and folds his hands in his lap.

"Are you proud of yourself?" he asks in a low rumble.

"Depends on what you're talking about."

"You seem to have a proclivity for threatening your characters when you're challenged. I was just wondering if you were proud of that fact."

"When said characters are pissing me off, then yes. Yes, I am. Do you have a complaint to lodge as well?"

He glances away, his jaw ticking. "I'm quite content with how things are. However, I would ask that you help Charlie. She's having a hard time adjusting to life in this world."

I sigh, tucking my chin to my chest. I don't have time to babysit anyone. Emmett seemed to be handling them well enough. Now that he's unavailable or unwilling, they're apparently suffering. Or maybe Charlotte isn't meant for the outdoors. I assumed most of them would be able to adjust since they're just characters. I didn't think about where they sleep at night. Emmett said they disappear into the woods.

"Does she not like camping?"

"This is not about the living conditions. She struggles to connect with the others. Not that she says anything. However, the other women have meshed seamlessly, whereas she is left on the outskirts of their soirées. I would like you to fix it."

"Is that concern? I didn't think you cared whether she was happy or not. Only that the arranged marriage did its job of protecting your assets."

He shoves to his feet, his shadow looming over me. "She is not an asset."

"No. She's not. She's an unfortunate victim of your reckless behavior. Why don't you think about your role in this before you come crying to me about her lack of socialization."

He studies me, a glint of something in his eyes I can't quite read. A dawning realization flashes across his face before he slips his mask back into place. I hate it. I hate that he's right. I hate that he seems to know something I don't. And I hate I just dismissed Charlie's needs without a thought. I don't like who I'm becoming.

Gideon nods, then makes his way to the front door. I expect him to slam it on his way out, but he doesn't. Of course he doesn't. He has complete control over his emotions. Which is the problem with his character arc. He plays his cards almost as close to his chest as Sage. Belvina deserved to have her ass chewed. She deserved the threats I lobbed at her. Charlie doesn't.

"You wanna talk about it?" Emmett's voice is a balm to my battered soul, filling in the pieces I've lost along the way.

I shake my head. My throat closes at the effort I'm putting in to keep my emotions in check. If I don't look at him, I'll keep my shit together. I desperately need to him to say something else, though. Anything to take my mind off the conflicting feelings swirling through me.

"Gorgeous?"

I glance at him and burst into tears. Shock spreads across his face before he's dropping the rag in his hands and rushing for me. The deluge only gets worse when he pulls me into his lap, cradling my body close to his.

His hand runs down my back, over my hair, along my leg. It's comforting, but only makes me feel worse. Guilt lays just beneath the surface, reminding me of all my mistakes I've shoved aside.

"Tell me what happened. Was it Gideon? What did he say?" When the only response he receives are hiccups, he growls, "I'll fucking kill him."

I cling to him as he tries to set me aside. As much as I should, I can't let him go. Not yet. Tucking my chin to my chest, I try to get myself under control. He doesn't deserve the weight I'm putting on his shoulders.

"Sorry. It's not Gideon. He didn't do anything wrong. It was my fault." I try to unravel myself from him, but he tightens his hold. "I'm fine. Sorry."

"Why do you keep apologizing? You didn't do anything wrong. At least not to me."

"I'm fine. I didn't mean to break down like that."

Hiding from him isn't working. Rationally, I understand we might be okay if we just talk about things. Once we do, though, it might be over. Fear clouds the logical parts of my brain. I'm not ready to face the consequences of that conversation. The words sit on the tip of my tongue, waiting for the right moment.

He sighs, tangling our fingers together. "I'm sorry I shut you out."

"I understand," I whisper, still fighting the cowardice within me.

I'm not lying but refusing to open up might be just as harmful. I can't seem to force the words from my mouth to explain how I'm feeling.

As soon as I tell him how much he means to me, the ball is in his court. Not knowing what he'll do, or say, or how he'll react to my confessions terrifies me. Now I intimately understand how my characters feel when I force them to profess their love for one another. I'm not ready to accept his rejection if he doesn't feel the same way.

"I don't think you do. Since we got together, I've become used to being there for you. Taking care of you, supporting you with your writing, feeding you has been my focus. And I loved every fucking minute of it. When I couldn't be there…it was hard to handle. I should have talked to you about it, but I didn't want to put more stress on you." His hand falls away from me and he releases my fingers. "And now isn't the time, either. You need to focus on finishing your stories. We can deal with everything else after."

He slides me onto the couch, his jaw jutting out as he grits his teeth. His words hold a ridiculous amount of hope, yet his reaction says something else. If we leave it for later, I'm afraid our insecurities will pile up, blocking our path to each other. I swipe at my face, erasing the evidence of my breakdown.

"What if—"

"No. We're not playing the what-if game. Nothing good can come from it. Perfectly acceptable when talking about your ideas, but not with our relationship. It'll keep." He pushes up from the couch, avoiding my eyes.

I track his movements as he makes his way back to the stairs. He didn't even give me a chance to fix things. Even while admitting he shut me out, he did it again. I don't know how to get back to where we were.

This was supposed to be fun and light and temporary. I don't even know when It morphed into something more. I just wanted to find my happy ending. Maybe I was never meant to. Maybe Emmett was never mine to keep.

Chapter
Fifty-One

Emmett

I can't keep my gaze off Maddie as she laughs with one of her characters. I can't remember the woman's name, but she's floated on the outskirts of the group since she showed up.

Gideon slips next to me as I lean against a tree hidden in the shadows, far enough away from the festivities I thought I wouldn't be bothered. Thank fuck it's far away from Belvina's section. I doubt I could handle dealing with her. Then again, I'd rather not deal with anyone.

"Are you who I have to thank for that?" he asks, nodding toward the two women.

"What do you mean?" I counter, not in the mood for another cryptic conversation.

"I spoke with the writer a few days ago. She was not receptive to my request to include Charlie. Then suddenly your writer is planning this get together and helping her assimilate into this new world. I assumed you had something to do with the change."

As much as I want to blast him for riling Maddie up, she told me not to interfere. She said it wasn't his fault, but she often takes on more of the blame than she should. I shove my hands in my pockets to keep from punching him. It's hard since his face is particularly punchable.

"She came to the realization on her own. While she would love to bury your ass six feet under, Charlie didn't deserve to pay for your sins."

A beat of silence weaves its way around us while he contemplates my words. "She certainly doesn't. I'm afraid some things are unavoidable, however."

"You could treat her with respect. Talk to her about shit," I growl, reigning in my anger a little more.

He chuckles, the sound hollow even to my ears. "Perhaps you should take your own advice."

He stalks away before I can respond. I fucking hate him. I'm sure he's a perfectly fine character. When he comes at me with logic, though, it only pisses me off. I despise how right he is.

I thought explaining things to Maddie the other day would lead us to a better place. Unfortunately, it only made things worse. She's been avoiding me more, all while pretending everything is fine. It's not. There's a vibration in the air, warping the world around me. Gideon only told me what I already know. I have to talk to her before we reach the point of no return.

A lilting voice floats behind me, singing a haunting melody. I glance over my shoulder, and my chest tightens. I've never seen the ethereal woman before. Her image blurs slightly before solidifying and she smiles. I wonder if Maddie forgot to tell me about writing a ghost story. Facing her doesn't seem like the wisest decision, but I do it anyway.

"Hello, Emmett. I've wondered when you'd notice me." Her musical voice settles over me. It's beautiful, but there's a bite to it, like she's trying to worm her way into my psyche.

"Who are you?" I attempt to keep my tone neutral, and she cocks her head.

She waves away my question. "Not important. Perhaps it'll be found later. Did you hear it?"

"Hear what?"

I can't really deal with any more magical phenomena. I'm at capacity. Even being slightly removed from the chaos of the characters hasn't protected me. As long as it helps Maddie, I'm happy to throw myself into this world. I'd rather not be singled out by someone I've never seen before, though.

"You truly haven't heard—" Her eyes snap up, gazing over my shoulder.

A slight smirk plays on her mouth before she dissolves. The move reminds me of when Maddie releases her characters. They evaporate into a mist comprised of a myriad of colors. It's a surreal experience and one I've only seen when Maddie finishes a story. I spin around, expecting to find her with her computer. She's still talking to Charlie, though, oblivious to the interaction.

"Oh, you're totally fucked." Sage says, then licks the ice cream cone she's holding.

"Where the fuck did you get soft serve?"

"Magic. Duh." She rolls her eyes. It's the most human reaction I've seen from her. "As someone who has perfected the art of staying the fuck out of it, even I can see how ridiculous you two are being. She's going to finish a story today. Might want to pull your head out of your ass long enough to be there for it."

She walks away, and I bite my tongue to keep from calling her back. It's one thing for Gideon to notice shit going sideways. He was there the other day, and I have no idea what Maddie told him about what's happening between us. Sage stays far away from the others and their drama, though. The fact she's butting into our business now says something.

I make my way toward Maddie, intent on dealing with this regardless of how much strain it puts on us. I can't go another day like I have been. The more time passes, the more I feel as if I'm losing her. If I don't start making up for my mistakes, I'll ruin any chance I have with her.

Her eyes dart to me, then away, a nervous energy overtaking her when I approach. I hate this is what we've come to. As I press my chest to her back, she tenses. I slip an arm around her waist, and she melts into me. A shiver runs through her when I lean down, my lips brushing her ear.

"We need to talk," I whisper.

"Can it wait? I need to—"

"No. It can't."

She nods and makes her excuses to Charlie, who doesn't seem fazed by her abrupt departure. I whisk her away, leaving the merriment of the party behind. I grasp her hand and lead her to the shoreline. Usually, we retreat to the cabin to have these interactions in private. No one needs to overhear us, no matter what we're doing. I'm hoping the change of scenery will help.

"We honestly don't need to do this now, Emmett." She tries to tug away from my grasp, but I don't let her.

"Others are noticing the distance between us. I don't like it."

She scoffs, glancing out over the lake as the water laps at her bare feet. "So it wasn't an issue until others started to notice?"

"What? No. I'm saying I don't like the distance. We need to discuss what's happening or we'll come out on the other side without a clear path on how to fix things."

"Who was that woman?"

My brows pull low as I gaze at her. "Sage. She's one of your characters."

She rolls her eyes, and my throat goes dry. This isn't going the way I thought it would. I apologized before, then did nothing to change things.

"I know who Sage is. The woman in white, on the other hand, I don't know. She won't talk to anyone else. Except for you. Who is she?"

"No idea. She knew my name and asked if I heard it."

"Heard what?"

I shake my head. "Haven't got a clue. You want me to talk to her more? Figure out what her story is?"

Her feet stutter to a stop and I follow suit. Indecision wells in her eyes as she gazes at me. I wish she would open up, tell me what's going on in her head.

"Tell me what you're thinking," I murmur, the plea evident in my voice.

She tucks her chin to her chest. "Not yet. I just...I need to wrap my mind around this. If you want to talk to her, I won't stop you. Whatever's supposed to happen will happen."

My head swims, and a numbness spreads through my limbs. I clear my throat as a dryness takes over my mouth. Maddie doesn't look up, as if she's slipped into her own world. I try to squeeze her hand to reassure her, but I can't. Her fingers slip from mine and I sway. I slam my eyes shut, attempting to center myself again.

"Karma only listens when you refuse to act. This isn't a wait and see situation, Maddie."

She bites her lip, and her eyes fill with tears. I reach for her, but she steps away. The move cuts deep, severing something within me. She composes herself quickly as she throws her shoulders back.

"Listen, I like you. Maybe more. And you've been absolutely what I need during this entire wild situation. And I don't want to let you go. I really don't. I just…"

"What do you want, Maddie? Deep down in the secret parts of yourself, what do you want?" I hold my breath as she studies me.

"I want time to sort through everything. I want to finish these stories that won't leave me alone. I want to figure out what I've missed. Because there's something missing. And I don't know what it is or who it involves. I just need time." Exhaustion pulls on the lines of her face.

"Okay, gorgeous." She tumbles into my arms, and I hold her close. "I can do that. Just promise me you won't disappear on me."

"I won't," she mumbles into my chest. "I promise."

She tugs away after a minute, wiping the tears from her face. She smiles, but it doesn't reach her eyes. I wish I could take away her pain. If she just leaned on me, I might be able to help her. I can give her all the time she needs. As long as she doesn't cut me out completely.

"Do you want me to leave?" I ask.

"Absolutely not. How would that solve anything? If you leave, I won't have anyone. And I can't lose you, too."

I chuckle, running my hands down her arms. "I didn't mean actually leave. I meant, do you need some time alone?"

She smacks my chest as I laugh. "You ass. Don't scare me like that. Dammit, I hate this."

"What do you hate? Hopefully not me." I grin and cup her face, rubbing my thumbs along her jaw.

"Definitely not you. I just wish I could get a handle on my emotions. I feel like everything is falling apart around me and I can't seem to stop myself from spiraling. Which isn't exactly helping anything." She winces, closing her eyes.

I rest my forehead on hers. "You can still lean on me. I fucked up when I pushed you away, and I'll spend the rest of my life regretting that. But you can still count on me."

"Can we sit? My calves are going numb."

She groans as she drops to the sand and leans against me. When her head slips off my shoulder for the third time, I guide it onto my lap. As the sun marches toward the horizon, I watch the slight rippling in the middle of the lake. It's subtle, the space between the small waves growing the closer it comes to the shore. I'm sure there's a metaphor hidden somewhere in there, but I'm too tired to figure it out. Maddie would be able to. I'm pretty sure she's dozing, and I refuse to disturb her.

Peyton picks her way across the beach, waving at me as she approaches. I lift my finger to my lips, hoping she doesn't wake Maddie. She nods, tiptoeing to the other side of me, and sits.

"I just had a question about one of those scary guys," she whispers.

"There's a couple of them around here, so you'll have to be more specific." I thread my fingers through Maddie's hair over and over.

"Uh, the ones with the wings? Is that offensive?"

"I don't think it's offensive to point out the demons have wings. They're just a part of who they are. What's your question?"

She wrinkles her nose, probably stuck on not offending a demon. I don't blame her. They're on another level and I'd probably be leery of them as well. I assume they can't hurt me, though.

I wonder if, because they're all characters, they're able to harm one another. I'm not about to ask the demons whether that's possible. They'd take the idea and run with it. Hopefully with each other, but I'm not taking any chances.

"Do they have a love interest? Or are they each the others' love interests? I don't know how to word it." She sighs, running her hands through her hair. "I guess what I'm asking is, where are their partners? I heard Kol complaining about an Evalie, but I didn't have the balls to ask him who that was."

"From what Maddie has told me, Kol, Nix, Rune *and* Dez are all in a relationship with Evalie. She's currently missing in their story which is why she's not here. I don't know how the magic works, but Maddie didn't seem surprised."

Her emotions are written on her face, and I swear she cycles through all of them. "So all of them...they're all with her. And everyone is okay with that. Like no one is jealous of the other?"

"From what I understand, Maddie only writes a specific kind of jealousy and that's not it. Is there a reason you're asking?"

She struggles to wipe her face of any reaction, but her wide eyes give her away. "No reason. I just wondered. Are there any side characters here?"

"I think I should leave that question for Maddie." I'll have to warn her of Peyton's questions.

"Well, alright, but she scares me too. Not that she's scary, especially while she's snoring so adorably in your lap. I just don't want to bother her."

"I promise you she won't mind. She doesn't want to intrude on you guys, so she stays away."

She pushes to her feet and dusts the sand from her legs. "Okay. If you think she won't mind."

"She won't."

Peyton makes her way back the way she came, turning before she climbs over the fallen log. "Take care of her. We kind of need to keep her around."

I brush my fingers through Maddie's hair once more. "That's my job."

Chapter Fifty-Two
Maddie

"What the hell is wrong with you? I thought you and Emmett worked everything out last night?" Rylie hisses as I march toward the beach.

"We have. Sort of. We're in a better place, but I need time to sort through everything that's happened. So, we've tabled the big conversation for later and we're just dealing." Not that she needs an explanation. I probably shouldn't be so open with her since she's a character. Then again, it's a little like I'm talking to myself.

"Then why are you stomping around? And where is he? Because Sage said you were finishing someone's story today, and I assumed Emmett would be here for that now that you're no longer fighting." She's struggling to keep up with me, and I force myself to slow.

"Because I have another crisis to deal with before I do. And while I appreciate Emmett being with me, he's currently busy tearing down the makeshift walls in the lower level. I'll get to the release in a bit."

I'm not even a little tempted to tell her whose story I'm finishing. She'll punch me in the kidney or something. And I don't blame her. Aiden corners her every chance he gets to reprimand her for not finding a way out of here. I didn't expect him to change since they're stuck where their story was when they got here, but he's been more confused since I fixed his occupation just like I did

Austin's. Every time he tries to talk business, he gets a confused look on his face and wanders away. Even though he's still an asshole, I feel bad for him.

"Who are we cussing out today?"

"Peyton's men. They keep pulling pranks on the demons, and pissing them off. Hell spawn aren't exactly a bowl full of laughs. I'm afraid they'll retaliate, and it'll involve the removing of limbs. So I'm going to have a little chat with them."

She slows, and I stutter to a stop, glancing behind me. "You okay?"

From the corner of my eye, I catch a flash of white. By the time I look properly, the woman is retreating between the trunks. The ghost lady, as the others call her, has shown up more and more lately. The questions surrounding her build up in my head, blocking my creativity. I can't figure out if she's an actual character or an actual fucking ghost. The only one she speaks to is Emmett, which only sets me more on edge. I shove away the thoughts as Rylie scoffs.

"You really think I'm going to get near a bunch of demons? No fucking way, dude."

I roll my eyes. "I'm going to talk to Peyton's guys. They're a bunch of college students. They might be hockey players, but they are *not* demons."

"Oh, well in that case, I'd definitely like to see this, then."

She skips along next to me as I lead her to the beach. At first, I didn't mind all the people. The noise didn't bother me in the slightest. Now, their constant parties and bonfires wear on me. Emmett tried to implement quiet days where they either had to stay in the woods or read. It didn't last long, but at least he tried. I just started hiding in the lower level, blasting music Emmett would scrunch up his nose at while he worked. We've settled into some semblance of normalcy, but we're both avoiding the elephant in the room.

"Oi! Xander!"

A man with brown hair whips around, his grin falling from his face when he spots me. I gesture him over, my eye twitching. Grey and Kolby trail behind.

They probably already know what I'm going to say. Won't stop me from reaming them out.

"What the fuck do you think you're doing? Would you like to see what your intestines look like as they're hanging outside of your body? Perhaps you'd like to watch Grey get beat with one of your limbs? Or discover how far blood can spurt when Kolby gets stabbed in the heart with a shadow dagger? Sound like loads of fucking fun, doesn't it?"

Their faces drain of color as Rylie tries and fails to keep her laughter contained. I raise an eyebrow, crossing my arms as I wait for their answer. Kolby's throat bobs and he looks like he's about to puke. If he throws up, I might too, so I hope he holds it together long enough for me to get out of here.

"No, ma'am. Sorry ma'am. We'll stop, ma'am," Xander says with a shaky voice.

"See that you do," I snarl, then pivot and march back to the cabin.

We're almost up the hill when Rylie's pants filter from behind me. "Did you just have all those threats at the forefront of your mind, or did you write them down?"

"I didn't know what I was going to say. Half the time it just bubbles out of me. Doesn't help that I haven't been writing any darker shit."

"What does that have to do with anything?" She grabs my arm and pulls me to a stop. "Can we not talk and walk? This hill is a killer on my knees."

I tilt my head, fighting a grin as she drops her hands to her knees and wheezes.

"When I'm writing about darker stuff, those ideas get used up. When I'm writing other types of things, they just sit there, waiting to be written. It's hard to describe."

"Yeah, brains are weird, I suppose." She straightens and shakes out her hands. "Okay, so what's next?"

I spin around, mumbling, "Finishing another story."

"Are you going to tell Emmett? Can I join?" Her eagerness has me wincing.

"You sure can." She's going to fucking kill me.

"I wonder what it's like to dissolve like the others did. Does it hurt? Can you feel anything at all? Maybe they all remember it, like a dream they once had that sticks with them."

Rylie's talking as if she isn't one of them. As if her character status changes because she was here before the others. I bite my tongue, unwilling to burst her bubble. She'll find out soon enough what it's like. At least she won't have to wait long.

As we round the corner of the cabin, a disgusted noise erupts from Rylie. Emmett guards the porch, crossed arms and a scowl keeping Aiden at bay. I grab Rylie's arm as she tries to stomp past me. I tug her back to hide her around the corner.

"You think they're going to fight? Emmett is totally going to win."

"Don't sound so excited about that, Rylie. No, it just occurred to me—Aiden showed up. The stories are supposed to be frozen where they were when I got here. Do you think it's because he was on a plane already?" My head throbs the more I think about it.

"Does it matter? It's magic. Like a cure-all for every weird thing that happens."

I rub my temples, closing my eyes. "But there has to be rules. In every universe with magic, there are rules everyone abides by. Even when you break one of those rules, there has to be a reason it worked. I've been trying to figure out the rules, but I'm still so confused."

"But you didn't make the magic system, so maybe you're allowed to break the rules to a certain extent. Plus, there's a blurring of the worlds."

My eyes snap open and I stare at her. "What do you mean?"

"Duh. The worlds are blurred. Do you really think I'm living in a fantasy land? It's reality. Might be a different reality than this one, but it's real, nonetheless. We're seeing what happens when magic from one world collides with another."

She might be right, but without confirmation from the universe, I don't know what to believe. I always assumed my stories were merely manifestations of my imagination. Having them be another reality morphs my entire understanding of the cosmos, and I don't think I'll ever wrap my head around it. This is one of those things I'll have to let go and know I'll never fully grasp—like what happens when we die or whether ghosts are real.

"Did I just break your brain?" Rylie asks, wiggling her eyebrows at me.

"I don't know. But if the last few months hasn't already done it, I doubt this will." I shake my head. "We'd better get going before they get in a fistfight."

"I'd pay to watch that," she mutters as I drag her to the front. "Like I said, my money's on Emmett."

The two are still glaring at each other. While I was having an existential crisis, these two were having a staring contest.

"Ready?" I ask and Emmett's eyes snap to me.

"Sooner we get on with this, the better," he mumbles.

Rylie glances around as I climb the stairs and stop next to Emmett. I swallow hard, bracing myself for her questions.

"Maddie, where are they?"

Emmett's hand grips mine, silently giving me strength. "They're already here."

She laughs, tilting her head. "I get you're struggling with finishing some of the stories, but you can't write you and Emmett into a story to get out of it. I doubt the magic will let you break *that* rule."

Realization dawns over Aiden's face, yet it's more a look of horror, and he demands, "Tell me what you did."

"Hell would freeze over before I told you anything. You need to live the story to truly belong to it." I lift my chin when he seems like he'll argue.

Rylie holds her hands up, and I glance at her. "Wait. Wait, wait, wait. You can't be serious. Maddie, you need me. You can't send me back. Not yet. I have to—"

"There's nothing more for you to do here, Rylie. You've done more than was expected of you. It's time for you to find your own story. It'll be great. I promise."

"How do you know?" she spits out, even as tears fill her eyes.

"Because I wrote it, silly. Trust me."

Emmett leans close, whispering, "She looks like she needs a hug."

I shake my head, waiting for Rylie to accept her fate. Her jaw clenches, and she steals a glance at Aiden. He'll be pissed at me the entire time. He's a lost cause until Rylie breaks down his ego. She's asked me more than once whether I think she'll survive her story. I didn't have the heart to tell her what she'll have to go through before she gets where she's supposed to be.

"Are you ready to go home?" I ask softly, and she nods, still not totally convinced.

I pull in a deep breath as she mounts the stairs and I wrap my arms around her trembling form. I squeeze her tightly, hiding every emotion welling up inside of me. No reason to break down now when she's already a blubbering mess.

Aiden stands at least three feet away from Rylie as she takes her place. Emmett hands me my computer, smirking with a glint in his dark eyes.

He faces them and grips the back of his neck. "Going to need you to hold hands."

"What?" Aiden snarls, glaring at Rylie as if it's her fault.

"Works better when you're holding hands. We don't want one of you loitering around when the other disappears." Emmett turns away, hiding his grin. By the time he faces them again, he's composed himself.

Aiden grumbles under his breath when Rylie's hand slips into his. He jolts, tugging away from her. His fingers flex by his side as he stares at her. The tension between them when they link again is palpable, and I sink onto the stair, wondering what I've gotten them into.

"Let's hurry this up. I need to get back to my business," Aiden snaps.

I open my laptop and write the last few words, my eyes darting from them to my screen. They dissolve into the familiar mist I've become used to. A grin spreads across Rylie's face and she giggles. I suppose she got her answer about what it feels like to be released. Relief spreads through me as they wink out of existence.

Emmett tugs on my ponytail and I glance up at him. "You okay?"

"I think I am. I might feel guilty later, but right now I'm okay."

He sits next to me and I lean into him. "Why would you feel guilty?"

I sigh, biting my lip as I gather my thoughts. "I kind of blindsided her. I think if I tried to explain it to her, she would have talked me out of sending her back to her world. Maybe I'll regret it at some point, but we'll have to wait and see."

Slowly, I close the laptop and set it aside. While I have a lot of work to do, I need a break. I've been writing almost nonstop since my characters showed up. If I keep going like I am, I'll end up burning myself out. Emmett feeding me cheesecake isn't enough to stop another spiral.

I peek at Emmett, and my chest tightens. I need a day to relax. I need just one day that isn't filled with tension or worries. A quiet night where our future isn't taking over my every thought. I need a fucking break. Hopefully, we can pretend everything is perfectly fine between us.

Chapter Fifty-Three

Emmett

"What do you mean, she's taking a break?" Dray asks as he hands me a dagger wrapped in a shirt. "Be careful with that. I made it as dull as I could, but it's still got a tip."

I unwrap it gently, my eyes widening as I take in the intricate designs. "Where the hell did you get all the materials for this?"

He shrugs, pointing at the woods. "Magic? Shit just showed up. I made the guard a little bigger than I normally would. Don't want her hand to slip."

"Thanks," I breathe, wondering if I should ask him to make me one. I don't have use for a weapon, especially one this fancy, but it's beautiful.

"I tried to incorporate her writing into the designs."

I nod, even though I have no idea what he's talking about. I'm sure Maddie will notice the details I'm missing. She has a way with that sort of thing. And giving her this might be the start of an actual conversation. We've been pretending everything is fine, but the weight on my chest is slowly suffocating me. I can't take much more before I'll give in to the despair swirling beneath the surface.

"I'd ask what I owe you, but I'm pretty sure you can't take money back with you." I rewrap the knife, carefully covering the tip.

"Seeing as how I've been wearing the same clothes for fucking months, I doubt it. You can repay me by telling me what the hell is going on with the writer. Why's she taking a break?" He crosses his arms, one eyebrow creeping toward his hairline.

"She's been working overtime to get your stories done. It's a lot more work than you guys see. She just needs to replenish her creative well. I'm sure she'll get back on track after a few days." I can taste the lie on my tongue. It fills my mouth, leaving a sourness in its wake.

"Well, let me know if she needs anything changed on that. And don't let her fall down the rabbit hole. I'll keep the others away."

"How are you going to do that?" I appreciate it, but there's some serious characters left, including mafia men. Not to mention the demons.

He chuckles, dropping his hands to his sides. "I'll just send Ezio after them. Even demons are afraid of vampires."

He walks away, still snickering to himself. Part of me wishes he'd stick around, if only to keep my mind off Maddie. I've tried to give her the space she needs, and it's killing me. If she keeps avoiding the issues, I'll end up cornering her. Which is exactly the wrong thing to do.

As I turn to go back inside, I spot the woman in white. I think they call her the ghost lady. Seems appropriate, given her tendency to wink out of existence without warning. Maddie hasn't brought her up other than during our time on the beach. It might be time to force the conversation. If she's another character, Maddie will need to figure out what story she belongs to.

The woman gestures to me, but I ignore her. No way am I getting sucked into another mystical shitstorm. Her image flashes, catching my attention and I grumble under my breath. Gripping the dagger, I stomp over to her.

"What the hell do you want?" I growl, glancing over my shoulder at the cabin, then back.

"Do you know why I'm here?" A slight smirk dances at the corner of her mouth.

"I'm assuming you're one of Maddie's characters. So you'll be stuck here until she finishes your story."

Her expression doesn't change, and it's a bit creepy. I'm not sure she heard me. Walking away would be the sensible choice, but I can't seem to move my feet.

"Perhaps," she finally whispers, then disappears.

I shake my head and search the trees for her, but she's gone. Sighing, I make my way back to the cabin. With every interaction, I become more confused. I open the front door and find Maddie on the couch, reading. I settle next to her, leaning my head back.

"Tell me when you're at a good stopping point," I murmur as I shut my eyes. She hums and I let my mind go blank as I doze.

Several minutes later, she sets her book down and turns to face me. "What's up?"

I straighten and my stomach flips. "I got this for you."

She reaches for the shirt, but I yank it back. "If it's for me, you're supposed to give it to me."

"Just be careful." I don't want to give it away, but I'd rather she not poke herself—or me.

She unwraps it, then squeals, her hands flying to her mouth. "Oh, she's so pretty. Where the hell did you get this?"

I spin the dagger around and present it to her with a flourish. "One of your characters has a talent for making swords and things. I asked them to help."

"Oooh, Dray or Nix?" Her fingers close over the handle, and she lifts it closer to her face. "Is this dull?"

"Do not run your finger along the blade," I growl, and she drops her empty hand. "Yes, it's dull. Dray said you can still poke yourself with it, though. Maybe Sage can teach you how to use it before you finish her story."

She wrinkles her nose, setting the dagger down and picking up her book. "As much as I'd love to learn, I doubt I have the skill to pull it off. Plus, Sage has been glaring at me every time I see her. The last thing I'm going to do is bother her. Or give her a knife. I really love it, though."

She leans over and kisses me swiftly. When she sits back and opens her book again, a weight drops in my stomach. Of course, a gift isn't going to fix everything between us. I open my mouth, then snap it shut.

"How many stories do you have left?"

"Seven. Maybe eight. I mean, I'm almost done with four of them, but the others will take longer," she murmurs, flipping the page. Her eyes aren't moving, though.

"Maddie."

"Hmm?"

"Maddie," I grunt, and her eyes lock on mine. "What is going on with you?"

"I don't know what you're talking about."

I shove to my feet and pace toward the deck, then back. "The hell you don't."

She frowns and raises an eyebrow. "Why don't you enlighten me?"

"You stopped writing. You barely reacted when you released Rylie and Aiden. You've been avoiding me since you finished their story. Hell, you slept on the fucking couch last night. I give you that dagger and nothing."

"I said thank you. And I didn't sleep on the couch. I *fell asleep* on the couch. You could have woken me up. You chose not to. I haven't stopped writing, I just stopped talking to *you* about it." Her chin trembles, and a blush spreads across her cheeks.

"So, you're still punishing me for shutting you out." I'm not upset anymore. I know I'm at fault, but I've done everything I could to make it up to her. I just don't know what else to do.

"No, I'm not. I understand why you didn't talk to me. I knew it was your way of dealing with your emotions. Didn't like it, but I understood." She glances away and her spine straightens. "The problem was, I thought I could finally be there for you like you are for me. I was dealing with all that, then she showed up and I started questioning everything."

"Who? Everyone here is a character other than you and me."

She turns back to me, sadness swimming in eyes. "The woman in white. What if she isn't here for me? What if she's meant for *you*?"

"What the fuck are you talking about?" I spread my hands in front of me, pleading with her to see sense. "I'm not a fucking character, Maddie. Why would you think I want her when I have you? You're who I want. You're all I've ever wanted. And that isn't about to fucking change."

"But what if—"

"No." I slash my hand through the air. "No more what-ifs. Can't you see it? I fucking love you, Maddie. You can push me away and make up all the wild scenarios in your head you want. It won't change a damn thing about how I feel."

Tears splash down her face, and all the frustration drains out of me. My knees hit the carpet and I cup her cheeks. Brushing my thumbs across her skin, I search her eyes for an idea of what she's thinking.

"What's going on in that pretty little head of yours?" I whisper, and she lets out a choked sob.

She sniffs, her fingers wrapping around my wrists. I expect her to pull away from my touch, but she holds me there as she composes herself.

"I thought I was doing what was best. I thought I should let you go because I'd gotten it all wrong. And I've been trying to finish these stories, but none of them are coming out right. Nothing makes sense. I convinced myself she was the perfect person for you. That I was stealing you away from your soulmate or something."

I rest my forehead against hers. "You should have talked to me."

"I was afraid you wouldn't listen because you're convinced you're not a character." Her lip slips between her teeth and I tug on her chin.

I study her face, searching for some way to prove to her I'm not one of them. An idea sprouts in my mind and I grin. I push to my feet and grab her hand. We're halfway to the front door before she pulls me to a stop.

"Where are we going?"

"We're going to prove that I'm not a character. Trust me."

She's skeptical but slips on her sandals, anyway. I drag her to the edge of the forest. Thankfully, no one else seems to be hanging around. They're down by the lake, enjoying the last days of summer. The weather hasn't turned yet. Colder nights are just around the corner, and everyone can feel it.

"Emmett, we've already been in the woods. We found bigfoot in there." She giggles, warming me from the inside out.

I flex my hands, hoping she doesn't notice my nerves. I'm not a character, but I haven't gone into the forest since Belvina lured me in. She's on the other side of the cabin, though—far away from where she could influence me.

"We didn't go far enough in. Besides, you're not going. You're going to be here when I stumble my ass back through the forest."

"Bold of you to assume I was offering to go with."

"I was talking to Axel before he left, and he said it's a decent hike before things get fuzzy, then poof, you're right back where you started."

She huffs as she peers into the forest. "They also said sometimes it can take a few days. Who's going to feed me when you're off wallowing in the void?"

"Plenty of food in the fridge, gorgeous. You'll survive. Not going to be a problem, though, since I'm not going anywhere. I'll walk right back out because I'm not a character."

Her mouth parts and her eyes take on that faraway look she gets when an idea hits her. "What if—stop groaning—the food that's mysteriously showing up is from other people's houses? I saw this video once of a guy who made a waffle in a toaster and when it popped, nothing. The waffle was just gone. And all the comments were talking about things disappearing. What if we're just stealing from them?"

"Technically, we're not stealing from them, the magic is. So we can't be held responsible for the crime."

She levels me with a glare. "I'd be pissed if someone stole my cheesecake and was sitting on a deck just eating it without a care. Only assholes steal dessert."

"Let's just assume they're stealing from a corporation. They deserve to give back to the masses since they're so greedy." I grin, then swoop down and kiss her hard.

I walk into the forest and weave through the trunks. The leaves above me rustle and my hands twitch by my sides. I'd put them in my pockets, but I'd probably end up tripping with no way to catch myself. Every snap of a twig sends my head whipping around. Creatures chitter, their little feet creating a cacophony of noise. I didn't think it'd be this loud in here.

"What's up, Emmett?"

I swing around, my fist flying wildly behind me. Kol catches my hand easily, his grin never faltering.

"What the fuck," I breathe, bracing my hands on my knees.

"Easy there. Wouldn't want your heart to burst. Is that a thing with humans? I can never remember." He taps his finger on his chin.

"I'm a little busy, Kol. Do you make a habit of sneaking up on people?" I straighten, closing my eyes when my head swims.

He doesn't notice the distress I'm in. Or he doesn't care. "Mortals are so jumpy. Can't sneak up on demons. Why are you in the forest? Thought you hated it here."

"I don't hate the woods unless I'm being stalked." I glare at him before continuing on. Of course, he follows me.

"Okay, but where are you going?" He steps in line with me, swinging his arms as his wings wink in and out of existence, as if they're unable to resist the streams of sunlight filtering through the leaves.

"To the edge, I suppose. I'm proving a point." I'd rather not divulge all my fears to him. Demons probably feed off that shit or something.

"The writer think you're a character? That why the air's been weird around here lately?" He gives me a pointed stare. "Oh, look. Ghost lady showed up. Hey, Ethel!"

"Her name is Ethel?"

He chuckles, waving at her as she scowls. "No idea. Just picked it because it was close to ethereal. You figure out why she's here?"

"Why would I be the one to do that?"

His footsteps slow, then he freezes as if he's hit an invisible barrier. "Can't go farther than this, I'm afraid."

"This is where you disappear?" I search the trees, the ground, the fallen logs for any sign of this patch of the forest being any different.

"Straight into the void, popping out on the other side. Rune has a tendency to wallow in there. Says it's like the Nihil."

"And that is?"

"Just an old word for nothing. Down in Hell, it's literally a place of nothingness. Creeps me out, but Rune likes it. You going to actually do this?"

I give him a curt nod, staring straight ahead. My lids flutter shut as I pull in the scent of pine and damp moss, letting it fill my senses. Setting my jaw, I shove aside the nerves threatening to drown out my resolve.

"Need me to hold your hand?" Laughter tinges his words.

"Fuck off," I mutter, and step into the unknown.

Chapter Fifty-Four
Maddie

I wring my hands together, wishing I would have grabbed my phone. I might not be able to make calls on it, but the clock still works. Time warps and I check the sky. As if I'd be able to tell how many minutes have passed. I roll my eyes, then plop onto the ground and wait.

I swear it's been an hour since Emmett tromped off into the forest, determined to prove me wrong. I'd love to just blindly trust him when he says he's not a character. It would make my life so much easier.

The idea that I've been falling for one of my own characters, someone I made up in my head, has been bouncing around my brain. How fucked up do I need to be to create my own book boyfriend and literally bring them to life? Not only that, but I may have stolen him from his soulmate, the person he's supposed to live happily ever after with.

Searching the trees, I spot Ezio weaving his way toward me along the edge of the forest. The last thing I want to do is fight with him about his story. I'm starting to regret allowing him to walk in the sun. I expect him to lambaste me the moment he gets within a respectable distance from me. Instead, he gingerly lowers himself to the ground facing the forest.

"I'm not really in the mood, Ezio," I mumble.

He crosses his ankles and leans back on his hands. "Perhaps not, but the magic will not leave me alone. Therefore, I'm here until the sensation to speak with you goes away."

"What exactly are you supposed to speak to me about?"

"Hard to say," he murmurs. "Though, I imagine it's centered on that man you've been shacking up with and the lady."

I tense, biting my cheek. The pain does nothing to help. "Go on."

He sighs, shaking his head. "I fucking hate interacting. You realize this, right?"

"Stop stalling, you asshole." I glare at him and his fangs slide from between his lips.

He flexes his jaw and the fangs retract as he fights his baser instinct. I've joked with my author friends about being turned into a vampire. Doesn't mean I want to experience it. I don't know if I'd want to live forever, even if I was in Ezio's position. He has it easier than other vampires when it comes to Ella and Dray.

"Very well. Perhaps you're searching for the wrong answers. You've allowed your imagination to run away with your rationality. You're viewing this situation as if it's one of your stories." He spits the last word out as if he isn't a character. "It's no wonder you've sabotaged your own happiness in lieu of building a new fictional world. Seems as if you do that quite frequently."

"What the hell, man," I grumble under my breath.

"I'd apologize, but I'm afraid I've forgotten how. However, I will leave you with something Ella wanted me to pass along."

I close my eyes, knowing her words are about to destroy me with some adage or metaphor. They'll worm their way into my psyche, hitting me right where it hurts. For some reason, when I'm writing their story, she'll spout something out of the blue I wasn't expecting. It destroys me for days afterward.

"The stories you write are not more important than your own. Sometimes fate works in ways we don't understand, and it's not our job to decipher them." He rolls his eyes, the most human reaction I've seen from him.

Ezio disappears, and I close my eyes again. I'll mull over Ella's words later when I'm no longer teetering on the edge of a cliff. Ezio's eat away at me, though.

What if I have been searching for the wrong answers? If I take out the magical elements of this place and look at things rationally, I'd never assume Emmett was meant for someone else. The problem lies in the fact that we *are* in this alternate universe. Nothing is as it seems.

My eyes fly open when there's a thud next to me. Kol grins as if he didn't just get thrown to the ground. I tip my head back, but the sun is exactly where it was just minutes before.

"Where the hell did you come from?" I ask, my tone harsher than I planned.

"Emmett and I were walking through the woods. I just took the shortcut back. Too bad for him. Then again, he kind of seemed like he didn't want to be hurtled through the void and dropped back into existence, so maybe stumbling through the forest isn't such a bad thing." He stands, dusting off his hands on his pants. "Hope you got your answers, because that boy is in deep when it comes to you."

I roll my eyes, tamping down the elation bubbling in my chest. "He's not a boy, Kol."

"Honey, I'm a demon. They're all boys to me."

He winks, then vanishes in a puff of smoke. I really wish they'd stop doing that. It's disconcerting. Not to mention entirely rude. I was in the middle of a conversation the other day with one of them and they just disappeared. Good way to get out of a lecture, I suppose.

When Emmett finally trips from the trees, I breathe a sigh of relief. It's not that I thought Kol was lying. Especially since he's not capable of it, but I needed to see the evidence with my own eyes.

"I really want to say I told you so right now," he says, collapsing next to me. "I won't, because that's a dick move."

He tugs me closer to him, and I wrinkle my nose and mumble, "I'm sorry I made you do that. You also need to go take a shower."

He laughs, kissing my temple, then pushes to his feet. He helps me up and leads me back toward the cabin. Issues like this are never resolved so easily in books. It'd be so much easier if they were. Then again, they'd be a lot shorter if everything was solved with a simple walk in the woods.

When we reach the porch, I push Emmett up the stairs and through the front door. He laughs, probably assuming I'm ready to jump his bones. He'll have to wait until he's not all sweaty. I kick the door closed behind me and shove him down the hall.

"You going to join me in the shower, gorgeous?"

"After you've used soap, sure. But I also saw Tate coming around the corner."

"You know, I saw Juliette making one of those flower crowns the other day. Later that night, Tate had one and was studying it. Not only that, but he wasn't scowling."

My feet stutter to a stop, and I rest a hand on the wall. An idea sprouts in my head, weaving together the threads of their story. Mentally, I tug them gently, filling in the plot hole I couldn't seem to figure out. My palms tingle, and a grin spreads across my face.

Skipping to the bedroom, I wave for Emmett to follow me. I snatch up my computer, cursing myself for taking so long of a break. Yes, I needed it, but I left it for too long. I shake my head as I open my laptop. It wasn't the break that did me in. My inability to open my damn mouth and talk to Emmett was my downfall. He's become an integral part of my writing process.

I freeze with my fingers poised over the keyboard. "I'm sorry. I should have talked to you. My mind spiraled and instead of talking to you, I just let it happen."

He sinks to his knees next to the bed and his hand slides to my knee. "We both fucked up. Hopefully, we both learned from it. And next time we'll do better."

I press my lips together, nodding. "We need to talk about the future. And how you constantly say you're put on this planet to be there for me, yet the reverse isn't true."

"The future. As if it isn't *our* future we're discussing," he murmurs. "I told you I loved you, Maddie. Do you really think I'd say those words if I didn't see a future with you?"

"I don't want you to give up your life for me. Your life is important, and I don't want it revolving around me without a way to return the favor."

His head drops onto the mattress, his hair brushing my thigh. I resist the urge to run my fingers through the short strands. His hand squeezes my knee, and my chest tightens. Can I really give him up? I don't have enough experience with relationships to make a sound decision. I wish I could call Chloe. She'd be able to break it all down and help me figure out my own feelings.

"You fill my life with happiness, Maddie. Plain and simple. You give me purpose just by existing. By needing me."

Realization dawns on me and I grit my teeth. Sometimes I hate being an author. Being so immersed in other people's stories sometimes blinds me to what the actual world is like. It makes me miss obvious things because my head is stuck in the clouds.

"Sit up," I snap, more upset with myself than with him. "I'm sorry."

"You don't need to apolog—"

"Stop. I'm sorry for not noticing earlier. I made our relationship into a book trope." I cover my face with my hands, groaning.

"Wait, which one?"

"Not good enough for him. It's basically self-sabotage with an extra dash of miscommunication thrown in for good luck. And I fucking hate it. I hate when people don't know their worth. Which is why I think I kept pushing you. I wanted you to know your worth. I thought I knew best what you deserve, even though you were telling me over and over what you wanted."

"What do you want? And don't you dare say a break."

"You." I smile, ignoring the nausea turning in my gut. "I would like to live here with you, which might not be possible. I want to wake up every morning next to you. And I want to eat all the food you make me. And I want to...I want to love you. That's what I'd like. Please."

His eyes soften and the corner of his lips twitch. "Well, since you were so polite about it, I'm sure we can figure something out. I'd kiss you, but even I can smell myself. Feel free to join me in about five minutes."

He pushes to his feet, and I track him as he makes his way to the bathroom. He doesn't bother closing the door. The water starts up and I focus on my screen, trying to remember why I was so eager to write.

Threads. Plot holes. Flower crowns. I run through the list in my head until the full picture comes into view. I pull up Tate and Juliette's document and read the last paragraph. Just as I'm about to add more, Emmett begins singing. My head whips around and I crane my neck to spy on him in the reflection of the mirror. The shower curtain blocks my view and I scowl. I've never heard him sing before. Apparently, it's another thing he's ridiculously good at.

I pull up another file and add singing to the list of traits I started for him. He might not be my character, but I'm sure one of the others I eventually write will steal some of his attributes. I've already used some of his dirty talk. Thank fuck he wasn't freaked out when I asked him if it was okay. For him, it became a challenge to see what would make it into a book.

I don't know why I thought we weren't perfect for each other. Ridiculousness and fear. Ezio was right. I deserve happiness just as much as they do.

Now that I've found my happily ever after, it's time for me to give it to the rest of my characters. Eventually, I'll need to deal with the woman in white, but she can wait. I'll find where she belongs afterward.

After writing a few more words, I give up and join Emmett.

Chapter Fifty-Five

Emmett

I set an energy drink on the small table next to Maddie and settle into my deck chair. The sun sets slowly, another day melting into night. The last two weeks have been blissful. I thought I'd seen her at peace before, but this is a whole new level. The aura around her is calm and confident, completely at ease with everything.

"Thank you. Love you," she mumbles, grabbing the can and drinking without taking her eyes from her screen.

My chest flutters at her words. Every chance she gets, she's telling me she loves me. I worried after I admitted my own feelings and she didn't say it back. I wasn't ready to give up, but it added to the nerves already building in me. It's as if she's making up for the hour between when I told her and she finally confessed.

"Who's next?" I ask after a few minutes. She sighs, snapping her laptop shut and turning to me. "You can keep working, sweetheart. We can talk about it later."

"No. I didn't stop because of you. These people are pissing me off and I need a break."

"Alrighty then."

I grab her computer and set it on the table, then wrap my fingers around her wrist and tug her toward me. She straddles me, looping her arms around my neck and my hands settle on her hips.

"How many do we have left?" I ask before nipping at her bottom lip. "We've already released five, including the scary fae lady."

"Just two. Sage and her men, who have been keeping to the forest, thankfully. And the demons who are upset with me, since they had to watch the numbers dwindle down to almost nothing. Every time I step outside, they're glaring at me. I've been trying to figure out the end, but my mind is scrambled." She rests her forehead against mine, her lids fluttering closed.

"Why don't you write it down? You've got enough sticky notes to cover the entire cabin."

She whines as she straightens, and I run my hands up her sides. "I would, but I'm terrified they'll pop into the room without warning. And I hate when that happens. But I need to plot this shit out or I'll forget something."

"Well, why don't you get started on that and I'll go pay them a little visit."

She scrambles from my lap and shakes out her hands. "Okay, but don't let them push you around."

"When have I ever let them do that?" I smirk, pulling her down for a kiss before she skips into the house.

I shove to my feet and approach the railing. The last thing I'm going to do is search for them. I scan the area until I find them fighting with Sage across the lawn. It takes me a minute before I realize they're not actually fighting. More like practicing. They move like they're made of water, flowing from one stance to the next with ease. As mesmerizing as it is, I want to get this over with. Maddie can deal with her plotting on her own, but I'd rather be there.

"Hey," I call, and Kol's head pops up, giving Sage an opening to stab him in the side.

He yelps, rubbing his ribs as he dances away from her. He glares at me before disappearing. The next second he's standing behind me, heat pouring off him. I spin to face him and cross my arms.

"Need all of you for this."

He nods and three more demons materialize in front of me. "We were kind of in the middle of something, but sure. Summon us."

"As if you don't have time on your hands. I need you four to stay out of the cabin. No popping in to badger Maddie." I don't have a way to keep them out, not physically, unless I find a way to ward the place. I have no idea if that would work, though.

"I fail to see how this applies to anyone except for Kol. However, we'll refrain from invading your space. Now, can we get back to practicing?" Rune asks, raising an eyebrow.

I wave him away yet can't help myself. "Have fun playing with your friends."

He scowls and they all vanish once more. I grin, wondering what my joke will cost me later. Ever since Peyton's guys pranked them, they've been laying traps for the others to stumble on. I'm back to avoiding the woods since I ended up trussed up and hanging from a tree. Maddie thought it was hilarious, but I'd rather not repeat the experience.

I make my way inside and swallow my laughter when I see how far she's gotten. "Do you need your computer?"

"Nope," she says, her voice muffled by the pen between her lips. "Got it all in my head."

I collapse on the couch, content to watch her while she works. There's already three dozen sticky notes plastered on the wall by the dining table. She scribbles on the next one and slaps it in place. I can't read them from here, but I doubt she wants me to. Every time I come close to her when she's writing, she turns her screen away and scowls at me. It's fucking adorable.

"So, I've got them back together and through the battle scene." She taps the small pieces of paper as she walks through her plot. "My problem is always the end. I don't know how to do lovey-dovey shit."

"Have they confessed their feelings to each other?"

"Some of them have, but she hasn't. She's going through some shit. Feels like she let them down, even though she did what was needed to survive. It's hard to work through. Especially while some of them are still holding out on her. Nix and Dez in particular are giving me the hardest time." She stares at the notes as if they'll morph into what she needs.

"Maybe you need to walk away from it. You've been going hard for the last two weeks."

I sneak up behind her and wrap my arms around her. She jolts, then sags into me. I brush my lips along her neck, relishing the shiver that runs through her body. When I slip my hand under her shirt, she sighs and tilts her head to the side.

"No one will be disturbing us," I murmur. "Take your clothes off, then put your hands on the back of the couch."

I drop my hands, digging my nails into my palms to center myself. She's irresistible, too enticing for her own good. She swishes her hips as she rounds the table, then braces her hands on the back of the couch, and glances over her shoulder, wiggling her ass.

"You're playing with fire, Maddie. Again."

She shoots me a cheeky grin. "I'd love to say something quippy, but I can't think of anything other than get the hell over here."

I grab the hem of my shirt and whip it over my head, tossing it on the table. Her gaze travels down my body, and a lovely blush blooms across her cheeks. When I reach for my belt, she licks her lips.

"My eyes are up here, gorgeous."

My pants join my shirt, and I make my way toward her. She tracks my movements and I rub my jaw. Stepping close to her, I smirk as she shivers. I skim my fingers down her spine, then over her hip and across her stomach. Her head drops when I slide my hand between her legs.

"Look at how wet you are already, and I've barely touched you," I murmur, and she shudders.

I stroke her lightly, and she groans, the sound resonating through me. Circling her clit gently, I grit my teeth. She soaks my palm, and I pull my hand away.

"Please," she whines.

I pop my fingers into my mouth, her essence exploding across my tongue. It's been too long since I've tasted her. My legs shake as the need to drop to my knees and bury my face between her thighs overwhelms me.

"Tonight, I'm going to tie you to the bed and feast on your pretty little pussy as long as I want."

"Now," she gasps, and I chuckle.

"No," I growl. "Right now, I'm going to fuck you hard and fast—exactly how you want it. I want you imagining everything I'm going to do to you later while my cum drips down your thighs."

She whimpers and her forehead lands on the back of the couch. I squeeze her hip and line myself up with her opening. Gripping my length, I slip the tip in and her pussy clamps down. She pushes back, trying to force me deeper. My eyes fall closed, and she does it again, forcing a moan from me. When she does it once more, I growl.

Grabbing both of her hips, I dig my fingers into her skin as I plunge into her. Her warmth envelops me, and I moan again. I thrust into her, each stroke harder and faster than the last. Needy noises fall from her lips and her nails burrow into the cushions.

"Fucking this pussy is one of my absolute favorite things in the world."

She shudders, her body tensing as an orgasm rolls over her. I slip an arm around her waist to keep her upright as I continue to pound into her. A beautiful flush spreads across her body.

"Emmett," she wheezes as her body goes limp.

My name on her lips sends me careening over the edge and stars flash in my vision. My body covers hers and I brace my hand on the couch next to hers.

"I love you," I whisper into her skin, and she spasms around my length.

"Holy fuck," she breathes, and I chuckle.

"Not the response I was expecting, but I won't complain."

I nuzzle her neck, and she turns her head. She smiles softly before pressing her lips to mine. It's sweet and gentle, emotions flowing from one to another—a silent vow of devotion.

"I love you, too," she murmurs, as if she's afraid I'll take my own confession back.

She wiggles and I straighten, still deep inside her. Later, we'll delve into our plans for the future. For now, I want to spend my time worshiping her. When she tries to move, my hand latches onto the back of her neck.

"You didn't really think I was done with you, did you?"

I pull out of her and she hums, her knees almost giving out. I lift her and carry her around the couch. My cock twitches against her ass and I harden once more. I doubt I'll be able to come again. I won't deny her, though. Sliding her down my body, she pants, clearly still worked up.

I set her on her feet and spin her around. "Sit."

She collapses onto the cushions, and I drop to my knees in front of her. I yank her ass to the edge, my chest thrumming with anticipation. Shoving her legs apart, I lick my lips. Her hand lands on my forehead and my eyes flick to hers.

"What are you doing?" She swallows hard, her thighs twitching under my palms as I hold her.

I smirk, tilting my head. "I'm cleaning up the mess you've made."

Her mouth drops open, and I swoop down. As I lick her from core to clit, her fingers slide into my hair and grip the strands. Her hips kick up as I continue to feast on her. I'll never get enough of her body. Her legs tremble as I suck the sensitive bud into my mouth. I plunge two fingers into her, then add a third and she erupts, her back arching as I stroke her.

"Fuck, fuck, fuck," she pants, and I grin against her skin.

Nipping at her inner thigh, I wonder if I could make her come again. She's still shuddering when I pull my hand away. She sleepily blinks up at me as I stand and grip my length. It's never been like this with anyone else. It's as if she was made for me, bringing me to the brink of ecstasy over and over.

Her eyes dart down, and I suck in a sharp breath when her lips part. "Imagining my cock in your mouth?"

She nods, her gaze fixed on my hand as I stroke myself. As much as I'd love her to, the need to be inside her once more overrides every other desire. I sit next to her, then yank her on top of me. Her knees settle on either side of my hips, and I plunge into her. I grip her waist, holding her still.

I want to etch this moment in my mind forever—the ecstasy engraved on her face, the love in her eyes, the completeness I feel. Nothing else compares to this moment as I finally find where I belong—with her.

Her nails dig into my shoulders, and I loosen my hold just enough to run my hands up her sides. Cupping her breasts, I brush my thumbs across her nipples, a fascination rolling through me at how she responds. She bites her lip as she rolls her hips.

"Ride me, sweetheart. Make yourself come on my cock."

Her chin quivers as she moves, grinding each time she sinks onto my length. Her pussy clings to me, fluttering when I hit the deepest parts of her. Her movements become erratic as she chases the high of another orgasm. I drop my hand to her clit and I rub it, whispering words of encouragement.

My stomach tenses as she explodes, collapsing on top of me. I grip her hips and plunge into her three more times before I'm groaning out my own release once more. Wrapping my arms around her, I hold her close, basking in the glow of being with her.

Chapter Fifty-Six

Maddie

"Are you sure you did it right?" Nix asks and I grit my teeth.

It's one thing when I doubt myself. It's something entirely different when my characters question my skills while standing right in front of me.

"I could still go in and kill you off if you'd like. There are three others who can carry on the story." I smile sweetly at him, and his face drains of color.

"I'm sure it's perfectly fine the way you wrote it," he mumbles, stepping behind Rune.

"That's what I thought."

Emmett slips next to me, and I shoot him a questioning look. He nods and I clasp my trembling hands together. I never thought this day would come. Even after I started sending characters back to their own worlds, I didn't think I'd get here.

A nervous energy thrums through my body and Emmett slides his arm around my waist. It's a comforting gesture I don't think I'll ever get sick of. I lean into him, soaking up the certainty of being with him.

"Do you guys want to hold hands? Might help get you to the right place," Emmett says. He's met with confused faces, and I bite back a giggle.

I grab my computer, then sit and open the device. Their story unfolds on my screen and a flash of relief hits me when it's all there. Every time I open a document, part of me wonders if it'll load. I've lost words before, and the panic is not something I want to revisit.

When I glance up, I suppress another giggle. They've looped their arms together as if they'll start skipping off into the sunset. This is the image I'll sear into my brain to warm me when I get stuck on a project. I wish I could take a picture. They probably wouldn't show up—like vampires in lore with mirrors.

"Alright, I don't know how the rules of your world will interact with the magic from this area, so you may or may not remember your time here. However, if you do, I need you to not dwell on it. You have shit to do." I give Dez a pointed stare, and he averts his gaze. He's the one who would try to deep dive into the lore of what happened.

"Happy hunting," Emmett says as I write their happily ever after.

"Wait, what the hell does that mean?" Kol cries as he dissolves into shadows coming from his skin. The rest are consumed by the darkness exuding from him.

"Well, that was different," Emmett murmurs.

I snort, rolling my eyes. "You just had to fuck with them didn't you?"

He grins, then sobers. "You ready for the last one?" Emmett's fingers weave through my hair, and I lean into his touch.

"They have no idea what's about to hit them. Sage kept whining about there being too much sun here. Probably didn't think I was going to send her ass back just to spite her." I smile, but even I can feel its falseness.

For as excited as I was to finish the demons' story, Sage's took a lot out of me. I'm surprised it only took me the last five days to finish both books, just in time to meet my arbitrary four-month deadline. I've been working through Sage's on and off for months now. It drained me emotionally, leaving behind a hollow sensation in my soul.

It'll be a long time before I can recover. The prospect of another break doesn't scare me like it did before. Emmett will be there to help. Leaning on him isn't nearly as terrifying as I once thought it was. It's probably the certainty of him sticking with me.

"Let's get this show on the road. Out of all these characters, Sage is the most deserving of a happy ending. Even if she doesn't believe it yet."

We weave our way through the cabin, my murder board from the demon's story still gracing the wall. I ended up taking some paintings down just to fit it all. I'll probably leave it up a little while longer. It's a physical representation of all the effort I've put in over the last few months. With each word I wrote, I learned a little more. Once my editor gets a hold of all these stories, I'll have my work cut out for me. I'll gain new knowledge, but I think she'll be impressed with what I've accomplished.

"Comfy?" I ask Sage, who's straddling the deck railing.

The corner of her mouth twitches as the four men I've made her love interests hover just out of reach. As much as they pretend they don't care, they do. For some reason, they think they can hide it. I plop down in my seat and rest my computer on my lap. Emmett takes the other seat, and a familiarity washes over me.

"What do you think you're doing?" Sage bites out, glaring at my laptop.

"Finishing your story."

"Thank fuck," Bishop mutters, running his hands through his jet-black hair.

Sage glares at him, then turns her scowl on me. "You can't be serious."

"*You* were the one who was complaining about the sun. Thought I'd send you back to your gloomy basement." I shoot her a cheeky grin and her nostrils flare.

"Like hell you will," Bishop growls as he takes a step toward me. Knight's hand whips out and latches on his brother's arm, halting him in his tracks.

I eye them, waiting for the tension to ease. It doesn't, which is no surprise. They're all a little on edge, whether they're stuck here or in their own world.

"Well, whether you like it or not, you'll be dropped right back into the story where I left it off. I have no idea how it'll be for you since this is the first time I've ever written out of order. I assume everything will be fine. And if it's not, well, too fucking bad."

Two of the men stalk toward me, but my fingers are quicker, writing the last few words. Sage tips her head back, a genuine smile blossoming on her lips. The men vanish with a pop I've never heard before.

Sage lingers and her gaze finds mine as her body blurs with the mist separating us. She mouths, *Thank you,* and tears well up in my eyes. I swallow hard as she finally disappears, the mist turning to droplets and hitting the deck.

"Way to go out with a bang, gorgeous," Emmett whispers.

Before I know it, he pulls me into his lap and cradles my body. I still need to deal with the lady in white. But she can wait. I have no idea why she's here or where she belongs in the grand scheme of things. Maybe she's the one who orchestrated all of this in the first place. If she is, it'll be hard not to punch her in the throat. She upended my entire fucking life.

Then again, if I didn't come here, I never would have met Emmett. I never would have had the experiences of meeting my characters in person. I never would have fallen in love.

"What do we do now?" I mumble as I tuck my head under his chin.

"I thought we'd see if the car will start. Go into town and figure out what's been happening in the outside world. I'm sure Chloe will want to hear from you."

Neither of us moves, content to bask in the sun just a little bit longer. My legs cramp before I'm ready to let go, and I stretch out my foot, hanging my knee over the arm of the chair. When I work the other one out, Emmett's grip on me tightens.

"What the hell are you doing?"

I push off his lap and almost end up on the deck. "My calves were cramping. We might need to get another one of those loungers since you broke the last one. Maybe we can drag one of the seven couches Chloe's uncle adorned this place with."

He stands and grabs my hand to lead me inside. "I'm not the one who broke it. And seeing as how none of the couches would hold up under an onslaught of rain, I think we'll have to figure something else out. You realize he might not even let us stay here, right?"

"I'm trying not to think about it," I mutter.

I don't have enough in my bank account to cover a down payment, much less a mortgage. I've mostly survived off Chloe's generosity at not making my rent high and whatever royalties I pull in each month. I don't even know if my entire business has fallen apart or not. Ryland said he'd keep an eye on some things for me, but he only knows to turn my ads off if they get wildly out of control. Leaving all the extras behind might have been the wrong move business-wise, but I never would have survived otherwise.

The thick layer of dirt covering my car has me wincing. Emmett climbs into the driver's seat, leaving the door open. I hold my breath as he turns the key. It starts right up. I'm not surprised, but I still exhale heavily. Part of me wasn't convinced I had actually finished. At least not enough for the magic to let us leave. As much as I love Emmett and love being here, I don't want to be stuck here forever. Living here and being trapped here are two completely different things.

I slide into the passenger seat, content to be driven around. "What if—"

"No. No, we're not going to talk about another what-if. Not when we're ten seconds away from driving off into the sunset," he grumbles as he flips on the wipers, trying to clean the windshield.

"First of all, it's not even close to sunset. Second, this is not a new idea. Do you think every time I get a new idea we won't be able to leave? It was helpful this time around, but I don't know how I feel about randomly being stuck here. Especially since I usually have a ton of plots and I have to wait to write them until I have the time to put into them."

He sighs, turning to face me. "I think if you back yourself into the corner again, maybe. I'm not an expert, though."

"Well, neither am I. Maybe we should ask the ghost lady."

"Why the hell would we do that?"

"Maybe she's the mastermind behind this whole thing."

He shakes his head, a grin spreading across his face. "Keep searching. She's definitely not the mastermind."

He puts the car in gear and circles around. He stops as we come to the top of the driveway. His hand covers mine, then laces our fingers together. I blow out a deep breath, waiting for my nerves to settle. Emmett eases forward and we roll over the invisible line. I press my lips together to keep my whoop of excitement to myself.

I bounce in my seat as he turns onto the dirt road. "Where are we going to go?"

"Figured we'd just drive around for now. I need to find my truck. If we get some internet access, we should try to order something to extend it to the cabin. Staying here will be a lot easier if you can actually work."

"My first order of business is to call Chloe. She's probably a little unhinged since I dropped off the face of the planet. She told me not to talk to her until I was done, but I'd usually bug her anyways."

He pulls closer to the ditch, though we're still blocking the road. I doubt anyone comes down here unless they have a cabin nearby. We never saw them this summer, which might be the magic. More likely it's because we're in the middle of nowhere. Emmett puts it in park, and I push from the car. He tips his head back and closes his eyes.

"I'll make it quick," I say while dialing her number.

"No rush. You kept me up half the night with your antics, so a nap is in order."

I roll my eyes, shutting the door behind me. He wasn't complaining about "my antics" when he was expounding on the excellence of my pussy.

The conversation is quicker than I expected. Her voicemail picks up and I tuck my chin to my chest, waiting for the beep. I've zoned out as she says the normal greeting, but I tune back in when I hear my name. I hang up and dial her number again, my leg jiggling uncontrollably.

"...Oh, and if this is Maddie, take all the time you need. Your stories deserve to be read. I'll be out of touch for the next few weeks. Don't worry. I promise I'll be there soon."

I hope she didn't get sucked into another shitty relationship. It wouldn't be the first time someone has used her issues with her family to bamboozle her into buying them the world. Tommy was the last in a long line of douchebags. I'm sure it's not easy knowing if someone is with you for your money or not. Unfortunately, she's only found the ones who don't care about her. She deserves someone who sees just her and not her bank account.

"No answer?" Emmett calls and I get back in the car.

"Voicemail. Let's drive."

Thankfully, he listens, not questioning me further. As he winds through the back roads, I gaze out the window. The trees march into the distance, obscuring the horizon. Emmett slows as we round a curve, and I catch a flash of white. Ghost lady's face comes into focus, a small smile forming. She lifts a finger to her lips and then she's gone. I crane my neck to find her, but the road curves again, blocking my view.

An idea sprouts in my head, threads of a story weaving together to create a tentative plot. It grows, forming a pattern of deceit and desire. Characters morph in my mind from faceless beings to individuals, all revolving around one person—the lady in white. I grin as I close my eyes, letting the strands of a new book take root.

The Last Chapter

I gaze at Maddie, our hands linked together while we watch the sun set over the lake. No one could have convinced me when she fell into my arms all those months ago that we'd be here now. I never thought I'd fall in love. Relishing the blanket of peace settling over me, I sigh. Maddie fills in the missing pieces of me and I've finally found home.

The End

The Author closes the laptop with a definitive snap, then leans back in their chair, letting the sense of accomplishment of another story burrow deep within them. The voices subside within the Author's head, giving them a slight reprieve from the constant battle for attention. Perhaps they've gone too far this time—tempting fate the way they have. The Author grabs a pen and pulls a journal closer. Flipping through the pages takes longer than it used to, not that they'll complain. They halt halfway through the book and scrawl Emmett and Maddie's names on the blank line, recording yet another happily ever after.

Thank You

Thank you so much for reading Maddie and Emmett's story!
Ready for another adventure?
Check out the other works by Emilia Abraham:
https://emiliaabraham.com

If you'd like to hear about the other stories that have been living in my head, sign up for my newsletter (including extra scenes & a novella), visit my website, or follow me on social media visit:
https://linktr.ee/emiliaabraham

Special Thanks:

K.B. Barrett Designs-Cover Artist and Formatter
Emily Michel-Editor
Emily Renee-Beta Reader
Krysten-Omega Reader

Other Works

Also by E. Abraham:

Shadows of Synd:

Under the Shadows-Book 1
Between the Shadows: Novella
Running From Shadows-Book 2
Becoming Shadows-Book 3
Shadows Within Us-Book 4
Beyond the Shadows-Book 5

Ruins of Rima:

Spin-off Series
Chasing Darkness-Book 1
Charmed by Darkness-Book 2

Available on Newsletter:

Extra Scenes, Bridging Epilogues
(Shadows of Synd-Book 1 & 2)
Cadence of the Xylophone (erotic novella)

<u>Also by Emilia Abraham:</u>

Stuck at Sundown
The Cryptid Chronicles: Bewitched by Bigfoot

About the Author

After many years of dreaming of becoming a full-time writer, Emilia Abraham took the leap, bringing her words to print. From sweet contemporary romance to spicy why choose and everything in between, she focuses on the happily ever after.

Emilia lives in the Upper Midwest with her husband (who's probably sick of listening to her expound on fictional men) and three kids (who try to steal her post-it notes). When she's not writing, she enjoys reading, playing video games, and consuming copious amounts of energy drinks.

www.ingramcontent.com/pod-product-compliance
Lightning Source LLC
Chambersburg PA
CBHW020327010826
48973CB00005B/1154